THE
LAST DAYS
OF
KRYPTON

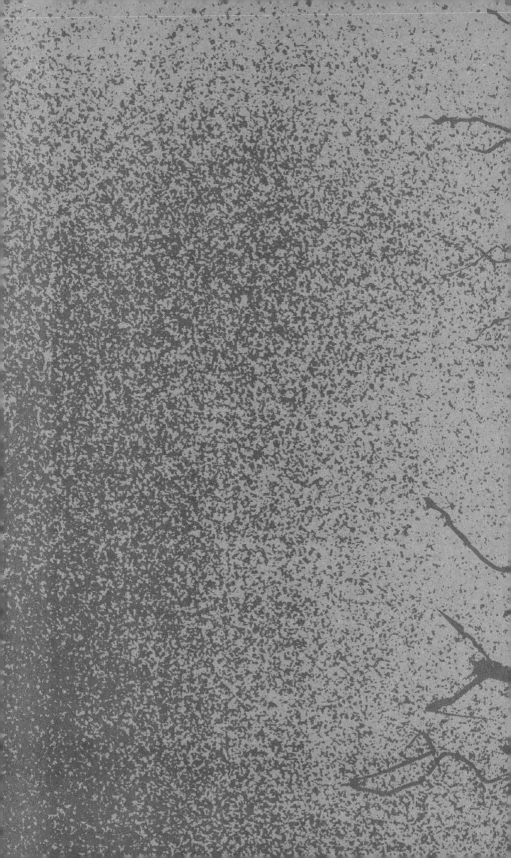

THE
LAST DAYS
OF
KRYPTON

KEVIN J. ANDERSON

Superman created by Jerry Siegel and Joe Shuster

HarperEntertainment

An Imprint of HarperCollins*Publishers*

HarperCollins books may be purchased for educational, business, or sales
promotional use. For information please write: Special Markets Department,
HarperCollins Publishers, 10 East 53rd Street, New York, NY 10022.

FIRST EDITION

Designed by Timothy Shaner, nightanddaydesign.biz

Library of Congress Cataloging-in-Publication Data is available upon request.

ISBN-13: 978-0-06-134074-1
ISBN-10: 0-06-134074-X

07 08 09 10 11 ID/RRD 10 9 8 7 6 5 4 3 2 1

To Julius Schwartz

I've always considered Julius Schwartz, or "Julie," as his friends called him, to be Superman's "fairy godfather." He worked for DC Comics for forty-two years and edited the line of Superman comics from 1971 through 1985, and after that he was a fixture at many conventions and gatherings. Years ago he gave me a gold Superman "S" pin at the San Diego Comic Con, and then when he saw me again months later he scolded me severely for not wearing it. I certainly learned my lesson, and I made a point of wearing that gold pin at every convention where our paths crossed (and he made a point of tracking me down to make sure I was). Julie died in 2004. Since I can't give him a signed copy of *The Last Days of Krypton*, I can at least put his name here. Thanks for everything, Julie!

ACKNOWLEDGMENTS

Destroying a world is not an easy job (although my wife tells me I do have a "high celestial body count" in my novels). Among the many people who helped me with *The Last Days of Krypton*, I would like to thank in particular Paul Levitz, John Nee, and Steve Korté at DC Comics, all of whom immediately saw the potential in this project as soon as I suggested it. Chris Cerasi at DC and Mauro DiPreta at HarperEntertainment did a terrific job as tag-team editors, using their expertise from both the comics and literary sides to help me polish this book into its final form. My agent, John Silbersack at Trident Media Group, ran interference through the various contracts and licensing challenges. At WordFire, Inc., the team of Diane Jones, Louis Moesta, and Catherine Sidor assisted greatly with the preparation, development, and proofreading of the manuscript, and my wife, Rebecca Moesta, did what she always does . . . which is far more than I could possibly list here.

FOREWORD

Science fiction fandom began in the 1930s, and two such fans were Jerry Siegel and Joe Shuster, the former a writer, the latter an artist. From their singular passion came the ultimate science fiction creation, Superman, *that strange visitor from another planet who came to Earth with powers and abilities far beyond...* No reason to continue; you know the rest. *Everyone* knows the rest.

Superman was born out of a love for science fiction, so it should be no surprise that the story of Krypton, Superman's doomed home planet, would be trusted to Kevin J. Anderson, one of the best science fiction writers working today.

Kevin was given a task as daunting as any of Superman's legendary deeds. He had to put together a history of a world that over the past sixty-eight years has had countless conflicting stories created for it. Did Krypton die of an earthquake? Or did a comet hit it? Or maybe the sun went nova and destroyed it in its burning wake? What were Krypton's people like? Were they benevolent, self-indulgent, emotionless, or loving? And what about Brainiac . . . what about Argo City . . . what about . . . what about . . . ?

These are questions that have been asked and answered by millions of fans many, many times.

But now it is time for a new story that brings those diverse histories together, yet forges its own path. We all know Krypton's outcome, but

Kevin gives us a new, thrilling tale unlike any we've seen before. It is both familiar and surprising.

Re-creating a rich, real, complex history out of such convoluted lack of continuity is an undertaking I would never have wanted to do. But Kevin did and succeeded, and he has now given us a history of a world most of us grew up knowing and caring for. And somehow, with that same flash of inspiration Siegel and Shuster showed when they created Superman all those years ago, he has put it all together in an extremely fast-paced book that has *something* for every fan of Superman, no matter which era they love, which Krypton they grew up with, which Superman they idolize.

—Marv Wolfman, author of *Crisis on Infinite Earths,* writer/creator of *New Teen Titans* and *Blade the Vampire Hunter*

CAST OF CHARACTERS

∞ǁ⟨⊗⟩ˈᴛ ‖·◇ ∞⟨⟩ǁ⟨⟩ǁ∞ˈᴛ⟨⟩ ⟨⊗⟩

DRAMATIS PERSONAE

JOR-EL—Krypton's most revered scientist

ZOR-EL—Jor-El's brother, an accomplished scientist in his own right and leader of Argo City

ALURA—Zor-El's wife, an expert in botany

YAR-EL—father of Jor-El and Zor-El, a genius who now suffers from the Forgetting Disease

CHARYS—mother of Jor-El and Zor-El, a researcher in psychology

FRO-DA—Jor-El's head chef at his estate

LOR-VAN—a well-respected artist and muralist

ORA—Lor-Van's wife

LARA—Lor-Van's daughter, also an accomplished artist as well as a historian and aspiring writer

KI-VAN—Lor-Van's young son

DRU-ZOD—head of the Commission for Technology Acceptance in Kandor

COR-ZOD—Dru-Zod's father, former head of the Kryptonian Council and legendary politician

NAM-EK—Dru-Zod's ward, a burly mute

BEL-EK—Nam-Ek's murderous father, killed by Kryptonian Sapphire Guards

AETHYR-KA—an independent woman cut off from her noble family, a former classmate of Lara's

BUR-AL—fourth-level assistant in the Commission for Technology Acceptance

VOR-ON—young man from a minor noble family

HOPK-INS—minor worker in the Commission for Technology Acceptance

GUR-VA—an insane criminal known as the Butcher of Kandor

SHOR-EM—the leader of Borga City

DONODON—alien visitor to Krypton

KIRANA-TU—dry and humorless female doctor

THE KRYPTONIAN COUNCIL

JUL-US (Council Head)	AL-AN
MAURO-JI	BARY-ON
CERA-SI	SOR-AY
POL-EV	RUL-AR
KOR-TE	JUN-DO
SILBER-ZA	

ANCIENT HISTORICAL FIGURES

JAX-UR—ancient warlord, generally considered Krypton's most terrible tyrant

LOTH-UR—cruel father of Jax-Ur

SOR-EL—ancestor of Jor-El, one of the leaders of the Seven Armies

KOL-AR—one of the leaders of the Seven Armies

POL-US—one of the leaders of the Seven Armies

NOK—ancient chieftain

KAL-IK—adviser to Nok, who sacrificed his life to speak the truth

HUR-OM—legendary star-crossed lover depicted in a Kandor opera tapestry

FRA-JO—legendary star-crossed lover depicted in a Kandor opera tapestry

DISSIDENTS

GIL-EX—leader of Orvai in the lake district

TYR-US—leader of the metal city of Corril in the mountains

GAL-ETH—vice mayor of Orvai

OR-OM—industrialist in a mining town

KORTH-OR—refugee from Borga City

ZOD'S RING OF STRENGTH

KOLL-EM—younger brother of Shor-Em, head of the Ring of Strength

NO-TON—a nobleman and scientist

MON-RA	POEL-OR
RAN-AR	BAL-UN
DA-ES	WRI-VO
ZHON-ZA	MIR-XA
FRER-SI	NAER-ZED
CREN-TE	YRI-RI
OEL-AY	TRES-OK

THE
LAST DAYS
OF
KRYPTON

The red sun of Krypton loomed in the sky, an unquiet giant. In its gaseous layers, planet-sized convection cells churned like the bubbles in a hellish slow-motion cauldron. Wispy coronal streamers danced across the gulf of space, disrupting planetary communications.

Jor-El had been waiting a long time for a flare storm like this. In his isolated laboratory he had monitored his solar probes, eagerly making preparations. The moment was at hand.

The visionary scientist had set up his equipment in the large, open research building on his estate. Jor-El had no assistants because no one else on Krypton understood exactly what he was doing; in fact, few others seemed to care. The people of his planet were content. Too content. By contrast, Jor-El rarely let himself feel complacent or satisfied. How could he, when he could easily imagine so many ways to improve the world? He was a true anomaly in the "perfect society."

Working alone, he calibrated beam paths through crystal concentrators, used laser-alignment tools to adjust the angles of intersecting reflector disks, checked and double-checked his gleaming prisms for any flaws. Because his work pushed the envelope of standard and uninspired Kryptonian science, he had been forced to develop much of the basic apparatus himself.

When he opened the set of louvered alloy panels in the roof of the research building, scarlet light flooded into the laboratory. Soon, the solar flux would reach the level he required. Keen scientific curiosity gave him more incentive than his awe for the red giant, which the priests had named Rao. He monitored the power levels displayed on flatcrystal gauges.

All the while, the sunlight outside blazed noticeably brighter. The flares continued to build.

Though he was young, Jor-El's distinctive thick hair was as white as bleached ivory, which gave him a regal appearance. The classically handsome features of his face looked as if they were modeled directly from the bust of an ancient Kryptonian nobleman, such as his revered ancestor Sor-El. Some might have thought his blue-eyed gaze distant and preoccupied, but in truth, Jor-El saw a great many things that others did not.

He activated his carefully arranged crystal rods, setting up a harmonic melody of wavelengths. On the rooftop, angled sheet-mirrors clashed their reflections into a central concentrating prism. The crystals stole only a precise segment of the spectrum, then diverted the filtered beam into parabolic mirrorpools made of half-transparent quicksilver. As the sunstorm's intensity increased, the quicksilver mirrors began to ripple and bubble.

According to plan, Jor-El quickly withdrew an amber crystal and inserted it into its proper grid point. The slick facets were already hot against his fingertips. The primary beam splintered into a luminous spiderweb that connected the labyrinth of mirrors and crystals.

In moments, if his experiment worked, Jor-El would break open a doorway into another dimension, *a parallel universe*—maybe even more than one.

The large and lonely estate many kilometers from Kandor suited Jor-El. His research building was as large as a banquet hall. While other Kryptonian families might have used such a space for masques, feasts, or performances, Jor-El's once-celebrated father had built this entire estate as a celebration of discovery, a place where every question could be investigated regardless of the technophobic restrictions imposed by the Kryptonian Council. Jor-El put these facilities to good use.

For an experiment of this magnitude, he had considered calling his brother from Argo City. Although few could match Jor-El's genius, dark-haired Zor-El, despite his occasional temper, had the same burning need to discover what was yet to be known. In a long-standing cordial rivalry, the two sons of Yar-El often tried to outdo each other. After today, provided this experiment succeeded, he and Zor-El would have a whole new universe to investigate.

Jor-El withdrew another crystal from the control grid, rotated it, and reinserted it. As the lights glowed brighter and the colors intensified, he became entirely engrossed in the phenomena.

Sequestered in their stuffy chambers in the capital city, the eleven-member Kryptonian Council had forbidden the development of any sort of spacecraft, effectively eliminating all possibility of exploring the universe. From ancient records, Kryptonians were well aware of other civilizations in the twenty-eight known galaxies, but the restrictive government insisted on keeping their planet separate "for its own protection." That rule had been in place for so many generations that most people accepted it as a matter of course.

In spite of this, the mystery of other stars and planets had always intrigued Jor-El. Not one to break the law, no matter how frivolous the restrictions might seem, he was nonetheless willing to find ways around it. They could not prevent him from traveling in his imagination.

Yes, the Council had disallowed the construction of spacecraft, but according to Jor-El's calculations, there could be an infinite number of parallel universes, countless alternate Kryptons in which each society might be slightly different. Jor-El could therefore travel in a new way—if only he could open the door to those universes. No spacecraft was necessary. Technically, he would not be breaking any rules.

In the center of the spacious lab, he set a pair of two-meter-wide silver rings spinning to establish a containment field for the singularity he hoped to create. He monitored the power levels. He waited.

When the intensified solar energy reached its peak, a shaft of collected light plunged through the ceiling lens into the center of Jor-El's laboratory like a shaft of fire. The multiplied beams gathered into a single convergence point, then ricocheted into the very fabric of space. The focused blast pummeled reality itself and tore open a hole to somewhere else . . . or nowhere at all.

The silver containment rings intersected, spun faster, and held open a pinprick that expanded in an equilibrium of energy and negative energy. As blinding light poured into the small speck of emptiness, the rip grew as wide as his hand, then the length of his forearm, until at last it stabilized, two meters in diameter, extending to the edge of the rings.

A circular portal hovered in the middle of the air, perpendicular to the ground . . . something a curious person could simply walk into. Behind that opening Jor-El knew he might find new worlds to explore, infinite possibilities.

On a pedestal in front of the hovering doorway, the crystal control array glowed hot and intense. To stabilize the volatile system, he pulled out the subsidiary power crystals, then tilted the quicksilver parabolas to deflect the main beam of sunlight. The power dissipated, but the singularity held. The dimensional portal remained open.

Dazzled, Jor-El stepped forward. Many times he had felt the delicious thrill of discovery, the rush of success when an experiment either produced the results he had predicted or, almost as exciting, something wonderfully unexpected. This doorway had the potential to be both.

When the strange portal did not waver, he cautiously slowed the spinning silver rings so that they hung motionless vertically in the air. Though eagerness tempted him to take shortcuts, his analytical mind knew better. He began his testing process.

First, like a child tossing a pebble into a still pond, he found a small stylus on his worktable and gently threw it into the opening. As soon as the slim implement touched the unseen barrier, it winked out, vanishing entirely and appearing on the other side, in the other universe. Jor-El could barely see a blurred reflection of it floating beyond his reach. But he could see no details of the strange place he had discovered. He ached to see what was there.

Filled with wonder, Jor-El approached the empty gateway. He saw nothing—*literally nothing*—a bottomless void in the air. He wished he had someone with him. Such a great moment should be shared.

He shouted into the opening. "Can anyone hear me? Is anybody there?" The portal remained silent, a vacuum that drained all light and sound.

For his next test, Jor-El attached an imaging crystal lens to a telescoping rod that he removed from an unused piece of equipment stored against a wall of the research building. He would carefully extend the imaging crystal through the barrier, allow it to record the surroundings, then withdraw the tool. He would review the images and determine his next step. He would have to test the air, the temperature, the environment in that other universe.

Sooner or later, though, he knew he was destined to explore.

Holding his breath, Jor-El extended the telescoping rod and pushed the imaging crystal into the edge of the void with the slightest, most delicate touch.

Suddenly, as if a great wind had swallowed him whole, he found himself yanked to the other side, sucked through the opening along with the rod and the imaging crystal. In less than a heartbeat, he was nowhere, suspended in a black and empty void—adrift, yet more than adrift, for he could not feel his body. He sensed no gravity, no temperature, no light. He didn't seem to be breathing, didn't need to. He was just a floating entity, completely aware and yet completely detached from reality. As if through a dirty window, he caught a glimpse of his own universe.

But he could not get back there.

Jor-El shouted, then quickly realized that no one else could hear him in this whole strange dimension. He yelled again in vain. He tried to move but noticed no change whatsoever. He was lost here, so close to Krypton, yet infinitely far away.

CHAPTER 2

Working with her fellow apprentice artists around the wonderfully exotic structures, Lara couldn't decide if the design of Jor-El's estate was the result of genius or madness. Maybe the two things were too similar to be distinguishable.

Rao shone down on "light chimes," ultrathin strips of metal dangling on fine wires that spun under the pressure of photons, producing a racket of rainbows. A milky-white corkscrew tower without doors or windows rose at the center of the estate, like the horn of a giant mythical beast, tapering to a sharp point at its apex. Other outbuildings were unique geometrical structures grown from hollowed crystals and covered with interesting botanical designs.

The bachelor scientist's manor house was a sprawling labyrinth of arches and domes; interior walls met each other at irregular angles, intersecting in unexpected places. A visitor walking through the chaotic layout could easily become disoriented.

Though Jor-El spent most of his time in the cluttered research building, he had apparently realized that something was missing on the estate his father had left him. Chalk-white external walls of polished stone beckoned like pristine canvases that practically demanded artwork. To his credit, the great scientist had decided to do something about it, which was why he had called in a team of talented artists led by Lara's famous parents, Ora and Lor-Van.

Lara wanted to make her own mark, apart from her parents. She was her own person, an adult, independent and filled with her own ideas. Given the chance, she imagined creating a distinctive showpiece that maybe even Jor-El himself would notice (if the handsome but enigmatic man ever bothered to emerge from his laboratory). One day Krypton would recognize her as an imaginative artist in her own right, but that wasn't enough for her. Lara wanted to go beyond that, and she wouldn't limit her possibilities. In addition to being an artist, she considered herself a creative storyteller, a historian, a poet, even a composer of opera tapestries that evoked the grandeur of Krypton's never-ending Golden Age.

Her long hair fell in ringlets past her shoulders, each strand the color of spun amber. As an exercise, Lara had tried to paint a self-portrait (three times, in fact), but she never quite got the startling green eyes right, nor the pointed chin or the rosebud lips that curved upward in a frequent smile.

Her twelve-year-old brother, Ki-Van, with his faintly freckled nose, inquisitive eyes, and tousled straw-colored hair, had also come to the work site, which he seemed to find more marvelous than any exhibition in Kandor.

Around the main buildings, teams of artists in training clustered around Lara's mother and father. More than just underlings and assistants, these were true apprentices who learned from Ora and Lor-Van so that one day they could add their own genius to Krypton's cultural library. They mixed pigments, erected scaffolding, and set up projection lenses for transferring patterns that the master artists had scribed the night before.

If her parents did their jobs well, Kryptonians would no longer focus on Yar-El's tragic fading and confusion that had marked the poor man's later life as he succumbed to the Forgetting Disease. Instead, they would remember Yar-El's visionary greatness. Surely, Jor-El would be grateful to Lara's parents for that. What more could he ask of them?

With the limberness of youth, Lara sat cross-legged on a lush patch of purple lawn, a strain of grass found in the wild plains that surrounded Kandor. She stared at what she considered to be the most puzzling objects on the grounds: Twelve smooth sheets of tan veinrock stood around the estate's open areas, each one two meters wide and three meters tall, with irregular edges. The obelisks were like flat upraised hands, blank and unblemished. Eleven of the flat stones were arranged at precise intervals, but the twelfth was startlingly offset from the others. What had old Yar-El meant by that? Had he intended to cover the obelisks with incomprehensible messages? Lara would never know. Though he was still alive, Yar-El was long past explaining the visions locked inside his head.

Lara propped her sketchplate on her knees. She used a charge-tipped stylus to change the colors of the coating of electromagnetic algae, drawing what she had already painted in her imagination. While her mother and father painted epic murals showing the history of Krypton, Lara had made up her mind to use these twelve blank obelisks for a more symbolic purpose. *If* Jor-El would let her do it. She grew more and more excited as she made plans for each of the flat panels.

Satisfied with her ideas, Lara froze the images on the sketchplate and climbed to her feet, brushing flecks of purple grass from her pearlescent white skirt. Exuberant and determined, she hurried over to the scaffolding where her parents were discussing the best dramatic portrayal of the Seven Army Conference, which had taken place thousands of years ago and changed Kryptonian society forever.

Lara proudly held out her sketchplate. "Mother, Father, look at this. I'd like to have your approval for a new project." She was full of energy, ready to get to work.

Lor-Van had tied his long auburn hair back in a neat ponytail to keep it out of his way. His expressive brown eyes showed his love for his daughter—as well as long-suffering patience. He tended to indulge Lara whenever she came up to him with one of her new (and often impractical) schemes, but he still seemed to view her as a child rather than an adult in her own right.

Her mother, though, was harder to convince. She had short hair, amber-gold like Lara's, but streaked with gray; as always, a few smudges of pigment dotted Ora's cheeks and hands. "What have you done now, Lara?"

"Produced a work of brilliance, no doubt," her father teased, "but beyond the capability of mere mortals like us to understand."

"Those twelve obelisks," Lara said before she could catch her breath,

pointing back toward the nearest one. She forced an evenness, a determination, into her voice. "I want to paint them, each one different."

Without even a glance at the sketches, her mother turned away.
"That's beyond the scope of our project here. Jor-El hasn't given us
permission to touch those."

Lara pressed the issue. "But has anyone actually asked him
about it?"

"He's inside his laboratory, working. No one should disturb him. I
had to send your brother to the perimeter of the grounds because he was
making too much noise." She looked to her husband. "Maybe Ki should
be back in Kandor attending classes with the other children his age."

Lor-Van snorted. "He is learning far more here. When will the boy
ever get such an opportunity again?"

But Lara persisted with her own question, not accepting the easy
answer. "Has Jor-El ever commanded us not to disturb him while he's
working, or are you just making an assumption?"

"Lara, dear, he's a revered scientist, and we're here on his estate at
his invitation. We don't want to overstep our welcome."

"Why are you so afraid of him? He seems perfectly kind and nice."

"Now, Lara," her father said with a tolerant smile, "we aren't afraid
of Jor-El. We respect him."

"Well, I'm going to go ask. Somebody has to clarify our param-
eters." She turned determinedly away, ignoring her parents' words of
caution.

Lara signaled at the door of the research building, which was as
large and ornate as a temple of Rao. When the door beacon elicited
no response, she rapped hard with her knuckles, but again heard only
silence. Finally, she impulsively poked her head inside. "Jor-El? Am I
disturbing you? I need to ask you a question." She had chosen her words
carefully. What true scientist could deny a seeker of knowledge who
simply wanted to ask something?

"Hello?" Though she knew he must be inside the brightly lit lab, she
heard only the echoing hum of equipment. "I'm one of the artists, the
daughter of Ora and Lor-Van." She hung on her words, venturing farther
inside, waiting to hear from him.

Jor-El's spacious laboratory was full of crystals that glowed like a light bank. The huge chamber was a wonderland of unusual apparatus, half-dismantled experiments, equipment racks, and exhibits. The man seemed to lose interest in a project once the challenging part was over, Lara thought. She could understand that.

Still, she couldn't find the distinguished scientist. Had he secretly left the estate? "Jor-El? Is anyone here?"

In the center of the laboratory hovered a motionless pair of silver rings that enclosed a . . . hole. And pressed up against the intangible surface membrane, she saw Jor-El floating there, gesturing wildly, his features blurred and oddly squashed. Though his lips moved, he made no sound.

Lara hurried forward, her sketchplate and drawings forgotten. She raised her voice. "Are you trapped?" Though he tried to answer her, she couldn't hear what he was saying.

Frowning, she went around to the back of the silver-ringed frame, and on the other side found Jor-El staring out at her again, as if he'd been sealed inside a two-dimensional plane. Curiosity spurred her on. "Is this an experiment of some sort? You didn't do this on purpose, did you?" The desperate expression on his handsome face was the only answer she needed. "Don't worry, I'll figure some way to get you out of there."

Drifting in the numb and empty void, Jor-El experienced a moment of bitter irony: For so many years he had dreamed of a place of absolute quiet where he would not be disturbed, a place where he could let his thoughts wander and follow them through to their conclusions. Now, trapped in this dead and surreal silence, he wanted only to get out.

In the initial moments of being trapped here, he had lost his telescoping rod and the imaging crystal. As soon as he had reoriented himself to face the window to his own universe, he had poked at the opening with the rod in his hand, but the barrier recoiled, somehow at a different polarity from this side. The imaging crystal had shattered, the rod had bent and shot out of his grasp, tumbling off into the nothingness. Jor-El just hung there like a disembodied spirit.

Some time later, almost like a consolation prize, his stylus drifted into reach. Jor-El grasped it, not knowing what might eventually become useful.

He had no way to measure how much time had passed. He calmed himself and turned his mind to the challenge rather than succumbing to panic. Normally, when faced with an insurmountable problem, Jor-El would have used his best calculating devices, worked with endless strings of equations, and followed his mathematics to often startling conclusions. Here, though, he had only his mind. Fortunately for Jor-El, his mind was enough. Time to think!

He applied himself to the physical explanation of this hole in space, trying to learn how he had been transported here and why he couldn't simply step back out. Once created, the portal would be self-sustaining; he doubted he could close it if he wanted to. He pondered the resonances in his crystal control array, the coherent beams of red sunlight and the quicksilver parabolas, until he devised a technique that just might work to get him out of there. But from this side of the barrier, Jor-El was completely helpless. He needed someone to help him from the opposite side.

Then, as he stared out into the laboratory, he spotted a face, a beautiful face like that of an ethereal dryad. Her lips moved, but he could not make out her words through the barrier. When Jor-El shouted back at her, she clearly couldn't hear him either. They were cut off from each other, separated by a gap between universes.

Jor-El thought he recognized the young woman, having seen her once or twice outside. Yes, she was with the muralists he had invited to embellish the structures on his estate. Maybe she would think to call for help—but who could help him? No one else, except possibly Zor-El, would understand his apparatus or what he had done. But it would take his brother days to arrive from Argo City.

The young woman paced in his field of view, deep in thought. Jor-El found it maddening that he had concocted a possible solution, yet was unable to communicate it to her. If he could just get the young woman to reverse the polarity on the central crystals, he might be dumped back out. But Jor-El didn't know how to tell her this.

Demonstrating amazing patience, the woman cleared her sketch-plate and began to write down the Kryptonian alphabet. He quickly grasped what she was doing. It would be a slow process, but since she could see his face, she would have him spell out words one symbol at a time.

Jor-El clung to a thread of hope and began to compose his message.

Lara stored her drawings in her sketchplate, cleared the screen, and got to work on the problem. At first she scribed questions that he could answer with a simple nod or shake of his head. Was he in trouble? *Yes.* Was he in pain? *No.* Was he in immediate danger? A hesitation, then *no.* Did he want her to help him? *Yes.* Did he know how to get back out? A pause, then *yes.*

Soon it became obvious that she wouldn't gather enough information this way. Finally, tapping one letter at a time with the stylus and waiting for him to choose, she painstakingly picked out his message.

Reverse Polarity.
Master Crystal.
Main Array.

With a look of consternation, Lara wrote, *What is the main array?* and *What is a master crystal?* and *How do I reverse the polarity?* But she could get only one question answered at a time.

It was often said that Jor-El spoke of things incomprehensible to the average Kryptonian. He created a gulf between himself and the majority of citizens, who were perfectly content to accept the status quo. By the time she spelled out his equally incomprehensible second answer, she still didn't know what to do.

Experimental Hub.
Solar Focusing Grid.
In Lab.

Lara looked around, but the whole chamber was full of exotic equipment, none of which made any sense to her. Which question was he answering? She found a great many crystalline panels, glowing arrays, humming equipment. At last she decided to do what she did best, a form of communication that didn't depend on mathematics or technical terms.

Lara used quick strokes of her stylus to sketch everything in the chamber. Again, through the meticulous process, she lifted the plate into his field of view and showed him the images. By pointing to each apparatus with the stylus, she gradually narrowed down what he was talking about.

At last, precisely following Jor-El's instructions (as she understood them), she located the set of controlling crystals. Jor-El grew obviously tense, but Lara felt only excitement. She wondered if the poor man was beginning to doubt his own theory, but she strangely had no such reservations. She believed in him.

Lara selected what he had called the "master crystal," which glowed a bright emerald green. When she slid it out of its socket, the crystal's light died away; she turned it around and reinserted the opposite end.

Suddenly, the glassy shaft glowed a bright scarlet. The hovering silvery rings that framed the dimensional hole began to spin like thin, razor-edged wheels, then flipped over, reversed position—

—and ejected Jor-El headfirst from the other universe. Sprawling onto the floor where he had fallen, he brushed off his serviceable white pants and tunic—which were unstained from his ordeal—and shook his head to clear it.

She ran to him, took his trembling arm, and helped him to his feet. "Jor-El! Are you all right?"

He could barely find words to speak. At first he flushed, then grinned. "What a fascinating experience." When he looked at her, his blue eyes sparkling, he seemed to see more of Lara than anyone else ever had. "You saved my life. More than that, you saved me from being trapped forever in that . . . Phantom Zone."

She held out her hand. "My name is Lara. Sorry for the unorthodox way of making your acquaintance." She decided to wait awhile before asking his permission to paint the twelve obelisks.

Rao's turbulent storm created a silent light show of auroras that night. Colorful, ethereal curtains spilled across Krypton's sky.

Since she had been his rescuer, Jor-El invited Lara to dine with him out on the balcony of the manor house. This gesture of gratitude was not a mere formality; it was the right thing to do. He had laughed when her parents apologized because their brash daughter had disturbed his work. If Lara hadn't interrupted him in his laboratory, who knew how long he might have been trapped in that empty place? He very much wanted to have dinner with her, and to get to know her better.

Now the two of them sat together in the warm, calm night, eating from many small plates, each of which contained a savory delicacy. Jor-El was something of a loner, not much for casual talk, but conversation with Lara proved to be surprisingly easy.

Using a dainty pearl-tipped prong, she picked up a spiced morsel of eggfruit from a gilt-edged plate, leaving the last piece for him. "When I've attended fancy banquets in Kandor, the food is usually so lovely that the taste can't possibly live up to its presentation." She removed the lid from a small enameled pot, drawing a deep breath of the warm peppery steam that rose from stewed fleshy leaves wrapped around edible skewers. "This, though, is all delicious."

"I instructed my chef, Fro-Da, to prepare a special meal, but I don't usually pay much attention to eating. Too busy with other things." With his fingers he took a small triangular patty. He had no idea what sort of meat it was or what ingredients Fro-Da had put into the sauce. "I've been to banquets where the dinner is more of a performance than a meal."

Lara brightened. "Nothing wrong with a performance, if that's what you're looking for. I enjoy the levitating ballets of Borga City and Kandor's opera tapestries, but when I'm hungry, I just want to eat." They both laughed.

As if eavesdropping on their conversation, the portly chef arrived and presented the colorful dessert course with a minimum of fanfare. "We allow our food to be a celebration of itself," said Fro-Da. Jor-El tried to thank him, but the chef disappeared along with a flurry of helpers who cleared away the dishes.

The two of them looked up into a dark sky suffused with pastel colors. In previous years, Jor-El had designed and constructed four telescopes of various apertures on the rooftops of his buildings. Though the Council would never "waste time" staring into the heavens, Jor-El had taken it upon himself to produce a detailed sky survey. He gazed at the stars, cataloguing the different types, searching for the other planets he knew were out there. He could not travel to those amazing worlds, but at least he could look. Perhaps later he would show Lara some of the distant marvels through his largest telescope. But for right now, he was having a surprisingly pleasant time just sitting here.

Prominent overhead hung the remnants of Koron, one of Krypton's three moons and once the home of a thriving sister civilization. No Kryptonian could look into the sky without feeling the poignant loss. Jor-El mused as he followed Lara's gaze, "Have you ever tried to imagine how much power it would take to destroy an entire moon? What kind of science was behind it?"

"Science? *Science* wasn't responsible for all that death and destruction—Jax-Ur was. I've read about that tyrant in the epic cycles. No single person has changed Krypton's history more."

Jor-El was startled by the vehemence of her reaction. Lara certainly wasn't afraid to state her own opinion. He'd merely been interested in deciphering the physics behind the astonishing weapons. *Nova javelins,* they'd been called. What sort of device could crack open the core of a world and cause such inconceivable destruction?

More than a thousand years ago, Jax-Ur had attempted to conquer all of Krypton, as well as the other colonized planets and satellites in the solar system. The people of Koron had refused to bow to him, so the warlord threatened to use his doomsday weapons. When they still refused to capitulate, Jax-Ur launched three nova javelins. After the weapons had shattered the whole moon, the warlord revealed that he had at least fifteen more in a hidden stockpile.

But Jax-Ur had spread his forces too thin; his conquests were too swift and too widely separated. Seven rebel generals gathered desperate armies from independent city-states that had survived the warlord's depredations. The seven armies converged at the great river delta in the Valley of Elders, risking everything to defeat Jax-Ur. One of the warlord's trusted advisers betrayed him—whether for noble reasons or just to save his own life, no one was sure. The traitor poisoned Jax-Ur before he could launch more of his weapons, and the despised warlord died without revealing where his stockpile was hidden.

Jor-El let his imagination roam. "If I could find one of those nova javelins, I could determine how it worked."

"Let's hope nobody ever discovers that stockpile. No one should have access to such weapons. That's why dangerous technology is forbidden on Krypton."

He gave her a wan smile. "Oh, yes, I know that too well. I have butted heads many times with the Commission for Technology Acceptance."

After the defeat of Jax-Ur, the leaders of the seven armies established a long-standing peace, and Kryptonians turned their attention to other ways they could salvage their civilization. Since Jax-Ur had learned how to build his nova javelins from an alien visitor, the leaders of Krypton chose to block themselves off from any outside influence. The Seven Army Conference had banned all interstellar travel, all contact with potentially destructive races, and all dangerous technologies.

Lara stared up at the shattered moon. "I loved reading the historical cycles. In those days every life was part of an epic. Kryptonians had passions and dreams."

Jor-El could not entirely veil his sarcasm. "But now the Council says we have everything we can possibly need and should be content. No new discoveries. No progress."

Her thin eyebrows drew together, making a gentle furrow on her forehead. Her green eyes had the most amazing sparkle. She seemed so very alive. "But if we don't aspire to improve ourselves, it removes the zest from life."

Jor-El looked at her and smiled. "I couldn't have said that better myself. I'm hungry for all different kinds of science—physics, chemistry, architecture, optics. Astronomy is my main passion."

Lara touched her fingertips to his arm, startling him. "Look at us— an artist and a scientist. At first glance we seem completely different, yet we're more alike than I could have guessed. My parents want me to specialize in mural painting, like they do, but I also love music, history, epic cycles. I don't want to be locked into only one area of expertise."

"Yes, I understand. Well, not those things, specifically. I've never been able to figure out tone symphonies or opera tapestries. Clinically, I recognize that they require significant work and imagination, and a certain level of skill. However, I can't help but scratch my head and wonder what it all means."

Her laughter was like music. "Ha! Now you know how most people feel about your science. It's all a mystery to them."

"I never thought of it that way."

"You don't know this, Jor-El, but I insisted on participating in this project with my parents because of you. You've always fascinated me— you and what you represent. I wanted to be where real history is taking place."

"History?"

"History isn't always old legends or records. History is being created every day, and you're creating more of it than any Kryptonian alive. You may well be the greatest genius ever born on this planet."

Jor-El had heard such things before, but always discounted them. Now he felt embarrassed to have her say it. She laughed softly when she saw him blush.

He quickly pointed up at the sky. "Look, the meteors are about to start." He was too shy to look at her, but he knew she was staring at him with that warm expression on her face. Each month as the moon's rubble orbited Krypton, gravity tugged at the debris. Fireworks streaked across the night sky, radiating from Koron as if the moon were still exploding.

Lara was captivated as the shower intensified. Streak after streak, meteors scratched like bright fingernails across the sky. Shooting stars flared out, then vanished. "I've never seen so many."

"That's the advantage of living outside the city where the skies are dark. In Kandor, the bright lights make it impossible to see most of the meteors. The trails are made by ionized gas caused by the frictional heating of—"

She brought his words to a halt with more laughter. He couldn't understand what was funny, but Lara continued to grin. "Sometimes, Jor-El, a scientific explanation serves only to dilute beauty. Just watch and enjoy it."

Sitting close to her, he forced himself to lean back and stare at the night. "For you, I'll try." He did indeed see the beauty of the meteor shower for its own sake, and he felt a surprising elation to be watching it with her.

While Lara continued to marvel at the particularly bright bolides, Jor-El's thoughts wandered back to the Phantom Zone. Even under such pleasant circumstances he couldn't stop his scientific mind from working. He had created a hole to another dimension, though it wasn't what he had expected. Not a doorway to wondrous new worlds, but a trap. He had hoped to venture into numerous parallel universes, but now he could see no benefit to that empty place where he'd been trapped alone and adrift. Before the Commission for Technology Acceptance allowed him to keep such a discovery, he would have to demonstrate some incontrovertibly practical application.

When the meteor show had died down, Lara stretched. "It's late." Jor-El realized that the sparkling rubble of Koron was close to the western horizon; he had been lost in thought for a long time. "Thank you, Jor-El, it's been an unforgettable evening."

"An unforgettable day. And tomorrow I will take the Phantom Zone to Kandor." He stood to lead her back toward the guest quarters where her parents, younger brother, and all the artist apprentices were staying. "I need to meet with Commissioner Zod."

CHAPTER 4

∞⚷◇‼◇⟶⊤♀⟨ 4

Kandor's grand stadium was a perfect ellipse with high walls, colonnades, and stately arches. All strata of Kryptonian society attended the spectacular hrakka races, sitting shoulder to shoulder in seats carved from polished bloodstone.

Pennants bearing the crests of Krypton's prominent noble families adorned the parapets of the grand stadium, and the spectators sat within section boundaries so they could cheer for their favorite charioteers. They whistled and shouted for whichever racing teams they considered to be the most exciting, and their fickle attentions changed throughout the course of the competition.

Veinrock stairs crusted with crystal dust led from one seating level to another like stone waterfalls. Prominent, private boxes were reserved for special viewers. The eleven members of the Kryptonian Council sat in the middle tiers with the best view. Below, the tan gravel of the track had been raked smooth for the beasts to run on when they emerged.

Commissioner Dru-Zod found the event both uncomfortable and uninteresting. The ruddy afternoon sunlight was too bright, too hot. Though ventilation systems dispersed cool air into his viewing stand, Zod still felt sweaty. Outside, the environment was too difficult to control, and he didn't like things out of his control. The stands were overcrowded, and he could smell the teeming populace even from his private box.

Nevertheless, the Commissioner pretended to be enjoying himself. Leadership was all about appearances. The great hrakka races were a cultural event, a circus thrill for people who had nothing important to accomplish. Zod had plenty of more important things to do, but he couldn't accomplish them unless he played to the expectations of the people. Everyone in the capital city gathered for this monthly spectacle. It kept them happy. It kept them calm. It kept them under control.

Zod's designated box was located in a dustier tier, two levels below the elaborate private boxes of the Council members, where the view wasn't as good, but Zod didn't care a whit for the spectacle. Since he supervised the Commission for Technology Acceptance, the eleven-member Council considered his position to be subordinate to their own. They thought that Zod happily did their bidding. They were fools. The smile on his face was perfect; neatly barbered dark hair and a trim beard and mustache gave him a distinguished appearance.

For the day's event, he was joined by Vor-On, the younger son of a noble family with no prospects whatsoever. "Will your charioteer win today, Commissioner Zod? Shall I place another wager?" He smelled of too much perfume masking too much sweat. Vor-On was little more than a sycophant, embarrassingly glad to have Zod's attention.

After many years of practice, Zod kept his voice carefully controlled. "I expect Nam-Ek will win, but such things cannot be guaranteed."

Vor-On squirmed, barely able to contain his enthusiasm. His rusty hair was cut with straight bangs and a square back; the style, which was very popular this year, had so little finesse it looked like an inexpensive wig. "You're planning something, aren't you? You've got the victory in your pocket. What's the surprise, Zod? Tell me."

"If I tell you, then it will not be a surprise." Zod did not bet, and he was not in this event for profit. He was certain, however, that his man Nam-Ek would meet or exceed expectations; in that, the muscular mute was quite predictable.

Zod leaned forward, bored. Misters sprayed cooling moisture into the air. Food vendors tried to sell cold drinks. Clownish performers in gaudy clothes carried streamers and ribbons, dancing along the packed track far below, overseeing the final preparations while doing pratfalls to amuse the audience. The anticipation built moment by moment.

In the midst of all the tedious hubbub, Zod spied something interesting. Over in the gaudy stadium box of the noble family of Ka, the guests wore extravagantly ornate and absolutely impractical costumes dictated by fashion and not by common sense. The men and women sat with high collars, spiky sleeves, cinched waists, and crinkled fabric studded with so many jewels that they couldn't possibly bend over to duck, should an assassin hurl a dagger at them. He found it both amusing and disgusting.

But what caught Zod's attention was a lovely young woman who didn't seem to belong there at all. Her raggedly cropped dark hair was mussed instead of coiffed. She wore no jewelry. Her eyes were like black pools, her features all the more bewitching because they did not pander to Kryptonian standards of beauty. Her tight black leather pants and loose dark jerkin were designed more for comfort and serviceability than for show. She lounged, rather than postured, on the stone bench.

Zod immediately sensed that this woman was unlike all the dull nobles he dealt with every day. "Vor-On, who is that intriguing creature over there?"

The eager young noble followed Zod's gaze, and a distasteful frown flickered across his face. "You cannot be interested in *her,* Commissioner!"

"Why must I explain myself? I asked a simple enough question."

"Yes, Commissioner. Of course, Commissioner. She's the third daughter of the house of Ka, something of an outcast, an embarrassment. When her parents tried to disown her, she retaliated by deleting her family name. She insists on being called simply Aethyr."

"Wonderful."

"Shameful! She intentionally refuses to live up to her family's great lineage."

Zod scratched his beard, contemplating. "Because she does things they disapprove of?"

"Certainly, Commissioner. She doesn't like her family, and they don't like her. I don't know why she insisted on coming to the chariot races, why she would want to be seen with them in their box."

Zod restrained his smile. Even if his naïve companion couldn't comprehend the reason, he understood the answer very well. Aethyr probably relished the very discomfort she caused, and she did it on purpose. He found it charming. Looking around, he saw members in the other noble boxes glancing at the Ka seats, frowning at Aethyr, then quickly turning away. So painfully obvious, so artificial. Kryptonians were like players in a stale performance.

"Don't you see? This is her rebellion, and she flaunts it in front of her family." He laughed. "Watch how the closer she comes to them, the more they flinch away. It's all a game to her. Aethyr is smarter than every member of her family. She is a diamond in the rough, Vor-On. In fact, she's quite beautiful."

Vor-On responded with horror. "Maybe—*if* you could see past all the dirt and her flaws. And those . . . clothes!"

"If she wished, Aethyr could dress herself in clothing that other people told her to wear, but nothing can artificially create that sheer charisma."

The preparation horns sounded. Fanfares played over tuned resonator systems, drowning out the background noise of the audience. Even under the blazing red sunlight, ornamental lights sparkled from the tops of fluted obsidian columns around the Council seating area. Vor-On immediately turned to the track, glad to concentrate on something more appropriate than Aethyr.

The ground-level gates rolled up, and the beasts emerged from the shadows of the darkened pens. Teams of hrakkas—brawny, short-legged lizards with jagged head crests—plodded forward, three tethered to each floating vehicle. The green-and-tan creatures strained in their yokes as each team hauled its chariot out into the open. The scaly hides bore the marks of noble family sponsors.

Zod narrowed his eyes to watch as his own man emerged. Bushy bearded and broad shouldered, Nam-Ek stood tall at the helm of his vehicle, holding the reins in one thick hand. Zod covered his smug smile as the audience began muttering about the unusual beasts hooked to Nam-Ek's chariot.

The mute had tamed black-skinned lizards from Krypton's wild southern continent. Adorned with horns and spines along their bodies, ebony scales, and scarlet head crests, these were feral creatures accustomed to hunting and gutting their own prey. As a trainer, Nam-Ek could be as fierce as the beasts, and he had whipped the three into line. The burly driver appeared utterly confident.

When all chariots were in place at the starting line, bald and grand-fatherly Council Head Jul-Us stepped up to the main podium. Among all the resounding cheers, Zod could manage little more than polite applause. Although old Jul-Us was well liked in Kandor, Zod despised the man for his high position. *He* should have been the head of the Council, but due to political backstabbing and faithless "allies," Zod had been shunted aside and put in charge of the minor Commission as a consolation prize. Though he had eventually reaped more power from that position than any Council member realized, Zod would never forget being unfairly spurned.

All eyes were upon Jul-Us as he raised a long scarlet crystal over his head, a symbolic shard containing a burst of light. Below, all of the chariot drivers marshaled their impatient hrakkas, ready to jockey for position as soon as they received the signal.

To his credit, the Council Head was not a man who demanded atten-tion and praise from the people of Kandor. He said simply, "Let the races begin!" and snapped the scarlet shard in two, releasing a blazing flash.

The hrakkas lunged forward, tugging at their harnesses and charg-ing down the packed track. With wiry muscles and long claws that dug into the gravel, Nam-Ek's black lizards pulled ahead. On either side of the big mute, the rival hrakka teams strained and pulled, trying to keep up with the feral beasts.

The crowd cheered for their chosen teams, waving pennants, calling last-minute wagers. Some whistled, some issued catcalls. Standing like a beatific stone deity in front of his box, Jul-Us watched the great races.

A thready voice tinged with barely controlled fear interrupted Zod's concentration. "Commissioner, I demand to speak with you!"

Forcibly calming himself, Zod looked smoothly over his shoulder. Close behind him, in a bright red cape and puffy sleeves, stood Bur-Al, his fourth in command at the Commission for Technology Acceptance. The man was an administrator, a functionary with neither backbone nor vision. "Why are you interrupting my enjoyment of the race? My man Nam-Ek is in the lead."

Bur-Al crossed his puffy-sleeved arms over his chest. "Commis-sioner, this issue would be best discussed in private."

Zod gave him a withering glance. "Then why come to a place with thousands of people gathered around?"

The other man seemed taken aback by the question, then blurted, "I've discovered your secret. I know what you've done with all the technological items you considered dangerous, the things you censored."

"Please confine your ravings to a more appropriate venue." The crowd shrieked and applauded. So far, Vor-On hadn't even noticed the mousy visitor. Finally the Commissioner sighed. "Very well, meet me downstairs in the private stables after the race is run, where we will not upset the rest of the crowd. Nam-Ek tends his hrakkas there, and you know he can't speak a word. Now leave me alone."

Enraptured by the spectacle, Vor-On raised his hands. "Did you see that, Commissioner? It was amazing!"

On the track, one of the chariots had wrecked. Nam-Ek pulled on his reins, encouraging the creatures without needing to whip them. The black beasts plunged ahead around the circuit, trampling the gravel, racing faster and faster. Zod sensed that Bur-Al was still behind him, fuming and antsy, but he ignored the man. Finally, the administrator went away.

Some noble families who had invested in opposing teams began to complain loudly about the black hrakkas. Behind closed doors before the running of the races, two racing officials had also questioned the legality of using the new species. Nam-Ek had looked forlorn and agitated, unable to verbally express his anxiety, but Zod, as always, had been the voice of reason, telling the officials to look at the letter of the rules. In the dusty old records, no one had defined exactly what a "hrakka" was. In the absence of any established rule to the contrary, the hidebound officials consented to let Nam-Ek's team compete in the races.

Now, as the charioteers entered the third lap, two of the opposing teams closed the gap, pushing the green-and-gold creatures beyond their limits of endurance. Zod could see that those hrakkas would probably die at the end of the race, which would no doubt cause a scandal in Kandor.

As one of the golden hrakkas pulled abreast of Nam-Ek's chariot, the nearest black beast turned its head and lashed out with a whiplike tongue, pulping the rival hrakka's eye. The wounded creature reared up, maddened, and clawed at the next creature in its harness. Suddenly the

chariot toppled over in a tumbling crash. The driver, wearing a protective suit and antigravity belt, ejected himself from the wreckage, unharmed, while the beasts lay injured and dying.

Wide-eyed, Vor-On looked at Zod as if he knew all the answers. "Is that allowed?"

"It is not forbidden by the rules."

"How could it not be forbidden? This is . . . horrible."

"One might call it innovative."

Zod felt a thrill as he watched. Nam-Ek's hrakkas lashed out with their long tongues to strike at the team on the right, also driving it into ruin. By now, the big mute had an indisputable lead. Zod didn't even need to watch the rest of the race; the outcome was a foregone conclusion. He let Vor-On pick over the refreshments that servants had placed in the Commissioner's box.

While all eyes were focused on the climax of the races, no one noticed Zod slip quietly away. He had to get down to the stables and begin his preparations before Bur-Al arrived.

The black hrakkas exuded an oily scent from musk glands behind their powerful jaws, but the stable smells did not bother Zod. He had built these pens adjacent to the big arena; they were dim and cool, and also very private. To his fellow noblemen, the stables showed that the Commissioner spared no extravagance to keep Nam-Ek, his chariot, and his hrakkas in fine form. For Zod, though, the stables served as a perfect place for unobserved meetings.

After the hard-fought race, Zod met his charioteer in the comforting shadows, standing aside as the victorious mute pulled the three black hrakkas into their pens and fastened thick chains to anchors on the wall.

Sweaty and exhilarated, Nam-Ek gulped directly from a bucket of cool water. He grinned at Zod, who patted his hefty shoulder in sincere congratulation. Though he must be famished, the mute would not eat until he had tended his hrakkas. The black lizards would also be ravenous from all the energy they had burned during their run, but Nam-Ek

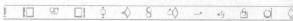

was careful not to feed them just yet. In their condition, they would gorge themselves and get sick.

The big charioteer rubbed a handful of oil into the hrakkas' hides, giving their scales a perfect obsidian sheen. He worked meticulously, massaging the beasts' muscles. The hrakkas growled and hissed and purred, but they made no threatening moves against Nam-Ek. They were also accustomed to Zod, who often came to the stables to do his thinking, frequently using Nam-Ek as a silent sounding board. He found it refreshing just to be able to speak his opinions without being interrupted by foolish comments.

After he explained to his muscular companion what he needed, Nam-Ek gave a brusque nod. Zod could still hear leftover noises from the crowd outside as people filed out of the stadium, chattering to one another, excited by the outcome of the race.

He looked up and saw a thin figure at the doorway. Bur-Al had come exactly as Zod had instructed him. The Commissioner leaned against the stone-block wall near the pens, looking at his fourth-level assistant. "I had hoped you would come to your senses by now, Bur-Al. You made some alarming accusations."

"Not just accusations. I have proof, and you know what I'm talking about. Don't even try to bribe me!"

"Who said anything about a bribe? I would never dream of it." *You're not worth the investment.*

Bur-Al gathered his courage. "I was a great admirer of your father, and it makes me ashamed to see that you don't follow in his footsteps. You put personal ambitions ahead of the perfection of Krypton."

"I thought Krypton was already perfect. And do not bring my father into the discussion. He was a great and visionary leader."

"In that, at least, we agree. But you have broken the law! All dangerous inventions submitted to the Commission must be destroyed. But that isn't the case, is it?" Bur-Al actually seemed to think he had the upper hand here.

"If you are so convinced, and if you insist that I cannot bribe you, why in the world would you broach the subject here? Why confront me with this? It seems foolish and naïve."

Bur-Al was flustered, as if he hadn't considered the question himself.

"I wanted to look into your face when I made my accusations. I wanted to see your eyes—and you've shown me that I am indeed correct."

Zod sighed. The man was an idiot. "Why should you need that, if you have incontrovertible proof? You haven't thought this through very well, Bur-Al."

The young man sniffed, taking the insult as a badge of honor. "I apologize for not being as well practiced in deceit and scheming as you are, Commissioner."

Zod walked over to where Nam-Ek had just finished oiling the third hrakka and stood wiping his hands on a rag. "You give me nothing to work with, and most serious of all, you have wasted my time. These few minutes of nonsense with you are minutes that I can never have back. Very inefficient." Bur-Al clenched his small fists at his sides. Zod turned to Nam-Ek. "The only redeeming factor is that I can make the event entertaining."

The charioteer clasped the thick chains with his bare hands, twisted them, and uprooted the anchor from the wall. The black hrakka stood up, thrashing, snarling. Nam-Ek broke the second chain, then the third.

"They are very hungry after the races," Zod explained. "You can make up for the waste of my time by at least saving me money on food."

The hrakkas bounded out of their pen before Bur-Al knew what was happening. The black lizards fell upon the hapless man, snapping and tearing. They gutted the young administrator, and blood sprayed in the air. A fanfare of resounding exit music played outside in the stadium, drowning out his screams. The last of the departing audience members cheered and laughed. Apparently the clowns were running along the track again, raking the gravel.

Bur-Al lay twitching in the sand and dust, and the three hrakkas continued their meal in the dim stable.

Zod said in a deadpan voice, "By the red heart of Rao, this is terrible. I simply don't know how they could have broken loose."

Nam-Ek could not tear his soulful eyes from the feeding frenzy. Zod could see the mute's misery, and his heart went out to the big man. "It'll be all right, Nam-Ek. I won't let them do anything to you."

Because murder was exceedingly rare on Krypton, no one would

suspect anything sinister. The deadly animals had simply gotten loose. An accident. Hrakkas were predators, after all, and had shown their penchant for violence during the running of the races. They were a hazard.

Nam-Ek pointed a blunt finger toward the three lizards, and Zod realized that his silent friend was distraught that the animals would now have to be destroyed. "I am sorry, Nam-Ek. There's nothing I can do about it." He racked his brain, unable to think of another way. "I'll get you new pets. I promise."

Clearly resigned, Nam-Ek nodded, and Zod felt a slight pang of guilt. It had seemed like the perfect way to get rid of Bur-Al, but perhaps he should have been more careful, should have thought of a subtler method that would not have jeopardized Nam-Ek's beloved hrakkas. "I promise I will make it better."

Once he was sure that his silent and muscular friend was all right, Zod calmly went out to sound the alarm.

CHAPTER 5

Even in Zor-El's beloved Argo City, most Kryptonians were too comfortable, their ambitions were too few, and they noticed too little of the world around them. They had forgotten the heady taste of danger. Zor-El, on the other hand, found it exhilarating to place himself in hazardous situations—at least when it was scientifically necessary.

According to his seismic sensor network, a tremendous volcanic eruption had occurred eight days earlier, and even now the aftermath contained enough hellish fury to incinerate him if he made a single misstep. The dark-eyed, ruddy-faced scientist stood alone among the brimstone and chaos of the wild southern continent—no safety nets, no guards, only his own wits and reactions. Many Kryptonians would have thought him mad to take such a risk.

Sulfurous smoke and fumes boiled into the air, and bubbling pools simmered around him. Zor-El let the hot breezes blow his black hair into a ragged mane around his face. His reddened eyes stung, and smoke and grit stained his cheeks.

He was enjoying himself immensely.

The ground shook again, and a geyser of scarlet lava shot up and arced back down like the mating plumage of a flamebird. After the massive seismic event, the fury that burbled beneath the planet's crust would take a long while to die down—if it died down at all. Zor-El wasn't convinced it ever would.

Over the years, suspecting that Krypton was by no means tame and

peaceful, geologically speaking, he had deployed a network of sensor stations at hot spots across the landscape. And Zor-El had grown more and more disturbed by the readings. . . .

Since he also served as the leader of Argo City, political duties demanded much of his time, but Zor-El never failed to monitor his geological stations. Argo City was a thriving metropolis on a narrow tropical peninsula off the main continent's southeastern coast. When the unprecedented volcanic eruption had occurred across the ocean on the distant southern continent, he had learned about it immediately. Judging by the readings, the explosion must have vaporized the mass-equivalent of a mountain, spraying ash, smoke, and poisonous vapor into the air. Had the southern continent been inhabited, the lava alone would have wiped out every settlement within hundreds of miles.

The ash and smoke had colored Argo City's sunsets with flaring oranges and reds. While the city's artists were inspired by the sheer beauty and color, Zor-El had explained to his wife, Alura, what the burning sky truly meant. "I must go down there and see for myself, take direct measurements. We can't ignore these danger signs. Something is brewing in our planet's core, and I have to find out what it is."

Cool and intelligent herself, Alura understood his scientific need for answers. "And once you know, what can you do about it?"

"That's a premature question. I've got to understand a problem before I can fix it. And if the task gets too difficult," he added, flashing a smile, "I'll ask Jor-El to help."

So he had packed his instruments and supplies and departed in a silver-winged aircraft. The sleek high-altitude vessel had a small enclosed cockpit, a cargo compartment in its belly, and streamlined wings that gathered wind and copious solar energy to drive its levitation engines.

Alone in the bright silence, Zor-El had circled up above Argo City, cutting through the morning sea mists. From this height, he could view his entire beautiful city, which was practically an island connected to the main continent only by a thin isthmus and five golden bridges. Argo City looked more marvelous than any map or painting.

He had streaked southward, leaving the curving coastline behind. As he gained altitude, Zor-El extended the flyer's razor-thin wing panels. The prevailing winds pushed him south, and the turbulence grew worse as he approached the isolated continent. The plume of gray smoke rose like a towering anvil into the sky. Volcanic ash powdered the flyer's viewscreen and dulled the reflective alloy of the hull, reducing its energy-absorbing abilities, but he pressed forward, eyes intent, brow furrowed.

From high above, Zor-El studied the mottled terrain, black rocks freshly formed by cooling lava, yellow-and-brown smears that indicated oozing sulfur compounds. As he circled the raw blast crater, he was amazed to note the extent of the destruction. The titanic eruption had knocked down countless trees, flattening them like crushed straw for kilometers around. The ecological impact was incalculable. How many creatures had gone extinct in only a few days? And how many more would die in the coming months and years with the continent so devastated? Only the hardiest life-forms could possibly survive.

Zor-El had retracted the flyer's wings and landed on a small patch of level ground outside the active lava area. Lava continued to boil from beneath scabs on the terrain, flowing out like extremely hot pudding. Whenever the lava encountered pools of stagnant water, steam plumes rocketed into the sky.

Exhilarated by the chaos around him, Zor-El climbed out of the flyer and gathered his pack and equipment. The air was oven-hot on his face. Each breath dried his mouth and seemed to sear his lungs. Alura had prepared him for this, though. Back in Argo City, with her vast botanical knowledge and greenhouses full of exotic species, she had picked a sealed bud—fleshy, soft and moist, the size of an outstretched hand. She had explained what to do with it, and now he silently thanked her.

Before setting out across the volcanic field, he pulled the bud from his pack. When he stroked the tight sepals at the base of its broken stem, the fleshy petals opened to form a soft and protective cup large enough to cover the lower half of his face. Zor-El placed the petals firmly over his mouth and nose, where they gently adhered; then he tentatively drew in a breath. He could barely smell the flower's perfume, but the air he inhaled was sweet and fresh, filtered through the stem and the active membrane of the petals. He drew another breath, satisfied.

He trudged across sharp rocks that were still hot. The sound around him was a background roar. A bright splash of lava flowed like spilled blood across the blackened ground. When he reached the edge of the molten river, he stared directly into the fury for a long moment, then got to work.

Zor-El opened his pack and removed the prized new tool he had invented—a diamondfish, half alive and half machine. It was shaped like a powerful swimmer, its scales formed of purest diamond to protect the delicate internal circuitry, its body run by a network of circuit paths as well as biological nerves. The diamondfish twitched in his hand as he activated it. When it turned faceted eyes toward him, he looked the gleaming creature-device in the face. "Tell me what's down there."

He switched on a small force-field generator (another of his inventions), which projected a shimmering protective sheath around the mechanical animal. "Swim deep, as far as you can go." He gently tossed the diamondfish into the air. It twitched and wriggled as it plunged into the hot, scarlet current. As if playing, the diamondfish splashed about in the molten rock, then dove downward.

From his pack, Zor-El removed a contact screen and activated it. Picking up the signal from the creature-device, he monitored the diamondfish as it swam deeper. It tasted the magma, ran the chemical constituents through integrated analyzers, and followed the intense thermal currents deeper.

As Zor-El looked around at the sterile, barren environment, he could feel the ground trembling beneath his feet. The diamondfish's continued readings gave alarming indications of rising pressures in the planet's core. He couldn't be sure exactly what it meant. Zor-El suspected that some inexplicable radioactive shift was occurring far beneath the crust. Elements were converting, creating strange mineral instabilities. But how? He had to know.

With another convulsive upheaval, the river of lava churned. The magma level dropped, then bubbled up again in a fresh burst. He was astonished when the molten rock abruptly changed color, as if a vat of dye had spilled into it. Instead of the intense orange and scarlet, a gush of some new mineral compound appeared—a bright emerald green seeping into the flow like a spreading stain. Zor-El had never seen anything like it. Then the thermal currents swallowed up the green, and the lava ran red again.

The dutiful diamondfish swam deeper and deeper, hotter and hotter.

On Zor-El's contact screen the readings became even more damning. The situation in the mantle was worse than he had feared.

Then, with a flash of static, the signal vanished. The diamondfish had been programmed to keep going until the extreme temperatures terminated it. He felt briefly sorry for the brave little creature-device, but it had served well. More important, it had given him vital, but baffling information. Something unimaginably powerful but inexplicable was shifting deep beneath his feet. The larger question was to determine whether this was a fascinating curiosity or an impending planetary disaster.

Zor-El began making plans to bring much larger teams here with heavy equipment. More than likely, he would have to pull his brother into the effort if the scale was as great as he imagined. Though Jor-El was more of an astronomer than a geologist, more theoretician than engineer, his insights would be vital. Even from the preliminary glimpse of data, Zor-El guessed that this problem was too large to be ignored.

He breathed through the flower mask on his face, and fumaroles and geysers continued to hiss around him, blurring his vision. As he rummaged in his pack, though, something gave him an instinctive shudder, a feeling that he was being watched even in this blasted place. The dark hairs prickled on the back of his neck.

He stood and spun, ready to fight. Suddenly, he saw movement among the black rocks, no more than a shadow—four shadows. Their color was the same as fresh lava rock and newly cooled obsidian, but the motion was lithe, fast, predatory. Crawling over the terrain low to the ground came four vicious-looking giant lizards. Hrakkas.

They were stalking him.

Zor-El drew a quick breath through the filtering flower. His mind spun as he tried to find a way to protect himself. He had not come here to the southern continent to fight. Because most indigenous creatures had been wiped out in the eruption, these hardy lizards must be very hungry. Their normal prey had been decimated, and the steaming landscape offered very little to eat, even for scavengers.

Careful to make no abrupt moves, Zor-El held his pack in front of him, the only shield he had. He estimated how far away his landed flyer was. Judging by their powerful reptilian legs, he assumed the hrakkas could run faster than he could, especially over the sharp-edged rock field.

The dark lizards warily circled him, and he watched their every movement. He counted four, but that didn't mean there weren't more of them unseen among the jumbled terrain. They hunted like a pack and could very well be setting up a trap. The creatures blended into their surroundings, except when they opened their jaws, and the flash of white teeth gave them away.

Because the smooth black crust could be eggshell thin, Zor-El had been careful picking his way to the edge of the lava flow. Now he scanned the ground along his escape route and mentally mapped his path, planning ten footsteps ahead. When he saw the black lizards closing in, he bolted.

Zor-El had taken no more than five steps before the creatures gave up all attempts at stealth and bounded after him. He jumped from one large rock to another, hoping each foothold was solid and stable. With one arm wrapped around the pack, he heaved great breaths through the flower mask. His foot slipped, and a sharp rock cut a long gash in his ankle. He ignored the pain, kept running.

Smelling blood, the hrakkas closed in. The nearest one stepped on a thin-shelled area and broke through, and its clawed forelimb dropped into the still-molten rock underneath. It yowled and hissed, pulling out a smoking stump, the rest of its paw incinerated. Sensing easy prey, a second hrakka dashed in, opened its jaws, tore open the belly of its wounded companion, and began to feed, ignoring the chase.

With half of the hrakkas out of the way, Zor-El had to worry about only two more of the black lizards. When one lunged at him, he spun and shoved his pack into its gaping mouth. He jammed it firmly into the beast's maw and twisted to shove the lizard aside. The momentum nearly bowled him over, but he let go of the tangled pack and sprang in another direction.

The hrakka tossed its head back and forth, trying to rip open the object or free its teeth. The other hrakka dove in, fighting for whatever "prey" the other had caught. Both creatures ignored Zor-El.

In the struggle with the pack, the filtering flower had been knocked from Zor-El's face, and now each breath felt as if he were gulping an open flame. Panting, he increased his lead, furious at the hrakkas. His data had been inside the pack—along with the readings the diamondfish had taken! All evidence of the drastic changes occurring in Krypton's core! Now how could he show Jor-El?

Irrationally, he considered going back to fight for what was rightfully his—until a fifth, previously unseen black lizard burst out from between two boulders and dove at him. Zor-El tried to dodge, but his escape was blocked by a sheer drop-off and a streaming flow of scarlet lava.

Zor-El struck back with his arms and fists. The lizard's sharp scales and jagged crest cut him, lacerating his forearm and his side. The hrakka snapped its jaws, raked him with its claws, but Zor-El fought back and finally pulled away.

The hrakka bounded onto the jagged rocks near the edge of the flowing magma, then came back at him. Zor-El kicked it in the ribs. The lizard scrabbled sideways on the shaking ground where steam and sulfurous smoke burbled up. Just as the hrakka coiled itself to spring again, the rocks collapsed beneath it, and the bank of the molten river gave way. The hrakka scrabbled for a foothold as it slid into the lava, where it was incinerated alive.

Zor-El somehow managed to keep his balance. Before he could inhale the searing air to breathe a sigh of relief, the continued turbulence of the eruption sent a spray of liquid stone into the air. Instinctively, he raised his bleeding arm to shield himself, and globules of lava splashed onto his side and his forearm, like a rain of tiny branding irons.

Crying out from the pain, he staggered away. The hot droplets of rock kept burning deeper into his skin. He gagged from the smell of sizzling flesh and burned hair. With his other hand he clawed at his arm and side, but the heat had cauterized the wounds.

Overwhelmed by waves of pain, he couldn't tell how badly he was injured. With great determination, Zor-El drove back the agony. He had a greater mission now. He *had* to survive. He had to get back to Argo City because of what he had discovered. He had to see his brother. In the worst-case scenario, the very fate of the planet might be in his hands.

Though each breath burned his mouth, and he could barely see, Zor-El somehow made it back to the stable ground where he had landed his silver flyer. Panting and shuddering, yet strangely exhilarated from the endorphins flooding through him, he hauled himself up into the cockpit. He refused to let himself faint.

Zor-El powered up the levitation engines, extended the ash-covered wing panels in an attempt to drink in more solar energy, and finally lifted off into the buffeting thermal currents. As the craft rose away from the southern continent, far from the stark and dangerous lava field, he saw another bright flash of emerald green, the new form of mineral lava burbling up from Krypton's depths.

CHAPTER 6

∞⚷◇‼◇⚷Ṭ♀♌ 6

Even though he viewed the world in terms of mathematics and science, the raw beauty of Kandor took Jor-El's breath away. With its temples to Rao, the shining pyramids, and the great Council ziggurat, Krypton's capital city was the pinnacle of civilization. Some exotic buildings had been grown from active crystals; other edifices were hewn from lustrous white veinrock or speckled granite polished to a sheen that reflected the red sunlight.

Early that morning Jor-El had departed from the estate on his personal flying platform, an open levitating raft that skimmed smoothly only two meters above the purple and brown grasses of the vast Neejon plain. He stood relaxed at the control pedestal, holding the accelerator and guidance handles, looking ahead at the approaching metropolis. Behind him he towed a cargo floater wide enough to carry the silver-ringed frame of the Phantom Zone and its crystal control array.

When he reached Kandor, he surrendered his invention to the city security forces, which were named the Sapphire Guards for their deep-blue armor. He gave them the Phantom Zone and the control console for processing and delivery to the Commission for Technology Acceptance. The guards knew who he was and stared at him with amazement, as if he were a great celebrity; Jor-El barely noticed. Their reverence for his previous accomplishments, though, made them listen very carefully when he warned them to treat the hovering "gap" in the air with extreme care. He left the framed singularity with them for safekeeping until he could make his case to Commissioner Zod.

Because of his boundless imagination, Jor-El had done this many times before, always optimistic about the prospects of a new technological innovation. All too often, though, his most exotic ideas were deemed too dangerous for a safe and peaceful Kryptonian society, and then they were censored and destroyed. In spite of his many successes, the frequent defeats frustrated Jor-El. The Commissioner (following the orders of the eleven-member Council) was prone to overreact . . . most of the time.

Jor-El wasn't so sure about the Phantom Zone, though. It had not turned out to be a portal into parallel universes as he had anticipated, and after his frightening ordeal inside the empty dimension, even Jor-El was uneasy about the possibility that it could be misused. Placing a call via public communication plate, he steeled himself and requested a meeting with Commissioner Dru-Zod.

However, Zod was involved in the funeral preparations for his fourth-level assistant, Bur-Al, who had been tragically killed in the hrakka stables. The Commissioner could not meet with him until late that afternoon.

In the meantime, Jor-El decided to watch the proceedings of the Kryptonian Council, which was in session. The government temple was a huge stepped pyramid at the very center of the city. Each corner was adorned with crystal shards, and atop the pyramid, focusing lenses displayed a high-resolution image of the red sun, projecting the incandescent face of Rao like a spotlight above Kandor.

Jor-El casually entered the observation gallery, following a tall, orange-haired instructor who ushered a group of well-behaved children to reserved seats as part of a class project. He made no mention of who he was, tried to keep a low profile. Even though he wasn't part of the Council itself, Jor-El had been invited to serve many times. He had always declined the offer, claiming that he had more important things to accomplish. His attitude startled and perplexed the Council members, who couldn't conceive of anything "more important," but that only increased his mystique. Even so, they kept the invitation open, offering to create a pending seat for him, if he ever decided to take up politics, like his brother from Argo City. Jor-El did not see that day coming any time soon.

Inside the immense hall, tiers and tiers of stone benches were carved out of the inner walls to accommodate thousands of spectators. Today, surprisingly, the audience tiers were filled. People in fantastically expensive and exotic formal attire crowded shoulder to shoulder with workers dressed in drab uniforms. Something interesting must be on the docket for this session. Jor-El rarely paid attention to the news.

The eleven Council members sat next to one another at a high bench many meters above the floor, where they loomed godlike above those who chose to speak. Jor-El himself had appeared before the eleven powerful representatives on several occasions. Though the Council considered him Krypton's greatest scientific hero, he could rarely get them to budge from their conservative stance.

Armored Sapphire Guards marched in, leading a prisoner across the tiled arena floor. The man was weighed down with transparent shackles and further restrained by a stun collar around his throat. His clothes were torn and blotched with reddish-brown stains that Jor-El guessed must be old blood. His blond hair was unkempt, his eyes wild-looking, his long face haggard. The prisoner moved with a feral clumsiness—stumbling, cringing, but always alert for a chance to escape. Members of the crowd hissed and drew back, as if the very wrongness of this man might contaminate those in the nearest lines of seats.

The Sapphire Guards hauled the prisoner in front of the Council, then took a step back to let the shackled man stand by himself. The security men remained tense and alert, close enough to seize the prisoner if he should become violent.

When old Jul-Us stood up in his white robes, he no longer looked grandfatherly or kind. He spoke in a booming voice. "Gur-Va, you have committed a heinous crime. You were caught in the Kandor zoo soaked with the blood of your victims, their torn bodies at your feet."

Gur-Va lifted his blond head, pulled back his lips to expose long teeth. "I am a predator. They were prey. What I did was only natural."

"What you did was an abomination!" said Kor-Te, a Council member who had thick silver hair that hung to his shoulders in waves, intentionally emulating the style of Krypton's classic leaders. "All details of this incident should be struck from the record so that future generations need not be sickened by it!"

Jor-El was astonished by the statement. Kor-Te practically worshipped past decisions and mandates; he read and quoted from the Council annals and documents as if they were holy scripture. In Council business Kor-Te believed that all important discoveries had already been made and that all matters had already been decided. To him, any question could be answered by digging through the annals and finding the appropriate quotation. It was inconceivable that such a man would propose striking an event from the historical record.

Jor-El leaned forward, fascinated. He turned to an intent gray-haired woman next to him. "What exactly has this man done? Whom did he kill?"

The old woman's expression overflowed with disgust and disbelief. "He's the Butcher of Kandor—broke into the zoo and went from cage to cage with his long knives, slaughtering rare animals. He chopped apart the last living flamebird. He decapitated the drang. He slit the throats of both rondors on display. It was senseless and appalling."

Above the arena floor, Council member Pol-Ev called for a series of evidence images to be projected. Pol-Ev, the dandy on the Council, had so many clothes and robes with trendy folds and ruffles it was hard to tell whether he followed fashion or set it. His hair was swirled and primped and pomaded, and he always wore a distinctive cologne that added a lingering background aroma to the entire chamber. Now, though, he looked ready to faint.

Crisp holograms showed mangled carcasses in merciless detail. Amid gasps and outcries from the spectators' gallery, several people became audibly ill; others, greenish and pale, stumbled out of the Council temple. The orange-haired teacher nearly fell over himself as he hurried his group of young students out of the tiers of seats.

Jor-El could hardly believe the sheer violence of what he saw in the display. The drang, a purple flying snake, had been hacked to pieces. The snagriff, a winged dinosaur, had been hamstrung in its cage and, once it had dropped to the ground, Gur-Va had gutted it while it was still alive. The heavy rondors, nearly hunted to extinction because their curved horns supposedly cured many illnesses, lay in a pool of their own blood; one had managed to crawl to its watering pond and slumped over the rim, near its mutilated mate.

Standing in the arena, Gur-Va seemed maliciously delighted to see the images. Why would anyone commit such a senseless act? What purpose did it serve? What could this man possibly have meant to accomplish? The utter irrationality of it made Jor-El reel.

Trying to steady himself, he viewed this as a problem, a puzzle. Something had corrupted Gur-Va's personality, broken him from sanity. The bloodthirsty temperament of this twisted man was a throwback to violent and primitive times. Where did such destructive impulses come from?

Such ferocious criminals were true anomalies on modern, peaceful Krypton. Inspired in part by his father's psychological deterioration from the Forgetting Disease, Jor-El's mother had spent a great deal of time trying to understand the mysteries of the Kryptonian mind. But psychology was not a mathematical, precise science.

All eleven Council members were so appalled that they remained silent for a long moment before turning to each other in quiet, urgent discussion. Jul-Us did not take long to pronounce the obvious sentence. "Your senseless actions are inconceivable. You are a danger to yourself and to all life on Krypton."

The prisoner started laughing. "Show the images again—especially the snagriff. That was my favorite!"

In consternation, the old Council Head raised his voice. "We will hold you deep underground in a cell from which you will never escape, and where you will never again see the red light of Rao. We do this for the safety of our people, and the protection of your soul."

Gur-Va didn't struggle as the muscular Sapphire Guards hauled him away, his transparent chains and shackles clanking. Jor-El felt an empty nausea inside. The punishment seemed harsh and terrible, but what else could be done with such a dangerous atavism? The audience muttered in approval. This was the most severe sentence the Council could impose. Only one or two criminals per year suffered such a fate.

Recently, another scientist had proposed that the worst criminals be sealed in capsules, placed in suspended animation with mental reconfiguring crystals fixed to their foreheads. Over the course of decades, the

scientist suggested, the reconfiguring crystals might heal their damaged minds. But the Council members did not consider that solution feasible. Where else could such violent criminals be placed, except in an impregnable underground cell?

Suddenly Jor-El realized what he should do, what he must suggest to the Commissioner. A hopeful smile crossed his face. Perhaps his new discovery did indeed have a practical application.

He looked forward to presenting the idea to Commissioner Zod.

Two blocks from the majestic governmental ziggurat, the Commission for Technology Acceptance was headquartered in an unpretentious side building, as if to emphasize the fact that Zod's status was far inferior to the Council's. As far as Jor-El could tell, the Commissioner ignored the implication.

When he arrived for his scheduled afternoon meeting, Jor-El noticed a weighty, somber feeling inside the office building. The windowfilms had been phased so that the huge sun bathed the rooms in muted, warm light. He recalled that the Commission staff had just returned from the funeral for their coworker.

Commissioner Zod stood to greet Jor-El, offering him a pleasant smile despite the gloom. Zod's office had a spartan feel, without the grandeur and ostentation of other buildings in Kandor. "How have you decided to challenge me today? Something to delight my sensibilities or something that will make me worry?"

"A little of both, Commissioner—as always." Despite the man's cordial reception, Jor-El could never forget that Zod was his adversary, a hindrance if not an actual barricade to progress.

Seeing Jor-El's expression, the Commissioner shook his head in a mixture of disappointment and reproof. "I believe you enjoy making my job difficult."

"I prefer the term 'challenging.'"

No one could doubt that Jor-El had done remarkable things for Kryptonian society—more efficient transportation monitoring to minimize accidents, new techniques to illuminate large structures through photonic excitation of crystal lattices, highly sophisticated medical scanning devices that could study ailments on a deep cellular level, advanced agricultural harvesting machinery that significantly increased crop yields. The average Kryptonian believed Jor-El could accomplish virtually anything he set his mind to.

Ever since the restrictions to progress had been set down generations ago, all new inventions needed to be submitted to the special Commission for Technology Acceptance, which would determine if any new technology had the potential to be used for dangerous purposes. The nightmare of Jax-Ur and his nova javelins had never been forgotten, and the people had no incentive to take risks. Zod's job, like that of his predecessors, was to crack down on any item that did not fit within a narrow definition of what was "acceptable."

"I wish we had more scientists like you," the Commissioner had once told Jor-El, sounding very sincere. "Alas, not everyone's character is as unimpeachable as yours. If only I didn't have to worry about your work being corrupted and used for evil purposes."

Jor-El could not disagree. In recent years incidents of bizarre and violent crimes had grown more and more frequent—for no apparent reason. Having seen the wild look in the eyes of the Butcher of Kandor, he shuddered to think what a man like that could have done with some of his inventions. . . .

Zod called for his security men to bring the item to his office. "Let us see what you've brought me this time."

Jor-El let enthusiasm guide his words. "I've created a hole in the universe that leads to a dimension I can only describe as a Phantom Zone. It's pure emptiness."

Two burly Sapphire Guards arrived, guiding a levitating platform that held the stilled silver rings and the blank field they enclosed. Because the singularity was composed of nothing at all, bounded by positive and negative energy, the frame was remarkably light. The guards barely had to strain their large muscles as they brought the containment frame into the Commissioner's office.

Zod's eyes widened. "By the red heart of Rao! You always manage to astonish me."

After the Commissioner dismissed the guards, Jor-El explained his experiment. "During yesterday's solar storm, Rao's energy was sufficient for me to punch through the fabric of space and create a kind of singularity. It's a doorway, or a portal, and it is stable."

Zod leaned closer to the fuzzy blankness that hovered in the air, but Jor-El quickly blocked the other man. "Be careful not to touch the field. I discovered how sensitive it is. I was trapped there for hours until a . . . friend . . . released me."

"Intriguing. So you fell through that hole into another dimension?"

"Only temporarily, Commissioner. With a relatively simple control panel, modified from standard equipment, it is possible to release an individual from the Zone. I need to spend more time conducting experiments, perhaps even with volunteer test subjects. I've been in there myself, and I came out unharmed, so there's no real danger." He offered his annotated plans. "I have brought the prototype control panel from my estate."

Zod tapped a finger against his lips, calculating. "And what possible practical use could this Phantom Zone have?"

Jor-El jumped at his chance, perhaps the only chance to get the device approved rather than censored. "A very real and relevant application occurred to me during this morning's trial in the Council temple."

"Ah, the Butcher of Kandor? Unfortunately, I was busy with the funeral of my poor assistant."

"We have no real way to punish or secure such a person. We don't know how to rehabilitate the damaged minds of our worst criminals, and it has been centuries since we considered such barbaric penalties as execution. The Butcher was sentenced to spend the rest of his life deep in an underground cell. Personally, I consider that a very inadequate solution."

Zod was unaffected by Jor-El's logic. "And what do you propose?"

"Sentence our worst criminals to the Phantom Zone instead of sealing them in underground cells until they die. In that other dimension, they have no physical needs, experience no pain, and can cause no further damage. Think of it, Commissioner—those criminals would be left to contemplate their crimes in passive and permanent isolation. If the Council ever determined they were sufficiently repentant, we could release them."

Zod scratched his neat beard. "Intriguing. Such violent criminals do make us nervous and uneasy. Your Phantom Zone would be a very effective way of sweeping them under the rug."

Jor-El flushed. "I wouldn't put it in such a crude fashion."

"I was not criticizing you. It seems little different from locking them away in an underground cell—and much more secure." He let out a long sigh—a sigh that Jor-El knew all too well. "But I must consider the worst-case scenario." Zod walked slowly around the silver rings, looking into the central gap as if he might find an answer there. "What if this singularity fell into the wrong hands? What if it were abused?"

Jor-El stiffened. "Naturally, we'd have to keep it under heavy guard, to be used in only the most extreme circumstances."

"And what if the guards themselves were corrupted? What if an enemy mounted a surprise military assault?" Zod shook his head. "The Council members are very strict in cases such as this—one practical application does not cancel dozens of possible abuses. I cannot in good conscience grant this Phantom Zone our stamp of approval. Too many drawbacks."

Jor-El had a sinking feeling in the pit of his stomach, but he did not meekly turn away. His voice had a rough edge of anger. "Commissioner, using those criteria, you'd forbid the use of fire because someone might burn his fingers. How will our lives ever improve?"

Zod folded his hands. "According to our beloved Council, there is no need for improvement on Krypton." Did his voice have a hint of sarcasm? "Unfortunately, I have no recourse but to seize your Phantom Zone, your blueprints, and all related materials. I cannot allow this device to tempt the twisted elements in our society."

Jor-El clenched his jaws, biting back further argument. He knew full well that he would not change Zod's mind, and he had no choice but to admit defeat for the moment, though he chafed under the harsh, narrow-minded, and nonsensical restrictions.

"I *will* keep trying, Commissioner," he said, making it a promise.

CHAPTER 8

After Jor-El departed in frustration, Zod could barely control his excitement. He left instructions with the outer receptionist that he was not to be disturbed, then turned to study the vertical silver rings that enclosed the Phantom Zone. Jor-El's discoveries were often frivolous or useless, but occasionally the man produced something that struck the Commissioner with awe. The scientist had outdone himself this time.

At his summons, burly Nam-Ek arrived within minutes, as if he had been waiting for the Commissioner's call. Zod locked the office door securely after him. With childlike curiosity and uncertainty, the bearded mute peered through the shimmering silver rings. When he raised a hand to poke at them, Zod lurched forward to stop him. "Careful, it's dangerous! I don't want to lose you." Nam-Ek gave him a grateful look.

Though his front office was small and plain, Zod went to the back wall and operated a secret lift chamber from a hidden panel. "Store that down below with the other items, where it will be safe."

Nam-Ek obeyed without question. After the back wall slid open, the muscular man dragged the rings through the covert door onto the lift platform. Together, the two men rode the humming elevator to the hidden room beneath the Commission's main offices. Without so much as a grunt of effort, Nam-Ek wrestled the silver rings into an open area.

The empty blankness of the Phantom Zone beckoned to Zod. He believed Jor-El's report, of course, but he wanted to see direct evidence for himself. This could well be the most powerful object in his special collection. He walked around the rings, looked at the flat opening from both sides, but could determine nothing. "Fetch me a servant, Nam-Ek. I don't care which one."

Without hesitation, the broad-shouldered man strode to the lower entrance of the underground chamber. The doorway was hidden, mounted behind the far wall of a forgotten storage room. Nam-Ek opened it and began to prowl through the halls of the Commission building's lower levels.

Zod remained behind, looking at all the devices on display as he pondered possibilities. Here, he kept all the important innovations that he had censored over the years. For the good of Krypton. As far as Jor-El and the handful of other visionary scientists knew, their "unapproved" inventions had been destroyed, but the Commissioner had assembled a veritable museum of marvels, available to himself and no one else. No one else bothered to see the potential; those eleven cretins on the Council were incapable of original thought.

Alone with his toys, he marveled at one object after another: a "Rao beam"—an intense burning ray that could be used for important construction work but also, obviously, as a potential weapon. Powerful engines that could drive a rocket into space. Memory crystals that could cause a person to forget or remember anything that a controller desired. Self-guided levitating daggers that could be directed to a specific target—what had Jor-El been *thinking* with that one?

Zod rationalized his acts by following the letter of his mandate—in a sense. Though he kept them for himself, he *did* remove potentially dangerous discoveries from the hands of the people. But he simply could not bear to waste such brilliance. Who could guarantee that Krypton would never need these discoveries? It was insane to discard such amazing items just because shortsighted politicians were afraid of change. He trusted himself to be a good steward for the world, unlike the pampered and self-congratulatory members of the Council. He certainly didn't trust *them.*

Zod's resentment toward the eleven inept blowhards had been building for a long time. He saw them for what they were: mere symbols. Though they had power available to them, they did nothing with it.

He was the son of the great Council Head Cor-Zod, who had ruled well, married late, and lived to a ripe old age. The man had taught his son the nuances of power and government, how to get things done and take satisfaction in his accomplishments. In his younger years, Zod had always assumed he would have a Council seat of his own when one became available; in fact, he had expected to step in when his father died.

But the other Council members had snubbed him. Rather than offer him a seat equal to their own, they had appointed Zod to the relatively unimportant Commission for Technology Acceptance. It was a humiliating blow at the time, a consolation prize. The supercilious leaders claimed he was "too young, not yet ready to become a Council member." Mastering his temper, Zod had listened to their excuses and rationalizations. To fill his father's seat, the Council appointed a wealthy nobleman named Al-An. Zod soon realized that Al-An had extravagantly bribed the Council.

Until that moment, Zod had been so confident in his legitimate claim that he had never considered paying off the other members. He'd been too naïve to see how corrupt the Council was. He had believed in fairness, in a sense of duty and achievement, and now his expected career had been destroyed because of it. Though he felt outraged and cheated, he contained his fury.

Zod had learned a valuable lesson from his father, though. "Power lies not in a name or title, but in what one does with it." And, oh, he intended to do something with what power he had.

Taking that to heart, he had once mused aloud to Nam-Ek, "They could have given me a meaningless appointment as a Council member, and I would have accomplished nothing beyond wearing a fine white robe with my family symbol. I could have endlessly debated issues that would never be decided. Instead, they gave me something far more valuable: a position I can use."

Rather than throwing a tantrum upon being bypassed, Zod stoically accepted his work in the Commission. Unlike the Council members, he understood how much power that position could generate, if handled properly.

Even for routine daily business, the eleven-member Council required a unanimous vote to enact any law . . . virtually assuring that no meaningful decision could ever be made. As a recalcitrant member he would have indeed had power, since a single dissenting vote could derail any new project, law, or proclamation. But that was only the power to stall, not to succeed. Zod believed he had a much greater destiny. He wanted to leave his mark on Krypton.

Over the years, he had quietly made the Commission for Technology Acceptance one of the most powerful and important entities in all of Kandor. The Council didn't even realize what they had allowed to grow right under their noses. Now, looking at all the wondrous devices he had collected, Zod felt quite satisfied.

Before long, Nam-Ek returned, practically hauling a wide-eyed servant into the hidden chamber. Though his shoulders were bowed, the servant looked in amazement at the exotic technological artifacts before noticing Zod. "Oh, Commissioner! How may I help you?"

"What is your name?"

"Hopk-Ins, sir." Zod had never even heard of his family . . . one of the lower classes, certainly. The man continued to gawk. "I've worked here for fifteen years and never suspected—"

"Of course you never suspected." Zod turned to Nam-Ek. "Throw him into the Phantom Zone. I want to observe what happens."

Nam-Ek grabbed the scrawny man by the back of the collar and hoisted him into the air. Hopk-Ins began kicking and squirming. "What are you doing?"

The mute threw the much smaller man like a rag doll into the middle of the silver rings. Hopk-Ins wailed—then abruptly vanished.

After being sucked into the void, the servant looked as if he had been squashed between two thin panes of crystal. He was flattened but still alive, and frantically trying to get back out. The silence was absolute.

Zod clapped his hands together. "Even better than I had hoped! Most intriguing." He could think of several ways to use this device.

The hapless Hopk-Ins was lost forever inside the Phantom Zone, unless someone reversed the polarity in the control array, as Jor-El had explained. Zod had no intention of doing so. For him, the benefit of the Phantom Zone would be to get rid of inconvenient people; he didn't need to worry about how they could be brought back. It was much cleaner than murder.

Nam-Ek was amazed, and a broad grin spread across his face. Zod again felt a paternal warmth in his chest. From the moment he'd taken Nam-Ek under his wing as a boy, they had trusted each other. "And now I have another job for you."

No one was supposed to know about this secret chamber, and he was annoyed that a simpleton such as Bur-Al had discovered its existence. What if the fourth-level assistant had left some sort of proof or testament for others to find? That worried Zod, and he did not intend to lose his toys.

He handed Nam-Ek a map. "Years ago, I set up a bunker in the Redcliff Mountains. I want you to secretly move these treasures. There's too great a chance they could be discovered here. Take as many days as you require, but do it yourself. I can rely on no one but you."

CHAPTER 9

The arena stables were Nam-Ek's own place, and he enjoyed spending as much time there as he could. He had liked animals since he was a child. Commissioner Zod often gave him expensive and exotic pets that no one else in Kandor owned, but Nam-Ek didn't really care how rare they were or how special their breeding might be. He just liked the animals. Any animals.

At least once a year, the Commissioner would set aside a day on which he took Nam-Ek to the extravagant zoo in Kandor so that he could see the incredible creatures. The big man wished he could share that excitement with his beloved mentor. Zod simply didn't see the same wonder, but even so he did this for Nam-Ek, and the mute couldn't imagine a greater gift.

Now in the dim shadows of the stables, he hunkered down in the dry, sweet-smelling hay. Now that the black hrakkas were gone, four heavyset, slow-moving gurns had become his pets. Though gurns were as common as dirt, Nam-Ek had a special fondness for them. The stocky creatures were covered with matted gray fur that gave off a pungent musk; their stubby horns were little more than knobs. Others considered the herd creatures to be stupid, saw them as nothing more than walking meat, but Nam-Ek saw them as friends . . . friends from childhood. He loved them.

He had also loved his black hrakkas—trained them, fed them, oiled their scales . . . but they were gone now, taken from him. Nam-Ek understood that they were dead. Just because he could not speak didn't mean he was thick-witted. Because the hrakkas had killed that man after the chariot races, they'd been "destroyed" or "euthanized."

Nam-Ek had stood with tears in his eyes and his huge fists clenched at his sides as Sapphire Guards had muzzled the reptilian beasts and dragged them away. He had wanted to oil their scales one last time, to clean the blood from their teeth, but the guards wouldn't let him. Nam-Ek felt sickened to think about what had happened to the black lizards. Had the guards clubbed their skulls, or simply given them poison as a "humane" way of killing them?

Through it all, Zod had never belittled Nam-Ek's misery, did not try to brush aside his grief. Later, though, he had offered him more pets. He had shown Nam-Ek pictures of strange specimens, unusual animals that he had never seen before. Instead, the mute picked simple, common gurns. Zod had tried to talk him into something more special, but Nam-Ek thrust an imperious finger toward the picture. Gurns. He wanted gurns.

Zod gave him four of the herd creatures and would probably have provided a thousand if Nam-Ek had truly wanted them.

Gurns made him think of good times in his youth, but also nightmarish ones. Alone in the stables he stroked their shaggy, thick heads and rubbed the rounded ends of their horns. The gurns made him feel like he was a little boy again—a normal boy, before all the terrible things had happened. . . .

Nam-Ek had been brought up on a gurn farm. He'd had a mother, a father, and two older sisters, and he'd led an uneventful life cultivating thick lichen fields on a rocky plateau. The gurns stripped the old tough lichen from the rocks and provided fertilizer for the fresh tender crop.

He'd been ten years old when it all changed, when Bel-Ek, his father, went berserk. Nam-Ek had been too young to know what might have shattered the older man's psyche. All he remembered was that one night Bel-Ek had murdered his wife, strangled his two daughters, then came after him.

Young Nam-Ek had climbed through a window and fled across the dewy grasses. He made it to the stables, where he hid among the restless animals. For hours, Bel-Ek had searched for him, stalking through the night, bellowing his son's name. His father held a long cruel knife in his hand. The sharp curved blade, designed for harvesting lichen from the rocks, dripped with blood in the light of Krypton's two remaining moons. Nam-Ek had crouched among the warm and shaggy beasts, holding his breath, afraid to utter a sound.

The door to the stable building smashed open, and his muscular father stood there silhouetted against the night. The shaggy gurns were restless, but the boy hid among them, trying to be small and silent. He held on to their matted fur, buried his face in the thick animal smell to keep himself from whimpering. Even so, Bel-Ek had spotted him. With a roar, the man strode forward, raising the killing blade . . . just before a group of Sapphire Guards had shot him down.

Later, he learned that his mother had sounded an alarm before she died. The security troops had responded too late for the rest of his massacred family, but they had saved Nam-Ek. The boy was so traumatized he'd never spoken again.

That had not deterred ambitious young Commissioner Zod from protecting the speechless orphan. Aware of the horrors Nam-Ek had endured, Zod took the boy and sheltered him. Yes, Zod had tried to get him to talk, but did not press, did not grow impatient and shout. Most important of all, the Commissioner accepted Nam-Ek, gave him a home, made him feel safe again. Nam-Ek could never repay his mentor for that. For years he had believed he would never again feel safe in his life. But Zod made him safe.

Nam-Ek was angry when he heard criticisms of his mentor. Even the Commissioner didn't know that Nam-Ek had secretly killed four people who had spoken out against Zod. He felt it was the least he could do.

Now he would dutifully take away all the precious items stored in the chamber beneath the Commission headquarters, as Zod had commanded him. But first Nam-Ek had another important task, something he had to do.

The halls of Kandor's prison levels were sparsely populated even during the day, and only a few token Sapphire Guards remained in place at night, as a formality. Kryptonians had a lax and contented view of security, and even the Butcher of Kandor had not shaken them enough to make fundamental changes.

Though he was a large man, Nam-Ek could move with predatory stealth. Anyone who recognized him as Zod's ward would no doubt assume he was on an important task for the Commissioner.

Using Zod's access codes, the big mute could easily manipulate the systems. He understood much more than most people gave him credit for. In the sleepy stillness, he passed underground and descended winding staircases into the intake level of holding cells. He glided along as smoothly as a rain droplet trickling down a polished window. His first task at a substation panel was to deactivate the security imagers. Assuming it to be nothing more than a routine malfunction, the night staff would request that it be fixed during the next work shift.

As he came closer to his quarry, Nam-Ek's big fists bunched and released, bunched and released. He thought of the Kandor zoo, remembering how much joy those animals had given him—the drang and its amusing antics, the ferocious-looking snagriff, the lumbering rondors. Zod had taken him to the zoo only two months earlier, and now Nam-Ek would never see those creatures again.

Extinct. What could possibly be a severe enough punishment for such an unspeakable crime? He had brought a long knife and a pulse scalpel, though he hoped he could do most of this work with his bare hands.

When he was in position, he used Zod's access crystal to send a signal that called away the two guards stationed at the Butcher's holding cell: a hint of smoke detected in a records complex three levels up. Nam-Ek lurked around the corner in a recessed doorway as the two armored guards jogged off down the hall, chattering with excitement and surprise at having something to do for a change.

As soon as they were gone, Nam-Ek moved in. He wasn't sure how much time he would have, but he intended to accomplish as much as possible.

Using the guards' controls, he unsealed the armored cell door and blocked the opening with his massive body. The Butcher of Kandor sat in the chamber, looking up with mad, bloodshot eyes and a deranged grin on his face. "Come to free me?" He sprang to his feet. "Shall we go on a hunt?"

Nam-Ek stalked forward, grabbed the Butcher by his clumpy blond hair, and yanked his head back. It would have been easy just to snap his neck and be done, but that would not be satisfying. Not satisfying at all.

The prisoner snarled and thrashed like an animal in a trap. Nam-Ek hauled out the pulse scalpel and jammed it into the criminal's throat, dispensing a burst just deep enough to mangle his larynx, severing the vocal cords and cauterizing the wound at the same time. The man would die soon enough, but not until Nam-Ek allowed him to. Now they were both speechless.

Though the Butcher writhed and clawed, the big mute easily held him in place. Using the blunt fingers of his left hand, Nam-Ek scooped out one of the man's eyes, plucking it free and setting the bloody orb on the cell's cold, hard bench where it could be a lone witness to what happened next. He wanted to let the Butcher keep his other eye, for now, so he could see what would happen to him next . . . like the animals in the zoo had seen their bloody fates.

The Butcher snapped his teeth together and spat, but only hollow wheezing noises came from his mangled throat. When he clawed Nam-Ek's cheek, the bearded mute grabbed the prisoner's hand and broke all of his fingers—a small, petulant gesture.

And it was just the first step. Nam-Ek took out the knife.

In the end, what this heinous man had done to the poor zoo animals seemed gentle compared to Nam-Ek's savage artistry. . . .

Afterward, with justice and revenge served, he thought no more about the rare creatures or the man who had killed them. There would be an uproar about the shocking murder in the prison cell, but Nam-Ek did not worry. No one would suspect him.

CHAPTER 10

∞⊡◇‼◇⊶T̤◊ 10

When his battered silver flyer finally arrived back in Argo City, Zor-El was burned, exhausted, and greatly disturbed by what he had seen on the southern continent.

While on approach to the lovely city, which sparkled with lights in the darkness, he considered calling for a medical team to meet him on the landing pad. His burns were excruciating, and he could feel hardened pebbles of lava inside the meat of his arm and his left side. But Zor-El did not want his people to see him staggering and weak, hauled off to a hospital. During the return flight across the ocean, he had used the medkit in the cockpit to apply basic first aid.

Landing at night, he left his ash-dusted craft on an empty pad not far from his villa and staggered away before anyone could see him. With unsteady but determined steps, he headed toward his wife, his home. Just smelling the cool, salty air that blew in from the ocean rejuvenated him.

Chains of lights looped between the graceful spires of the five golden bridges that connected the peninsula to the mainland. From the terminus of the bridges, roads led out to the farmlands, the mountains, and the lake district. Cross-country highways led off to Borga City, Ilonia, Orvai, Corril, Kandor, and other villages and mountain communities.

But nothing could compare with Argo City. The Kandor snobs could have their capital, as far as he was concerned. Here the warm, tropical climate made for pleasant days and balmy nights. Ocean mists rolled in regularly to irrigate the lush plant life that graced the streets, buildings, and arboretums. He loved it here.

The city's circulatory system—a network of glassy-smooth irrigation canals—carried as much traffic as did the paved streets and pedestrian paths. At regular intervals, small bridges arched over the flowing water; each bridge was owned, tended, and decorated by a different family. Hanging vines, flowers, and berries adorned every structure. The city itself—his city—gave Zor-El strength.

He walked through darkness to his villa with its colonnaded entrance and Alura's two brightly lit geodesic greenhouses. Only a few more steps. His wife was trained well enough in medicine; she could tend him.

He stood at the door, opened it—and somehow she was there to greet him. Alura had shoulder-length black hair even darker than his own, arched eyebrows, and a high forehead, which often showed her focused concentration. Zor-El had always considered her a counterpoint for his passion and energy. Before she could say anything, he collapsed in her arms.

Alura responded in a calm and professional manner, immediately getting to work—exactly as he had known she would react.

"Volcanoes," he said. "Instability in the core."

"Quiet, now. Let me tend your injuries. Explanations later."

"But it's important . . . "

Holding him up, she helped him walk down the vine-draped corridors toward their living chambers. "Telling me won't do any good now. Whatever the emergency is, you'll have to stay alive to do something about it." She let him drop onto their foamweave bed as if he were a lightning-struck tree falling in the forest.

Sheets had never felt so cool, and no bed had ever been so comfortable. But the moment the stress and weariness began to drain from his body, the pain of his burns and wounds became paramount. Sweat burst out on his forehead. Zor-El clenched his eyes shut.

Alura leaned over him. Flowers and plants filled the walls, the corners, the alcoves, creating a potpourri of scents. She snatched a smooth, dark-green seedpod from a potted bush and leaned over his face. "Breathe this. Inhale deeply." She crushed it in her fingertips.

A mist of thin, acrid plant juice sprayed into his sinuses, making him dizzy. "Wait, I must . . . " Then he couldn't remember the rest of his sentence, couldn't speak another word to explain what he had endured. He dropped into an emptiness as black as the lava fields of the southern continent.

Zor-El awoke fuzzy-headed and aching, but much improved. Flower arrangements had been pushed close to the bed—blossoms and aromatic leaves and herbs chosen by Alura for their specific healing properties. He saw coral-colored lilies the size of pillows and blue roses that smelled of pepperspice and sweet berries.

Alura used her botanical genius to breed special plants for medicinal uses. She had developed flowers that produced fragrances or pollens laden with stimulants, analgesics, antibiotics, immune-system boosters, antivirals, and other drugs. During his sleep, Zor-El had been surrounded by a bouquet of the strongest medicines his wife could arrange.

Now, as he struggled to sit up, he noticed that the bedside table was stacked with documents, messages, and urgent requests—items of important Argo City business. With a groan, he turned in the other direction and saw Alura there, watching him. He smiled at her, and she smiled back.

"Now, it's time you told me what happened to you—and where these came from." She tapped a nightstand on which rested six small dark chunks of hardened lava. The pure black was stained rusty brown from his dried blood. While he had lain unconscious, she had extracted them from his wounds.

His ribs and side were bound with thin, dissolving leaves overlain with tight bandages; his injured arm had been slathered with healing ointments and completely wrapped in gauze. Fortunately—he thought after looking at the pile of documents to review—it wasn't his writing hand.

He propped himself up on his elbows on the foamweave and told her about the eruptions, the ever-building lava pressure, the readings he had gotten from the diamondfish, and how he had lost all his data in the

hrakka attack. "I have to go to Kandor immediately. I need to see Jor-El. He's got to know what I learned. No one else suspects —"

She pushed him back down. "You have to recover first. A minimum of five days."

"Impossible! Jor-El and I —"

"Very possible. In geologic time, five days is nothing, and you cannot save Krypton if you drop dead in your tracks because you won't take care of yourself." She indicated the stack of documents and decrees. "These may be shorter-term emergencies, but you have responsibilities to Argo City as well. You made that choice."

Zor-El sighed. "Yes, it was my choice." Unlike his brother, who entirely eschewed politics (though he could have been a driving force on the Council), Zor-El devoted at least half of his effort and energy to guiding his city and leading his people. Alura was right: Even if Jor-El agreed with his assessment of the rough data, he couldn't do anything about the planet's unstable core without a long-term effort. There would be many more investigations, many other measurements.

But the people of Argo City needed him now. He reached over with his good hand and began sorting through the documents. He could take care of most of them from his bedside and delegate the rest.

Alura brought him a drink of potent juice and left him to himself. "Sleep when your body tells you to, and I won't complain if you awaken to do work."

He tried to shift his focus to more mundane matters, but he couldn't stop thinking about what he and his brother could do together. He was two years younger than Jor-El, a genius in his own right, but his brother had always achieved more in science, made more spectacular discoveries, pushed the boundaries of Kryptonian knowledge. Another man might have been bitter about that, but not Zor-El. When he was barely a teen, he'd had an epiphany: Rather than resenting his pale-haired brother for what he was, Zor-El could excel in an area that his sibling wasn't really very adept at—politics and civic service.

Although Jor-El grasped esoteric scientific concepts better than anyone, Zor-El more easily mastered people skills, pragmatic problem solving, organization, and practical engineering. While Jor-El developed bizarre new theories (most of which were censored by the Commission for Technology Acceptance, unfortunately), Zor-El administered public works in Argo City. He had new canals installed throughout the peninsula, set up fog catchers, designed new boats for efficient fish harvesting, extended the main wharves. The city's population turned to him with their problems, and they also listened whenever he made requests.

Though he was impatient to make a presentation to the Kryptonian Council, he did as Alura instructed. He healed.

Finally, two days before his wife believed he was ready to travel, he got up and packed for his trip. He could have sent a direct message via the communication plates, but he preferred to do this in person. Since he had lost all his hard data, he wanted to face his brother, describe exactly what had happened, and get his advice. With Jor-El's aid, he could speak directly to the Council, and they would not be able to brush off his claims as hysteria.

Or maybe his brother would decide there was little to worry about, that a simple geological explanation could account for what he had seen. Zor-El could only hope that was the answer . . . but he couldn't be sure.

After Alura changed the bandages on his severely burned arm and side, he kissed her and set off for his brother's estate.

CHAPTER 11

∞⌐◊‼◊⊷T♀◊ ‖

Angry, but not surprised that Commissioner Zod had confiscated the Phantom Zone, Jor-El insisted on doing something useful before he left Kandor and returned to his estate. He had plenty of other important projects to occupy his time and his mind.

With Rao staring like a gigantic bleary eye from the western sky, Jor-El used his access to ascend to the very top of the Council ziggurat. On the highest open-air platform, sharp-tipped condensers sprouted like steel thorns around a viewing radius, projecting a highly detailed holo-gram of the giant red sun. Even at night, collectors from the opposite hemisphere captured the solar image and projected it to Kandor exactly half a day out of phase. Therefore, according to the priests and politi-cians, the sun never actually set in Kandor.

Many Kryptonians saw the projected orb as an object of worship or a beacon to the heavens. Intrepid artists, diligent philosophers, and rev-erent priests smeared protective creams on their faces and sat on special benches around the safe perimeter. Wearing masks or goggles to shield their eyes, they gazed for hours into the bright face of Rao, searching for inspiration or enlightenment in the churning gases.

For Jor-El, though, the high-resolution projection was useful as a solar observatory. Oily ripples of heat made the air shudder around the hologram, which, like a caged beast, never seemed to stay still. The star churned and roiled, its plasma layers boiling. Magnetic field lines trapped dark sunspots; feathery streamers of the corona wafted outward.

In addition to the telescopes he had placed on his own rooftops, Jor-El had constructed a similar—if smaller—solar observatory on his estate. Here atop the main Kandor temple, though, the image clarity was greater. Among his many fascinations, the life cycle of the gigantic sun had occupied much of Jor-El's time over the past several years.

He adjusted the thick goggles over his face and walked around the blazing image, always studying. One of the artists sketched furiously, using his fingers to make swirls and patterns in colored levitating gels; Jor-El could see many technical inaccuracies in the young man's representation, but he didn't think *precision* was the artist's goal. A middle-aged woman wearing a philosopher's gown with a ragged collar sat cross-legged on the hard tiles in front of a bench; she nodded cordially at Jor-El, though he didn't recognize her. The group of red-robed priests did not take their eyes from the swollen sun. The power and fury of the red giant was enough to inspire religious awe, and not surprisingly, some people worshipped Rao as a deity.

Jor-El was one of the few who dared to suggest that their god might be dying.

Eschewing the available seats, he stood on the fringe of the three-dimensional image, as close to the shimmering heat as he could stand. The solar storms, the magnetic anomalies, the dark sunspots like diseased patches—all were signs of an unstable sun. How could the priests, the Council, the artists, and the philosophers not recognize such obvious danger signs?

The bloated red star was undergoing its final stages of evolution. After countless millennia of converting hydrogen into helium, the fuel at the core was running out, leading to more complex nuclear reactions. Unsettled by its new diet, the sun had swelled over the past millennia, expanding until it had swallowed up all of the solar system's inner planets. The engine at Rao's heart would keep burning until it used up the remaining fuel, and then an abrupt collapse would initiate a shock wave sufficient to create a cataclysmic supernova.

That could happen at any time. Maybe tomorrow, maybe thousands of years from now.

A year earlier, Jor-El had warned the Council that the red sun would eventually explode. After listening to the evidence, old Jul-Us had spoken slowly. "Over the past hundred years or so, other scientists have also mentioned such a catastrophe as a means to frighten the gullible."

"Even if we believed you, no one can stop the changes in Rao," said Kor-Te, who was always confident in the security of the past. "The sun has burned without incident for all of recorded history."

But Jor-El had found an ally on the Council in its youngest member, Cera-Si. "We can't ignore a problem simply because there's no immediately obvious solution. Jor-El's science is impressive. We would be foolish to ignore him." When Cera-Si had been appointed to the Council, he'd begun his work with great dreams and interesting ideas. Jor-El had placed hope in him, but although Cera-Si had a more open mind than some of the older members, he didn't have the fortitude to persuade others.

The young man had long flaming-red hair that he bound behind his head with a single gold ring. Because of the red hair, the Priests of Rao had courted him for years, trying to recruit him as one of their number. But he had no patience for the hours of wearing goggles and solemnly staring at the giant red sun. Cera-Si had trouble sitting still and was famous for requesting frequent breaks during long and ponderous Council sessions.

"We need to think in the long term. There are ways we can prepare." Jor-El began to list options. "We must think beyond Krypton. We can explore other planets. We can be ready to evacuate our people, if it becomes necessary."

Al-An just laughed, looking at the other Council members to see if they would join in.

"That goes against the prime resolution of the Seven Army Conference," grumbled Silber-Za, the only female member of the Council. She had long yellow hair, a bright smile, and a razor-edged temper that she directed toward those who dared to challenge her. She was also the reigning expert in nuances of Kryptonian law. "Doing so would expose us to outside contamination. It could be the end of us."

Jor-El jabbed a finger toward the high ceiling. *"Rao* will be the end of us if it goes supernova."

"There's no reason not to let Jor-El continue his studies," said Mauro-Ji, another occasional ally. He was a cautious Council member, always willing to give each question due consideration. "It seems only prudent. I say he should draw up his plans, document his ideas. Centuries from now, when and if the sun does become slightly more unstable, our descendants might be glad that we had such foresight."

"That does seem prudent," Pol-Ev conceded. "Let the historical record show that we did indeed plan ahead."

Jor-El had nodded his appreciation to Mauro-Ji. He knew the man had his own reasons for keeping on the scientist's good side. Centuries ago, the noble Ji family had been powerful and prominent, but in recent years their holdings had fallen on hard times. After they had invested heavily in a new set of vineyards to compete with those in the Sedra region, a blight had killed the vines, and an earthquake had leveled one of their large manor houses. Mauro-Ji often invited Jor-El to social events, weddings, and feasts, as if proximity to the esteemed scientist might increase his own standing. Jor-El wasn't sure that anyone could benefit from being his friend, given the vagaries of Kandor's high society.

After looking at his supernova data, the Council members had discussed the matter interminably before finally agreeing that he should continue his work, just in case. Jor-El had hoped they would begin a full-scale investigation with many other scientists, exhaustive probes, and contingency plans. Instead, they saw the unstable sun merely as a theoretical issue, a problem of esoteric scientific interest rather than immediate urgency.

At least they had not commanded him to stop his work. Jor-El could only hope there would be enough time to save his people if anything terrible should happen. When the star went supernova, the shock wave would disintegrate Krypton and its moons. In all likelihood, the population would have only hours of warning. So he had to plan ahead.

He turned away from the giant rippling hologram as turbulent Rao continued its slow-motion upheavals. When the diligent young artist caught his attention, still playing with his colored gels to form a three-dimensional sculpture of the sun, Jor-El realized that there were so many more important investigations to do.

He needed to get back to his estate, where he could continue to work undisturbed, without the interference of unimaginative people. Yes, once he returned, he would launch another probe into the glowering red sun.

Somebody had to take the initiative.

CHAPTER 12

∞ ⌂ ◊ ‼ ◊ ⌐ T̤ ◊   12

As soon as Jor-El had departed for Kandor, Lara began sketching furiously, planning a distinct image for each of the obelisks arranged around the estate grounds. After she had rescued him from the Phantom Zone, Jor-El gladly agreed to let her paint the mysterious stone slabs. (Apparently, even he didn't know why his father had erected them.) Lara had never been so excited about a single project.

On her sketchplate she planned a thematic arc across the twelve obelisk stones, alternations of chaotic colors and precise geometric lines. She didn't think Jor-El would understand the nuances of unbounded abstract artwork—he was such a literal person—but she could bring him around if he gave her a chance to explain. The eleven perfectly separated obelisks would each demonstrate one of the powerful foundations of Krypton's civilization: Hope, Imagination, Peace, Truth, Justice, and others. She would pair each concept-image with a particular historical figure who embodied those ideals.

The outlying twelfth stone offered the greatest challenge. Why was the single obelisk set apart from the others? Obviously, Yar-El had considered this stone to have a greater significance. Did it symbolize how he felt—that he stood apart from the eleven Council members in Kandor? After she finished sketching her other designs, Lara went to stare at the blank outlier stone. She had to think of something sufficiently important to paint on it, and so far she hadn't come up with the right idea.

As they completed their own massive project, Ora and Lor-Van had noticed a difference in their daughter's attitude; Lara frequently caught them giving her sidelong smiles and amused glances. They seemed to know whenever she was thinking of Jor-El. Well, let them think what they wanted! She went back to work.

Her young brother, bouncing a half-levitating green ball, walked up to her. He leaned over her shoulder to look at the sketches. Ki-Van tossed the ball high above his head, then ran around his older sister as he waited for it to slowly descend so he could catch it. "You're trying to show off for Jor-El, aren't you?"

"I am creating a new project," she replied too quickly. "This is Jor-El's estate, so I hope he'll be impressed."

"Mother and Father say you like Jor-El. They say you want him to notice you." Even though he was a good-natured boy, Ki had a knack for being annoying.

Lara said defensively, "He already has noticed me, thank you very much."

Ki tossed the ball up in the air again, waited for it to drift back down into his hands. "I think he likes you."

"You don't know what Jor-El thinks at all." *But I hope you're right, little brother.* "Now leave me alone so I can concentrate."

The creative technicians and apprentices began to take down the scaffolding against the long wall of the main house, where her parents had completed their intricate mural. The artwork showed the seven armies dramatically rallying against Jax-Ur. Too distracted to continue her sketches, Lara paced around the work site, admiring the art. She noted with satisfaction that her mother and father had accurately painted the Valley of Elders. After all, Lara was one of the few living Kryptonians who had ever visited there.

Back then, she had wanted to be a historian, an archaeologist, a documenter of her civilization's past. Her teachers had expressed frequent skepticism about her career choice, though. "History has already been recorded, so you would be wasting your time. The chronicles were written long ago. There is nothing to change."

"But what if some of the details are incorrect?" she had asked, but

no one gave her a satisfactory answer. From that point on, Lara had begun to keep her own journal, recording her impressions of events so that there might be at least one independent chronicle.

Several years ago, after completing their cultural and historical instruction, Lara and five fellow students—all considered audacious by their conservative instructors—had left Kandor to see the long-abandoned places for themselves. Among their group was an opinionated young woman named Aethyr-Ka, the rebellious child of a noble family.

On their expedition, the group had been rained on, and some of the mapped "roads" had turned out to be little more than quagmires of mud. Paths were overgrown with foliage. The marshes were infested with biting insects—not at all like the romantic glory Lara had seen in legendary images or read about in poem cycles. She and her companions had trekked out to the Valley of Elders and stood at the intersection of two rivers where Kol-Ar, Pol-Us, and Sor-El had fashioned the resolution that turned Krypton forever away from the dangers of ambition and greed.

While Lara had stared awestruck, Aethyr had simply shaken her head. "So this is where it all began. This is the place we should blame."

"Blame?" Lara had asked. "This is where we gave up all warfare, all violence and death."

"We gave up a lot more than that. Have you looked at the noble families lately? Have you studied Kryptonian history over the past several centuries?"

"Of course I have!"

"Then you can explain in a sentence everything we've achieved since proclaiming our society 'perfect.' Stagnant, more like!"

"What about . . . Jor-El? Think of all that he's accomplished." Even years ago, Lara had been fascinated by the great scientist.

"The exception proves the rule, dear Lara," Aethyr said with a superior expression. "You can think of only one man who embodies Kryptonian ideals anymore. Our noble families have become decadent and lazy."

"I'm not," Lara had said.

Aethyr chuckled. "Neither am I. Perhaps the two of us will set a new standard for our generation."

Now, sitting alone and staring at the blank twelfth obelisk, Lara thought again about that journey to the Valley of Elders. She still had her detailed record of the trip, what they had seen, descriptions of how it felt to be surrounded by the immensity of true history. Jor-El's ancient ancestor had been revered, but Sor-El was long in the past; modern-day Kryptonians were far more interested in gossiping about how his father had lost his mind to the Forgetting Disease and fallen from grace. It was terribly unfair. Lara hoped that, in some small measure, her work would begin to turn opinion around for old Yar-El.

Her mother startled her, coming up close behind. "You're daydreaming."

"An artist doesn't daydream. An artist simply waits to be inspired."

"And you find inspiration in daydreams about Jor-El?"

Lara flushed. "Please don't distract me. This is important work."

"Of course it is." Lara didn't acknowledge her mother's amusement, nor did she admit how long she had been thinking about Jor-El.

CHAPTER 13
∞⛯◇‼◇⊷T̈♀◇ 13

From atop the Council temple the holographic image of Rao blazed through the darkness. Zod could see it from the balcony of his private penthouse, and he stared at the hovering solar image until his eyes hurt. As the city lights began to sparkle, he scanned the other magnificent buildings on the skyline, all of them brightly illuminated. The people of Kandor liked to laugh at the darkness, and Zod often laughed at them.

Outwardly, he waited with calm patience, but inside he felt great anticipation. He wondered if Aethyr-Ka would arrive early to show her eagerness to meet him . . . or late, to toy with his emotions . . . or if she would show up at all. He had no guarantees, and that was what made it so intriguing. He sensed a kindred spirit in this brash, independent woman.

After she had caught his attention at the chariot races, Zod had immediately sent a few spies to make quiet inquiries about her while he dealt with the bothersome fallout of Bur-Al's death. He easily learned that most of Vor-On's dismissive comments and assessments reflected the general opinion. Aethyr enjoyed breaking the rules, and she relished provoking strong reactions, much to her family's dismay. She didn't live her life in the same tedious, washed-out manner that most Kryptonians did.

Deciding that he wanted to meet her as soon as possible, Zod had recorded a message crystal. With his most sincere and meaningful smile (he had been practicing that), he requested that she join him for a fine private dinner. At first, to impress her, he had listed his formal credentials; then, not wanting to sound pompous, he deleted them all. Aethyr would scoff at such pretension.

But Zod's assistants had a difficult time actually tracking her down. Aethyr had no stable address. Her family did not know (and claimed no interest in) her whereabouts. One of his spies finally found her poring over crumbling maps in an archives center and museum.

When they delivered the Commissioner's message to her, Aethyr had held the rose-colored crystal in the palm of her hand, warming it with her personal heat. The image of Zod's face wafted upward and congealed so that he seemed to be speaking directly to her. She listened to his invitation, then flustered Zod's men by declining to give an answer. Any answer at all. She simply went back to her maps, digging out records of ancient historical sites. . . .

Now, as he waited on the balcony on the evening after his meeting with Jor-El, Zod was sure Aethyr must at least be curious. He had planned carefully for the assignation, choosing exactly the right bottle of wine from the Sedra region of the coastal highlands. His servants set out a selection of chilled seafood caught by nomadic fishermen, fresh fruits drenched in nectar, and a braised fillet of gurn held in a thermal field to keep it warm. Everything was perfectly calculated and staged.

Aethyr arrived four minutes early—another surprise. Not early enough to imply anticipation, not stiffly punctilious, and not arrogantly late. When he opened the door, he was caught by her large dark eyes, like a robber bird trapped in the fine mesh covering an orchard. As before, Aethyr wore none of the ridiculously formal costumes other nobles loved to flaunt; instead, her clothes absolutely suited her, showing off her lean figure. She wore no jewelry, and her short, dark hair was unadorned.

"Welcome, Aethyr. Thank you for coming." He gestured her inside, but she remained at the threshold of his penthouse.

"I came so that I could decline your invitation in person, Commissioner."

She obviously expected him to reel, to protest, to react with indignation. Instead he smiled and answered in a neutral voice, "And why is that?"

"Because I don't play political games, and this seems like one. Too many unanswered questions."

"Such as?"

Aethyr arched her eyebrows. "What could the great Commissioner Zod possibly want from me? You gain no political clout with my family through making my acquaintance."

"Maybe I have no interest in your family. Maybe I find you beautiful. Maybe I think you're intriguing."

"Maybe I think you're used to getting what you want. I'm not a bauble in the marketplace to be had because you toss a few coins in my direction."

He gestured inside again, slightly more insistent. "Why don't you at least share a glass of wine with me while you explain yourself. Tell me what you have against me."

She chuckled. "I'd be happy to drink your wine. I assume you've brought out a rare and expensive vintage in an attempt to impress me?"

"Absolutely." Despite what Aethyr said, Zod could tell she was enjoying herself, pleased with the discomfiture she had inflicted. He poured her a glass of the ruby-red wine. She took a large sip without going through the motions of staring at its color in the light, sniffing its aroma, or swirling it around in the glass. He waited for her to make a comment, but she didn't. "Do you like it?" he finally pressed.

"It's wine." She shrugged, then changed the subject. "I understand you've been busy, Commissioner. The funeral for your assistant?"

Zod frowned. He never wanted to think about that idiot again. "Poor Bur-Al is gone, and the vicious hrakkas have been destroyed. We have other things to discuss."

"Do we?"

He was finding this quite amusing. "Most women in Kandor would leap backward off a cliff for the chance to have dinner with me."

"I'm not most women."

"I know. That's why I asked *you* here."

She looked down at the meal extravagantly spread out on the private little table. "I don't like seafood." She walked to the balcony and looked at the skyline. "I have no interest in the stuffy leaders of Kandor or the clumsy establishment. They always want to change me."

Zod came to stand next to her. "How do you know I'm not different?"

She finished off her wine in a single gulp. "Since you haven't proved otherwise, I can only assume that the great Commissioner has much invested in maintaining our stagnant status quo."

"You might be surprised." Zod's eyes were gleaming. "If modern society is so distasteful to you, tell me what you would change. What do you want to do with your life?"

"I do whatever I like. I'm about to go off into the wasteland to study a large set of ruins. I think I've found ancient Xan City."

"Where Jax-Ur made his capital long ago? No one goes there."

"Exactly. That's why I have to."

Zod delicately sipped his wine. "When you come back, return here. Have dinner with me and tell me your adventures."

"I doubt there would be any point." She walked back to the door of his penthouse. "You can finish the rest of the wine by yourself. As you said, it's an expensive vintage. Don't let it go to waste."

And then Aethyr was gone. Zod stared after her, and a slow smile curled his lips. The fact that she had so easily dismissed him made her that much more intriguing.

CHAPTER 14

∞⌐◇‼◇⟶⊤♀◊ 14

Jor-El arrived back at the estate long after the artists and their crew had retired to their guest quarters for the night. He realized he had hoped to encounter Lara, but then decided he didn't want to tell her how Commissioner Zod had taken the Phantom Zone from him. He still stewed over this, but he had other important work to do, and he was anxious to dive into it.

He slipped into his private study and worked for many hours drawing up plans and calculating trajectories for the following morning's solar probe launch. He didn't even notice when the sleepy chef delivered a quick meal for him, and he ate without looking up from his blueprints.

But he often found himself distracted by thoughts of Lara. Normally, Jor-El resented distractions, but now he didn't mind. That had never happened before. He was curious to note these unusual feelings.

Forgetting about his equations, he analyzed his growing attraction for Lara as if it were an experiment, but he couldn't fit his emotions into a suitable framework. And it had happened so quickly! He had a perfectly clear memory of everything she had said during their evening together, each time she had laughed. Not only was Lara beautiful and talented, she was also *interesting*.

He finally went to bed, but sleep was a long time coming.

Early the next morning he emerged, fully dressed but bleary-eyed. He walked across the quiet, dew-spangled lawns from the manor house to the large research building. He had a two-hour window to launch his probe toward the red giant sun, but he wanted to finish the project before too many people might see the rocket plume even from far-off Kandor.

Lara interrupted him, calling his name as she ran out of the artists' guest quarters. "Jor-El, I'm glad you're back. I want to show you something. Follow me." She took him to the first obelisk stone she had painted, to show off what she had done. With the launch of his solar probe forgotten for now, he dutifully admired the placid image of a man whose head was shaved except for a thin, curly crown of silver hair above his ears. Around the face, the background was a confusing discordance of slashes, hues, and shapes. "Look at this obelisk and tell me what you see."

He frowned. "I see a man's face surrounded by pretty colored lines." She waited. Jor-El looked at her, then back at the painting, concentrating. "Is there something else?"

With a sigh and a wry smile, she said, "This panel is called *Truth,* and that is Kal-Ik, a man executed during the ancient city-state wars. I copied the facial features directly from a bust in the Kandor cultural museum. Do you know the story?"

"I think I heard it once, but I didn't pay much attention. . . . "

Lara stood very close to him, both of them facing the portrait. "All the advisers of the chieftain Nok insisted that his war was going well, that the battles would easily be won, that all of his soldiers would fight bravely for their chieftain. The so-called advisers shielded him from what was really happening. They continued to say what the chieftain wanted to hear, just so they could save their lives. But Kal-Ik knew this was not the truth. He demanded an audience with Nok and told him the grim reality. The chieftain grew angry, and when the advisers demanded that Kal-Ik retract his statements, he insisted that truth was more important than his life. So they killed him for it. Shortly afterward Nok was defeated."

Jor-El said, "I probably would have done the same in Kal-Ik's position. An unpleasant reality is preferable to a kind delusion."

"That explains the history. Now to explain the artwork." Lara took him closer to the obelisk and carefully guided him through what she meant by the opposing lines, the symbolism in the conflicting angles, the abstract shapes around the figure of Kal-Ik. Jor-El blinked with a dawning realization as he made the connections. He seemed almost abashed. "I didn't know that it all made any sort of . . . sense before."

"Art makes sense, Jor-El, but you have to look at it through a different set of mental filters. It isn't all quantifiable, cut and dried." She took him to each of the other eight obelisks she had completed in the previous day, similarly explaining the concepts she meant to convey. By the time they finished, he was delighted with these new revelations. She had done swift and brilliant work.

He wasn't looking forward to the day when Ora and Lor-Van left with their daughter and their crew back to the city. Maybe he could find some way to invite Lara to stay. He hoped so.

Without even thinking, he took her hand. "Now it's your turn to come with me. I need your help."

Behind the research building, he had built a paved launch zone with angled rails and scorched blast deflectors. Each one of his eight probe rockets was no more than two meters long, thin cylinders filled with concentrated explosive fuel directed through a thrust nozzle. The top of each launch tube held a transmitting probe, a scientific package that collected particles from the hurricane of the red giant's solar wind.

Lara stared around, seeing the evidence of the hot fires from previously launched rockets. "My brother showed me this place, but we did not know what you used it for. Nobody seems to know."

Jor-El was puzzled. "Nobody asked."

He asked Lara to assist him in carrying one of the remaining in-system rockets. Each data package was simple and redundant, but it provided him with the direct measurements he needed. His probes studied the outer layers of the swollen red giant. Each month, he shot a probe into space and then recorded the flux levels, magnetic field lines, and the composition of the solar wind.

If anyone in the Council was aware of the streaks of light that arced into the starry blackness, they simply discounted the phenomenon. A few of them might have realized that Jor-El was up to something, but since they were not interested in the answers, they didn't ask questions.

Lara did not shy from lifting her end of the heavy cylinder and helping Jor-El to load it onto the polished launch rail. "This has the power to fly beyond our atmosphere? It can go all the way to Rao?"

"So far, only one of my rockets has failed. The chemical fuel has enough thrust to reach the target, but frankly it's not difficult to hit a celestial object as large as our sun. You just have to get close."

"And then what?"

"Then I can continue my uninterrupted monitoring of the solar cycle. Rao is in its final stages of life. A supernova could happen at any time."

Lara didn't even seem particularly alarmed. "But you have developed a plan to save us."

He had to catch himself from laughing. "You have a great deal of faith in me."

"Yes, I do."

"I have a few ideas."

Jor-El had indeed made plans, letting his imagination run free. He had drawn up designs for a huge fleet of arkships, gigantic vessels that could be built only with a concerted worldwide effort. The ships would be vast enough to take most, if not all, of Krypton's population. Jor-El didn't believe in thinking small. He had spent months dabbling with the designs, fine-tuning all of the details.

Sadly, because the Council had forbidden space exploration for so many years, Jor-El had no idea where such arkships could really go. Even with the best Kryptonian science, no one had yet proposed a workable faster-than-light stardrive that could take them to a new world. Nevertheless, he continued his sketches and his blueprints . . . just in case.

Once his new probe rocket was installed, Jor-El used his highest-resolution calipers to check the launch angle. The chemical fuel would take the projectile up above Krypton's atmosphere, directly into a tight intersecting orbit with the outer layers of the red giant. He knew the sensor package would transmit the vital data back, and he already feared what he would learn.

For the moment, though, he enjoyed the open expression of delight on Lara's face as she watched the ignition of flames, the thin cylinder streaking up off the launch rail and leaping into the sky, followed by a bright orange and black trail of smoke. How much more thrilling it would be, he thought, if Krypton had allowed him to build a real spaceship, a vessel that could carry a real person up into space and out into the unknown to see all the amazing things the universe had to offer. . . .

For now, he had to content himself with these small scientific launches.

Hearing the roar of the burning rocket, many other artists, including Lara's parents, rushed out of the guest quarters. They stared up into the sky, seeing the dissipating trail of smoke. Lara's mop-headed young brother raced over to her, begging to know what had happened. She frustrated him by refusing to answer, simply smiling in awe.

"Thank you, Jor-El. Now I have to get back to work." She clearly didn't want to go. "I need to finish the rest of the obelisks."

CHAPTER 15

∞⚬◊‼◊⊸Ṱ◊ 15

Without sending a message ahead through the communication plates, Zor-El arrived from Argo City with his urgent news. Jor-El rushed forward to meet the dark-haired man as his high-speed floater settled down in front of the main house. When the two embraced, Zor-El winced in pain.

"You're hurt!" Jor-El saw that his brother's left arm was wrapped in a thick bandage, and his reddened complexion showed blisters and peeling skin from recent burns. "What happened to you?"

"It's a long and frightening story. I need your help."

"And you'll have it—that goes without saying." Jor-El quickly took the other man by his uninjured arm. "Come inside. Tell me everything."

In the shade next to a wall of rippling water that flowed down polished bloodstone, Zor-El sat back with a heavy sigh. He noticed the artists and scaffolding, the dramatic murals on the external walls, even the portraits painted on many of the mysterious obelisks, but he did not comment on them.

Zor-El's dark eyes were still red from exposure to the acrid smoke. "I've documented severe seismic activity, deep quakes that are sure to rock all of Krypton very, very soon." He explained what he had discovered in the southern continent, to his brother's growing alarm, and then he dejectedly admitted how he had lost the data. "I don't know what it

means, but I wanted to share this with you. I've never seen anything like it. That's why I came to you."

"The pressure in the core is building." Jor-El's expression was grave. "We could go see our father. Perhaps he can help."

The dark-haired man was surprised at the suggestion. "But he won't even know we're there."

"Nevertheless, we could use his wisdom now. We have to hope for some kind of reaction."

Originally a summer cottage, the isolated dacha had been built in the forested foothills two hours' journey from the estate. As his condition grew worse, old Yar-El and his wife, Charys, had chosen to live here in the shelter of tall trees, far from public view. The intimate home was constructed partly of fast-growing crystals, partly of stone, and framed and adorned with polished blackwood. Intricate wind chimes hung from rugged wooden rafters. As the two brothers arrived, the resinous forest air was utterly still, and only a rare tinkle of tones wafted around the small home.

Their gray-haired mother was outside tending her garden, a precisely arranged network of colorful herbs, vegetables, and blooming flowers. Though her face looked pale, and her shoulders were stooped, Charys straightened from her work to greet them with a genuine smile. "My boys!"

Jor-El stepped forward to hug her with his brother right behind him. "It's been too long, Mother."

"It's been too long for both of you," Charys scolded. She set down her gardening tools and led them up the walk to the porch. "Sometimes it gets lonely out here with only your father for company. I still prefer it to living in Kandor, though. I grew tired of the pitying stares from everyone I met, of so-called friends expressing sympathy. The worst were those who looked at me as if it were my fault—as if something I did cost Krypton the great mind of Yar-El."

Zor-El was quick to show a flash of anger. "Who did that to you?"

"Now, don't you worry. Come inside. Maybe your father will know who you are today, but I can't guarantee it."

The shadowy house smelled of sun-warmed wood and polishing oils. Jor-El looked around the kitchen area, remembering the meals their mother had made for them when they were young. In a conservatory room that looked out on the wooded hills, old Yar-El sat in a chair like a mannequin, silently staring into the blacktree forest.

"Look who's come, Yar-El! Don't you want to greet them?" Gently touching his shoulder, Charys turned the chair. The old man's gaze remained fixed in a straight line, but she directed his head toward the two brothers. Jor-El looked for any sign of recognition, any flash in those once-brilliant eyes. His father didn't blink.

"He's quiet most of the time." She lovingly stroked his smooth cheek; Jor-El could see that she shaved him every day. "I can remember the way he was. I had many wonderful years with Yar-El, and two wonderful sons. That should be enough for any person."

She forced a smile, making herself appear strong and undefeated. "I sit with him while I work on my psychological treatise. I've made a great deal of progress in the last several months, and I'll submit it to the Academy soon." Charys looked at her husband with a wan smile. "Yar-El would be pleased to know that even after his . . . collapse, he's still providing ways for us to increase our understanding. I watch him, quantify my observations, record my thoughts, and draw conclusions. That's what he would do. My husband wouldn't want to let such a striking problem go unsolved."

"Too few people suffer from the Forgetting Disease to warrant a large-scale research effort," Jor-El said. "The doctors call it incurable, with unexplained causes."

"Is that good enough?" She snorted. "I don't believe it's just an obscure bacterium or undetectable virus. I believe the Forgetting Disease is a symptom of what is happening to all of Krypton's society."

Jor-El had already read his mother's theories and agreed with her thesis, though it frightened him. For so long, Kryptonians had had everything they needed; they lived happy lives, free of ambition or purpose, devoting themselves to comforts and diversions, simply whiling away the days. Although violent criminals were true abnormalities, genius and innovation were equally rare. That was one reason why genuinely brilliant men like Yar-El and his two sons managed to invent so many new things. Few other people made the effort.

Sadly, Jor-El's father had lost touch with the world around him. People in Kandor muttered that the man had been too brilliant for his own good, that too many ideas had created a bottleneck in his head. In his last year of sanity, Yar-El had become increasingly manic, then swiftly lost his awareness of reality. Now catatonic, unable to break the logjam of thoughts, the old man was lost in another universe . . . a Phantom Zone in his own mind. Jor-El shuddered at the comparison.

Charys had spent years trying to understand both what had happened to her husband and what was causing the increasing number of anomalies on Krypton. According to her theory, everyone had been forced to be "average" for too many generations. "One cannot constrain an ever-growing thing without consequences," Charys had said.

If society inhibited the bell curve for too long, radical spikes would appear at either end. Some anomalies took the form of unorthodox geniuses like Jor-El and Zor-El, while others were heinous criminals who demonstrated their "genius" through violence and destruction rather than creation. Like the Butcher of Kandor.

Jor-El leaned close to Yar-El, looking deep into his eyes, but the old man did not focus. "Father, we need your wisdom! You have to help us with this crisis. Zor-El has discovered something very disturbing."

Charys turned to them. "What crisis?" She glanced from one brother to the other.

Jor-El quickly described the situation while his brother added details. With a grave nod, their mother said, "You both need to go to Kandor to explain the problem. If the Council has any sense, they'll devote Krypton's resources to a concerted analysis and solution."

"*If* they have any sense," Zor-El emphasized.

"I was hoping Father would hear the problem."

Charys spoke encouraging words into her husband's ear. "These are our sons, Yar-El. Can you speak to them? They need you. Krypton needs you."

Suddenly something changed. Their mother picked up on it first, but

Jor-El also noticed a difference in his father's breathing. The old man shifted his body. He blinked and seemed alive again. Yar-El looked first at Jor-El, then at his brother. "My sons—good sons! Listen to me." The two leaned toward him, eager for any insight he might offer. "Do not be afraid to have children." Already the light was fading from Yar-El's eyes. "I am very proud of the ones that I had." He focused on some far-distant point, and his breathing went back to the shallow, mechanical rhythm of inhale and exhale.

Charys was visibly moved. Even though Yar-El hadn't been able to help his sons, his words acted like a tonic on her. "He hasn't reacted that way in a long time! He saw you. He *knew* you."

Jor-El tried not to let his disappointment show. "But he offered no insights on the crisis at hand."

Charys looked from one brother to the other. "Then you will have to solve that problem yourselves."

CHAPTER 16

∞⚬◊‼◊⚬T♀◊ 16

The pulsing red heat of early afternoon drove most Kandorians inside their buildings of veinrock or filtered crystal. Shops and offices closed down, and the pedestrian walkways were nearly deserted. But the plodding business of government continued inside the Council temple.

While his brother scanned the posted schedule, Jor-El insisted that no other prominent hearings could be more important than the ominous readings from the southern continent. Now that Zor-El had identified the problem, they both felt an urgent need to *do* something about it. Zor-El had already begun making plans to dispatch another team to verify his data, to take more extensive measurements of the continuing eruptions.

But first they had a major obstacle to overcome: the Council itself.

The two sons of Yar-El entered the central ziggurat. Jor-El frowned to see only a sparse audience in the tiers of public seats; he had hoped for a full hall with thousands of attentive ears to hear their momentous announcement. "My news will have to speak for itself," Zor-El said.

Side by side, the brothers descended five steps to an arched waiting foyer before the wide, empty speaking arena. A harried chamberlain intercepted them. "You wish to address the Council? I will add you to the schedule at their earliest convenience. We will contact you when—"

Jor-El coolly stood up to the man. "Come now, the leader of Argo City and Krypton's preeminent scientist do not need to be announced. Besides, I have a standing offer of a seat on the Council if ever I choose to accept it." As the ineffective chamberlain spluttered, the two men marched past him onto the vast expanse of colored hexagonal tiles that comprised the speaking floor.

Council Head Jul-Us was conferring with three members who leaned close to him, all exchanging documents and nodding. Without waiting to be acknowledged by them, the brothers faced the towering bench.

Startled by their unexpected appearance, old Jul-Us turned from his documents. "This is most unexpected." Jor-El appeared so rarely before them, and he had such a prominent reputation, that heads turned. The eleven members viewed him with a sort of surprise and reverence as he came forward with his brother.

Jor-El raised his voice to the Council Head. "Zor-El has come from Argo City with a grave announcement that warrants your utmost attention."

With a troubled expression on his grandfatherly face, Jul-Us glanced at his fellow Council members, all of whom looked either confused or annoyed by this deviation from the routine. "Very well, Jor-El. We can table our business for the moment. Your brother wouldn't have traveled a great distance on a mere whim. I trust this is important?" He folded his big-knuckled hands and leaned forward to listen.

Jor-El wasted no time with niceties. "Gentlemen, Krypton is doomed." His words, stated so baldly, caused a stir among the eleven members. *"Unless* we do something about it."

Even his brother was startled at the dramatic approach, but Jor-El knew he had to seize their attention. "Zor-El, tell them what you've seen."

The other man tossed his dark hair. "I've been to the southern continent, where I witnessed massive volcanic eruptions and unrelenting seismic instability. I saw it with my own eyes, and nearly died to bring my observations back here." He raised his still-bandaged arm, almost in a gesture of defiance. In no-nonsense terms, he explained what he had seen and the obvious conclusions to be drawn. "I took readings, but I didn't know what they meant. I came here to ask my brother for help. On his advice, we are presenting the information to you. This is a problem that affects all of Krypton, and all of Krypton must work together to study it—and solve it. Not just me, not just Jor-El . . . not just Argo City and not just Kandor. *All of us.*"

"Your words are alarming," Jul-Us said with a deep frown.

"Some might even say premature and impetuous," Silber-Za added, a scowl on her face.

Zor-El was ready to defend himself, visibly controlling his temper, but red-haired Cera-Si interjected, "Wait, the Council has enough respect for these two men that we should discuss their concerns. Does anyone here wish to question the wisdom of Jor-El?"

Mauro-Ji leaned forward, tapping his fingers on the flat table surface in front of him. "We'll give it a very thorough consideration, I promise. We will look at the issue and debate the seriousness of this supposed emergency."

"Debate? There is not time to entangle this matter in endless discussions and committees. First we must set up a full-scale study group and begin collecting data without delay. In Argo City—"

"This is *not* Argo City," Pol-Ev cut him off, adjusting one of his many rings. Even down on the speaking floor, his cologne hung thick in the air.

Seeing his brother's growing frustration, Jor-El broke in. "I wholeheartedly agree with Zor-El. I suggest we perform planetwide seismic studies—send probes not just across the southern continent, but distribute them across Krypton. We need to assess the extent of the problem. From what he has told me, I believe there is a real reason for concern."

When old Jul-Us frowned, his face became a wadded ball of soft leather. "So, you claim that instabilities are building up in our core and that somehow"—he spread his hands, as if looking for a reasonable explanation—"our whole planet will just spontaneously . . . explode?"

"Didn't he say that about the sun Rao, too?" Al-An muttered loudly.

Jor-El squared his shoulders. "Yes, that is exactly what I am saying. None of you can deny that our cities have noticed a substantial increase in seismic tremors in recent years. Remember the rockslide in Corril only six months ago? Three major mines destroyed —"

"Which my son Tyr-Us is rebuilding along more stringent construction codes," Jul-Us said, as if that would solve the whole problem.

"Besides, we have always felt tremors," said Kor-Te. No doubt he had memorized every prior incident.

"Ah, then you have also noted the evidence," Zor-El added smoothly. "It is obvious for anyone to see."

Before they could wander into other bureaucratic dances, Jor-El laid out the basic plan he had developed. "Without delay, we've got to find some way to release the pressure building up in our core. Who knows how close we are to a critical point? Zor-El took readings at only one of the thermal plumes."

"A global problem requires a global response," his brother added. "All cities must join in the effort. We are all in this together."

Jor-El narrowed his eyes, sounding determined and hoping that no one here decided to call his bluff. They all knew he was far more intelligent than any of them, frighteningly so. "Perhaps I should accept that provisional Council seat you offered me some time ago. It is the only way I can be sure you will focus your efforts on the necessary work. With my vote, I could veto any other distractions until this matter is resolved."

"That is not necessary," Pol-Ev said quickly. "Krypton would benefit most if you dedicated yourself to your real work."

Jor-El stared them down. He could tell he was making them nervous. They didn't want him to serve on the Council any more than he wanted to do so.

"Jor-El is right about our priorities," Cera-Si said eagerly. "Provide us with the data you collected, and our objective experts will review it. As soon as the threat is verified, the Council can develop action groups. Both of you should lead them. Then we will send representatives to other cities, see if additional groups wish to join us in the effort."

"I, for one, intend to look at this data very carefully," Kor-Te said. "Do you have it?"

Zor-El looked at his brother awkwardly, but Jor-El sighed. "Tell them."

Mauro-Ji leaned forward, putting his elbows high on the bench. "Is there some problem? If your data is so conclusive that you would rush—"

Zor-El met the skeptical eyes of those staring down upon him. "I lost my data. There was another eruption, and I was attacked by hrakkas. My equipment was destroyed."

With a sarcastic chuckle, Silber-Za tossed her long yellow hair. Apparently, their entrance had interrupted discussion on a civic matter she had personally submitted to the Council. "Then your claims seem premature. Even if your brother supports you, we cannot authorize dramatic changes in planetary policy on the basis of your word alone, Zor-El."

"Why would you doubt my word?" He could barely control his anger.

"It's not an unreasonable request." Mauro-Ji sounded conciliatory. "Just mount another expedition. Gather more data. Come back here and submit it to us. At that point, we will develop our response."

"Yes, we really should do everything according to the rules," Kor-Te added. "That is how it has always been done."

"Another team will easily confirm what I found," Zor-El said. "But I had hoped to get a head start on such a large problem, a full-scale research group rather than just me."

"Rash decisions are often bad decisions," Jul-Us intoned, folding his hands together. "Thank you both for a most interesting presentation. However, it's up to this Council to assess the real threats and priorities for Krypton. At such time as we deem this problem to be significant, we will invite the two of you to participate in the study group."

Though not satisfied, Zor-El saw that they could ask for nothing more at the moment. "We will get the data as soon as possible."

Jor-El straightened, looking directly at them. He could sense impatience building within him just like the pressure in Krypton's core. "And when we do, I expect the Council to act promptly and decisively."

Old Jul-Us nodded sagely. "Of course." The eleven members were already picking up their documents and debating other civic matters.

Zor-El growled as they passed down the echoing hall, "This isn't the way things work in Argo City. My people listen, they cooperate, and get things done without dickering endlessly over trivial matters." He shook his head. "They are deluding themselves. They are delaying—"

"They are the Council."

CHAPTER 17

∞⌂◊‼◊⊸T̈♀◊ 17

When Jor-El came back to the estate, Lara could tell he was frustrated by what had happened with the Council. His brother had departed directly for Argo City; she'd barely been introduced to him.

Trying to change Jor-El's mood, she showed him the new paintings she had done. By now, Lara had finished the portraits on eleven of the twelve obelisks. Though she continued to touch up the details, each of the symbolic panels was complete and (even if she said so herself) quite remarkable.

Her parents had already wrapped up most of the artwork along the estate's buildings, and many of the apprentices were being sent back to Kandor; Ora and Lor-Van would spend several more days documenting nuances in the murals, so that others would interpret them properly. The famed artists were in great demand, and they already had a major new project lined up in the capital city. But Lara wasn't so anxious to leave.

"And what about that last obelisk?" Jor-El asked, apparently glad to be distracted from his other troubles. "What do you intend to paint there?"

"I'm waiting to be inspired." On an impulse, she blurted, "In all the times you've been to Kandor, have you ever taken a few hours to actually *see* the city—the museums, the humming galleries, the architecture of the crystal temples? There are so many things I'd like to show you, Jor-El. With my parents' influence, I can get us fine seats for the next opera tapestry."

He was obviously not thrilled with the idea. "I don't like opera tapestries. I don't understand them."

"And I don't understand your physics, but that didn't keep me from getting you out of the Phantom Zone," she countered. "All it takes is a little care and attention. Come with me to Kandor. Let me show you."

"An opera tapestry?" he said again, as if pleading with her to choose something else.

"A new epic just debuted, 'The Legend of Hur-Om and Fra-Jo.' It has a grand scope, star-crossed lovers, tragedy, and a happy ending. What more could anyone want?" He took her question literally and was about to answer with something specific, but she cut him off. "Trust me in this, Jor-El."

"All right, I'll trust you. Go ahead and arrange it."

They spent most of the following day in Kandor, even though they had no plans until the evening's opera tapestry. Jor-El was not accustomed to the luxury of simply finding things to do, but Lara's relaxed mood gradually rubbed off on him. Once his brother did collect the necessary data, he would have to devote all of his time to saving the world. For now, though—just a few hours—he allowed himself to enjoy being with Lara.

After a while he no longer even checked the solar clocks, though he did insist on stopping by the offices of Council members Cera-Si and Mauro-Ji, the two men most likely to implement a mitigation plan for Krypton's tectonic instabilities. Jor-El spoke with each man briefly, reminding them that he trusted his brother and his predictions, that they must not ignore this potential for disaster. Cera-Si and Mauro-Ji both promised to do their best—but only after they had incontrovertible proof.

Lara took him to a museum, a sculpture garden, and a quick dinner before heading to the opera pavilion, whose design looked like an unfolding nest of tourmaline parabolas. She settled beside him in the dim auditorium and leaned close to make an amusing comment; Jor-El barely heard her words, distracted by her nearness.

On his estate, Jor-El had always thought he had everything he wanted. Off and on over the years, he had pondered the possibility of a politically advantageous marriage, though he had never seen much point in it. Mauro-Ji made no secret of how beautiful and well connected his two daughters were, but the young ladies were so obsessed with transient fashions and esoteric gossip that Jor-El could hardly bear an hour in their company. Though many women pretended to adore him, Jor-El always sensed that they were more impressed with his fame than with *him*.

Lara, on the other hand, wasn't trying to woo him for political or financial gain. She liked him because she *liked* him, and he very much enjoyed her company in return. She neither brushed aside his science nor insisted on comprehending it. "I don't need to understand the details of your *work,* Jor-El," she had said. "I need to understand *you.*"

Lights dimmed, casting an ebony blanket of simulated night on the theater walls. The stages levitated, and a holographic representation of the old and ornate city of Orvai appeared, setting the scene.

Lara's eyes sparkled. "Now instead of you explaining science to me, let me explain the opera tapestry to you."

"I hope you're a patient teacher. When does this story take place?"

"It's a legend. It takes place in some vague 'long ago.' "

Someone urged them to be quiet. Lights strobed across the stage, and actors appeared. The singing began, and counterpoints of symphonic music clashed with the vocal melodies.

In the story, Hur-Om was a wealthy young man, highly opinionated but well respected. Fra-Jo was a beautiful young woman, just as passionate, from a rival family. The two disagreed on almost everything, so naturally they fell in love, though neither of them would admit it. Sparks flew with their every conversation; they opposed each other's propositions during numerous Council sessions. They debated furiously, but with each encounter they felt a strange pull tying their hearts together. Still, their stubborn personalities made them deny their mutual attraction.

Finally, Fra-Jo accused Hur-Om of loving her, and he accused her of loving him. Each indignant, they angrily parted company, vowing never to see the other again. Fra-Jo took to the sea, leaving Orvai and sailing off through the great lakes and onto the open ocean; Hur-Om marched in the opposite direction, leading a caravan expedition out into the desert.

Now, the levitating stages split, showing both stories simultaneously. From his seat, Jor-El had to flick his gaze back and forth to follow it all. Fra-Jo's half of the stage filled with water to show ocean waves through a transparent static barrier. Rain poured down as a storm tossed her boat from side to side. Finally she was cast overboard, left to drift, clinging to a few pieces of wreckage in the depthless sea.

On the opposite side of the stage, Hur-Om led his caravan into the scorched wastelands, but a quake shook the desert and shifted the dunes. Like a great mouth, the desert swallowed up his party, pack animals, and supplies. They all vanished into the gaping pool of sand, leaving Hur-Om alone and lost.

Somehow, though, through all their tragedies, the two characters managed to keep *singing*.

Lara repeatedly leaned over to whisper in his ear, explaining what was happening, pointing out nuances of stage direction, the shifting holograms of the sets, the lighting effects. In the building climax, the conflicting choruses drew together so that Hur-Om's voice and Fra-Jo's voice joined into a single song. With his last breath, parched and dying of thirst and heat exhaustion, Hur-Om sang out, admitting his love for Fra-Jo. Meanwhile, the woman, unable to swim any longer, dipping under the water and about to drown, called out her love for Hur-Om.

Then a miracle happened. Clouds broke, and rain poured down upon Hur-Om in the desert. On the other side of the stage, a sleek, gray dolphus buoyed up Fra-Jo; she held on to its fin as it streaked toward the distant shore. Meanwhile Hur-Om followed the run-off water into a canyon, then found a river, which guided him to the nearest village.

Many in the audience were weeping while others cheered. Jor-El just said, "That's not physically possible."

Lara chuckled. "But it is *metaphorically* necessary, and romantically required."

Jor-El accepted the story for what it was. Once he opened his mind and put aside his skepticism, he began to see an almost mathematical dance in the performance, a perfection to the music that he had never noticed before.

Afterward he took Lara's arm, and they waited in the mezzanine gallery for the crowds to thin. So many unexpected things in one day! They walked out into the gentle night, where people sat in outdoor cafés or strolled along the boulevards. Atop the Council temple, the flaring image of Rao spilled crimson light over the metropolis, even at night. Jor-El looked up to the speckle of stars that were bright enough to shine even against the glow of city lights.

When he saw a streak of light, he realized it was not one of the usual meteors falling down from Koron. This was a deliberate flaring trail that arrowed down toward the city, moving one way and then another, as if choosing a place to land. "Look! Up in the sky!"

Lara followed his pointing finger. "Is it a bird? Or an aircraft of some kind?"

"No, see the way it moves." Absently he took her hand. "I've never seen anything like it before."

In the middle of the great plaza, other people spotted the approaching craft and backed away as it came in for a landing. Jor-El pushed closer, anxious to see. The unusual ship was small, and its curves and fins were unlike any vehicle of Kryptonian manufacture. The markings on the silver and blue hull plates were in a language he could not understand.

Jor-El felt a thrill, certain that this ship came from outside. It had crossed the pathways between the stars and had somehow found Krypton.

After a long and silent moment, a hatch disengaged with a hiss. A metal plate lifted up and a figure emerged—humanoid, through of much smaller stature than a Kryptonian. He had pale blue skin, wide-set eyes that seemed much too large for his face, and a fringe of twitching worm-like blue feelers around his chin, like a beard of tentacles. His flat nose had thin vertical nostrils. He wore a baggy, slick jumpsuit that sported many pockets and pouches, each of which held a small tool or glowing device. He looked wizened, almost comical.

The Kryptonians were terrified. Heavily muscled Sapphire Guards hurried to the scene, but even they were not trained for this.

The alien stepped out, looked around, and twitched his beard tentacles. He startled them all by saying in a language they could clearly understand, "My name is Donodon. I have come to Krypton to speak to your leaders." He spread his arms in a gesture of welcome. "It is time for you to leave your isolation and join the rest of the galactic community."

CHAPTER 18

On her own in the wilderness, surviving by her instincts and abilities, Aethyr made her way across the trackless landscape. After weeks of searching, she finally arrived at the majestic ruins of Xan City, the abandoned stronghold of the deposed warlord Jax-Ur.

She had studied historical records, analyzed antique maps, followed roads long fallen into disuse. The ancient metropolis was not, in fact, difficult to locate. Aethyr felt disdain for most other Kryptonians who simply never bothered to look.

Originally, Xan City had been built at the intersection of major trade routes, when caravans crossed the baked plains from the coastal mountains to the great river network. Over the centuries after the tyrant's defeat, with gradual developments in technology and transportation alternatives, Kryptonians had stopped using the old caravan routes, and so the fallen capital of Jax-Ur had been left to decay in the wasteland.

And Aethyr found it.

The historic city had remained untouched by scholars or treasure seekers for centuries. Treasure seekers! She snorted at the thought. As if any of those were still around—such a profession would require ambition.

When Aethyr at last surveyed the ruins from a hill overlooking the once-impressive city, she drew in a triumphant breath. The tallest buildings had crumbled, the soaring towers snapped in half, leaving only the rubble of what had once been great boulevards and viaducts.

Others might have viewed this site with a sense of forlorn loss, but Aethyr saw the grandeur of a better time when Krypton's rulers had left a unique mark, rather than cementing the status quo for generation after generation. History called Jax-Ur a heinous tyrant, but Aethyr knew that history was often wrong. Each "objective" chronicler had his or her own bias.

As Rao sank like a hot coal to the horizon, she burned the skyline into her mind's eye: the fluted towers and cylindrical minarets, the soaring pyramids topped with delicate crystal. Every building had been designed to proclaim the glory of Jax-Ur.

The sky here at these latitudes was redder than she was accustomed to, the climate hotter and dryer. The grasses were seared brown, the rock outcroppings a rusty tan. The day's heat cooled abruptly with sunset, bringing dry and furious winds across the plains. Unruly breezes sighed among the broken-topped towers, whispering and whistling through the cavities as if the pinnacles were the components of a huge pipe organ.

Aethyr unslung her pack in a grassy hollow and decided to make camp outside the ancient tomb city. Savoring the anticipation, she wanted a full day to begin her explorations of Xan City. The sharply honed excitement made her feel more alive. She spread her blankets and chose not to bother with her geometrical tent structure. Aethyr preferred to be out in the open, free, staring up at the auroras and the stars.

She ate dried food, drank from her bottle of enhanced water, then closed her eyes so that she could listen to the winds moan through the broken towers. The haunting random notes rose and fell. Aethyr could almost imagine that it was the wailing of Jax-Ur's countless victims from so long ago.

This was a symphony she could comprehend, unlike the traditional composition called "Jax-Ur's March." Her professors at the Academy called it a work of Kryptonian genius, but Aethyr had always found the piece to be overblown; she wasn't even sure she believed Jax-Ur himself had commissioned the march. Her friend Lara had been certain, though. They had spent many weeks together debating literary and musical merit, discussing classics and works of genius.

Back in school, the two of them had done the impetuous and unconventional things that students usually did. The Academy considered it sufficient for a student to read the official records published in the archives. But Lara and Aethyr had not agreed. They and a small group of their friends had gone to explore for themselves.

For herself, Aethyr had wanted to be the first to go places, to do things other Kryptonians simply did not do. After graduating, Lara had settled down, presumably falling into conventional social behavior, but Aethyr had never given up. She wondered where Lara was now. . . .

She lay back in her camp, comfortable and warm, yet tingling with anticipation. All of Xan City waited for her. Tomorrow.

To amuse herself during the evening, she withdrew a personal flute from her pack. It was a simple, primitive musical instrument, small enough to carry anywhere. She blew into the mouthpiece and moved her fingers over the holes to play melodies of her own devising. Aethyr entertained herself with her own skill. She didn't need to copy anyone else's creativity.

Later, as she went to sleep, she considered Xan City—untouched, unexplored for decades, if not centuries. Tomorrow the ancient collapsed city would be her playground. There, Aethyr would look upon secrets that no one else on Krypton had the nerve to discover.

CHAPTER 19

During their time together, Lara had seen more of the real Jor-El than anyone else bothered to notice. She learned his fascinations, memorized his changing expressions. Jor-El was unaware of her surreptitious observation, too busy looking at all the things she pointed out to him. Lara was thrilled to have shown him as much as she did.

And at last, Lara knew what to paint on the final obelisk. It was perfect.

After the arrival of the alien spaceship—quite an unusual ending to their date!—Jor-El had not wanted to send her back to the estate by herself, but she gave him no option. "I don't need a bodyguard or a babysitter. I can take care of myself."

He had flushed with embarrassment. "I didn't mean—"

"Jor-El, you have to stay behind and deal with this. It's too important to leave in the hands of the Council members." Besides, since she had her inspiration, Lara wanted to get back to the last obelisk so she could surprise him.

Now, engrossed in painting the solitary stone near the corkscrewing tower, Lara didn't even notice how alone she was on the mysterious estate. Her parents had packed up their scaffolding and materials, ready to return to their Kandor studios. The apprentices had already departed with most of the equipment, like a legendary army retreating from an encampment. Ki-Van had gone back to his classes in the city.

Lara, though, intended to stay until she was done. She implied that

Jor-El had given her permission to do so, and she was sure he wouldn't mind. She also took time to write down her thoughts and impressions of him, documenting what the two of them had done in Kandor, describing the events leading up to the arrival of the alien spaceship. Maybe some-day she would write Jor-El's biography.

At the moment, though, art was her outlet. She painted the obe-lisk's background with sweeping colors to imply radical ideas, paradigm shifts, and the wellspring of scientific imagination. This stone would convey a rare and vital aspect of Kryptonian society, a quality that too few people still showed: *Genius*. And who better to symbolize that con-cept than Jor-El himself?

She applied another brushstroke and stepped back. She had out-done herself. The heart of the image was just the face of Jor-El—the real Jor-El.

Before he joined the others leaving the work site, her father came up behind her and watched her paint. "Haven't lost interest yet? You're putting far more passion into that one painting than I've ever seen you apply to any other project."

She blushed at his knowing smile. "It's an important project to me."

"I can see that you've paid a great deal of attention to Jor-El him-self." Lor-Van nodded toward the painting.

"I wanted to get the likeness right." She tried to keep a defensive tone out of her voice. "Not enough people bother to look at Jor-El. They consider him either a crackpot or a slightly sad figure."

"I can see that in your painting. And yes, your mother and I can also see that you're attracted to him."

Lara didn't deny it. "I think he's growing fond of me as well."

"How could he not?" Lor-Van said with a chuckle. "Just look at you."

"Yes, he has looked at me—and talked to me, and listened to me. It's probably a new experience for him." She hesitated, serious now. "Are my excuses to stay here that transparent?"

"Oh, they're reasonable enough for now. The key will come if Jor-El wants you to stay even after you run out of excuses."

"He just might." Smiling, Lara flipped her hair away from her face and turned back to her painting. "I intend to give him some very good reasons."

After saying their goodbyes, her parents and the remainder of their entourage departed for the studio in Kandor. When Lara looked again at the obelisk, she nodded to herself. Others viewed the great scientist as merely the sum of his achievements, but Lara's painting showed Jor-El's inner strength and genius, revealing that it was *he* who had created those achievements, not the achievements that created the man. She couldn't wait to see the look on his face when *he* saw what she had done.

CHAPTER 20

Once his brother had listened to his story and interpreted the seismic data, Zor-El fully believed in the impending disaster and knew that something had to be done. Jor-El had not even seen the actual readings, but the brewing disaster in the planet's core was severe enough to be obvious to him.

And regardless of the data itself, Zor-El had actually *been there.* He had witnessed the planet's restless heart in a more visceral way than his brother could ever believe. Zor-El had watched the eruptions, seen the chilling emerald-green mineral shift, and he *knew* that something wasn't right.

Similarly, having faced the eleven-member Kryptonian Council in Kandor, he was able to instinctively interpret their political mood. His brother was a genius in all matters related to science, but Zor-El understood the lumbering machinery of bureaucracy and governments. He grasped the herdlike lethargy of an entrenched decision-making body.

Zor-El headed back to Argo City, deep in thought. He could not let the whole planet die because of the shortsighted members of the government. If they wanted data, he would give them data, but after seeing the Council in session, he doubted even the data would be enough.

However, there were other ways to influence the momentum of a large government. It seemed petty, but momentum could be diverted by pressure from other sources. If he could secure other allies, influence independent cities to join him, then Kandor's government would take the path of least resistance and flow with the main current.

Jor-El would never think of such tactics. He would present the data and let the numbers speak for themselves, even if the Council was deaf to that kind of language.

Zor-El stopped briefly in Borga City on his way home, hoping to rally support, technical assistance, and funding from Shor-Em, the city leader there. Shor-Em was something of a stuffed shirt who pretended to pride himself on his forward thinking and public works. He made no secret of the fact that he expected to be appointed to a position on the Council as soon as another seat came open; the man had said more than once that he simply couldn't understand why the great Jor-El would ever have declined "such an honor."

Zor-El considered the man a colleague rather than a friend, someone with similar interests and civic problems. Though Argo City had the means to continue the seismic investigations alone, Zor-El firmly believed that other city leaders should participate. He had to gather a political rationale as well as a scientific one.

Borga City was located on the other side of the Redcliff Mountains, where several drainages created an expansive marsh carpeted with spiky grasses taller than a man. Rivulets of brown and green water tangled like the threads of a crumpled tapestry interweaving the marsh.

The city itself was suspended above the swampy ground, a complex of interconnected platforms made from multicolored alloy plates and interlocked boards of treated wood. Tethered to huge pilings sunk deep into the muck, the platforms were held aloft by colorful balloons adorned with jewels. To fill their balloons, Borgans captured lighter-than-air gases that boiled up from the swamp.

In peaceful times tourists often came there to take in the marsh vapors and enjoy one of the many independently floating spas. Boatmen netted fat water beetles that were considered a culinary delicacy; others harvested reeds and grasses for the renowned fabric artists who lived on their own platforms.

Zor-El crossed the extensive marshes only to find Borga City in an uproar. Shor-Em and his ambitious (not to mention abrasive) younger brother, Koll-Em, had once again been feuding. With their parents long dead, Shor-Em had blithely assumed control of the city government as a natural consequence of his birth order. The younger brother demanded a place on the city's council and called for drastic changes, many of which were ill advised. Change for the sake of change—simply because Koll-Em disliked the old order of things—was no way to run a city, Zor-El knew. Shor-Em had ignored his brother for some time, first passively and then more blatantly.

When Zor-El arrived, Koll-Em had just been cast out of Borga City, evicted for staging a clumsy attempt to overthrow his brother. The people were horrified by the very idea, and Koll-Em had fled in angry disgrace. Zor-El waited patiently to see Shor-Em, who sent a messenger with a curt response that he was "preoccupied with urgent matters at the moment" and that he would "be happy to discuss the concerns of Argo City in some months' time."

Zor-El departed without leaving a formal response. He preferred to go back to where he could make his own decisions, where people cooperated for the good of society. Back home . . .

CHAPTER 21

∞ ⸗◇‼◇⸗T̪◊   21

The arrival of the alien visitor threw all of Kandor into turmoil. When the Kryptonian Council called an emergency session, Commissioner Zod insisted on attending. Though he was not part of their anointed group, Zod believed he was the only one who could see the opportunity, and the real danger, here.

When the great Cor-Zod had been in charge as Council Head, he would have rallied the other ten members behind him and made a swift and reasonable decision. Now, though, Jul-Us and his lackeys would most likely run around in aimless circles like panicked gurns trying to flee a thunderstorm. Now picking up his father's mantle, Zod felt it was up to him to keep his eyes open and determine the proper response at the proper moment.

Word passed swiftly through the city. The people, both fascinated and frightened by the diminutive blue-skinned alien, were not certain how to react. And Kryptonians did not deal well with uncertainty.

In recent days, many citizens had already been appalled by the shocking murder of the Butcher of Kandor in his own protected cell. No one particularly mourned the loss of the detestable criminal, however, and the mystery remained unsolved. Although some trace in the information systems hinted that Zod's own access crystal had been used at the time of the murder, he knew nothing about it; he also had a perfect alibi, since he had been with Aethyr-Ka at the time. Though he didn't care about the Butcher, he was intrigued by the crime itself.

Such fascinations, though, were far overshadowed by this mysterious alien. Giant crystal screens broadcast flickering news images within the facets of the tall transparent towers. Crowds gathered outside the imposing Council temple early the next morning, because the tiers of audience seats had already filled up. Bells and resonant chimes announced the impending important session.

Zod thought the eleven Council members must be wringing their hands behind closed doors, at a loss as to how they should respond. And the blue-skinned visitor hadn't even told them what he wanted. Their flurry of indecision only proved their own potential weakness. If Zod had been in charge, he would have told them to be calm, to be strong, to face the wizened alien without fear.

If he had been in charge. . . .

Donodon waited patiently in a lower anteroom outside of the speaking arena. Alert Sapphire Guards kept watch over him, ready to prevent the visitor from taking any aggressive action, though the burly men were clearly uncertain that their weapons would be effective. The gadgets in the pockets of Donodon's comfortable baggy jumpsuit might well be weapons, but no one had the nerve to confiscate them. The alien remained quiet and content, seemingly innocuous. His beard of feelers twitched and wriggled sinuously, either tasting the air or sensing vibrations.

Inside the echoing chamber, Zod claimed an important seat reserved for prestigious observers, as was his due, and he waited. Finally, wearing white robes emblazoned with their family symbols, the eleven members filed in, attempting to look imposing from their lofty positions. When they had taken their seats, Jul-Us commanded the great doors to open into the arena below.

Pointed forward by the Sapphire Guards, the elfin alien strutted in, smiling as he crossed the floor of hexagonal tiles, which looked like a game board. But this was no game. Donodon stopped and stood looking up at the Council seats that towered high above him. He slowly blinked his enormous eyes and twitched his beard-feelers.

Without introduction, the alien spoke. "Greetings, Council of Krypton!" The audience stopped muttering, as if hundreds of people held their breath at once. The blue-skinned alien bent backward to look at the high benches. Clearly finding the situation unsatisfactory, he brushed his hands along his lumpy pockets, searching for something. "My apologies, but staring upward like this is not conducive to a productive conversation."

He selected a device from one pocket, held it close to his beard-feelers as if sniffing it, then swapped it for another gadget. He paced in a small circle, looking down at the hexagonal tiles, and pointed the glowing end of the device at the floor. "I see, yes, this will do it."

Four Sapphire Guards approached the alien on the speaking floor, but paused, afraid he might open fire with his glowing device. High above, Jul-Us sat, his face reddening. He shouted, "Explain yourself! We have not granted you—"

Donodon seemed oblivious to the reaction. As he used his small device, the thick tiles in the floor popped loose and bounced off to the side like discarded puzzle pieces, exposing packed sand and dirt under the foundation. Still gripping his strange tool, the alien played the beam over the ground, turning in a full circle. As if by magic, a structure began to build itself out of the loose grains. "Do not worry," he said offhandedly. "I will restore everything when we are finished."

Sand and clumps of dirt piled together, building higher, until a cork-screwing ramp rose up. Dizzying patterns, ornate decorations, and alien hieroglyphics adorned the sides. Pillars sprouted from around the platform's base to shore it up. The growing podium lifted Donodon above the speaking floor until he reached the level of the flustered Council, where he could face them directly. "Much better!"

Finished with his demonstration, the alien switched off his hand-held device and tucked it back into an available pocket. "Simple electrostatic rearrangement and binding of sand grains. Nothing to fear." He looked down at the complex structure. "Though I admit I may have been showing off."

"Intriguing," Zod whispered from his reserved seat in the audience tiers. Despite the alien's unassuming demeanor, Donodon had just demonstrated extraordinary powers. Was there a threat implied? Zod wondered how much more the creature could do. Jor-El himself would have been impressed.

Donodon stretched his wrinkled blue face in a broad grin. Atop his platform he turned in a slow circle, surveying the hundreds of people in the audience, as if storing and cataloguing their images inside a sharp mind. He paused briefly as he faced Commissioner Zod's private box, then turned to the Council bench again.

"Why have you come here?" Jul-Us demanded. Zod detected a faint quaver in the old man's voice.

"We Kryptonians prefer our privacy," barked Kor-Te, so nervous that he could barely keep his seat.

Donodon brushed a few stray sand grains from his jumpsuit. "A pebble beneath a flowing stream can't ignore the water that exists all around it. Your solar system exists as part of the twenty-eight known galaxies, whether you like it or not."

"We've done fine for more than a thousand years. We protect ourselves," said Silber-Za. "Krypton wants no trouble with outsiders."

Donodon responded with a sincere-looking smile surrounded by his fringe of wormlike tentacles. "I did not bring trouble, but an opportunity, a new beginning for Krypton." He nodded down toward the muscular armored guards who stood wary but impotent. "There is a galactic security force that patrols and protects all civilized planets. With them, societies such as Krypton can remain safe from the dangers that abound in the universe."

"We have been safe. Haven't we?" Pol-Ev looked around. He moved a heavily ruffled collar out of the way of his waxed and pointed beard. "Krypton has always been safe."

"It appears you haven't been entirely safe. I saw your destroyed moon from space."

"You spied on us?" Cera-Si's face turned nearly as red as his long hair.

"I did due diligence in order to better welcome Krypton into the fold of galactic society. Believe me, there are outside threats you cannot even imagine." Donodon smiled. "Someday you may be glad to have a superior protective force around."

Al-An, usually the tiebreaker and peacemaker on the Council, said, "What is your stake in this? Are you a representative of this . . . enforcement group?"

"I am an explorer who seeks the right opportunities. That is all."

In a huff, Silber-Za said, "So you want us to submit to the rule of an intergalactic police force?"

Donodon's tendrils wriggled with apparent agitation. "You misunderstand what I said." The blue-skinned alien selected a device from another pocket, adjusted its settings, and sprayed a glowing rectangle in the air that shimmered like a projection screen. He displayed a host of images, monstrous villains, destroyed worlds, enslaved populations. "You have been safe thus far, not because the dangers don't exist, but because none of them have found you yet. Rest assured, they will. Krypton cannot remain hidden forever."

Zod leaned back as a thrill shivered down his spine. "Exactly." He could already imagine several ways to prepare the world for the inevitable; the Council certainly wouldn't do it.

"You threaten us?" Old Jul-Us pretended to be indignant.

"I only suggest that you would benefit greatly from the protection and peace offered by an alliance with other civilizations."

Unannounced, a pale-haired figure passed through the arch and strode bravely across the tiled floor to the base of the granular podium the alien had created. He extended his hands, shouting upward. "Council Head Jul-Us, all Council members—think of everything this rare visitor can teach us! I have come to speak on his behalf."

From high above, Donodon peered down at the unexpected visitor. From his own seat in the special balcony, Zod leaned forward, not at all surprised to see Jor-El take charge like this. The scientist's face seemed to be shining with hope and fascination. He boldly stepped to the base of the sand-and-earth pedestal, calling upward as if he and Donodon were the only two adults among a group of children. "Please excuse the Council's abrupt reaction. This is all very new to us."

"Jor-El, your interruption is unprecedented!" Jul-Us said.

"Everything about this event is unprecedented. We must learn more about this emissary before jumping to rash conclusions. It is the only logical way to proceed." He placed his hands on his hips, forcefully meeting the gaze of the Council Head. The other members muttered to each other. "And you all know that I am the best-equipped person on all of Krypton to engage in these discussions."

"He does have a point," Cera-Si said, loudly enough to be heard in the hushed audience chamber.

"But *we* are in charge here!" Silber-Za insisted.

Turning back to look at the eleven Council members, Donodon

said, "While I must respect your traditions, *I* shall choose my own comrades." The visitor made a gesture with another device, and the platform began to dissolve, falling back down into the hole in the floor, the grains streaming smoothly back to their original positions with a hissing, rushing sound. The hexagonal floor tiles flipped up into the air, then reseated themselves, interlocking perfectly.

The crowds in the viewing stands responded with an appreciative gasp.

When he reached the floor level, Donodon strolled forward until he stood in front of Jor-El, barely reaching the height of the man's chest. "Thank you for intervening. Are you the leader of Krypton?"

The scientist laughed, surprised by the question. "No, no. I am Jor-El—a scientist, not a politician."

"I see, yes. Then you and I have much in common." Donodon craned his neck and faced the Council again. "I think I will continue my discussions with this man." It did not sound like a request.

The old Council Head was taken aback. Several of the other members muttered, all of them looking pale, few of them having the nerve— Zod wasn't surprised—to do anything.

Jor-El looked from the amazing visitor up to the governing body. "Council Members, I will take Donodon to my estate. There I will keep him safe."

"And the people of Kandor will be safe as well," Pol-Ev said.

"Why yes," Jor-El said. "Yes, they will." Moving briskly, as if certain the Council would change its mind if given enough time to do so, the scientist bowed formally to Jul-Us, then to the audience of rapt Kryptonians, and then ushered the diminutive alien out of the great hall.

Zod was already on his feet and rushing to the private Council chambers. He did not dare give them the chance to ruin this if they were allowed to make their own decisions.

Most of the audience had streamed out of the great temple, buzzing with conversation. They watched as Jor-El and Donodon went to the alien's compact starship, already talking so intently with each other they barely noticed the awed crowd that followed them.

The eleven members of the Council were left alone, having allowed control of the situation to slip through their fingers. Retreating, Jul-Us quickly called them all to meet him in his spacious private chambers—as the Commissioner had known the old man would.

He gave them enough time to convene there. Then he strode down the hall to the tall closed doors covered with patterned yellow metal. As boldly as Jor-El had strode into the speaking hall, Zod flung open the doors and stood framed in the entry to the crowded room.

The eleven members turned toward him in a panic, as if he were brandishing a weapon. Zod just smiled. "You have much to fear," he said.

He knew that without his help they would continue their "discussions"—bickering, sharing paranoias, and wallowing in helpless despair. Zod expected nothing better from the eleven incompetents.

"Commissioner, this is a private session," Kor-Te said, swallowing hard to cover his own anxiety.

"Relating to a very public problem." Without being invited, he stepped into the chamber and closed the doors behind him. "Naturally, you are worried about what Jor-El and that alien might do together."

"We should have stopped them from leaving. We should have commanded Jor-El to stay!" said Jun-Do, a mousy Council member who seemed very brave now that he was safe in this closed room.

"It is too late for that," Zod said. *You should have thought to issue some sort of command during the original meeting,* he added silently, *but you were all too afraid.* He understood that their greatest fear was the fear of change itself. He had been disgusted with the ineffectual leaders before, and now their actions (*in*actions!) only reinforced his opinion. How his father would have been sick with disappointment. "But I can offer you an alternative."

He could almost hear their indrawn breath. Jul-Us looked at him with an expression full of appreciation. "What is it, Commissioner?"

"Jor-El and this alien will be sharing information, discussing technologies. Donodon's ship itself is a scientific marvel. Since I am head of the Commission for Technology Acceptance, I should be there. I will go to Jor-El's estate and observe what they are doing. Let me take care of it." He applied one of his practiced smiles. "With your permission?"

Jul-Us did not need to consult his fellow members. "Please do so."

CHAPTER 22

∞⌒◇!◇⟲T♀⟲ 22

Though uneventful, the trip from Kandor aboard Donodon's vessel was intense, exciting, and brief enough that Jor-El didn't mind being cramped within a tiny vessel designed for a small-statured passenger. What thrilled him most was the knowledge that this was a real spaceship that had actually gone from star system to star system.

The small blue alien was truly a kindred spirit. Eager for information and insights, Jor-El had discussed Krypton's isolationism, how he was forbidden from investigating space travel or trying to contact other civilizations, although he still made extensive studies of the stars with his own telescopes.

Studying the ship's controls, Jor-El asked, "How do you navigate? How do you deal with emergencies?"

"I have a tool for every emergency." Donodon proudly patted one of his lumpy pockets. "This ship is made of discrete components but operates as an organic whole—so sophisticated that even I can fly it without trouble."

"I want to know more. I want to know everything about the whole universe out there."

Donodon made a burbling sound of amusement. "You could spend your life finding the answers, and there would still be many, many more questions." His skin was cool and moist, and he exuded a natural scent somewhat reminiscent of tart fruit.

Jor-El beamed. "Exactly as I prefer it."

"I have been to many marvelous planets and wonderful civilizations. My ship's log has a record of all of my journeys."

"I'd like to see them."

"That would take years." The alien's overlarge eyes blinked.

"What could be a better use of my time?"

Donodon displayed items from his ship's database, quickly skimming through a few of the marvelous planets. "Let me show you the fabulous landscapes of Oa, Rann, and Thanagar." He called up another sequence of images. "And the fungus caverns of Trekon, the flying islands of Uffar, the lavender seas of Gghwwyk. It is difficult for me to choose a favorite."

While sharing ideas with Donodon, telling him of his many other inventions, including the Phantom Zone and the solar-probe rockets, Jor-El grew both relaxed and excited. Suddenly, this alien visitor had opened many doorways in his imagination, made him feel that so many things were possible, that he was not alone.

When he had described his studies of the swollen red-giant sun, Jor-El expressed his concerns about the possibility of Rao going supernova. Instead of the skepticism the Kryptonian Council exhibited, Donodon simply nodded slowly and gravely. "I see, yes, that is a problem. We must bring in other experts, but my people can certainly help Krypton evacuate, should the need rise."

"I have drawn up plans for arkships. Will we have time?"

"Perhaps. Probably. There are certain indicators before a supernova occurs."

Jor-El could barely contain his exuberance, a long-forgotten enthusiasm coupled with relief. He began to believe Donodon could help Krypton with its many problems.

When he described the instabilities in the planet's core, as Zor-El had discovered, the tentacle-faced alien seemed more uncertain. "That is not my area of expertise, but with my ship I could possibly acquire the necessary data. By combing through my library and making use of your own technology and equipment, perhaps we can construct a deep mapping probe that can peer directly into your unstable core. It would be simple."

Jor-El already felt his pulse racing. "That would require an immense amount of power."

Donodon shrugged, as if he did such things every day. "I have traveled across several galaxies, and my ship holds the legacy of hundreds of civilizations. I do not believe that looking through a planet's crust is an insurmountable problem."

As she painted alone, finishing the last obelisk, Lara heard a noise in the sky, which seemed overloud in contrast with the quiet of the estate. Glancing up, she saw a glint of silver, black, and blue—the alien's oddly contoured ship coming here, to the estate! She paused in her work, looking up in amazement and delight. Her mind had been filled with questions and worries, but now it seemed that Jor-El must have contacted the alien and convinced the Council. She wasn't surprised.

Lara stepped back as the circling craft landed on the lush violet lawn. When the hatch opened, she saw two figures crowded inside. One was the diminutive alien in his baggy jumpsuit, and the other was Jor-El, as she had expected, wearing a boyish awed grin. He emerged, stretched his cramped muscles, and ran a hand over his tousled white hair. When he saw her standing there, his smile only widened. "Lara! I've brought us a visitor."

She stepped forward. "I can see that. Did the Council send you here?"

He flushed. "We didn't exactly give them much choice. They're probably still discussing it."

Donodon's feelers wafted around his face like thick tendrils of smoke as he peered at the unusual scenery and architecture around him. "A remarkable estate." He noticed her last painted obelisk even before Jor-El did. "I see, yes. Kryptonian artwork is indeed superior to much that I have seen from other worlds."

Jor-El finally spotted her portrait of him, and he stared, speechless. His surprised, even embarrassed expression was all the reward she could possibly have asked for.

CHAPTER 23

He had already made up his mind that the alien visitor would have to die. Zod had thought it all through.

Now that the Council had granted him their blessing, he gathered his rarely worn formal robes, donned the insignia of the Commission for Technology Acceptance, accepted a pompous writ of justification from old Jul-Us (as if Jor-El would require such a formality), and prepared his private vehicle for departure the following morning. He wanted to give Jor-El and Donodon enough time to begin their own technological mischief. He knew they would.

In the back of Zod's mind, disturbing ideas leapfrogged each other. The arrival of the alien visitor, the possibility of opening naïve and ill-prepared Krypton to a flood of outside influence, had changed everything. He knew it could rapidly spiral out of control.

Zod had spent his whole life pulling strings, manipulating people who believed they were in power, building his position for the good of Krypton. By controlling the Commission, he had remained unobtrusive while becoming one of the most powerful men on Krypton. However, if Kryptonians opened trade and interaction among all the populated worlds in the twenty-eight known galaxies, Zod would become an insignificant speck of lint in a vast cosmic tapestry. And that wasn't how he saw himself at all. If the blue-skinned alien were to inform outsiders of what he had found here, Krypton would never be the same.

No matter whether Donodon's intentions were good or evil, the future course of Krypton and the salvation of a clearly crumbling civilization required that the alien be killed before he could leave or before he could cause too much damage here.

And Nam-Ek was the only one he could trust to do it. Looking at the big man as he flew the official vehicle swiftly across the grassy plains toward Jor-El's estate, Zod smiled to remember how they had become bonded to each other.

After the terrible tragedy in Nam-Ek's youth, the noble houses of Krypton had remained uneasy about the speechless boy, sure that because something had been irrevocably *wrong* with his murderous father, therefore the son must be flawed as well. But Zod had taken the mute under his wing, insisting that no child should be punished for the failures of his parents. He had sheltered Nam-Ek, given him a home, teachers, and an ever more important place in his life. Zod never again spoke to Nam-Ek about his irrational, murderous father. No one could understand why Bel-Ek had done what he had done.

Zod was not blind to the fact that inexplicable crimes were happening with increasing frequency. It did not surprise him. The very nature of the Kryptonian race was to soar, to aspire to things, but a rigidly pacifistic society had eliminated all safe outlets for minds and emotions to grow. A society could not survive in peace if the peace lasted for too long.

However, the disruption the blue-skinned alien was about to cause would tear the fabric of Krypton apart. Zod very clearly realized that something drastic had to be done . . . but he couldn't allow anyone to guess how far he was willing to go.

When they arrived at the estate, Zod wanted to make it seem that he and Jor-El were easy acquaintances who visited each other often. After landing the vehicle, Nam-Ek remained beside it, muscular arms crossed, obviously ready to intervene should he perceive any threat to the Commissioner.

Zod immediately spotted Jor-El and the alien outside working together, engrossed in a complex mechanical sculpture of mirrors, lenses, prisms, and light-catchers they were constructing, like a technological kaleidoscope. Donodon used many of his small gadgets to help with the assembly.

"Greetings, Jor-El." He bowed slightly. "I am here on formal business. The Council has requested that I come here to observe you and your strange guest."

Jor-El's face was smudged with grease and dust. He looked up with a pleased smile. "Commissioner, as you can see we have gotten right to work. We are developing a seismic scanner that can penetrate directly to the planet's core."

Donodon stood at his side. "Jor-El tells me we could be on the verge of a means to save your planet."

Strewn across the purple lawn near an overturned fountain (which appeared to have been dismantled to provide more working room, or maybe a few stray components) lay a dizzying array of pieces. Some of them had come from Jor-El's laboratory facilities; others had apparently been stored as spare parts on Donodon's ship.

"Intriguing. I am glad to see you two getting along so well."

The ancient alien tucked away a few loose tools. "Yes, Jor-El and I have much in common."

"And how long will you stay here with us, Donodon?" Zod pressed, hoping he still sounded friendly.

The alien stood in a relaxed stance; one of his probes had almost worked its way out of a pocket in his jumpsuit, and he deftly tucked it back in before sealing the seam. "I journeyed to Krypton to study your people, and I am learning everything I could possibly wish to know. I am in no hurry to depart."

Zod maintained a pleasant tone as he pried for further information. "Are others of your race coming? Does the galactic police force monitor your whereabouts?"

"I am a solo explorer, and I travel my own route. Oh, every few decades I return home to share the information from my ship's database." Donodon looked directly at Zod, his face-feelers quivering. "I am fully aware that my arrival presents Krypton with a difficult choice. Will you open yourselves to the rest of the galaxy, or will you remain in total isolation?"

"That is a vital question, but our Council is not particularly swift to act—as both Jor-El and I know, though for differing reasons." Jor-El looked sidelong at him, as if trying to determine what Zod was up to.

The Commissioner realized he would have to be more careful. "You are the first outsider to find us in many, many centuries."

"I see, yes. But if I can stumble upon Krypton, then others can as well. Will you welcome them or hide from them? I hope you make the correct choice."

"I fully intend to."

Donodon turned back to the device, inspecting its framework. He pointed with a thin, blinking cylinder. "We have installed one of my secondary power sources into the penetrating scanner, and I believe it should project sufficient energy to let us visualize deep down."

Zod looked at the construction, fully aware of the many dangerous things Jor-El had submitted, and surrendered, to the Commission in Kandor. What could Jor-El's mind and this alien's concoct together?

"It sounds very powerful, enough to make me concerned." Zod paced among the components. An idea was already forming in his mind. Yes, many dangerous things . . . "Is this seismic scanner another device I'll need to lock away for the protection of all good Kryptonians? Does it pose any risk?"

Jor-El's eyes flashed, and he tensed. "None whatsoever."

Donodon nodded gravely. "Every object has the potential to be used for harm, but one should not imagine danger where none exists. Otherwise you will live your whole life in fear."

Zod was not entirely convinced, but he did have an idea. He would have to watch them carefully. "And when will you test this probe? How soon will you know if it functions?"

"And how soon will we know if my brother's concerns are justified?" Jor-El added, looking at the blue-skinned alien. "Another day. Two at the most. We are putting our fullest effort into this task."

"I can see that." He came to a decision. "Then, since I have the full authority of the Council"—he withdrew the pretentious writ Jul-Us had given him—"I would like to remain here and be a part of the test."

Jor-El was taken aback. He considered the Commissioner with more than a hint of suspicion. "You are welcome to stay at my estate for the next day or so, provided you do not interfere. We have important work, and the Commission did ask me to provide them with proof of the danger in the core."

"*If* it exists."

"It exists."

"I would not dream of interfering. I will simply watch. You will barely even know I am here."

As the two worked, they ignored the Commissoner's presence. He didn't mind. He watched the scientist and the alien continue to modify their frivolous, flashy device. They shared insights about theoretical physical principles that went far above Zod's head.

Meanwhile, Nam-Ek waited dutifully by the vehicle, but Zod would find him a place to sleep. Jor-El would pay even less attention to Zod's burly bodyguard, and that was good.

The young artist, Lara, daughter of Lor-Van, was also there at the estate, supposedly completing a project. She seemed oddly out of place as she watched, mystified by what Jor-El and Donodon were doing. She acknowledged Zod with a nod, but he paid little attention to her.

Within a few hours, he had already seen what he needed and had already decided what he wanted Nam-Ek to do. It was swift and impulsive . . . and decisive.

No one on the Council could suspect his plan. The big mute would do the difficult work, and he would do it well. The Commissioner had seen a way to remove the potential problem, as well as to increase his own control of the situation . . . and of Krypton itself.

CHAPTER 24

∞⌂◇‼◇⊷T̈◇ 24

Returning home, Zor-El drew a deep, exhilarating breath of Argo City's salty air. He stood on the central golden bridge that spanned the bay separating the peninsula from the mainland, letting traffic flow around him. Once again, he did not want to call attention to his arrival. Doing so would mean having to admit that his warning to the Council had been ignored.

Great pillars in the seabed supported the long bridge above the water. Looking south, he could see another bridge farther down the coast and then, at the tail end of the peninsula, the misty outline of the last bridge. To the north he could see two other bridges, five in all.

Long ago, the Argo City elders had launched a competition: The greatest architects would present their best bridge designs, and judges would decide which were the most beautiful, the most durable, the most innovative. Five of the proposed structures were so magnificent that the elders could not choose; they decided to give no prizes, but to erect all of the bridges as testaments to Kryptonian ingenuity.

As Zor-El walked across the span, he admired the calm waters of the bay, the glorious towers of Argo City, the lacy suspension cables of the bridges. A knot formed in his stomach. If the strange pressure buildup in the core continued unabated, all this would be destroyed—and soon.

Alura was waiting for him in the villa, and her expression told him that she already guessed how the Council had responded. "Jor-El agrees that the readings indicate a very real danger," he said, "but the Council refuses to consider the problem until I provide them with more extensive data."

She stroked his long, dark hair. "Then that is what we must do."

"I know, and it will be a large project. I tried to convince the leader of Borga City to offer his assistance, strictly as a gesture of support, but he was preoccupied with his own internal matters."

"So we'll just have to do it ourselves."

"Yes. I expect to mount an expedition and send a preliminary team as soon as possible." He looked at her with hardening determination. "Even if I don't get much cooperation from Kandor or Borga City, I am the leader here, and I can make decisions as I choose."

He winced as a twinge of pain from his recent injuries shot through him. Alura frowned with disapproval. "You should have rested another day or two. Here, come into the main terrarium."

She gently took his bandaged left arm and led him into one of the transparent domes. The air was filled with the perfumes of flowers, warm resins, and oils from shrubs and herbs. One large plant with thick, soft stems had burst into bloom, displaying seven radically different flowers, each blossom exuding a distinct, potent scent. Root tendrils emerged from a basket of loose, peaty moss, at the ends of which Alura had installed tapered, transparent vials. Liquids dripped from the ends of the distended roots, drop by drop, to fill each vial with a different substance.

She removed a tube of clear yellow-green fluid from a root, held it up to the light, and nodded. "While you were gone, I created this to help your burns heal." She cut away the loose cloths that bound his arm and side to reveal angry red skin and dark scabs. During the long trip, Zor-El's energetic passion had been enough to drive away the pain, but now he could feel the underlying ache.

She snapped off a blossom and squeezed it over the healing scabs; with deft fingers she began to rub in the greenish liquid like a salve. "This will prevent infection, and it should smooth the skin. There'll still be scars. You're always going to carry the mark of this."

He flexed his fingers. "Scars are nothing. Each time I look at my arm or my side, I'll be reminded of how blind the Council was."

Then, as if Krypton itself were listening to his complaint, the floor of the greenhouse shuddered. The plants in the terrarium cases began to sway, rustling against one another. Increasing vibrations made the tiles and shift out of alignment.

Zor-El grasped his wife's shoulder, pulling her out of the way as one of the transparent panes of the greenhouse split. It shattered, dropping shards onto the floor. Outside, he heard a tinkling crash as a poorly balanced flowerpot toppled from a balcony and smashed into the thoroughfare.

The quake lasted no more than a minute, but it seemed like an eternity. When it was over, Zor-El's stomach felt leaden. "Those will occur much more often as the months go by." He grabbed Alura's hand and hurried with her to his tower that overlooked the open sea. "I need to check my seismic probes. That may have been the worst of it, or we may be at the weak fringe of a much larger event."

In the high observation tower, he had installed receivers for the scientific apparatus he had already deployed across Krypton, including automated buoys out on the oceans. As he watched, the readings went wild. "Look at how the underground tremors spread!" Shuffling papers, he scanned the patterns his devices had detected during the past few days while he'd been in Kandor. He saw that three more massive eruptions had occurred down in the southern continent; the seismic signatures were unmistakable. "This is definitely not normal. The core is changing more dramatically than I predicted. How can the Council ignore this? Maybe these readings will be enough to show them."

Alura went to the balcony where cool breezes wafted around the tower. Out on the open sea, colorful pleasure craft dotted the waves. Kite-driven fish skimmers floated along, scooping up the day's catch. Catamarans with bright blue or red sails tacked along the coast, their passengers diving overboard to swim in the warm water. The red sun reflected off the sea. It all looked so peaceful.

A signal came in from one of Zor-El's drifting buoys. The seismic trace was massive, an undersea signature nearly as great as the largest volcanic eruptions in the southern continent. He could barely believe what he was seeing. "What we felt here was only a minor temblor, less than a tenth of the actual quake."

She turned away from the ocean view. "Where was the epicenter?"

"Deep underwater, far out to sea."

She looked relieved. "Then it won't harm anyone."

Zor-El felt a profound uneasiness. He had more questions than answers. "I can't be certain what the effects of such a powerful deep-sea quake might be."

Crystal bells began chiming from the shoreline watchtowers, then louder alloy tones clanged as the alarm increased. Zor-El crossed the tower room to the emergency communication plate, where he received a frantic distress call from a far-outlying fishing boat.

"—swamped! A rogue wave came out of nowhere and slammed into us! Fifteen lost at sea. Our ship is floundering."

On the balcony, Alura stared at the water. "Zor-El, look at this. The ocean, it looks . . . wrong."

He rushed out to see what appeared to be long, low wrinkles in the water far off, but approaching at an astonishing speed. Rolling closer and closer, a series of waves, each as tall as the greatest buildings in Kandor. "By the red heart of Rao!"

A breakwater of rugged black rocks extended out to shelter the city's edge, and a thick seawall had been built up to protect against hurricanes and high surf. As he watched, though, Zor-El knew it couldn't possibly be enough. He wanted to evacuate the city, get everyone across the bridges to the mainland, but there was no time. It would be only a matter of minutes before the first wave struck the coast.

Zor-El ran to the communication link and summoned all emergency personnel. "Prepare for worst-case rescue and recovery procedures. A disaster is approaching the likes of which Argo City has never seen."

Sickened, he watched the first frothing wall of water engulf several colorful catamarans close to shore. Responding to the clamoring alarms, four fishing craft had reached the piers; their captains had lashed the boats to pilings and scrambled onto the docks.

A cluster of fishing kites simply vanished beneath the first growing wave. Swimmers who noticed the oncoming threat too late were swept away from their boats, and the boats themselves were picked up and dashed against the rocks like a child's toys.

Holding Alura, Zor-El clenched his burned fist at his side, as if through sheer willpower he could drive back the set of waves. But no one on Krypton had such strength.

As it continued to roll along toward the shallower water at the coast, the terrifying wave actually grew higher, more destructive. By the time it smashed over the breakwater, then pushed on toward the high seawall, it was at least five meters high.

People were running along the piers trying to reach the stairs that led to the top of the seawall, but they too were swept away. The piers were smashed, the seawall hammered as if by some great monster pounding at the gates. Spray flew up as high as the tallest buildings.

The water was sucked away for an awful, tense moment in the trough between the first and second waves, and then the second one hit.

Zor-El looked down from his tower. The ocean, so peaceful only a few minutes ago, now looked like a boiling cauldron filled with a soup of wreckage and floating bodies. Much of the debris began to march back out to sea, drawn by the deadly undertow between the next two waves.

After five seconds of sickened awe, Zor-El snapped out of his shock and ran out of the tower and into his city, shouting to the emergency crews to initiate rescue operations. His mind raced through all the layers of the response. And the train of waves kept coming. Before he could get out of the tower and onto the streets, a third hammer hit, causing a surge through Argo City's canals.

"How many more will there be?" Alura cried, following him.

"I saw at least four . . . and others may not be far behind."

Search teams would have to find the injured and give immediate medical attention. Many victims swept out to sea might still be alive, but they would drown soon; he would send flyers out to search for survivors clinging to drifting wreckage. Others would have to keep watch for additional deadly waves. Boats and flyers must travel the coastline, looking for seacraft washed ashore, picking up stranded people.

And that was only in the first few hours.

Next, he would have to restore power in any sections of the city and outlying villages that had been cut off. Fresh water would soon be a problem, so he had to ensure a proper supply. The sheer cleanup would take weeks, the rebuilding would take months. Tens of thousands would be affected by this.

Then he had to worry about food, reconstruction materials, transportation. He'd have to repair the piers and replace the boats, which were vital for Argo City's food supply. He would make reconstructing and reinforcing the seawall a high priority, because he knew that other quakes and tsunamis would eventually come.

Given the dangerous buildup in Krypton's core, Zor-El was sure this was only the beginning.

CHAPTER 25

∞⌐◊‼◊⊸T̈◊ 25

In the fresh early morning light, Jor-El finished adjusting the internal generator and ran a few quick diagnostics of the penetrating scanner before climbing back out of the contraption. He wiped his face, but succeeded only in smearing a grease spot.

The deep seismic probe was ready to test, and he could tell that Donodon shared his excitement. He found it amazing that two people with such vastly different origins could relate to each other in so many areas.

From their first brainstorming, both of them wrapped up in the problem, the two had decided to build the new invention right at his estate. On the purple lawn in front of his research building, Jor-El had dismantled a large ornate fountain to make room for the glittering machine he and Donodon were constructing. Using levitators and magnetic pulleys, he had pulled aside the fountain's wide elliptical bowl, tipped over the columnar stand that looked like a petrified tree trunk, and stacked them together off to the side to create room for the scanner that would look deep into the heart of the planet.

Unfortunately, despite his supposed watchful interest in the project, Commissioner Zod had decided not to stay for the demonstration. The Commissioner had never been particularly warm or understanding, cordial but resistant to Jor-El's work . . . and consequently Jor-El saw the man as a roadblock, an impediment to progress. He didn't consider the Commissioner to be a fool (unlike several members of the Kryptonian

Council); Zod was extremely intelligent, but he simply did not see eye to eye with Jor-El.

And now, even before he could watch the remarkable new seismic scanner in operation, a showpiece of cooperative technology between Krypton's best science and Donodon's knowledge, Zod had made his excuses. He claimed "pressing business" in Kandor, and he had left the night before.

No matter. Jor-El had Lara here at his side, and that was much more important to him. He was eager to show her what he and Donodon had come up with.

When he called her for the big demonstration, he wore his best white robes emblazoned with the serpent-in-diamond family crest of the House of El. With a grand gesture he indicated the finished cylindrical machine on the lawn near the large, dismantled fountain. The framework and power source came from the alien's supplies, but Jor-El had integrated his own focusing crystals and concentrating lenses to add the power of Rao to the machine.

Even silent and motionless, the device looked magnificent. The seismic scanner had waited alone all night long, seemingly impatient to begin its work, but Jor-El and Donodon were forced to delay until dawn's intensifying red sunlight would let them begin their work.

Lara came out to stand beside them, and Jor-El proudly showed her the completed machine. "Today we will see what's really changing deep inside Krypton."

She smiled, captivated by the intricacies of the probe. "I'm sure you didn't do this on purpose, but by following the mathematical needs of your design, you've constructed an amazing sculpture of conflicting angles and reflections."

Jor-El was both pleased and embarrassed. "You mean I'm an artist now?"

"I wouldn't go that far!"

He wished Zor-El could have been here to witness the proof of his suspicions, or to experience relief at being proved wrong. Jor-El had tried to contact him using the communication plate when he and Donodon began their design, but his brother had not yet returned home, apparently having taken a long side trip. This morning, when he'd attempted to contact Argo City again, all communication lines were down; he could not get a signal to his brother, which he found odd. Such disruptions frequently occurred during severe solar storms, but Rao had been relatively quiescent. Jor-El could not fathom why Argo City wouldn't respond.

Regardless, after this successful test, he would have a wealth of data to share with his brother. Then, working with Donodon, they could figure out how to solve the problem—if it existed.

Donodon was already hunkered down on the grass. The alien's smile of anticipation made his chin tentacles quiver. He climbed to his feet, checked that all of his pockets were securely fastened. "We are ready."

A small control pedestal stood next to the blocky base of the dismantled fountain. "Stand here with me to watch," Jor-El said to Lara.

He rotated one of the crystal rods until it illuminated, and the penetrating scanner began to shine. Shutters and reflective flaps opened to expose a power collector that drank in Rao's light. The cylindrical body rotated, picking up speed. Mirrors shifted angles to receive the output from the solar battery, added to the power source Donodon had supplied; then they began to revolve about their axes, flashing glints of light.

The alien stepped close to the whirring device and withdrew one of his handheld tools. Pointing the end in the air above his head, he drew a floating rectangle in front of him, then filled it in as if spraying the frame full of information. His ethereal screen began to display data being projected by the throbbing probe, layer after layer of rock, then lava, currents of molten stone as the view rushed deeper and deeper.

Jor-El found it dizzying. Lara laughed in amazement. "This is . . . beautiful!"

The heavy engine hummed, and the screen hovering in the air showed impossible thermal chaos. "I see, yes . . . there is your problem. Just a little deeper." The alien stepped closer, his facial tentacles twitching with fascination.

When Jor-El checked his set of control rods, several of the crystals glowed amber. He pulled them out and reinserted them, but the warning color continued to intensify. "That isn't supposed to happen."

The lights from the penetrating scanner flashed on and off. The internal engines began to groan, then emitted a shrieking, tearing whine. Suddenly all the control crystals turned a blazing red. Donodon rushed toward the scanner in an attempt to fix the problem, but Jor-El could see it was already too late. He shouted a warning to the blue-skinned alien and grabbed Lara. He dragged her to the ground behind the shelter of the heavy fountain just as the throbbing device exploded with a scintillating, searing flash.

Jor-El pushed Lara's head down, tried to cover her with his own body. A shattering, shrieking hail of broken fragments peppered the tilted fountain and sheared off the control rods of the standing podium. In the last instant he saw diminutive Donodon raise his hands to shield himself. Shards of crystal and gleaming metal hurtled into him, propelled with explosive force.

With a crash and a groan, the cylindrical device toppled over, like a mortally wounded behemoth, all its prisms falling in upon themselves. Showers of crystal continued to tinkle around them with incongruously musical sounds.

Wearing a stricken expression, Jor-El noted the blood flecks all over Lara's slashed clothes, then glanced down to see that he, too, had been sliced by dozens of the razor-edged shards. He didn't yet feel any pain. "Lara, are you hurt?"

"I don't think so. At least, not badly."

Leaving her, he bolted across the purple grass. Broken fragments of crystal crunched under his feet. "Donodon!" His voice was ragged.

The alien lay sprawled on his back. More than twenty spearpoint shards had slammed into his body, delivering multiple mortal wounds. His jumpsuit was shredded, and brownish-green blood oozed from the cuts. Jor-El dropped to his knees, grabbed the alien's head. "Donodon, I'm sorry. I don't know what went wrong."

Blood trickled from Donodon's mouth. The fringe tentacles were limp. He reached up with a gnarled hand. Even his throat had been cut, and he bled profusely. He managed to gasp no more than a fading rattle; then he died in Jor-El's arms.

Blood smeared Jor-El's hands. Lara knelt beside him. "It's not your fault."

But the scientist stared at his dead friend in abject horror. "It *is* my fault. The probe . . . something was wrong."

He and Lara sat listening to the final collapse of the destroyed machine. The last fragments settled to the ground, still reflecting the light of Rao.

Neither of them saw the muscular form of Nam-Ek slip away from the hiding place from which he had secretly watched the results of his sabo-tage—just as Commissioner Zod had commanded him to do.

CHAPTER 26

∞ ⛧◇‼ ◇�⟐ 26

The Kryptonian Council reacted to Donodon's death with horror, disbelief, and helpless panic—as Zod had known they would. They had always been fools, and now they were fools faced with a dilemma.

The Council had absolutely no idea what to do. In times of great urgency, when difficult decisions needed to be made and action needed to be taken, Zod wished that someone would just take firm control. That was what the people needed. Finally, after his impulsive act of pure inspiration, the doors of possibility would open for him, and the long-overdue changes would be swift and permanent. Even Cor-Zod would have admired how carefully his son had laid down every thread in the pattern. . . .

The recent earthquake and tsunami that had smashed Argo City had already thrown the Council into turmoil. Zod saw a measure of irony in the Argo City disaster—maybe Jor-El's brother could take satisfaction in having obvious, if tragic, proof of the planet's seismic instabilities. Jor-El did not need his alien seismic scanning device after all. Since other city leaders were rushing supplies and relief to the damaged peninsula, however, the eleven Council members in Kandor were more worried about the repercussions of Donodon's death. They were plainly terrified.

Sure enough, the Council declared another emergency session and summoned Jor-El to face their wrath, their justice. He was the perfect scapegoat, and in his own shock and grief, Jor-El might even accept whatever punishment the Council decreed. Zod guessed that he would wear his own mantle of guilt heavier than anything the government leaders could ever impose. Zod bided his time, waiting for the right moment.

Feeling heartsick at what had happened, the stunned scientist had already rushed to the capital on his own. Such a monumental failure and miscalculation from the great *Jor-El* was even more unsettling to the public than the alien's death itself. Even Jor-El couldn't seem to believe what had happened.

"I accept full responsibility." He stood below the Council in the speaking arena, raising his hands. His face was as white as the robes he wore, but he still carried a weighty dignity about him. Dressings covered dozens of wounds on his hands and his cheeks. "I did not intend for this to happen. Donodon and I were working together. It is a terrible mistake."

"It is terrible, to be sure," Jul-Us said sternly. Since the Council session was closed and the access doors were barred, all the tiers of stone seats remained empty. His voice echoed in the cavernous chamber. The mood here was the complete opposite of when a confident Jor-El had faced them at his brother's side, taking charge and demanding that they listen to his warning. Zod knew he could use this to his advantage.

"In all our centuries of records, there is not a single comparable incident!" said Kor-Te, sounding both disappointed and confused. The Council members drew strength from each other's indignation.

Personally, Zod was quite pleased with how events had turned out. He had not known how effective Nam-Ek's sabotage would be, and he had resigned himself to losing the great scientist in order to light the fires of panic. Even that would have been acceptable to him, but fortunately, Jor-El had survived. If carefully guided, the man could still play a very important role.

Jul-Us raised his gnarled hand for silence from the other members, though each of them was frothing with the need to speak. The Council Head looked down from his bench. "Will the alien's people view this as murder? Will they demand retribution?"

"Murder?" Jor-El was appalled, then rallied and stood straighter. "Don't be ridiculous. How can you think that? How could anyone think that? It was an accident." He lowered his voice. "Donodon was my friend. He himself helped me build the device."

"He should not have come to Krypton in the first place," Pol-Ev muttered.

"And yet he did," Al-An moaned. "Now what are we going to do?"

"It was his own experiment that killed him," Jun-Do pointed out.

Knowing that it was time to make sure the questions and accusations followed the desired path, Zod stood from his own seat. He was careful to balance the necessity of placing Jor-El in his debt with the need to maintain the Council's suspicions. "Once again, we all see the dangers of unproven technology. My Commission warned Jor-El numerous times." He held up a hand to cut off a flurry of comments. "But he has a good heart and a strong sense of honor. I do believe he meant no harm. The alien insisted there was no risk. As did Jor-El."

He rubbed his trim beard. He knew exactly what seeds to plant. "In fact, it may be a blessing that Donodon was killed. Have you considered the implications? Who can say what the outsider might have communicated to his superiors once he left our world? His friendship might have been a ploy. Would he have revealed our vulnerabilities? Our secrets? To alien invaders, Krypton no doubt seems a lush fruit ripe for the picking."

Jor-El turned to him, looking stung and angry. "Donodon's race was *peaceful,* Commissioner. They were explorers, travelers—"

"Then why was he so eager to talk about his powerful galactic police corps?" Silber-Za demanded in an icy voice. She had bound her blond hair back in a severe arrangement, held in place with sharp pins. "If we refused to accept the rule of *their* law, would they have used their powers against Krypton?"

Despite his clear misery, Jor-El still stood up for himself. Now he seemed angry. "We have absolutely no reason to doubt Donodon. He said they were a force for good."

"As defined by whom?" Zod continued, speaking now for the benefit of the easily manipulated Council members. "Those who hold such power tend to use it for their own purposes, not to the benefit of others."

"Commissioner Zod is right," said Mauro-Ji, amidst the muttering of the other members. "No doubt every one of those villains Donodon displayed for us also believed they were doing something 'good.'"

Cera-Si nodded. "I'm sorry, Jor-El, but the very fact that other planets need such a police corps proves how dangerous it is out there! I see now that Krypton has been absolutely correct to remain isolated."

The timing of the Sapphire Guards could not have been better. They entered carrying the small cloth-wrapped body on a stretcher.

Mere moments after news of the tragedy had arrived, Zod had issued swift instructions, thinking faster than the Council members could. The security troops had rushed to Jor-El's estate, seized Donodon's lacerated body, wrapped it up, and carried it back to the Council temple. They had also confiscated the alien's numerous devices and tools, plucking them from his mangled jumpsuit and then locking them in a vault beneath the government chambers.

Seeing the wrapped corpse now, the Council members were struck silent. Jor-El turned his head away in anger, grief, and shame.

"I have also ordered a team to bring the alien's spaceship here to Kandor, where my Commission will dismantle it properly." Zod nodded, smiling coolly. The Council members approved, looking both surprised and relieved that someone would show such initiative. "We will take it apart, so we do not have to worry about the dangers of that spacecraft."

Though he appeared defeated and overwhelmed, Jor-El turned quickly. "Do not destroy that ship, Commissioner. We can learn—"

"Your curiosity has caused quite enough damage, Jor-El," Silber-Za snapped. "There's no telling what dangers Krypton now faces because of you."

Zod continued to push them to the edge of fear. "There is no need for panic." But his tone said exactly the opposite. "We can hope for the best. When Donodon's people discover what happened, it is possible they will listen to our explanations. Jor-El is clearly sincere. It is possible they won't suspect us of treachery. It is possible they are a gentle race, a force for good, as Jor-El believes them to be. It is even possible they will just forgive him and forget anything terrible ever happened."

"It's possible they'll leave us alone," Al-An added, his voice quavering.

Zod looked at Jor-El with an expression of cautious hope before he hardened his voice again. "But I do not believe it. We have to prepare for the worst. How will Krypton protect itself as a sovereign planet? We must change our ways. Instead of forbidding technology that might be turned against us, now we need to embrace it! We must shift our emphasis, pour all of our creative efforts into defense." Naturally, he expected to be personally put in charge of all of the weapons preparations, as a first and crucial step.

The Council members were unanimous in their shock. "That is inconceivable, Commissioner!" Cera-Si cried.

"Inconceivable perhaps—but necessary. If it turns out we do not need the weapons, then we will not use them. But better to have them just in case. We must begin immediately. We may not have much time." Zod carefully controlled the intensity in his voice. If he appeared too eager, the Council might suspect his plans. "No one can tell when vengeful outsiders will come."

"Completely unacceptable, Commissioner." Jul-Us shook his head gravely. "It would change who we are as Kryptonians."

Zod wanted to strangle them. He had set everything forth so carefully. He quelled his fury, controlled his voice. "I respectfully disagree. Any reasonable person can see—"

The Council Head continued in a ponderous tone. "No, no, if Krypton begins a sudden military buildup, it will be seen as proof that we are lying, that this was no accident. No, the only thing we can do is hold Jor-El accountable. The blame clearly falls on his shoulders. He invented the device that killed Donodon, and Donodon himself was involved in the misadventure. Those two played with dangerous technology. They let it get out of control."

Mauro-Ji said, "Yes, we must have a full and open trial. Jor-El can present his case, show any evidence he chooses. That will demonstrate the fairness and impartiality of our justice system."

Old Jul-Us slowly turned to look at his fellows on the Council bench. "And when we find Jor-El guilty, it will prove that we meant no harm to Donodon. Then the outsiders will leave us alone."

Jor-El's shoulders sagged, and it was clear to everyone there, even Zod, that he would be convicted no matter what evidence he presented at the inquisition.

CHAPTER 27

Disgraced, Jor-El saw no alternative but to place himself in quiet exile while the Kryptonian Council decided his fate. Though he believed the tragedy was an accident, and he could not accept that Donodon's vengeful race would bring destruction to Krypton, he had no desire to talk to anyone.

Many members of his estate staff were frightened, and he gave them leave to go stay with friends or relatives. Fro-Da wouldn't budge, though, insisting that he would make a fine meal every night; the plump, curly-haired man saw exquisite food as a cure for any unpleasant turn of events. Regardless, Jor-El felt very alone.

He had thought matters could not get worse, until a second team of Sapphire Guards came to ransack his estate on orders from the Council. They had already taken Donodon's ship and all of the alien's tools and possessions. Now, though, while he stood helplessly watching, the guards removed several half-completed engines and "threatening" devices from his research building.

They also found the seven remaining small rockets equipped with solar-analysis probes at the launching pad behind his main research building. He had received data from the last sensor package he'd launched, but he still intended to send monthly probes to monitor the red giant's fluctuations. Donodon had offered his assistance. . . .

Now, though, the Sapphire Guards took them all away. "These are potential weapons, clearly precluded by Kryptonian law." Though the guard captain seemed somewhat awed, even intimidated, by the great scientist's presence and his technology, he instructed his men to load the rockets onto a transport platform. "I am sorry, Jor-El. They are to be confiscated."

Jor-El tried to explain. "They are scientific probes used to study Rao. They go above the atmosphere to take readings!" He drew a deep breath. "The Council gave me express permission to study the sun so that we can prepare if it enters its final supernova phase—"

"That is not my decision to make." The big-shouldered man seemed apologetic. "You will have to appeal to Kandor." The guards finished loading the apparatus without a further word to Jor-El, though they continued to give him sidelong glances. Angry, he watched them depart. They were only following the orders of the frightened, misguided Council.

From Argo City, even as rescue crews combed through the wreckage and tended the injured, Zor-El sent a supportive message on the communication plate. His dark hair long and loose, Zor-El looked drawn, his exhaustion and shock barely kept at bay by sheer adrenaline and determination. "I would be there at your side if I could, Jor-El. You know that."

"Yes, I know it. And I also know that Donodon's technology could have scanned the core and gotten the data we needed to convince the Council. The seismic penetrator would have changed everything. But now it's too late."

"I'll still get the data, Jor-El. Even after the tsunami, I am sending a team to the southern continent. We were doing it before the alien arrived. We can achieve this ourselves."

Jor-El looked intently at his brother's face on the screen. "You need my help. Saving Argo City should be our priority, not my personal troubles—"

Zor-El cut him off. "Don't worry about me. Many workers from all across the world responded to our need with all the willingness and enthusiasm I could hope for. I just have to give them guidance." His image grew larger and more intimate as he leaned closer to the viewer. "You know you did nothing wrong, Jor-El. Don't surrender without a

fight. I believe in you, just as you believed in me when I told you about the core instabilities."

Jor-El found the strength within himself. "Yes. I have to make the Council see beyond their fear."

Not wanting his disgrace to rub off on her, Jor-El urged Lara to return home to her parents and brother in their Kandor studios, but she responded with cool stubbornness. "You need me, Jor-El, more than at any other time in your life." She tossed her amber hair and looked him directly in the eyes. "You need me."

"Of course I do, but you shouldn't be with me. You know that, Lara."

"Why? For the sake of appearances? For a genius, you can be incredibly dense sometimes." She placed both of her hands on his shoulders, stood close enough that he could feel her warmth, smell her scent, see the bright sunshine on her skin and hair. "I don't care what anyone thinks, as long as you have faith in yourself. I believe in you, and I intend to stay for as long as you need me."

Jor-El let out a strained laugh. "You may be stuck here for quite some time, then."

"Then that's the way it will be."

Sensing that he needed a new perspective, Lara took him by the arm and dragged him out to look at the spectacular murals her parents had painted. He stared with a leaden heart at the last obelisk, the one separate from the other eleven. Lara's recently completed portrait of him looked so brave and wise, so determined. *Genius*. Jor-El wanted to be *that* visionary man again. The device he and Donodon had built should have provided vital information, but instead it had caused unexpected tragedy. A simple miscalculation . . . or a fundamental design flaw. Working with Donodon, he had learned much about the alien's technology, had glimpsed only the tip of the iceberg of possibilities. Had *he* done something wrong? Jor-El accepted that he would have to pay for that mistake, rather than let his whole planet suffer. It was what truth and justice demanded of him, just as in the legendary story of Kal-Ik that Lara had told him.

In a determined, almost scolding tone, Lara said, "Stop feeling sorry for yourself. That hurts me more than all of these cuts." She held out her bandaged arms.

She took his hand again and led him across the grounds to where the dismantled fountain showed white marks, chips, and scratches from the flying debris. That fortunate barricade had saved both of their lives. Nearby, broken crystals, shattered mirrors, and fragmented components of the seismic scanner lay strewn across the scarred garden. "*Study* this. Find out what went wrong. I'm surprised the Sapphire Guards haven't already taken every scrap."

For her sake, he straightened. *Had* he made an error in his calculations? Had he assembled the pieces incorrectly? Was Kryptonian technology incompatible with the alien's systems? Had the power conduits been insufficient to carry the load he had distributed into the scanner? He drew a breath as possibilities crossed his mind. "You're right. I'm a scientist. I have to learn all I can while I still have the chance. I can solve the problem."

"Yes, you can."

He gazed at her, feeling a deeper emotion than he had ever experienced before. "I'm sorry, Lara. After all of my grandiose blueprints and prototypes, I intended to make something that would show the Council the urgent need to do something. I should not have been so impulsive."

"Don't be ashamed because you were enthusiastic and decisive. Being impulsive is not a bad thing at all. Even though a terrible accident happened, you're still a good person—and I love you for it." She smiled at him unabashedly, as if daring him to contradict her. "Yes, I do love you, and I think you feel the same about me. That's why we need to make some good come out of this."

He blinked at the realization and then couldn't stop himself from smiling. "Yes, Lara. I love you. There's absolutely no question in my mind, even under these circumstances." He stopped, then looked at her with an intensity that surprised even him. She had encouraged him to be impulsive, and so he plunged ahead in a rush of words without pausing to think. "In my dedication to my work, I sometimes forget what I need most—like sleep and food and . . . you. It's been hard for me to *stop* thinking about you for quite some time. Lara . . . I want to be your husband, and I want you to be my wife."

Jor-El could not breathe for several seconds, and he turned away, his thoughts spinning, his heart pounding. Suddenly he realized that he was being incredibly selfish to ask. He was in disgrace, and the Council could very well sentence him to permanent imprisonment. How could he ask her to make such a sacrifice?

He realized that she was smiling. "It's about time you asked. I can help you get through this crisis—and everything afterward." She slipped her arms around him.

He looked all around him, indicated the wreck of the seismic scanner as if that symbolized the magnitude of his crashing dishonor. "I can't let you be dragged down with me."

"Then I'll have to keep you from being dragged down, won't I? If I'm at your side, I can help hold you up."

Jor-El hugged her for a long moment. He knew she would do exactly that. Just by looking at her, he could tell Lara was sincere. Marrying her was truly what he wanted. And it was what she wanted, too.

CHAPTER 28

Xan City was a metropolis of ghosts and ruins and forgotten lives. Aethyr drank in the lost wonders with her dark eyes and painted in details with the brush of her imagination.

After moving her camp into the city on the second day, she began her explorations in earnest, taking notes and capturing images for her own satisfaction, not for any stuffy department of historical studies back at the Academy. Most people were content to reread old records, without having any desire to touch and see and smell what Krypton had been like during its violent yet glorious days.

The ancient warlord had constructed and armored his blocky watchtowers and graceful crystal minarets to withstand any attack from outside enemies. The architecture was reinforced with heavy beams and arches. Yet even those defenses had not withstood the slow and inexorable assault of time. Crumbling roofs had slumped down; windows were shattered, leaving holes like the gaps in an old crone's smile. Toppled, grandiose sculptures were so badly weathered that Aethyr could not tell what they had once represented.

Even so, with minimal rebuilding, she believed that Xan City could once again become a thriving population center. No one on Krypton would ever make the effort, of course; her race had lost the spark of ambition and progress. And so the dead city continued to fade into the dusts of memory.

The centerpiece of Jax-Ur's capital was a vast plaza where smooth interlocked tiles remained set in place, impervious to weeds, weather, and even the low seismic tremblings that so often made the ground cringe. With breezes ruffling her short, dark hair, Aethyr thought she could hear the long-faded cheers—or screams—of the huge crowds that the warlord had commanded to attend him. In ancient lettering, Aethyr read the ominous name of this place: Execution Square.

In the middle of the plaza she paused to look at the remnants of an ancient statue, a towering figure carved of black stone. Its details had been scrubbed away by countless seasons and storms, but even damaged and worn the figure had an oppressive magnificence. Around the main figure, carved from softer stone, were five pale lumps showing only the faintest outlines of arms, bent legs, and bowed heads . . . defeated subjects kneeling before him.

She laughed aloud at the monolithic sculpture. "Behold, the great Jax-Ur, warlord of Krypton, destroyer of the moon Koron!" She bowed in a gesture of mock respect. "So this is all that remains of you, king of kings, mightiest of the mighty?"

According to Krypton's legends, Jax-Ur had summoned the generals of all the armies he had defeated, commanding that they kneel before him. The conquered men had bent their knees here in the great square and sworn their fealty—after which Jax-Ur had executed them all anyway. "I will not tolerate defeated men as my generals," he had said.

Back then, arrogant Jax-Ur had never dreamed his empire could fall. He had invincible armies. He had a hidden stockpile of nova javelins and had already demonstrated his willingness to use them. But even Jax-Ur failed in the end. Everything, it seemed to Aethyr, succumbed to history.

She could spend weeks here in Xan City, as long as her supplies lasted. She found a capped-over fountain, from which she managed to pump out fresh, sweet water. As she splashed her face and took a deep drink, she wondered if Jax-Ur himself had moistened his parched throat here. The very idea made the water taste more delicious.

Wandering among the ruins, poking into alcoves and collapsed structures, Aethyr found two yellowed skeletons. Would-be treasure hunters, she assumed. She had no way of telling how long they had rested here. The bones appeared to be gnawed and chipped, as if by serrated jaws. She scoffed at the remains, feeling no kinship with plunderers who would die empty-handed. Aethyr did not intend to leave Xan City without discovering something major.

During the broiling red heat of afternoon, she took shelter in the colonnaded ruins of what had once been an old temple. In the shadows she saw topaz-shelled beetles scuttling about, each the size of her hand. They lunged upon and devoured plump spiders, then disappeared back into crannies. Their clacking, chirping noises grew louder as the afternoon waned. The whole city must be infested with them. How ironic that a population of insects had conquered the remnants of a once-titanic empire.

Hearing a skittering sound, she saw two of the beetles approaching her cautiously, their antennae waving in the air. They opened and closed sawlike jaws. She crunched both of them under her heel, then smeared the ichor on the flagstones.

She went from building to building, most of which must have been dwellings. Other structures were silos and storehouses in which she found amazingly preserved food supplies. Though she could not make out the faded drawings on the labels, tonight she would treat herself to a feast that Jax-Ur himself might have eaten.

After Rao had set, she moved her camp over beside the pitted Jax-Ur statue in Execution Square. The warlord's dominating presence made Aethyr feel secure, as if he would frighten away anything that might endanger her.

She built a fire, not so much for the warmth as for the glad comfort of the crackling flames. She opened the jars of food she had found, breaking ages-old seals and smelling the contents. One stewlike mixture was savory and piquant, flavored with spices totally unfamiliar to Aethyr. She dipped her finger into the sauce, tasted it, then heated the entire serving. Another container held some sort of pickled vegetable, but it was brown and bubbly and smelled foul. She tossed it into the corner of the fallen-down ruins, where it spilled against a broken fluted column.

She watched, both amused and fascinated, as four topaz beetles scuttled out of the shadows, startled by the noise of the clattering container. They returned to devour every scrap of the spoiled pickles. More and more beetles emerged from the shadows, waving antennae in search of their share of the food, before ducking back into shelter.

Strictly as a precaution, Aethyr gathered a pile of rocks and shards from the broken statues. Beneath the looming shadow of Jax-Ur, she looked again at the city's towers, the broken windows, the randomly arranged alcoves and black balconies. Oddly, the very randomness seemed somehow calculated, a pattern that she could see only at the edge of her awareness.

She opened another container to find a smooth, sweet pudding with a sugary crust on top and chewy lumps inside. She ate it, enjoying every bite, though afterward her stomach felt heavy and her ears were filled with a slight buzzing. Perhaps the pudding was some sort of drug, a sensory-enhancement or thought-deadening substance. Feeling herself grow sleepy, she shook her head.

A lone beetle scuttled forward, as if its companions had dared it to make a foray in her direction. Aethyr picked up one of her rocks, aimed carefully, and smashed the beetle's carapace. It let out a thin squeak as it died. Four other insects rushed forward and fell upon the carcass, ripping away the shining shell and eating the soft goo inside.

The buzzing in her ears grew louder, and Aethyr looked again at the fallen buildings, sweeping her gaze from thick towers to the remains of Jax-Ur's palace. From here, she could make out shadow-enhanced carvings, geometric projections, and deep-cut alcoves. The placement of the windows and openings made no sense—until she stopped thinking of them as windows. Instead, she viewed them as a design, a code. As she looked back and forth, trying to decipher the letters or symbols, they finally made sense.

Musical notes.

She and her friend Lara had both studied ancient Kryptonian compositions, especially the pompous "Jax-Ur's March." According to legend, the warlord had demanded that the eponymous march be played at each of his appearances. Aethyr recalled the old notation and translated the notes. Fighting back a strange temptation to giggle, she began to hum and sway, making her finger follow along with the notes. Yes, she was sure of it.

Aethyr sat down, a little off-balance from the intoxicating dessert, and withdrew the small flute from her pack.

Five more beetles approached from different directions. Impatient,

Aethyr killed them all with thrown stones, thereby providing a cannibalistic feast for another batch of beetles.

She placed the flute to her lips, concentrated, and played the thin, piping tune. Fumbling with the melody at first, she stopped and wiped her lips, which felt numb and swollen. This time when she played "Jax-Ur's March," the clear music pierced the silence of the ruins. In response, as if she had awakened them, the topaz beetles began to chirp a thrumming song of their own.

Aethyr was sure she sensed something shift deep beneath the city, machinery awakening, ancient generators coming alive. Frowning, she played the melody again from start to finish. Yes, indeed, a rumble was coming from far below Execution Square, and it was not a seismic tremor. With her vision growing annoyingly fuzzy from the drugged dessert, she blinked repeatedly and looked around the square, hoping to see something out there.

The carefully laid flagstones were marked with faded colors, large geometric patterns across the expanse where crowds would have gathered. Columns and sculptures stood in random places around the perimeter, and as Aethyr looked at them from her new perspective, she noted that these objects were not mere decorations or ornaments. The hollow stones, embedded metal plates, and ancient hanging tubular chimes could all serve as simple yet serviceable musical instruments. And each object bore a marking, a camouflaged musical note, now that she knew to look for it. Viewed from near the central statue, she could see they were laid out in the order of the melody.

What would happen if she played the famous march with the instruments Jax-Ur himself had hidden here?

She picked up a still-burning wooden stick from her campfire and strolled unsteadily over to the metal plate, which was subtly marked with the first note in the march. Along the way, she stomped on two more beetles. One actually scratched her ankle with its sharp black legs and she kicked it away, concentrating on her new quest. She pondered the arrangement of the strange and antique musical instruments.

She struck the first object like a gong, and as the note slowly faded, she ran to the next, a hollow stone, and hammered the second note. Moving over to a cylindrical chime, she smashed out the third note.

Slowly and ponderously—but without mistakes—Aethyr played music that had not been heard here for more than a thousand years.

The sound beneath the ground grew louder, building to an engine's roar. Crystals embedded in the long-abandoned towers started to glow in the night. Aethyr stood awestruck. Astonishment flushed away the ringing in her ears and the numbness in her thoughts.

Now phosphorescent lights began to glow in the weathered flagstones of the area, illuminating distinct though faded circles randomly distributed around the broad area; each circle was more than four meters wide. Eighteen of them.

The glowing rings started to vibrate, and the circles split in half along a neat line that cut along the diameter. The circular plates were hidden trapdoors, sealed for untold centuries, and the halves swung downward. Each open hole now revealed a shaft that was lit from beneath by stuttering, weak green light. Eighteen hidden pits right in the middle of Jax-Ur's Execution Square.

Squadrons of ravenous beetles squeaked and whistled, then beat a hasty retreat to their hiding places. Aethyr ignored them.

Stagnant air and curling steam wafted up from long-closed pits. Careful to keep her balance, Aethyr peered down into the nearest circular opening. This treasure was worth far, far more than anything she had ever seen in her life.

CHAPTER 29

Lara contacted her parents in Kandor to announce that she and Jor-El were going to get married. In the background of the screen, young Ki yelled teasingly, "I knew it! I knew it!"

Lor-Van seemed about to burst with pride, though her mother voiced reservations. "Don't rush into something you can't undo. What if Jor-El is found guilty?"

"Jor-El is Jor-El," Lara said firmly. "I love him, and I know he's a good man, regardless of what the Council says."

Her father tried to console her, hearing the worry she could not quite cover up in her voice. "We know Jor-El as well. We can't believe the terrible things they say, and yet the evidence. . . . You yourself were there."

"Yes, I was, and I saw the accident. And I still stand by Jor-El."

Her parents looked at each other in the image screen and simultaneously came to the same conclusion. Lor-Van said, "Then you have our support, Lara. We will be there for you."

Ora hesitated. "I assume the wedding will take place soon? Jor-El's hearing . . . "

"It will be as soon as I can manage it. Trust me!"

Before they ended the communication, her parents shared their own news, that they had begun exhaustive preparations for their most ambitious project yet: to adorn an entire administrative spire with complex friezes and colorful crystalsilk weavings. Lara was excited to hear their descriptions, but her concentration strayed back to helping Jor-El.

Even with the components of the destroyed seismic scanner spread out on the grounds and catalogued, Jor-El still couldn't determine what had gone wrong, and he worked obsessively to find out. Even though it would not change the guilt the Council no doubt intended to pin on him, still he needed to know. He called up his blueprints, recalculated every possible light angle. Though he could not duplicate Donodon's technology, he even built another prototype of the red sun generator, which operated perfectly at up to three times its designed capacity. It made no sense.

Outside in the afternoon sunshine, they worked together on the problem. Though Lara had an artistic rather than a technical background, she insisted on helping him. "I can't match you in the theoretical arena, but every small task I take out of your hands gives you more time and energy to devote to clearing your name."

Jor-El, however, knew it wouldn't be enough. He needed a much more powerful ally if he were to have any hope of changing the Council's decision.

Commissioner Zod arrived unannounced at the estate five days after the death of Donodon. Jor-El came forward, feeling a knot in his stomach. He could not interpret the Commissioner's motives; at times he seemed to support Jor-El, while other times he seemed intent on destroying him. "Do you have news from the Council?" He wasn't sure he wanted to hear the answer.

Zod waved his hand casually. "They take an interminable amount of time to do anything. Don't expect a decision soon."

Lara remained close at Jor-El's side, suspicious. "Then why did you come here, Commissioner?"

"Why, to help you plan your defense at the trial. You need my assistance. You must know that I am one of your staunch supporters."

Jor-El couldn't believe what he was hearing. He didn't know any such thing. Though he respected the man for his single-mindedness, he had always disagreed with Zod's entrenched attitude against progress. "That's not like you, Commissioner. As you so pointedly reminded the

Council, you warned me time and again about uncontrolled technology. It was my invention that caused this disaster."

The other man shrugged. "Yes, and if I could spin the planet backward and reverse time, I would urge you never to build your dangerous device. But it is too late for that. We must put the past behind us."

"That still doesn't explain why you are on our side, Commissioner," Lara said. She watched the man closely, trying to figure out what political advantages he saw to helping Jor-El.

Zod scrutinized Lara, as if trying to fit her into the equation alongside Jor-El. As if admitting a terrible mistake, he said, "When Donodon was killed, I had an epiphany. When I faithfully censored dangerous technologies to keep Kryptonians from hurting each other, I failed to imagine that we might need to protect ourselves from outside enemies. We may be a gentle and peaceful race, but the rest of the galaxy is not so harmless. Outsiders have noticed us now, and you have a better chance of saving Krypton than anyone else. But the Council doesn't realize it." Zod sighed heavily. "I fear the time is going to come when our world needs your genius, Jor-El. It would be a mistake to lock you away. I intend to speak on your behalf at the trial, for the good of Krypton."

Jor-El looked down at the carefully labeled components spread out across the lawn. "There may be more to this mystery. I just found a foreign residue that seems to be some sort of unstable high-energy chemical. As near as I can tell, it is the same concentrated substance I use to launch my solar-probe rockets. I don't know how it could have gotten into the seismic scanner, but I intend to run further analyses to identify the compound. That may be the key. What if someone tampered with the device? The explosion might not have been an accident."

Zod appeared troubled. "Intriguing. It is best if you give me those samples, Jor-El. If there is indeed some suspicious contamination, then *you* cannot be the one to analyze it. The Council will never believe you didn't plant this so-called proof yourself."

"Jor-El would never do that," Lara said.

"Of course he wouldn't." Zod gave a meaningful shrug. "On the other hand, the device should never have exploded, either. Let me take your samples back to Kandor. I will have my own experts study the chemical signature. You are not alone in this, Jor-El."

Jor-El nodded slowly in reluctant agreement. "That would probably be best."

The Commissioner turned, looking behind the large estate buildings as another floating vessel approached, this one guided by the burly mute Nam-Ek. On the craft's open flatbed, large objects were covered with thick cloth, draped and shapeless. As if afraid of being overheard, Zod lowered his voice. "I have brought you something, Jor-El—something you must keep hidden for the time being."

Jor-El looked at Lara, then back at the Commissioner. "What is it?"

Nam-Ek brought the floating vehicle and its bulky cargo over to where his master stood. With a flourish, Zod removed the tarpaulin to reveal large components, engines, computer systems, and sleek blue-and-silver sections of hull plating. "My Commission team members carefully disassembled the alien's starship, but it is far too valuable to ignore. Regardless of the Council's fears, I simply could not allow Don-odon's ship to be ruined."

Jor-El came forward, breathing quickly. "You kept the components intact? I heard you announce to the Council—you said you had destroyed it."

"The Council doesn't need to know." He smiled thinly. "Someday, Krypton will know the wisdom in this—I know you can see it already."

Jor-El brought Lara forward. "His navigation system, his database of planets, his starship engines. We can do *so much* with this!"

"Unless the Council confiscates it again," Lara warned.

"We will just have to keep them from finding out." Zod rolled his eyes. "I cannot bear to leave such a technological treasure in *their* hands, can you? Until this distraction is over with, we must keep these components safely hidden. I trust that sooner or later we will need you to understand those starship systems, Jor-El. Someday I may ask you to build a whole fleet of Kryptonian space vessels to defend our planet. Whom else can I trust?"

Zod walked across the lawn with the big-shouldered mute matching his every step, and Jor-El followed him. He lowered his voice to a conspiratorial whisper. "My Commission offices in Kandor are not safe from inspection. Is there a place that we can hide the craft here?"

"I could haul it into my main research building and get to work even before my inquisition. . . . "

Zod shook his head. "Too obvious, and too dangerous. We need a place where no one will think to look."

Jor-El turned in a long slow circle, and finally his gaze rested on the prominent tower with its spiraling pearlescent walls. He paced around the perimeter of the structure, running his palm along the smooth wall, tapping and searching for any indication of an entrance. To Jor-El the enigmatic structure symbolized all the undiscovered things that remained in the universe.

"A long time ago, my father said I would know when to open the tower, when I would make use of what's inside. I can't think of a better time than now." As he tapped with his knuckles, he found a patch that seemed to be made of a different sort of material, thinner, like an eggshell. "Here. We could get mallets and construction hammers from one of the work sheds."

But Nam-Ek simply balled a huge fist and swung, not even wincing as his hand impacted the wall. The pearlescent barrier shattered, and shards tinkled down to expose a doorway wide enough for two men to stand in side by side—wide enough for the small spaceship.

Inside, a milky-rose light bathed the tower's main room: red sunshine filtered through the translucent wall. Years ago, before he'd sealed the structure, Yar-El had set up a pristine laboratory with alcoves, tables, equipment—everything ready for use. Jor-El was delighted with the discovery.

When Nam-Ek had unloaded the dismantled starship components inside the secret tower laboratory, Zod looked at the strange objects with keen interest, then stepped back out of the tower. "Do you have construction resin? We should seal the opening again for the time being, so that the ship remains hidden. I do not want you to work on it . . . not yet. We need to take care of the Council first."

As a loyal citizen, Jor-El didn't like keeping secrets from the legitimate government, but he certainly understood why this was necessary. The Kryptonian Council's obstructionist attitudes could well bring about the downfall of Krypton—in more ways than one. "Yes, I can keep it safely hidden . . . for now."

CHAPTER 30

30

Only seven days remained before the scheduled inquisition. Jor-El had planned his defense, rehearsed his speech so that he might sway the eleven Council members, though he doubted more than a few of them would listen. Nevertheless, he did not intend to go down without a fight.

In the meantime, Zod had sent the samples of chemical residue back to Kandor for analysis, but they had heard no results yet. Jor-El did not know how the chemical proof could help his case, but he very much wanted to know what had gone wrong. He needed to understand.

But another problem presented itself. "We should find someone to marry us." Jor-El turned to Lara with bright blue eyes.

She stood with him inside the main research building where she had first rescued him from the Phantom Zone. "I will not let you face the Council unless I can tell the whole world that we're husband and wife. We will show them our strength together. Just let them try to keep me from accompanying you when you receive your sentence."

Commissioner Zod entered the large laboratory carrying selected excerpts from old Council sessions and citations of archaic passages from Kryptonian law. He had stayed at the estate for two days, assisting Jor-El with his legal defense, finding documentation and historical precedents that might allow the Council to change their minds. Lara still wondered why the Commissioner would devote so much attention to the scientist's case, but they could not afford to turn down his assistance. Zod seemed to be their only powerful ally.

"Forgive me for eavesdropping. You two are to be married? A last-minute romance?" She found something unsettling about his smile. "Intriguing."

"We haven't had the time to prepare," Jor-El confessed. "And time is running out."

The Commissioner seemed to be making mental calculations. He looked sidelong at her, as if he still didn't remember her name. "And would marrying this woman make you happy?"

"Yes," Jor-El said, without a tinge of doubt in his voice. "Lara makes me feel not only happy, but at peace."

Zod's whole demeanor shifted. "Then I shall perform the ceremony myself. I insist."

Jor-El and Lara looked at him in surprise. "I thought we'd find a priest of Rao or, considering the circumstances, a dutiful civil official."

"As Commissioner, I have the full authority to perform legally binding ceremonies. This wedding will be my gift to you, and I do it because I am your friend. Worry no further. It will be done."

Though she was happy, some instinct told Lara that the Commissioner wasn't quite as altruistic as he pretended to be. But she shook those thoughts from her mind, for Jor-El's sake. They didn't have the luxury of being choosy right now.

The small ceremony would take place at the dacha in the forested foothills, with only a few attendees. Jor-El's mother would host the event, whether or not Yar-El was aware of what was happening around him.

On the morning of the wedding Jor-El sent a priority message to Argo City, briefly pulling his brother away from the salvage efforts. "You know, it's my wedding day, but it seems that nothing is the way I would have planned it."

Zor-El looked haggard, though still fiery-eyed, on the communication plate. His manner was gruff from making snap decisions every hour for the past several days; he looked as if he had not slept in a very long time. "It's not the wedding that counts, Jor-El, but the marriage. Are you satisfied with what you're doing?"

"Lara is the right woman for me, of that I'm completely certain."

"Then I am happy for you. I wish I could be there to stand beside you." He spread his hands helplessly. "The power is still not restored in all areas. Much of the water supply is contaminated. We haven't even tallied the dead—"

"I understand, Zor-El. So many tragedies all at once. Do what you have to. We will get through this."

When they departed for the dacha, Jor-El stroked Lara's hair tenderly. "If I ever get my life back again after this trial, I promise we'll have a reaffirmation ceremony. We will do it right."

She clasped his hand. "This is all we need, Jor-El. I don't need choirs and mirror-kites. I don't need pavilions decked with banners, banquets of fantastic delicacies or a guest list that includes all the prominent personages of Kandor." She gave him a quick kiss on the cheek. "All we need is each other. That's enough."

Charys greeted them on the wooden porch, beaming with an excitement and satisfaction that Jor-El hadn't seen on his mother's face in years. She had strewn the small house with flowers picked from her gardens, and each breath was heady with sweet perfume.

Yar-El sat in his chair, a blanket on his lap. His wife had combed his hair and dressed him in a fine formal robe, and she herself had donned an ornate gown. The old man wore a distant smile, as if he had at least a nebulous grasp of what was happening. Jor-El rested a hand on his father's bony shoulder; he seemed to have much to say to Yar-El, but was unable to say it.

Zod wore his Commissioner's outfit, adorned with a prominent gold sash. Burly Nam-Ek stood outside the door of the dacha, as if guarding the wedding against outside attack. Lara chose her best dress from among the possessions she had brought with her to Jor-El's estate. She didn't know why she had ever packed a clinging lavender gown of the softest ruffled fabric, but now it became a perfect wedding dress.

Lara's mother and father, having postponed their work on the crystalsilk tapestries, arrived at the last moment, though they had hoped to decorate the dacha for the wedding. Her little brother looked as if he had dressed hurriedly for the event. All three were very impressed to meet Commissioner Zod in person. They had brought three looping glass sculptures (handmade) and a bell-mouthed vase for display during the ceremony.

Lara's parents graciously greeted Jor-El's mother, and Lor-Van talked pleasantly to Yar-El. "I don't know if you can hear or understand me, sir, but I must express my admiration for your work. I am an artist, a fairly well-respected one, but you were both a scientist and an artist. The things you created were so very influential. . . . "

The old man gave no sign that he knew Lor-Van was speaking to him.

Ora took her husband's arm. "The ceremony is about to start." A fidgeting Ki sat next to his parents, flashing a wide grin every time Lara glanced his direction. She stood beside Jor-El in front of the broad windows that let in streams of sunshine. Lara grasped his hand as if she never intended to let go.

Commissioner Zod chose an abbreviated ceremony, getting right down to business. The dacha's skylights had been opened so that even more of the late afternoon's sunshine poured down upon them. "Together you stand beneath the face of Rao. You declare your love to the universe, to your friends and family, and to each other."

"We do," Jor-El and Lara said in unison. They hadn't even needed to rehearse.

"Your love is like gravity, a force that pulls you forever toward each other. Let nothing pull you apart."

"Let nothing pull us apart." Jor-El and Lara clasped hands.

To signify the marriage, Lara's parents had brought two pendants they had designed specially for the occasion. Each pendant sparkled with a ruby struck from the same stone; the gems were joined down to the very molecules of their crystal structure.

Now Zod looped one pendant on a chain over Jor-El's snowy head, then placed its identical partner over Lara's. "Let these hang over your hearts, which now beat as one." Zod raised his hands, as if he had just sealed a bargain. "You are now wed. Let me be the first to declare you husband and wife."

Jor-El faced Lara, and she stared into his eyes, finding everything she had hoped for there. Her parents applauded loudly, and her little brother let out a raucous whistle.

With tears in her eyes, Charys squeezed her husband's shoulder.

Yar-El stared off into space while she stroked his hair, then kissed him on the forehead. The older woman looked up at the newlyweds. "And now for a gift from me. From us. You need time alone, even if it's only for a day or two."

"Not now, Mother. My inquisition is—"

She wouldn't be dissuaded. "If not now, then you will never take it. I don't care about your trial or your other troubles or your plans and experiments. You need this, and I have just the place." Her expression became wistful. "When we were married, Yar-El constructed a fabulous palace for us up in the arctic. He called it a palace of solitude, a retreat where we could be by ourselves, unbothered by the cares and stresses of Krypton.

"That palace is still there out on the ice cap. I wanted Zor-El and Alura to use it, but instead they went to the reefs outside of Argo City for their honeymoon. I've waited for you to be married, Jor-El, so that you and your lovely wife—" She reached out to clasp Lara's hand; her voice shuddered, and tears welled up in her eyes. "It is a perfect place for a newly married couple."

Lara was barely able to catch her breath. "It sounds beautiful."

"No, we can't." Jor-El shook his head. "I have to stay here. My defense—"

Zod stepped up to them with a smile, though his eyes seemed troubled. "Your mother is right. No one on Krypton believes the renowned Jor-El will break his word and flee. If you give me your promise that you will return in time, then as Commissioner I grant you leave to go. Be happy while you can."

Lara said cautiously, "That's very generous, Commissioner. But with all that's going on, the preparations—"

"It is the least I can do. You both know that we have done all we can. There are no further preparations, no additional studies, no new evidence. Jor-El will face the Council, and I am confident we will prevail. Remaining here serves no purpose. Once Jor-El receives a pardon, we will have a vast amount of work to do. And if he is sentenced . . . " Zod spread his hands helplessly and looked at Nam-Ek standing by the door. "Then that is all the more reason for you to take this opportunity before it's too late."

CHAPTER 31

31

Zod and Nam-Ek flew back to Kandor at night in an open vessel. They stood side by side on the humming platform with the night air blowing gently around them. The stars overhead were veiled with colorful streamers of auroras, and three bright orange meteors streaked across the blackness like the slashes of a bloody knife.

His time with Jor-El had gone well, and Zod was sure he had the scientist in his pocket, no matter what happened. He certainly hadn't expected to add a wedding to the activities, but that had tied the bonds of loyalties even tighter. By now the brilliant scientist had seen enough proof that Zod could get things done even when the Council members hesitated. Jor-El also had a passion for progress, though of a different sort. Ah, if Zod and Jor-El had the same goals, what things they could achieve for Krypton!

"I am glad Jor-El wasn't killed in the explosion after all," Zod mused aloud to Nam-Ek. "We still need him. Fortunately, everything turned out to our benefit, if only we can convince the stubborn Council to place me in charge of Krypton's defenses." His bearded companion nodded. "I have to be very careful, though. I cannot appear biased during the inquisition. However, if the great scientist is brought low and then I save him, Jor-El will be forever in my debt." So far everything had fallen perfectly in place.

After the wedding, Zod and Nam-Ek had briefly returned to the estate with the happy couple. While Lara packed for the wedding trip to the arctic place, the Commissioner and Jor-El went over a few last details, completing an inventory of the scientist's remarkable and useful inventions over the years. Zod promised to present the list at the upcoming inquisition, sure that it would portray Jor-El in the best possible light. Finally, late at night, Jor-El and his wife had flown away to the north, and the Commissioner began his return journey to Kandor.

Soon the glowing lights of the capital city lit the horizon, like an island of soaring towers, pyramids, and monuments in the middle of the broad valley. Kandor was a cluster of habitation and technology surrounded by sprawling outer settlements, suburbs, support industries, and warehouses. Agricultural fields quilted the flatlands in geometrical patches. Other vehicles and aircraft shot along main thoroughfares, fellow travelers like himself, though he had told Nam-Ek to take a quieter overland path. He didn't want to be near any traffic.

Zod could feel the energy and the pulse of Kandor as they approached. "I'll be glad to get home." He patted his companion on the shoulder. "And you want to see your animals, of course." With a boyish expression of pleasure, Nam-Ek nodded.

As they reached the outskirts of the shining city, Zod heard a strange humming in the air. Static electricity crackled along his skin, making the fine hairs on his arms and neck stand up. Sensing the disturbance, Nam-Ek also looked around, then turned his face to the night sky.

High above, a dazzling white light flitted about like a rogue spark from a campfire. Zod's brow furrowed. Another ship? Then he felt a cold lump in his stomach. What if Donodon's people had come back after all? As the single bright spot dropped lower, orbiting over the city skyline, growing larger and larger, he felt a thrill rush through him.

Earlier, he had raised the specter of a vengeful outside race only to manipulate the Council. It was a straw man threat to rile the already nervous citizens so they would be willing to consider drastic changes— changes that would benefit Zod. He had never actually believed Donodon's companions would come so soon!

When he studied the vessel more carefully, though, he saw that it was far more ominous than that other small ship. The strange new craft descended unhurriedly toward Kandor's skyline, and only when Zod could view it in relation to the towering buildings did he realize its sheer immensity. The new spacecraft seemed to be made of shadows and bright metal, sharp creases and precise geometrical planes that tapered to a lower point, like a gem that had broken free of its setting. The vessel had a grace despite its enormity, reminding Zod of a flower with razor-edged petals.

The thrumming in the air grew more overbearing. Nam-Ek pulled back on the controls of the passenger craft, bringing them to a dead stop far outside of the city. In the distance Zod could hear the faint sounds of people crying out, crowds rushing from buildings and looking up into the sky. Although traffic was minimal this late at night, he still saw ground vehicles and illuminated floater rafts swirling in eddies at the edge of Kandor. Some groups of travelers tried to rush back to their homes, while others struggled to evacuate the city.

Zod took the controls from Nam-Ek and accelerated the vessel forward again. "If this is an attack, the Council will never know what to do. I can rally the people to me, but only if I am there!" He suddenly saw this as a great and unexpected opportunity. "I can lead them—now!"

Deeply alarmed, the big mute grabbed his master's sleeve and shook his head, but Zod insisted on rushing toward the city, his city. "I know you want to keep me safe, but I have to try—"

Bright sparkles along the edges of the huge spacecraft's angled seams flared from orange to white, interrupting Zod's words. The ship lowered itself until it hovered directly above the central ziggurat of the Council temple, where the throbbing hologram of Rao blazed into the night. The outer metal planes of the alien vessel folded and rearranged themselves like the images in a dimensional kaleidoscope, and the razor-edged flower opened to reveal a tiny core of searingly bright light.

A moment of sickening silence hung in the air. Zod couldn't even blink. His heartbeat pounded in his ears; the whole Kandor valley seemed to be holding its breath.

A blinding pillar of solidified light dropped down to cover the small image of the red sun, as if using it as an anchor point. From the corners of the alien ship's folded hull planes, three perfectly straight beams lashed out like deadly whips, extending over the building tops. Separated by equal angles, the beams struck the ground at the perimeter of Kandor, blasting and boring into the ground. The bright lights fanned outward, sweeping around like the blades of a container opener. With the ease of a stylus scraped across a piece of paper, the three equidistant rays gouged a deep furrow all the way around the city, scribing a perfect circle.

Caught in the path of the piercing rays, several unfortunate ground-cars exploded. Outlying structures toppled, severed by the blast. The sounds of vaporizing rock and hissing steam roared like unending thunder. Bridges and roadways collapsed. Numerous hapless homes were simply erased in the path of destruction. A tethering field for Kandor's private dirigible airships vanished as the wave of disintegration passed by; frantically, two pilots cut loose their airships and attempted to float away, but both were caught in the beam, incinerated in an instant.

A city full of people screaming created an oddly operatic sound that rose into the air, but the alien ship continued its destruction, heedless of their cries. The beams cut a circular moat, encompassing most of Kandor, and then cut even deeper into the crust.

Just as the slash of light passed in front of the passenger platform, Zod veered the flying vehicle aside. He barely avoided slamming into the high-intensity blast. The Commissioner struggled to reassert control over the wobbling vehicle while gale-force thermal currents slapped against him in the open vessel, and molten debris spattered the side of the hull. Nam-Ek turned sideways, intentionally shielding Zod with his burly body; tiny embers sizzled into the big man's back, making his shirt smolder.

Nam-Ek knocked Zod away from the controls and brought the raft down in a rapid descent, slamming them into the dirt. They skidded to a halt only meters away from the deep, smoking cut in the ground. From the angry turmoil on the mute's face, Zod wondered whether Nam-Ek would physically drag him away if he persisted in trying to get back into Kandor.

The Commissioner brushed himself off and stared in awe. "By the red heart of Rao!" He could smell the electric ozone in the air, felt a wash of heat sear his face like the exhalation of a blast oven.

The three brilliant beams continued to wreak havoc, sweeping along the circumference again and again, cutting deeper into the crust with each pass. Streets were severed, outbuildings blasted into rubble. Dirt and smoke sprayed upward, accompanied by fountains of sparks and jets of steam from underground conduits.

When the sizzling boundary circle was finally complete and the smoke began to clear from the air, Zod could once again hear screams and panicked shouts, mingled with a cacophony of internal alarms. Sapphire Guards from their training barracks outside the city must be rushing into position, calling all reinforcements.

But the ominous alien ship wasn't finished yet. With the deep gouge ringing the core of Krypton's capital city in a perfect circle, a shimmering curtain spilled out of the invading ship and dropped until it enveloped the metropolis under a hemispherical bubble that sealed itself inside the mammoth groove.

Zod reeled, staring at the enormous artificial dome that now covered Kandor. "It's like a child's dollhouse in a terrarium." Everyone in the city was imprisoned, specimens in a gigantic zoo. Zod's mind raced, wondering if this might indeed be a retribution force of Donodon's people, or the powerful police force the alien had mentioned . . . or something entirely different.

Feeling isolated and helpless, Zod looked at the stranded citizens and vehicles on the nearest main thoroughfare outside of Kandor. A squad of Sapphire Guards rushed forward, firing their weapons to no effect. He wondered if he should take command of that guard contingent and tell them what to do. But *he* didn't know what to do, either.

"How do we free them? How do we drive away that enemy ship?" For the first time he could remember, Zod felt completely out of control, unable to do anything. He should never have let Jor-El go to the arctic. Not now.

Suddenly Zod swallowed as he realized that if he had not stayed to perform the wedding, or even if he had left Jor-El and Lara's estate one hour earlier, then he and Nam-Ek would also be trapped beneath that impenetrable dome. By sheer fortunate coincidence, they had been away from Kandor.

The dome throbbed, and the gigantic angled ship hung overhead, just waiting. He heard the pulse of energy from the containment dome mix with the still-sizzling sound of melted dirt and rock. Every breath he drew was filled with cold static electricity and metallic ozone. Despite his instinctive fear, he couldn't help but admire the incalculable power the craft possessed. Zod feared that something even worse might be in store.

Finally, after a long moment of building tension, the air itself groaned. The terrarium dome flared and began to contract, like a tightening noose. At first Zod couldn't believe what he was seeing. Nam-Ek stared, then shielded his eyes.

The dome pressed inward, encapsulating Kandor within a smaller and smaller boundary. Zod realized that the whole enclosed skyline was *shrinking*. Exotic lenses or condensing fields inside the projected dome reduced the size of the capital city, leaving behind only a ragged crater. As the boundary retracted, the alien ship followed it down above the containment dome.

Nam-Ek urgently tried to convince Zod to fly away to safety, but the Commissioner would hear none of it. Instead, he placed his hand on the mute's chest, easing him off the landed raft. Nam-Ek retreated onto the open ground, looking forlorn.

Zod's entire life was there in the capital city: his Commission, his strings of power, his connections, his home. None of the people there were his friends—in fact, he genuinely despised the Council members and many other bureaucrats who had stood against him over the years. Nam-Ek was the only one he really cared about, and the big mute was here with him.

But how could he stand by and simply *watch* this unprecedented act? He was angry, afraid, and almost wild to realize that he was utterly helpless in the face of this strange attack. Zod grabbed the controls of the flying platform, tried to take off, but Nam-Ek defiantly stood on the ground and gripped the side rail of the raft, holding back the vehicle with brute strength.

Zod spoke sharply from the control pedestal. "Do not challenge me, Nam-Ek! I am going closer, but I cannot do what I must do unless you are out of harm's way. Otherwise, I will be too worried about you." He softened his tone. "Besides, if I don't leave you here, then who will come and rescue me if I need it?"

Unable to argue with that, the big man reluctantly released his grip. He seemed convinced he would never see his mentor again, but Zod tried to sound reassuring. "I will be careful." He took one last glance at Nam-Ek's forlorn expression, then focused on the millions of Kryptonians trapped inside the shrinking city. Maybe he could get close enough, ram the invader ship, find some way to undo this disaster. He could save them all.

Lifting the floating raft again, he accelerated toward the ever-growing crater as Kandor continued to shrink. By the time he reached the edge, Zod could no longer see the alien vessel. The city had all but vanished deep inside the giant ragged hole, shrunk down to an unimaginably small size, and the enemy ship had followed it down into the depths.

Zod brought the craft to a lurching halt just before the abrupt drop-off, smelling the smoke and sulfur rising up into his face. He felt disoriented by the unreality of what he had just witnessed. Kandor . . . *gone!* He stepped off the landed platform and walked cautiously toward the edge, then stared down.

He was so shaken that at first he didn't see the bright light sweeping up toward him. Having done its awful work, the ominous alien ship began to climb out of the great pit. Zod staggered, pinwheeling his arms to get back from the edge.

As the ship rose above him, Zod stared up into the white light that still shone from the bottom of the complex craft. Dangling by an invisible thread beneath its hull, miniaturized Kandor hung like an absurd toy, a city in a bottle. The flat metal surfaces of the outer armor shifted and opened again like geometric petals, showing the interior of the strange vessel. Zod watched it draw tiny Kandor up through the gap, and then the plates folded shut like mandibles, swallowing the capital city.

Far off, other survivors milled about where severed bridges and roads led only to the smoking hole. But Zod had not followed the main route back home, taking his own path, as always. And now he seemed painfully vulnerable and obvious out in the open. He stood alone.

And after slowly circling the deep crater, the ominous vessel came toward him.

CHAPTER 32

∞⫶◇‼◇⊷Ṯ̣◇ 32

The palace of solitude in the arctic snowfields was breathtaking. Seeing it, Jor-El was reminded of his father's original genius and creative
imagination, before he had degenerated into forgetfulness.

As their enclosed two-person skimmer raced over the icy wasteland,
he and Lara came over a line of jagged black peaks buried in glaciers.
Various shades of red sunlight dappled the textures of blown snow and
polished ice. They saw the exotic angled structure of the palace nestled
against a cliff, like a spiny bush grown out of precious gems. Steam
wafted up from a fissure where volcanic heat created a warm oasis even
in the ice cap.

Lara caught her breath. "Everyone says Yar-El was such a brilliant
scientist—but he was an artist, too! Just like my father said at the wedding. It's beautiful."

Lara's parents and her little brother had rushed away from the dacha
immediately after the ceremony, called back to their sensitive project in
the city. Apparently the crystalsilk weavings had to be monitored precisely, or else the whole web would unravel and they would be forced
to start over. Lara insisted that she understood why they had to leave so
soon; after all, she had grown up in a family of artists.

"My father was a mathematical artist." Jor-El knew, however, that
simple equations without inspiration could not account for the marvel
he saw in the mountains of ice. Thin crystal sheets balanced against one
another at low angles, green and white structural columns that at first

looked like a randomly stacked pile of broken glass, but further study showed a complex order. As a counterpoint to the low angles, straight pinnacles like watchtowers jutted vertically above, yielding a perfect view of the clean, pristine arctic.

The fortress had remained untouched in the cold, white wasteland for years. He and Lara had the ice cap all to themselves in perfect peace, perfect shelter. They would keep each other warm.

Jor-El landed in a snow-swept area near a majestic front gate guarded by long spearlike crystals. Huge angled shards had grown out of the glaciers themselves, reinforced by metallic and polymer overlays to form the main structure of the palace. The pointed spires interlocked in a geometric tapestry more amazing than any architecture he had ever seen.

The two stepped out into the brittle cold air and stood at the palace's cold gateway, watching white breath curl from their nostrils and mouths. Peering through the hood of her parka, Lara gazed at the white and emerald spires with absolute delight. When Jor-El pulled her close, she felt very much at home in his arms. Here, for a brief while, they could hide from the rest of Krypton, ignore the Council and its accusations.

Once they had passed through the crystal-fenced entrance, the passageways of the palace were made of blue flowing ice, stabilized with polymer films. As soon as he and Lara entered, thermal gems began to raise the internal temperature, making the chambers comfortable.

She drank in the dazzling light that reflected from everywhere, and basked in the sheer sense of safety and privacy. "I couldn't ask for a more magical place for our wedding trip."

"How about better circumstances?"

"You and I are married now, and that is a *wonderful* circumstance," she said with absolute conviction. "We're together, for better or worse. Your problems are mine, and I'll stand beside you just as I stand with you now." She nestled against him. "No matter what happens. As dark as it seems, we will overcome this."

He nodded. "Even if the whole Council is against me, Commissioner Zod promised his help. Let's see if he's true to his word. And if he can't help after all, we will have to do it ourselves."

The palace's master suite was as large as a throne room. Light

sparkled through the faceted walls. Neither of them could imagine any Kryptonian resort being more appropriate. Lara gave him a mischievous smile. "We'll make do." She pulled him toward her for a long kiss.

All around them the cold arctic exulted in their union. Yar-El had had the foresight to include warm furs and soft sleeping pallets. Lara held her husband, delighting in every second with him, never wanting to let go. She didn't care about what might be happening in Kandor. In this place, Jor-El was hers alone, and she would lift the weight of the outside world from his shoulders.

Though only a scant few days remained before his trial, Jor-El and Lara managed to distract each other from their worries. Entirely.

Zod stood by himself on the edge of the vast pit, realizing that he couldn't run. Any being with the power to reduce an entire city to a mere plaything could easily catch one man, and he knew that the alien vessel had spotted him.

So he didn't try to flee. He stood with his hands at his sides, glaring up at the ship, showing no fear. Defiant. He had always believed that as the son of Cor-Zod, he had a great destiny. But now, before his very eyes, his dreams of power, his home, his possessions—all had been stolen away.

The mechanical, razor-edged ship descended to the flat ground outside the yawning crater, still glowing with residual energy. Finally, two of the metal planes shifted and folded inward to reveal a hatch that spilled out hazy yellow light. Silhouetted against the interior of his ship, a manlike figure emerged—an entirely different sort of visitor from the diminutive tentacle-faced Donodon.

The stranger stood with his hands on his sides, facing Zod. Tall and muscular, with sickly looking olive-green skin, he wore a tight body suit and matching boots. The alien was completely hairless, his skin so smooth it seemed to be coated with wax. Across his skull, several glowing red and gold disks were connected with silver lines, like circuitry paths that mapped out the constellation of his brain. The visitor's face showed no emotion, nor did he speak; he simply assessed the Commissioner.

Finally Zod shouted, "What are you waiting for? Are you not going to take me as well?"

"No. I have Kandor." The alien spoke in a matter-of-fact voice, not gloating over what he had done.

"And what do you intend to do with it?"

The alien seemed perplexed by Zod's anger. "As part of my collection, Kandor will be forever safe. I mean no harm."

No harm? Zod looked at the huge, deep crater. Even if the population inside the shrunken metropolis somehow remained uninjured, hundreds if not thousands of Kryptonians had been slaughtered in the process of uprooting the city. On the alien's skull, the red-and-gold disks gleamed, as if amplifying his thoughts. The ship's hatch opened wider, and the stranger gestured behind him. "You are welcome to see for yourself, if it reassures you."

Some distance away, Nam-Ek emerged from where he had hidden in the upthrust rubble. He stormed toward the edge of the crater in a misguided attempt to protect Zod. When the green-skinned alien turned swiftly, reacting to the threat, Zod shouted to the big mute. Without thinking, he placed himself between the alien and his big-shouldered friend. "Nam-Ek! Stop! I don't want you hurt."

At Zod's command, the burly bodyguard halted abruptly, as if he had reached the end of a leash. His expressive face was an agony of indecision, ready to tear the alien and his ship to pieces should his master be harmed.

Zod could tell that the fate not just of Kandor but all of Krypton might depend on what he did next. His thoughts raced ahead, calculating, assessing possibilities and discarding them. The eleven members of the Council were trapped in Kandor, completely cut off. Only he, the Commissioner, remained outside. Therefore, this was all up to him.

The open, bright spacecraft might be a looming trap, but the power that this alien exhibited, the audacity of what he had done to Kandor— the Commissioner longed to know much more. If the alien wanted to hurt him, Zod could do nothing about it anyway. He forcibly drove down his inner panic, his natural tendency to fear this powerful vessel and obviously destructive enemy. The only way to take the upper hand would be to show no hesitation.

He gave a cautious signal to Nam-Ek, then gathered his courage and squared his shoulders. He strode toward the alien ship, showing no fear. "I am Zod. I represent Krypton. Explain yourself to me."

The exotic humanoid gestured toward the hatch. "Come, I will show you all that you wish to know."

Zod walked up the ramp, determined to radiate an air of confidence. "What are you? Where do you come from?" The interior of the ship smelled of polished metal along with an exotic stew of scents: dirt, vegetation, lightning.

The disks on the smooth green scalp glowed golden. "I am a Brain Interactive Construct, an android. My planet is—was—called Colu. I was created and sent out to catalog worlds for the Computer Tyrants to conquer."

"So, a spy."

"A gatherer of data." With a small gesture of his synthetic hands, the android activated the polished white walls, converting them into projection screens. An image resolved out of many points of light to display a rocky, icy landscape, covered with vast industrial cities and cordoned-off camps on the outskirts where human slaves lived squalid lives. Colu. The image faded after Zod had absorbed it.

As he stepped deeper into the vessel's watery yellow light, he spotted tiny Kandor in its dome, a carefully preserved model city on display in a museum. And Krypton's capital wasn't the green-skinned android's only prize. He saw a dozen other bottled cities, each one a landmark of unusual architecture, bathed in artificial lights to simulate their respective suns.

One sample city was composed of black rock built up like pieces of a coral reef, and a tiny ocean swirled around the boundaries under the dome; another terrarium contained an intricately grown forest village; a third was filled with dirt and riddled with a labyrinth of tunnels, like a child's diggerbug farm. One specimen city had buildings that seemed to be made of melting wax; another was a floating cluster of lavender bubbles with butterfly-winged inhabitants flitting from place to place. The populations in each specimen dome seemed to be thriving.

"The Computer Tyrants are long forgotten except by me. I do this for myself. And for *them*." He looked at the domed cities. "I have saved them all."

Zod stepped closer to the energy dome that encapsulated Krypton's capital. He wondered if the tiny people inside could see his gigantic face looming over them. "Is that why you were sent here?"

"I came of my own free will." The android sounded very proud of the fact. "I am no longer the subservient construct the Computer Tyrants created."

Zod waited for him to continue, still puzzled by the alien's oddly nonthreatening attitude after having caused such horrific destruction.

"In order to make me a better spy, the Computer Tyrants twinned me with a slave boy. I took all of his emotions, his thoughts and his desires. I believe he took much from me as well." The android sounded almost wistful. Another image shimmered on the smooth wall screen, displaying a thin dark-haired youth with lean features and sunken eyes, haunted by a brief lifetime overloaded with fear and oppression. Even so, the image seemed almost . . . idealized.

"Once we were twinned, the boy should have been my longtime companion. The ship was ready to depart on my survey mission, but the boy escaped just before I took off. He surprised me." The wall image sparkled and vanished. "I miss him."

The green android seemed genuinely sad. "And so I went from star system to star system by myself. That was centuries ago. I studied many planets, searching for perfect cities." In separate projections around the ship's main chamber, more images showed spectacular landscapes of world after world, exotic places such as Zod had never imagined.

Then he saw a sparkling portrait of Kandor. "Krypton was one of my favorites," the android said.

Zod drove back his feelings of being overwhelmed. All those places, world after world raided by this creature . . . and no one on Krypton had ever known of the threat. Kryptonians had been obliviously, and intentionally, unaware of so much. The Council members had hidden their heads in the sand for centuries. Damn them! "Then why didn't your Computer Tyrants invade us?"

The Brain Interactive Construct stood close to Zod, also staring down at bottled Kandor. "Because I never told them about Krypton." His artificial face shaped itself into a placid smile. "The Tyrants had programmed me to feel their need to dominate biological life-forms, but after I was twinned with the young boy, I also understood other components of the equation. I valued peace and beauty. I valued harmony and personal interaction. Those were the things the poor slave boy longed for most." He lowered his voice. "However, when I had gathered all the necessary data, I returned to Colu, as my programming demanded of me. I had no choice."

Now shimmering images formed on all the wall screens, creating an overwhelming symphony of dark and bleak recordings. Zod saw scene after scene of total destruction, wrecked industrial cities, bodies and machines strewn through streets and across a barren landscape. "But when I arrived home, my planet had been devastated. All of the Computer Tyrants were annihilated in a great war. All of the slaves had rebelled against the machines."

"Intriguing." Zod thought he should feel relieved. "They won?"

"In a sense, perhaps. But every scrap of life was wiped out as well. Colu was dead." The walls grew blank again, as if the android could no longer bear to view the images. He stood stock-still, reviewing files in his cybernetic mind.

"I dug through the rubble for two years alone until I found intact data cores. When I uploaded everything that had happened in my absence, I learned that the cause of the destruction was none other than my own 'twin.' After the slave boy had shared with me, after I had become partially human and he had become partially machine, he understood how to overthrow the Computer Tyrants. He destroyed our world."

Grainy archival images showed the revolt, slaves throwing themselves against the minions of the Computer Tyrants, being slaughtered by the millions, and still coming, and coming, like fanatics. And leading them was an older, hardened version of the haunted boy who had been twinned with the android.

The alien hung his pale green head. "A powerful empire, nothing more than dust. If the boy had learned some key information through sharing with me, then I, by extension, caused the vulnerability that brought about the downfall of my planet." He looked at Zod, his expression now full of anguish. "How can I endure that knowledge?"

The Commissioner squashed any sympathy he might have felt for the pathetic android. "That doesn't explain why you stole Kandor—or

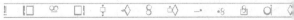

all these other cities. Just because your world was destroyed, what gives you the right to ransack other planets?"

"Ransack? I mean only to protect them, preserve them. When I take these precious cities back to Colu, I can restore them, put them into their proper places. Kandor was one of my most marvelous discoveries, and so I will keep it safe against anything bad that might happen. It is a good and noble deed."

Zod was aghast. "But stealing Kandor! Do you have any concept of what that will do to our society?" He had barely begun to think through such questions himself . . . and maybe the result wasn't all bad.

The green-skinned alien was unmoved. "As I learned on my own planet, nothing lasts forever, and these gems of civilization deserve to be saved. What if some terrible disaster were to destroy Krypton?"

Zod fought back a disbelieving snort at the suggestion that anything so calamitous would ever happen to his world.

The Brain Interactive Construct gazed at him. "If you wish, Zod, I can allow you to join your comrades. I can miniaturize and insert you into the dome, where you will be under my protection forever. It is your choice."

"I have no wish to live inside a specimen case."

Zod suppressed a smile as he began to realize what had unexpectedly fallen into his lap. New thoughts fought through his daze of disbelief. The Kryptonian Council was gone, the old government stripped away . . . but he remained. Only Zod. And Krypton's desperate population would demand a strong and confident leader, now more than ever. At last this was the opportunity to work the changes he had always known must be made. He had waited all his life for a chance like this.

Viewed from a certain perspective, this was a miracle, not a tragedy.

"No, I will stay behind to help my people recover from this great loss." Magnanimously, the Commissioner added, "You can have Kandor—and I will take the rest of Krypton."

When Zod emerged from the alien ship, he motioned for Nam-Ek to accompany him. The muscular mute was ecstatic to see his mentor unharmed.

Zod was flushed, his mind spinning. The Council, Kandor, Jor-El's inquisition—everything—simply brushed off the playing board! "It's going to be all right, Nam-Ek. In fact, everything will be just fine."

They turned to watch as the ominous ship lifted away from the smoking crater that had been Kandor. It flew off into the night, leaving Zod as the only real witness, the one person who knew the true story of what had happened.

And he could use that to his advantage.

CHAPTER 34

All of Krypton reeled from the sudden loss of the capital city. And, exactly as Commissioner Zod expected, the frightened people looked to him for guidance.

Immediately taking charge, he declared a planetary state of emergency, dispatched messages to all major population centers, and established his command post just outside the deep, steaming crater. Thousands of displaced refugees remained in the area, those whose homes were located outside the perimeter of destruction, as well as hundreds of Kandor citizens who had simply been away on that fateful night and had returned to find the city gone.

Unlike the tsunami at Argo City, the clean, abrupt loss of Kandor created none of the usual aftereffects of a natural disaster: few injured, no rescue efforts, no massive recovery operations. The capital city was simply gone. All that remained was a huge, deep scar on the Kryptonian psyche, as well as a blot on the landscape.

As the news spread, volunteers and spectators rushed in from Borga City, Orvai, Ilonia, Corril, and many smaller settlements. Some of them brought emergency supplies, tents, food, water, and construction materials. Soon the second wave came, stricken pilgrims who traveled to the crater just to stare in shock and mourn the loss of their beloved capital. Everyone assumed that the population of Kandor was dead, and Zod did not disabuse them of the idea.

The Commissioner walked among the people here, showing strength and perhaps a little compassion. He spoke briefly with one man who had been late returning from a visit to the mountains; his wife and three daughters had gone ahead to Kandor and were now gone, leaving him all alone. An aspiring sculptor came by himself all the way from the lake district; he fell to his knees at the crater's edge and wept for hours, though he had never previously been to Kandor.

Nam-Ek often stood alone at the lip of the crater, staring down into the pit, clenching and unclenching his fists. The big man no doubt still wondered if he could have fought the alien android and reversed the disaster. Zod quietly consoled him. The two stood apart from all the shell-shocked visitors and eager workers who swarmed around the empty site with little to do, not knowing where to begin work of such magnitude.

"In the end I believe Krypton will be stronger, Nam-Ek. Not only did the alien take our city, he also took away the useless Council. The more I think about it, the more it seems like an acceptable trade-off. With their obstructionist ways and their narrow vision, those eleven caused as much harm as any outside invasion. And I have a chance to make it right. Now, more than at any other time in centuries, Krypton needs a man who can be a true, efficient leader. A man like me."

As he looked around himself at the overwhelming crowds of stricken but resolute survivors and volunteers, Zod formulated his plans to utilize their angry determination. If he could cement them into a unified fighting and working force, these people would become his most dedicated followers. He had to act swiftly.

Zod's initial challenge was to establish a permanent settlement near the crater's perimeter. For the moment his goal was a clean and organized camp. The administrative and support realities of such a large group would swiftly make living conditions miserable . . . and if people were miserable, they could easily turn against him. As a precaution, he also recruited the remaining Sapphire Guards, who had lived outside the city in training barracks.

Without delay, he laid out the settlement on a grid and put together teams to erect large tents and serviceable shelters. They drilled for water, installed pumps, erected sanitation facilities. The food supplies brought by emergency workers were gathered into large community depots. Meals were prepared and served in a long communal mess hall.

Tireless in his inspiration, he organized the ever-growing crowds into work groups. So long as he kept the refugees busy and focused on the obvious threat of outside enemies, no one would have time to question his assumption of total authority. From his experience with the other lackluster city leaders on Krypton, he knew it would be more than a month before anyone else even thought to suggest a plan, and by then it would be too late.

At noon on the third day, after he had carefully practiced his speech, Zod stood at the center of the camp on a quickly erected stage. In a clear, commanding voice he issued his statement, and the shaken people looked up at him, comforted that someone had shouldered this heavy responsibility. The Commissioner doubted anyone else on Krypton would rush to volunteer for the job.

"Because we no longer have the Council to guide us, it falls upon me to keep our world safe. This unspeakable attack shows that we must change our passive and stagnant ways. We were isolated for so many centuries, foolishly believing that hostile outsiders would leave this planet in peace. But now they have found us!" He pointed vehemently toward the yawning crater, where wisps of yellowish-gray smoke continued to curl into the air.

Zod had already told a somewhat altered version of what he'd witnessed, and rumors continued to embellish the horrors of that night. He had changed the android's name to something more sinister than "Brain Interactive Construct." *Brainiac*. He had painted the android's story in the worst possible light, removing any hint of sympathy, making the green-skinned android the embodiment of everything unspeakable and frightening. He had not mentioned the possibility that the miniaturized inhabitants might actually still be alive.

"What if Brainiac returns for Borga City next?" Zod swept his gaze around, listening to the cries of dismay. "Or Orvai? Or Corril? Argo City is already reeling from the damage done by the tidal wave—how could they possibly defend themselves? How could any of us?" Zod had no intention of calming the already terrified people. Fear was a very efficient tool. "How many outside enemies are even now plotting against Krypton?"

His face was grim, yet full of an angry confidence. "Outsiders may believe that we are an easy target, that we have forgotten how to defend ourselves and how to fight—but they are sorely mistaken! We can do this *if you will follow me.*" He was not at all surprised when the crowd gave a rousing cheer. What else would they do?

After his speech, Zod returned to his command tent during the heat of the afternoon. A dark-haired woman sauntered up to him, put one hand on her hip, and raised her pointed chin. "Those were fine words, Commissioner. Maybe you are better than the other nobles and the silly Council members after all."

He was both surprised and pleased to see her. "Aethyr, you are safe!"

"That's one advantage to living in isolation and touring ancient ruins."

He let out a dry laugh. She had struck him as a definite survivor.

"Yes, you did unfairly dismiss me as a representative of the establishment you despised."

"I may have been too quick to make that assumption. I hated the old government for being ineffectual. To me, anyone who worked in that system had a vested interest in the status quo."

"Then you misjudged me."

"I can see that now."

He tried to gesture her inside his tent, but she remained where she was. He said, "If you have come to accept my offer of a special dinner, your timing is awkward. We may have to settle for food in the mess hall." Zod still found her beautiful, her haughty attitude intriguing. Remembering how fearlessly she had scorned the stuffy expectations of Kryptonian society, he knew Aethyr was exactly the sort of person he needed at his side now.

She turned slowly, looking at the camp, at the organized people already getting back to work, making progress. "You have accomplished quite a lot in only a few days and under the most extreme circumstances, Commissioner. The old Council would have taken this long just to decide which robes to wear while inspecting the disaster. Has any other city leader done more than wail and gnash his teeth?"

Zod considered, trying to hide his smile. "I doubt it."

"You'll disappoint me greatly if the old style of government crystallizes around you again." Her voice had a warning tone.

He wondered what she was getting at, found himself reluctant to play her game. "Who says I will allow such a thing to happen? The Council is gone."

She laughed now and gently touched his arm. "I was hoping you would say that. In fact, I can help you." Leaning close, she lowered her voice to a whisper. "I have an offer you can't afford to decline."

"Intriguing. What do you suggest?"

"I've come from the ruins of Xan City. I have walked through the ancient capital of the warlord Jax-Ur."

"And how could some old ruins possibly interest me? Especially now?"

"Because I've found Jax-Ur's hidden stockpile of doomsday weapons. His nova javelins."

Zod sucked in a breath.

"*Fifteen* of them. All are still functional, as far as I could tell." Now she took him by the arm and led him toward the cooler shadows of his tent. "Provided you offer me an appropriate reward—shall we call it a finder's fee?—I am certain you can think of some way to put those weapons to use."

Zod decided that this called for a celebratory meal after all. "Yes. I believe I can."

CHAPTER 35

∞⌐◇‼◇⟶T♀◇ 35

Jor-El and Lara's brief bit of solitude and joy in the arctic palace was far too short. On the third day they departed, dreading what lay in store for them back in Kandor. No matter what the Council decreed after his trial, Jor-El would always have these bright memories to hold on to.

As they approached the capital, though, they found that the whole world had changed.

Instead of the bright spires of Krypton's most magnificent city, they saw a complete holocaust. Lara let out a strangled cry as their covered flyer glided over the deep, fresh crater; Jor-El was too stunned to make a sound. The once-thriving capital was truly gone—the museums, the soaring crystal towers his father had built, the habitation complexes, the temple of Rao, the very heart of Krypton's civilization.

Lara pressed her fingers against the transparent plates of their aircraft as if she could reach down and touch the devastation. "Why?" was all she could whisper.

Jor-El forced himself to set aside his horror and concentrate on the observable facts. "Were we attacked? It's too clean, too perfectly delineated to be an explosion . . . almost as if someone scooped up or disintegrated the whole city. I don't understand it."

"My parents were there," Lara cried out suddenly, her voice hitching in a sob. "And poor Ki—he was only twelve! Jor-El, they're *gone!* After our wedding, they went back to Kandor." Her words stumbled to a halt as she thought of all the things that had been ripped away. She moaned.

"Gone!" She broke down inside the cockpit, trembled with both anger and confusion. Then she reached over and clung to her husband, as if afraid something terrible might snatch him from her, too. She seemed caught in a cyclone of vivid, extreme emotions. He wrapped his arms around her, caring for Lara as the craft's automated systems kept them level.

As he held her, Lara's whole body shuddered, a reaction that was less despair than grief and anger, coupled with a frantic need to do something. Knowing that nothing he could say would be sufficient, Jor-El simply kept his arms tightly around her, drawing her close, refusing to let go. The enormity of the situation roared like an intangible whirlwind around them. Finally he said with determination, "We have to find answers. We have to get to the bottom of this." He gripped the controls so tightly that his knuckles turned white as he brought the flying craft down to the ground.

They landed in the hastily assembled camp near the crater. The haggard and exhausted people they met there mumbled answers to Jor-El's repeated inquiries; many of them shook their heads in confusion. Most people honestly didn't know what had happened, while others said incomprehensibly that the magnificent capital city had been "stolen." Tears streamed down Lara's face as she watched the turmoil, completely at a loss.

Upon learning of Jor-El's return, Commissioner Zod found them. He greeted the shaken scientist with a quick, hard embrace. "Jor-El, my friend! By the red heart of Rao, I am glad to see you safe. Krypton needs you." Zod had exchanged his formal robes for more utilitarian clothes: durable trousers and a loose black vest. He seemed exhausted, but also frenetic. "This is the greatest disaster ever to befall our world. The losses are incalculable." Seeing Lara's grief-stricken expression, he offered her a sympathetic look. "Ah, yes. Your parents left the wedding before Nam-Ek and I did, didn't they? They must have been in Kandor when it happened." He shook his head almost dismissively. "Another tragedy to add to so many. Everyone has lost somebody. The only thing to do is get through our collective grief. We are Kryptonians, and we will survive if we all pull together." Zod gestured toward the enormous crater. "How can we even begin to measure such loss?" He looked at Jor-El. "It's a miracle we still have *you.*"

Jor-El summoned all the inner strength he had intended to use when facing the Council. Now even that ordeal seemed trivial. "I will assist in every way I can, but first I need to understand what happened here."

"It was an alien attack, just as we feared. Just as I warned about, if only the Council had listened."

Jor-El felt cold and sick. "Was it Donodon's people, after all?" He couldn't believe it.

"No, the evil android that did this to Kandor had nothing to do with Donodon."

Jor-El saw some of the wan refugees staring at him. "People will still think I'm responsible, after all the accusations. Will they want my help if they think I brought this down upon us?"

Zod scowled impatiently. "Then such nonsense must be silenced. I will see to it. We cannot waste time on casting blame and pandering to politics now." He grabbed the scientist by both shoulders and faced him. "We have to defend ourselves, prepare for another attack, and how can we do that without you? We need your genius, Jor-El. We need things that Krypton has never before imagined—and we need them now."

Without giving the two of them time to absorb what had occurred, the Commissioner led them along trampled dirt paths, past tents, equipment sheds, and guarded storage silos. Lara followed her husband, still in shock but obviously full of questions. Jor-El could see she was close to collapse, barely managing to walk. He desperately wanted to take her away from here.

In a crisp, businesslike voice Zod explained the immediate emergency measures he had taken and all the work that still needed to be done, and swiftly, to stabilize the situation. Zod became more animated, as if he had dispensed all the sympathy he deemed necessary for the moment.

He led them into the long temporary mess hall, where the air was redolent with the smells of soup, fresh-baked bread, and dried fruits. Dirty, tired people crowded next to one another on makeshift benches, wolfing down food with a desperation that showed their lingering fear. Every person was covered with dust and sweat. Some of them looked listless and broken, while others were argumentative, lashing out at those nearby because they could find no better target for their helpless anger.

Filled with purpose, Zod marched to the front of the food line, pull-

ing Jor-El with him. As the Commissioner shouted for attention, the murmur of conversation in the long tent died down. The workers and refugees turned on their benches to listen.

"I have wonderful news." Zod raised Jor-El's arm, clasping the scientist's hand in his own fist. "The great Jor-El has survived. Although Kandor is gone, he is still with us."

The white-haired scientist flushed to find himself the center of public attention, especially in such tragic circumstances. Only a few days ago, the people of Krypton had been convinced that his negligence had placed their world in danger. He did not want to be applauded by them.

Zod looked intently at Jor-El while the others wearily listened. "The slate is wiped clean. Our priorities are changed, and far worse alien threats face us. *Real* threats. We have wasted too much time and energy on irrelevant distractions." He smiled, looking very benevolent and paternal.

"As the provisional leader of Krypton and the de facto representative of the Kryptonian Council, I hereby pardon Jor-El of any charges pending against him. As of this moment, the matter is dismissed. There will be no inquest into the tragic death of Donodon. We cannot afford to squander our remaining resources. We need your help."

Jor-El was shocked. "But that doesn't resolve the issue—"

Zod cut him off. "We have been attacked. Our capital city is *gone.* What you can do for your people far outweighs any past mistakes. The Council was only seeking a scapegoat, after all." He picked up a tray and personally dished up a meal for Jor-El. "All Kryptonians share a common cause now. We must make our outside enemies fear us—and *you* can give us the means to accomplish that."

The conversation around them in the mess hall resumed. The people seemed heartened that Zod was directing them and also that Jor-El had come back. They began to believe Krypton might have a chance after all.

In addition to the temporary camp set up on the edge of the crater, many intact residences on the outskirts had opened their doors to the refugees and aid workers. Waves of volunteers from all strata of Kryptonian society continued to rush blindly to the site of Kandor, though few understood the scope of what they were coming to do. Though they could have returned to the comfortable estate, Lara refused, insisting that they were needed in Kandor to help heal the wound Krypton had been dealt. A desperate need filled her eyes, and she was driven to work herself to the point of collapse . . . and then she would fall into a deep gloom that made her nearly catatonic. Jor-El remained beside her every moment.

He wished Lara would confide in him, but he did not press her. He accompanied her as she, like so many other pale-faced and haggard refugees, trudged around the entire perimeter of the crater in a sort of obsession. They walked and stared, as if their procession could somehow bring back the lost city. Though the tragedies were individual, those who had been left behind shared a bond of mutual grief. Searching for answers, they traced the perfect circle around the great scar in what seemed to be an endless march.

Scribes interviewed the people in the camps, carrying makeshift datapads. They took down the names of lost ones and recorded stories and remembrances, filling pad after pad. Two of them, overwhelmed by the magnitude of the task, gave up in despair.

In the evening, Jor-El sat beside Lara on the flat ground in a tent not far from Zod's command post. Leaning back against the stiff fabric wall, she propped her sketchpad on her thighs and worked furiously, her gaze intent. Jor-El leaned close, sharing his warmth and love without interrupting her train of thought. She was weeping as she worked.

With swift, sure strokes of her stylus Lara drew an image of her mother and father in happy times. The details were perfect. She drew her grinning brother, Ki-Van, next to them with his freckled face and tousled straw-colored hair. After hesitating, she included a figure of herself. She then dropped the stylus, racked in sobs. She stared at the sketch for a long time with unbearable pain in her eyes. "I don't ever want to forget that this was my family, but drawing a picture can't hold them here."

Jor-El stroked her hair as she leaned her head on his shoulder. "You won't forget. I'm here for you." He brushed a fingertip across her tear-stained cheeks.

"Thank you." Lara looked up at him with a teary gaze. "You are my family now, Jor-El."

Zod dispelled any lingering resentment toward Jor-El by making a point of meeting with him daily. Everyone in the camp could see that the Commissioner and the great scientist were close companions, partners against the adversity Krypton now faced. Lara accompanied her husband, inseparable from him, though she said little. Her eyes remained red-rimmed and puffy, her expression drawn.

During one such discussion in the command tent, a woman with short, dark hair entered wearing a self-satisfied grin. "So, Lara! Do you remember an old friend from your student days?"

Surprise animated Lara's sad face. She couldn't seem to believe what she was seeing. "Aethyr-Ka! I haven't seen you since the Academy. I heard your family had cut you off."

"It was more the reverse, in fact." She grew serious. "But that hardly matters now. The Commissioner needs my help—and he could use yours, too."

Lara turned to Jor-El, heaving a sigh and finding the energy to explain. "Aethyr was one of the only students willing to visit historical sites with me. Camping out in the open, eating preserved rations, sleeping on the ground. What miserable times those were!" She sounded almost wistful, distracted for a moment from her deep loss.

Aethyr's dark eyes flashed. "Miserable? Admit it—you've never felt more alive." A troubled flicker crossed Lara's face, but the other woman pressed on "I'm certain we'll be seeing much more of each other. We must catch up on old times."

"*After* we restore some semblance of normal life for the people," Zod said sternly. "We all have work to do." He turned to Jor-El. "In years past you brought such intriguing inventions to my Commission, but the shortsighted Council forced me to seize them from you. Now it is time to revisit those old plans."

Jor-El couldn't keep the bitterness from his voice. "Your Commission destroyed most of my best work."

"I have great faith in your abilities. I give you full permission—in fact my most enthusiastic encouragement—to work without restrictions or inhibitions. Is that not what you always wanted?"

Jor-El wondered if Zod finally understood how deeply the Commission had hurt him over the years. Again and again, the man had capriciously declared Jor-El's greatest ideas to be unacceptable or dangerous. To expend so much effort and see it all wasted would have shattered a lesser man, yet even with his confidence undermined, he had continued to work, to invent, and to achieve breakthroughs.

Now the ground rules had changed, though, and the Commissioner needed more from him.

"Do what you were born to do. The whole planet is counting on you."

Jor-El realized he had been waiting all his life to hear those words.

CHAPTER 36

∞ ⟨⟩‼⟨⟩ 36

Even as the people of Argo City pulled together to recover from their own disaster, the loss of Kandor struck Zor-El with great dread. "Our world is in danger," he told Alura. They stood together in his observation tower, looking out at the deceptively calm sea. "Volcanic eruptions, quakes, giant waves, the buildup in the core—and now an alien attack. There's got to be something more I can do."

Alura was levelheaded and matter-of-fact. "Commissioner Zod is directing the Kandor volunteers and refugees well enough. You need to keep doing the same thing here. Argo City is your city. Rally and reassure them."

Zor-El wished he could send more assistance up to Kandor to help his brother, but he was barely able to cope with his own disaster. All along the coast, the massive rebuilding efforts continued. Since the tsunami had smashed the piers and battered the seawall, the people of Argo City had labored with remarkable solidarity. Rescue teams scouring the long shoreline had found only a few survivors among the hundreds of dead. Funerals were held day after day; Zor-El had personally spoken at forty of the services. During their mourning, however, the citizens also grew more determined.

Medical centers were overflowing; several of the city's power generators and water-purification plants remained damaged. A few main piers were repaired first so that boats could be launched again, and fishermen worked overtime to bring in aquatic harvests. When they produced more than enough for their own needs, they rushed extra supplies to the refugees at the crater of Kandor. It was the only aid they could offer.

Although Zor-El had been too overwhelmed to attend his brother's recent wedding, at least he knew Jor-El was married, no longer facing a trial, and assisting Commissioner Zod—all of which was comforting news. Krypton couldn't ask for a greater help.

In the meantime, construction crews reinforced and raised Argo City's seawall, after which Zor-El took the extra step of augmenting it with a greatly expanded protective field, based on the one that he had designed for his diamondfish probes. Unless something fundamental was done to relieve the pressure in the planet's core, though, more quakes would strike, further tsunamis would batter the coast, and restless volcanoes would continue to erupt.

Amid all the turmoil, Zor-El had finally dispatched a new survey team to the southern continent. Soon he would have all the evidence he needed . . . but instead of a useless, stagnant central government, Krypton had no government at all. With Kandor gone and Argo City brought to its knees, Zor-El didn't know how anyone could manage a project of such magnitude.

More swiftly than anyone could have expected, however, Commissioner Zod had jumped into the power vacuum. Zor-El wondered if the other man would acknowledge the far greater problem. "Maybe now I can speak to someone who will see reason."

"Do you think Zod has that vision?" Alura asked. "Will he hear you?"

His dark eyebrows drew together skeptically. "I don't know about Zod. He is intelligent and ambitious, but he's proved an impediment to progress so many times in the past."

"Many things have changed . . . "

"Yes. Let's hope that his mind has changed."

He and Alura left the villa and walked together through the bustling streets, along the burbling canals, crossing one ornate pedestrian bridge after another. The center of Argo City had recovered quickly, but still the sounds of construction reverberated everywhere. They passed homes bedecked with beautiful flower vines, multicolored herbs, blossoming ferns, and spore trees. Butterflies and pollinating bees descended

in droves, adding a pleasant background hum to the air. For today, at least, nature seemed oblivious to impending geological disasters and alien attacks.

Thin streams cascaded off the sides of buildings, trickling down in small waterfalls to strike fountain basins. Weary people came out to stand on their colonnaded balconies, took seats on stone benches, or leaned up against hedges. Even after the disaster, children still found reasons to play in the streets, resiliently discovering joy in life.

Since Kandor could not possibly be rebuilt, Zor-El considered suggesting that Argo City become Krypton's new capital, at least in the interim. Though he had no interest in serving as planetary leader, he and the heads of other population centers might provide the basis of a new council. A competent council. Zor-El began to doubt, however, that Commissioner Zod had any inclination to hand over the reins of power. That concerned him.

Instead of delivering ponderous speeches to swelling audiences, Zor-El simply walked through squares and gathering points, talking personally to the people, who listened and helped to spread his words.

"What do we do now, Zor-El? Is there a plan?" called a citizen with long white hair and a clean-shaven face. Zor-El recognized him as a man who designed and built barges.

"Krypton has no capital, no Council, no Temple of Rao." Zor-El straightened. "But Krypton still has its most important resource—people like you and me. And we have our determination."

"Is Argo City safe?" called someone else. "What can we do if Brainiac shows up here?"

He nodded sagely. "That is my challenge to you: prepare for the unthinkable. We've got to consider the long term. How do we save Krypton? How do we all survive?" Zor-El raised his burned hand as if it were a badge of honor. "Take heart. Argo City will carry the flame now. I'll remain in contact with my brother Jor-El, and we will get through this."

As the sun set over the mainland to the west, the sky presented a blazing and colorful spectacle. Every day the dusk grew increasingly beautiful, but Zor-El could think only of more ash, more fire, and more turmoil being thrown into the atmosphere.

CHAPTER 37

While he waited for Aethyr to arrive for their special planning session, Zod stood at the flap of his headquarters tent and looked across the expanse of hastily erected huts in the deepening twilight.

Settling in for what they expected to be long months or years of work, the people had already begun to decorate their shelters with tassels, family symbols, and reflective streamers as a way to defy the grimness all around them. As darkness fell, the many mourners gathered to sing and tell stories in what had become an impromptu tradition. Already numerous ballads and poems had been written about lost loved ones, lionizing the wealth and beauty of Kandor.

Spontaneously, refugees joined with well-meaning volunteers to make pilgrimages to the edge of the crater and throw flowers, ribbons, and other mementos into the deep emptiness. Priests of Rao had set up small temples to attract new worshippers in their prayers to the great red sun. Little shrines of glowing crystals and treasured images of loved ones littered the perimeter, so many that Zod worried they would soon begin to get in the way. Did every single lost person deserve his or her own memorial?

Six hollow-eyed boys and girls played together, throwing rocks into a deep puddle, but they seemed to take no joy in it. In the first week many survivors had drifted away from the crater to find temporary housing with distant friends or relatives. Others, without options or without the will to go anywhere, remained in the camp.

The Commissioner had waited long enough for this evening, but Aethyr treated it as no more than a casual event. She arrived wearing comfortable tan field clothes and a brown vest with pockets for tools or samples. Her billowy sleeves were smudged with dust. If she had worn a fine gown, costly jewelry, or intoxicating perfume, Zod would not have been so attracted to her.

Inside his command tent, a small table had been covered with fabric and set with a selection of savory appetizers. Warm, glowing crystals were distributed in the corners and on shelves. Aethyr lounged back in a seat across from him. "So, Commissioner, is this to be a romantic meal between the two of us? Shall I expect to be seduced, or is this a strategy session?"

Zod leaned across the table. "I've watched you, Aethyr. You're like me in many ways."

She chuckled. "What do you mean by that? And you didn't answer my question."

"People like us find nothing more intense than tactical and political discussions. Tonight you and I could decide the future of Krypton. Isn't that intriguing?"

With a confident smile, she reached over to clasp his hand. "So, the answer is seduction, then."

He called for the main course, a freshwater fish stuffed with nuts along with spiced vegetables roasted over an open fire. Jellied fruits crusted with sugar crystals and mounted on tiny skewers made a festive dessert.

Upon learning that Jor-El's personal chef had joined the ever-growing group of volunteers, Zod had quickly taken advantage of the man's talents. Fro-Da worked wonders producing great quantities of palatable, nutritious food for the camp's population. Tonight, though, the chef had prepared a very special meal for Zod and his guest.

With the bounty spread in front of them, Zod sent the smiling chef away with his thanks. When he curtly told Nam-Ek to keep away any eavesdroppers, he was satisfied that the bearded mute would kill anyone who tried to defy those wishes.

Zod got down to business with Aethyr. "I secured my position by acting swiftly. The people needed a leader, and I offered myself. No one else rose to the challenge. No one else has offered an alternative. I want to keep it that way—for the good of Krypton, naturally."

"Naturally. It must have been quite a shock for everyone to see government acting swiftly." She smiled. "Krypton's noble families are incapable of responding to sudden needs, but you can expect to hear complaints once they recover from their shock." Aethyr was persistent. "This is our window of opportunity. Right now, the people in this camp are united by tragedy. They're yours to command. They'll do anything you ask of them."

"But that won't last," Zod finished for her. "They rushed here, desperate to help, but soon they will realize that nothing can be done. There is no one here to save, no city left to rebuild. The suburbs and outlying fields and some industrial areas remain, but they are extremities without a heart or mind."

"Then buy time before the people begin to disperse. Give them something to do. Make up a harmless project in the short term and give them guidance for the long term."

"Intriguing." Zod ran a finger down his short beard. "I can formalize the project of gathering names, putting together a database of everyone who needs to be remembered. That will keep them busy. In fact, I'll even propose a massive memorial—a huge crystal wall etched with the names of everyone who vanished with Kandor. A pointless gesture, I know, but they seem to need an outlet for their sorrow."

"They'll throw themselves into it wholeheartedly and praise the name of Zod for his warm heart and his understanding of the people."

"You sound very cynical, Aethyr."

"Not cynical—pragmatic." She popped another morsel into her mouth and licked her fingers clean. "Also, once you reveal that you have Jax-Ur's nova javelins, you can claim to be the only person strong enough to defend Krypton against outside enemies like Brainiac. And that's the truth. What will you do if he returns?"

"I am confident that will not happen," Zod said, lowering his voice conspiratorially. "He is not quite so appallingly evil as I painted him. Brainiac already has what he wants, and he left the rest of Krypton for me."

Aethyr was surprised, then seemed to admire him. "Of course. You were the only one who spoke with the android, so you could alter the story to serve your own purposes. Then all your talk, your beating of the drums, your calling for a massive buildup of defenses—"

Zod folded his hands. "In order to gain power and unite the Kryptonian people, I need to show that I am *protecting* them. Peace and a common vision once bound us together, but I have found something even stronger: fear. With it, we will cement our hold on Krypton. The best enemies are fabricated enemies for two reasons: one, *we* have nothing to worry about, and two, the populace falls in line. And if Jor-El—my ally—develops new weapons as I have instructed him to do, no other would-be leader can hope to oppose me. Victory by fiat."

"What about Donodon's race?"

"It will be a long time before they discover he's missing, and longer still until they track him here." He picked up some of the seared vegetables, crunching them as he continued to talk. "In the worst case, we can offer Jor-El as the culprit, as the Council intended to do all along."

"So you have it all planned, then?" Aethyr had moved on to dessert and ate some of the candied fruits, then stabbed the empty skewer into the bones of the half-eaten fish on the main serving plate. The juice colored her lips a luscious crimson.

"Yes, I do."

"I have plans, too. You have succeeded in establishing calm, order, and productivity, persevering through great adversity, when no other city leader dared step up to the challenge. In the unlikeliest of circumstances, you, Zod, were Krypton's savior."

"Krypton's savior . . . " Zod leaned closer to her. He liked the sound of that.

"We must send loyal followers to all other cities to proclaim your heroism. You'll get the majority of the people easily enough, especially if you ally yourself with the more prominent noble families."

Zod could not hide his sour frown. "But the prominent nobles are the ones who want the position for themselves, especially Shor-Em in Borga City. He expected a Council seat as soon as one of the members retired." He let out a sardonic chuckle. "Of course, all eleven have now retired."

"Dru-Zod, son of Cor-Zod, I can tell you're an only child! Consider other members of the noble families, not just the oldest sons. Second, third, and fourth children. Think of all those sons and daughters born into privilege, yet denied any chance to become Council members. What about Shor-Em's younger brother, Koll-Em, who is far more ambitious?

Many younger nobles like him never had any opportunities open to them. They'll see *this* as their chance. If you offer *them* a way to participate in a powerful government—your government—they'll follow you anywhere." She reached out and traced a finger down the opening in his shirt, a sensuous tickle that could easily turn into a scratch.

"I begin to see." Zod took a long sip of his wine, admiring the dry Sedra vintage. Then he took her hand.

Aethyr shifted her position, coming closer to him. "Why do you think I rebelled against my parents? I had no interest in becoming a trophy that adorns some husband's arm. So I went out and did what I wished to do, much to my family's dismay." She pulled back, nearly hypnotizing him with her large eyes. "I can think of nothing more attractive than to see you do away with the old order—entirely."

He tried to kiss her, but she drew away, still talking. "Other younger nobles might not have expressed their dissatisfaction so blatantly, but they're much the same as I am. Younger sons and daughters of the most powerful families are given nothing important to do, nothing to challenge their abilities. Offer them some power and prestige."

She finished her wine in a single gulp and wiped her mouth. "Many of the younger nobles are truly lazy and decadent, but some of us do have ambitions. It's very different to be told that you don't have to do anything, as opposed to not being *allowed* to do anything."

Now she leaned forward to kiss him, pressing her moist lips firmly against his. He could still taste the heady wine on her mouth. "And how do I take advantage of this unexpected pool of candidates?" he asked.

"Offer them what they hunger for. Bypass the privileged older noble children and promote the lesser ones. Their loyalty will impress you." Her tunic came unfastened easily, and he roughly pushed the fabric down, baring her shoulders, then her breasts.

Zod's mind spun with the ideas Aethyr had presented, the tantalizing chance to re-create Krypton from scratch. She tore his shirt in her urgent need to remove it. They quickly moved to the thick sleeping pads, kissing deeply, tasting the exotic flavors of the meal and the spicy allure of the possibilities they both saw. They drank each other in.

Now unexpectedly exonerated, Jor-El began to assist Commissioner Zod in strengthening Krypton. He was wary that the ambitious Commissioner might be taking advantage of the tragedy to gather a great deal of personal power. On the other hand, Jor-El had witnessed firsthand the total paralysis of the old Council, and he couldn't imagine them trying to deal with the disaster. At least Zod was getting things done.

And Jor-El intended to do the same. He and Lara returned to his research building at the estate, where he assembled all his best ideas for the protection of his planet. First and most important, the Commissioner had decided that Krypton must be vigilant, alert for any alien attack force that might come against them.

With Zod's encouragement, Jor-El designed a large array of observation telescopes to scan the heavens and provide an early warning about any threats from space. This was a significant turnabout from his previous dealings with the old government, which had never given his proposals much serious consideration. So far, at least, Zod was giving the brilliant scientist free rein. That was a silver lining to the cloud of awful events that had happened.

As an astronomer, Jor-El had always been fascinated with the heavens, other stars, nebulae, black holes. He longed to see what was Out There. Previously, the dour Council had chided him for his preoccupations. "Distant worlds mean nothing to Kryptonians," old Jul-Us had once pronounced in a ponderous voice from his high bench. "It is best that you keep your eyes toward Krypton."

Now, everything had changed. Zod *wanted* him to turn his gaze outward.

"And those small rockets you built, the ones confiscated by the Council?" the Commissioner had said. "Find a way to modify them so they can carry explosives rather than scientific probes."

"I need to continue my solar studies," Jor-El said. "We must monitor the fluctuations in Rao."

"So long as you help create defensive missiles, we can both get what we want out of this situation."

Jor-El had never meant to "get something" from the situation. He merely intended to devote his work to helping Krypton recover from disaster and to stay safe.

He chose a perfect site for the observation network on the uninhabited plains not far from his estate and mapped out a broad-baseline listening post consisting of twenty-three parabolic telescope dishes. He made only clumsy sketches, but Lara proved to be a remarkable help by cleaning up his drawings until they were precise blueprints. From his command tent at the crater, Zod approved the plans with barely a glance. "You will have all the resources, equipment, workers, and materials you could possibly need."

Less than two days later, like an invading army, heavy machinery rattled away from the refugee settlement and rumbled across dry grasslands to the open land Jor-El had chosen. The volunteer workers seemed glad to participate in such a significant project.

Constructors cleared the grasses, plowed new access roads, excavated foundations, and sank anchor pilings down to bedrock. At Zod's command, foundries from the mines in Corril began producing the structural girders and conduits needed for the framework of the telescope dishes. Tyr-Us, the industrialist leader of Corril, complained about the imposition, but obeyed anyway. Anyone at the refugee camp who demonstrated an ability to perform skilled or technological labor was shipped away to help build the listening post.

Jor-El was amazed, even overwhelmed. In all his years of research, he had never been offered so much assistance. Previously, his projects had been mere experiments, prototypes to be submitted to (and usually confiscated by) the Commission for Technology Acceptance. Now, though, his dreams became large-scale practicality.

Lara spent the days beside him as his wife, his companion, and his sounding board. Though they had been married for only a short time, she could easily read his moods. Though the loss of her parents and little brother still weighed heavily on her, and she remained restless and agitated, she drew strength from Jor-El and gave it back at the same time. She wrote faithfully in her personal historical journal, recording firsthand all the activities around them; someday it would be a valuable—and accurate—chronicle of what had really taken place during Krypton's most difficult days.

As she watched the construction continue, Lara was pleased to see so many people following her husband's instructions. "You have an amazing second chance, Jor-El. Krypton needs you. I always knew you'd be found innocent."

He turned away from the rising dust and rumble, unable to hide a troubled frown. "I wasn't found innocent, Lara. I was *pardoned.* Those are two different things. People will still assume I'm guilty, but that Commissioner Zod simply needed something from me. A shadow of doubt will always hang over me."

"I don't think so, Jor-El." Lara placed her fingers on his cheeks, turned his face to hers, and gave him a kiss. "Look around you. Krypton is forever changed."

Unlike his brother, Jor-El had always held himself aloof from politics, avoiding the petty rivalries and arguments in the Council. Though he'd been repeatedly offered a seat among the eleven, he could imagine nothing more frustrating than to spend his days in bureaucratic quicksand. Better to let them worry that he could accept the appointment any time he wished.

The government had wasted time on decisions that improved one noble family's personal standing rather than Kryptonian society as a whole; they had misplaced priorities. With his science Jor-El felt he was doing far greater work than a political career would ever have allowed.

He had bypassed the Council when necessary, done what he believed was right, and completed his independent studies.

Now, however, he didn't have to worry about Zod's Commission seizing and locking away his greatest discoveries. Zod had once been his greatest rival and nemesis, but now he couldn't help but feel a sort of grudging gratitude toward the intense man.

Together, Jor-El and Lara watched the first tall girders being installed into pilings for the listening dishes. At the speed these people were working, it would be less than a month before he could begin thorough, round-the-clock observations. While the Commissioner was primarily concerned about alien invaders, Jor-El couldn't wait for the scientific opportunities this huge telescope array would offer. He could finally produce a complete sky survey in various wavelengths.

While his thoughts wandered, the ground suddenly began to shake, an ominous tremor building from deep underground. The girders of the partially built telescopes began to sway. Construction machines strained to stabilize themselves while the dirt bucked and heaved. Workers shouted from high scaffolding.

Jor-El grabbed Lara, and they ran out into the open, away from any tall structures. As the shaking reached a crescendo, one of the anchored telescope stalks toppled and crushed a lifting machine as its operator leaped to safety.

When the tremors faded again, Lara brushed herself off, trying not to look shaken. "Do you know what that was? What caused it?"

His brother's earlier concerns came thundering back to him. "It's what Zor-El warned us about—science that the Council didn't take seriously."

CHAPTER 39

Hoping to secure his power base, Commissioner Zod had already dispatched some of his passionate followers to Orvai, Corril, Ilonia, Argo City, Borga City, and many smaller agricultural and mining villages. Speaking Zod's praises, the messengers rallied the citizens, played upon their fears, and put him forward—humbly, of course—as the only man who could truly lead Krypton, "at least during these uncertain times." Zod had personally faced the evil Brainiac. He had been there from the very beginning, while other city leaders had stayed home for weeks, discussing the tragedy from the sidelines.

Meanwhile, arrogant Shor-Em had unilaterally issued a call for volunteer candidates to become members of a reestablished Council that he proposed in Borga City. Though the pompous nobleman commended Zod's continuing "temporary" efforts at the crater camp, he called the prospect of rebuilding Kandor absurd. Although the Commissioner privately agreed, he nevertheless encouraged his fanatically devoted workers to take offense at the insensitive pronouncement. By virtue of their indignation, they recruited even more followers.

Living with the painful reality of the gaping wound every day, his dedicated followers at the temporary camp couldn't help but recognize how slow and ineffectual the other city leaders had been. Zod was clearly the only viable alternative. Everyone had to see that.

Unfortunately, the majority of Kryptonians hadn't personally lived through the tragedy or witnessed the magnitude of the damage firsthand, and they were swayed by naïve and impractical suggestions, such as Shor-Em's. Zod knew he had to set them straight, and soon, before these complainers stumbled upon some way to oppose him.

It was time he decided, to see for himself what Aethyr had found in the ruins of Xan City. There he would find the tools he needed to consolidate Krypton and trump the blowhard claims of any rival leaders.

Promising to return in only a day or two, Zod departed from the burgeoning refugee camp with Aethyr and Nam-Ek. As their levitating raft raced away to the south, Zod looked back at the temporary settlement, shaking his head in disappointment. "If I am to lead Krypton, my center of power must be more than a group of tents, dirt paths, and primitive sanitation facilities. No wonder people listen to Shor-Em when he offers Borga City as a viable alternative."

Aethyr lounged back on a cushion at the side of the open-air vessel, smiling at him. "One problem at a time."

After a journey of many hours, they arrived at the ruins of Jax-Ur's ancient capital. Using this very place as his center of power, the warlord had conquered a world, destroyed an inhabited moon, and prepared to reach out across the nearby inhabited star systems. Only treachery had toppled him.

Zod reveled in the sensation of being surrounded by looming history. In the middle of Execution Square, he approached the weathered statue of the once-great warlord surrounded by the nearly unrecognizable figures of kneeling and defeated subjects. Propping his hands on his hips, he looked upward with a challenging smirk. "All your works have fallen into dust, Jax-Ur! Mine will be greater."

Aethyr said, "Then take Jax-Ur's mantle for your own, Zod. Why not follow in his footsteps? Be the savior of Krypton."

He looked at her strangely. "Jax-Ur is one of the most reviled men in our history."

She pointed out the obvious. "Only because history was written by those who reviled him."

"Then I had better write my own history to make sure that later generations will remember these events properly."

She was delighted with this solution. "Yes, you'll have to do that—and soon. Now, let me show you the weapons."

Not overly interested in history or technology, Nam-Ek prowled among the flagstones and the fallen columns. He enjoyed stomping on the topaz beetles, crunching their shells under his big feet, and stepping back to watch as other ravenous insects scuttled forward to devour the oozing carcasses. These were not his beloved animals. They were bugs, *vermin*—like anyone who opposed his master. Nam-Ek stomped some more.

With obvious anticipation, Aethyr played the notes of "Jax-Ur's March" on the crude and ancient musical instruments scattered around the square: a pitted tubular bell that still rang out low and clear, a hollow stone box that resonated when struck, a sheet-alloy gong that boomed like metal thunder. When she had completed the ponderous sequence of loud notes, the round covers of the underground silos ground slowly open to reveal the golden doomsday weapons standing upright in their cradles.

With shining eyes, Zod gazed at Aethyr, thinking that she looked more beautiful than ever, now that she had revealed her secret. He leaned over the lip of the nearest pit to stare down at the slender missile, with its smooth, bulbous tip that contained such untold destructive energy. He shook his head, nearly hypnotized by the elegant symmetry. Three of these warheads had been sufficient to blast Koron to rubble. Only three! "What could a warlord possibly do with *fifteen* such weapons?"

Aethyr lifted her softly pointed chin. "A man with such power could strike fear into anyone who might challenge him. Simply by possessing the nova javelins, a leader could ensure peace, prosperity—and total, absolute obedience."

Possibilities swirled in the Commissioner's mind. "Intriguing."

The pair descended into the shadowy control-room bunkers she had found underneath the ruins. Zod inhaled the smells of dust, stale air, cold metal, and old grease. The ancient equipment looked intact and undamaged, except for the slow deterioration of time. Only a few of the old illumination crystals still functioned in the large and silent banks of machinery.

"The systems are strange, the notions old-fashioned," Aethyr said, "but I don't believe it would take much to fine-tune them."

Later, when they emerged from the control bunkers, Zod admired the lost grandeur all around him. Studying the still-intact buildings and towers, he extended his hands as if he could feel ancient power rising from the ground.

"I like this place. It has a very solid feel, a sense of majesty. Think of how long it has endured." He smiled at Aethyr. "Yes, once all my followers are in place, this will be a clean, fresh start for a new world. *This* will be Krypton's new capital."

CHAPTER 40

After the setback from the severe quake, Jor-El revised his plans for the telescope array, reinforced the structures, and set the teams to work again. In only a week, four more giant observation dishes unfurled, like the petals of enormous wire-frame flowers. With the structures geometrically arranged along two intersecting baselines, each a kilometer long, the array looked like a technological garden. He wished his father could see this. Yar-El would have been awed by the site.

The sensitive telescopes and receiver dishes would warn of any impending invasion, and they would also collect copious pure scientific data. The heavens were rife with mysteries and possibilities, but the Council had not wanted Jor-El even to look for them. Now, under the pretext of defending the planet, Zod had given him all the permission he needed.

Jor-El also set his mind to pondering designs for new defenses, just as Zod had asked him to do. However, even though he convinced himself the weapons would be used only against Krypton's outside enemies, his mind often went blank now that he was *trying* to create destructive devices.

In the midst of Jor-El's efforts to complete the telescope array, his mother tracked him down, first by sending a message to the estate, then to the temporary camp at the crater, and finally to the telescope construction site. He watched her image on the communication plate, read her distraught expression, and suddenly knew that this message was what he had been dreading for many years.

"Your father is dying. This could be your last chance to say goodbye." Charys hesitated. The image flickered, and he realized that she had switched off the recording to gather her courage so that she wouldn't cry, so that her voice wouldn't crack. "I've already sent a message to Zor-El, but I doubt he'll make it from Argo City in time. Please hurry. I need at least one of you here."

Lara would not let him go alone. An angry breeze picked up, growing moist as gray clouds formed overhead, and Jor-El didn't even notice when the drizzle began. They borrowed a fast platform flyer from one of the construction crews, activated the passenger cover, and left the noisy and frenetic work site.

It was raining hard by the time they landed the hovering raft among the trees that enfolded the isolated dacha. Jor-El's knees shook as he stepped down from the vehicle. Cold droplets splattered his face and plastered down his white hair, but he hardly noticed the discomfort.

As they ran to the porch, Jor-El saw that Charys had allowed her garden to fall into weeds. After the blooms had been plucked for Jor-El and Lara's wedding more than a month before, the untended flowers had reblossomed in a riot of colorful petals. The fact that his mother had not cared for her prized plants told him more than any verbal explanations.

She opened the door, looking wan and lonely, her eyes hollow. "Come inside. I'm glad to have you here with me."

His face gray and pale, a sheen of sweat sparkling on his forehead, Yar-El lay on his bed, covered by a light blanket. His open eyes barely blinked as he stared off into his own universe. His breathing was shallow.

"He knows what happened to Kandor," Charys said. "It's not always obvious when he's aware of his surroundings, so I'm not sure how he learned the news, but he feels the loss of the city. That's what did this to him." Unnecessarily, she straightened the blankets, then stroked Yar-El's hair, keeping her hands busy. The older woman struggled to maintain her dignity. "Another day, Yar-El. Just hold on another day. Zor-El will be here as soon as he can."

They watched over the catatonic man in a long vigil, unable to find words. Surprisingly, old Yar-El blinked. His watery eyes flicked from side to side, then focused. He lifted a hand, weakly extending a finger.

Jor-El leaned closer. "Father, can you hear me?"

Yar-El pointed to the side of the bed, growing agitated. He clenched his fingers, then pointed again, attempting to grasp something. Lara saw that he was trying to reach the touch-sensitive notepad at the side of the bed. "He wants to write something. Do you have a stylus?"

Charys rushed to get a writing implement, but Yar-El took the tablet and made a sweeping stroke with his finger, drawing a curve that bent and rebent back upon itself. The old man clearly and deliberately formed the S-shaped symbol of their family crest, the serpent of deceit trapped within an impenetrable diamond. He let the pad fall onto the blankets that covered his lap.

With his other hand, he reached out to clasp Jor-El's fingers and said a slow, breathy word. "Remember." The effort took the last sparks of his existence. Yar-El sighed, slumped back into his pillows, and closed his eyes forever.

Zor-El arrived four hours too late in the swift silver flyer that had previously taken him to the southern continent. He and Alura, windblown and exhausted, ran from the clearing where they had landed, but to no avail. As soon as they stepped through the door of the dacha, Zor-El immediately sensed the pall of sadness. He looked at his brother, and Jor-El shook his head.

Yar-El lay at peace on his bed, and his younger son approached tentatively. "I suppose I mourned him a long time ago," he said in a rough voice. "With a mind like his, our father was effectively dead when the Forgetting Disease stole his thoughts."

The four of them stood together in shared grief while Charys collapsed in a chair, finally letting them see the toll taken by so many years of tending her unresponsive husband. "That's what I thought, but I was deluding myself. Now that he's gone, all the pain is back, as fresh and sharp as it ever was." She drew in a long, shuddering breath. "Now it's as if he died twice, and I've had to endure the same loss both times."

"He was lucid right at the end. He said something." Jor-El looked at his brother. *"Remember."*

Zor-El's dark eyes flashed, bright with a sheen of withheld tears. "'Remember'? What does that mean?"

"I think he wanted us to do what he could not." Gazing down at the old man, Jor-El realized how little he knew his own father.

Finding a small reservoir of strength, Charys announced, "We will hold the funeral at the estate, his original home. That's where he belongs."

After Yar-El's body was prepared, they returned to the manor house. Memories pressed down upon Jor-El, clear recollections of when his father had been brilliant, how Yar-El had spoken of his hopes for his two sons, how he had trained them both to investigate scientific possibilities and make intuitive leaps that few Kryptonians even attempted.

When Rao was high in the sky, the two brothers carried their father's bier across the estate grounds. Charys led the way in a slow procession with Lara and Alura on either side of their husbands. Jor-El could not help thinking that Yar-El deserved greater fanfare than this, a huge crowd, a funeral parade that wound through the streets of Kandor.

The little group gathered at the small private solar observatory Jor-El had built on a stepped platform behind the estate's main building, where it was unshadowed by trees or lichen towers. Although this was much smaller than the similar facility that had projected a huge orb of Rao atop the Council temple, Jor-El had spent much time here deciphering the star's turbulent flaws. The observatory's mirrors and focusing lenses had been swung aside to leave the projection zone empty. The brothers placed Yar-El's body at the center of the focal space.

Zor-El delivered a brief eulogy, but his gruff voice cracked, and his words ended quickly. Jor-El stood beside him, summoning his own thoughts, wrestling down the waves of grief. "Krypton should revere Yar-El for the great things he accomplished and forget his strange fall from grace." He swallowed a lump in his throat. "Even though we find that our heroes have feet of clay, we must never forget that they were *heroes* in the first place."

He and Zor-El each took one of the alignment rods and swung the curved focusing mirrors into place. As the observatory gathered the light of Rao, they slipped the magnifying lenses into position, removed the filter covers, and stepped back.

A fuzzy image of the red sun formed in the focal zone where Yar-El's body rested; then the image suddenly sharpened into an intense representation of the blazing star. The corona formed, followed by the churning layers of dark sunspots and thundering plasma. The heat condensed in a blinding flash. Yar-El's body vanished into white smoke, entirely disintegrated, becoming one with Rao.

Jor-El's face was dark and troubled. "Krypton needs us, Zor-El. It's what Father would want. We can't let him down. We can't let Krypton down. You and I know what's happening in our planet's core. The quakes, the tidal waves—it'll only get worse. Now that the Council is gone, you and I have to do something to save the world. Do we have proof to show Commissioner Zod?"

Zor-El's expression hardened. "I recently received word from my survey team. One member was killed in a fresh round of eruptions, but the others are returning with a complete set of data from the network of sensors they deployed." He pressed his lips together. "Soon we will know for certain."

CHAPTER 41

∞⚬◇‼◇⊸⊤♀◊ 41

By the time Zod returned from Xan City, satisfied and enthusiastic with his new plans, many of Krypton's ambitious younger nobles had arrived at the camp. They came to deliver extravagant loads of supplies or to volunteer for the work of constructing a new city or memorial. Back in their decadent, sprawling households, these young men had nothing significant to do.

Some of them were bleeding hearts who wrung their hands in misery at the loss of the Council and dreamed only of restoring Krypton to what it had once been. Zod had no interest in people like that. Aethyr, fortunately, pointed out others who were much more likely to serve him.

"For someone who doesn't bother with internal politics and household rivalries," Zod observed with an amused smile, "you certainly know a lot about the noble family members."

"I know a great deal about anyone who thinks along similar lines as I do. Koll-Em even tried to overthrow his brother not long ago—a botched attempt, but it shows how he thinks. He was banished from Borga City, and now he's here. Many more of the younger sons and daughters played their roles as dutiful children, but it was all an act. You'd be astonished at the depths of hatred some of them have toward their elder, privileged siblings. And we can turn that to our advantage. We have to. You and I won't succeed without their strength and support."

Zod sent out a discreet invitation to seventeen of the most ambitious younger sons, as chosen by Aethyr. Putting the pieces in place.

He met his special guests at the broken rim of the crater at dawn. The edge dropped off into a debris slope before plunging steeply into emptiness and the smoky unseen bottom of the pit. Nam-Ek stood behind the group, an intimidating presence.

Seventeen candidates: some eager, others skeptical, all curious. Zod observed them. Sharp-featured Koll-Em. No-Ton, a noble son who had studied science and engineering (not remotely comparable to Jor-El, but useful nonetheless). Vor-On, the eager sycophant who had tried to curry the Commissioner's favor at the chariot races. Mon-Ra, Da-Es, Ran-Ar, and others whose names he did not know yet. And of course, Aethyr.

These were talented men willing to break rules, those who had either bypassed family expectations and made something of themselves or chafed at restrictions and had every reason to despise the placid order of old Krypton. They had spent their lives being told what they couldn't do.

Many of them were barely out of their teens, with fire in their blood. What they lacked in experience and reasonable caution they made up for with radical enthusiasm. They were young enough to be naïve, convinced of their own righteousness, never imagining that their closely held beliefs might be wrong. They were perfect for what Zod had in mind.

At a glance, he could see that some were doubtful that Commissioner Zod would be any different from previous government officials—skeptical, just as Aethyr had originally been. He simply smiled at them. "The old Council is gone, and so is our old way of life. Not one of you will mourn that. Do not pretend otherwise." He could tell by their shocked expressions that he had grabbed their attention. "In order to achieve my goals, I need a cadre of close advisers to stand with me as I do what must be done, for Krypton's sake. Will you listen to what I have to say?"

The younger nobles glanced at one another, some muttering questions while others remained silent. Koll-Em said brashly, "It does no harm for us to hear you out."

"No one's ever taken us seriously before," Mon-Ra added. He had a well-muscled body, created by physical sculpting rather than hard labor.

"Come, let us descend a ways into the crater." Zod gestured to the sharp drop-off and the uneven switchbacked path Aethyr had marked out.

She stepped up to the lip. "The Commissioner needs you to touch what actually happened here. Feel it viscerally, grasp the power of one evil alien who uprooted a city and left a hole halfway through the crust. Make yourselves different from those who issue pronouncements while they sit in comfort halfway across the continent."

"Like my brother." Koll-Em's voice dripped with loathing.

"Down in the *crater?*" Vor-On said, alarmed. Only a moment ago, he had been bursting with excitement at the thought of being part of the Commissioner's inner circle.

"I have no use for timid advisers, Vor-On. You are welcome to stay in the camp with the other manual laborers."

The young man swallowed hard. "No, no. I'll come . . . if the rest of you do." He looked around. His square-cut hair no longer looked terribly stylish.

Zod took the first step onto the crumbling slope. Pebbles skittered downward, but he found solid footing. "Aethyr explored our route last night. It may be difficult going, but if a simple hike is beyond your abilities, you are not the people I am looking for."

None of the seventeen turned down the offer.

Aethyr led the group, picking her way from boulder to boulder, sliding on loose dirt, holding on to outcroppings. Some of the ground had been fused into glassy patches by Brainiac's powerful cutting beams. They scrambled deeper and deeper until they were far from the lip, away from the edge and any possible spies. Nam-Ek's burly silhouette waited for them on top.

Down here, the air smelled of sulfur and steam, foul water and bitter dust. Zod's hands were dirty and sore from gripping sharp-edged stones as he worked his way down. One tall, loose-limbed man, Da-Es, slipped and stumbled, dropping almost two meters before Aethyr snagged his tunic and stopped his fall. Da-Es regained his composure and brushed himself off. He looked with scorn at his torn clothing, a smear of blood, the scrapes and bruises.

"And? Do you want to return, climb up to the top?" Zod prodded him.

"My ego is more bruised than my body is," Da-Es said. "I want to hear why you've gone to such great lengths so no one will overhear us."

After a quarter of an hour of climbing, they reached a shelf of rock. Zod and Aethyr waited as all seventeen gathered on the stable ledge or balanced on rocky protrusions slightly above.

"As you can guess," Zod began, "this is not the sort of meeting where we serve refreshments or adhere to rules of order. This is a war council." The young men looked surprised; some nodded grimly. "Krypton is at war, not just against alien invaders like Brainiac, but also against those of our own people who would keep our great civilization stagnant, as in the old days."

Most of the seventeen muttered in agreement, Koll-Em the loudest.

"Many of us quietly disagreed with the entrenched Kryptonian Council, and now, too late, all can see that their fossilized attitudes left us vulnerable. Now that the footdraggers are gone, I cannot in good conscience allow that to happen again. Ever." Zod saw that his candidates were waiting anxiously to hear what he proposed. "The older members of your families were vested in the former status quo. They felt entitled to a privileged life. Some of them have already begun talk of reestablishing a Council identical to the old worthless one. They want to lead us back into our naïve and helpless ways."

Aethyr added, "We can't allow your fathers and older brothers to cripple us again."

"Of course not," said Koll-Em. "It's time for the older ones to step aside and let the more visionary people—like all of us—have our turn."

Da-Es said, "It's not fair that no one ever asks us our opinion."

Mon-Ra added, casually flexing his bicep, "We've always been prevented from helping when that's what we most wanted to do."

"But they're our families," said Vor-On.

Zod hid his brewing smile behind a grave expression. "I'm not calling your older brothers evil or stupid, but they simply do not realize the damage they've caused. Not even now! It is time for me to form a new advisory board and take useless variables out of the equation."

"Commissioner, you're talking about overthrowing the established noble families." Vor-On sounded very upset. "I wanted to *be* one of them, not *destroy* them." The young man looked at the others crowded on the ledge. The sulfur fumes were making his eyes sting. "You can't expect us to take part in this . . . this mutiny."

Zod let out a tired sigh. "Very well, Vor-On. I thought I could count on your support, but do what you think is best for Krypton." He held out his hand in a genial gesture. Relieved, the eager young noble accepted the hand, shaking it as Zod continued, "And I'll do what *I* think is best."

With an abrupt, violent jerk, he yanked Vor-On over the edge and released him. The young noble was dropping out into the open pit before he even knew he had lost his footing. His yelp of disbelief turned into a fading scream of terror. The walls were sheer, and the crater was very, very deep. The shout cut off when Vor-On struck something, but his body continued to slide and bounce for a long time afterward.

Ignoring the dwindling noise, Zod turned back to the group on the ledge, expecting to see a scramble of panic or horror. Instead, he saw only grim determination. Excellent. "So, are you willing to be my sixteen advisers? My inner circle? The position is yours if you choose to join me—if you help me make Krypton strong again and swear your loyalty to me."

"I swear it," Aethyr said proudly. "Only Commissioner Zod can save us from our own shortsightedness."

Koll-Em said, "Even if we fail, I would rather fail trying to be something than succeed in attempting nothing."

"I've listened to my brother's constant talk, and I know what he intends," said Da-Es, rubbing his scraped knee. "It would be suicide for us to do as the older nobles plan to. You have my support, Commissioner."

Very quickly, all of the others threw in their lot with Zod.

He admired his new inner circle. "In order to symbolize our unity and our vision, I name you my Ring of Strength. Together we will be unbreakable. We will encircle all that was best about Krypton. Follow my lead, obey my orders, and we will bring about a golden age greater than any Krypton has ever seen."

When they climbed back out of the crater, the whole group seemed changed, energized, reborn. As they emerged to stand firmly beside Zod and Aethyr with Nam-Ek in front of them, the Commissioner sent criers throughout the camp to gather an audience as swiftly as possible.

People came streaming from the canals and tents and work sites to hear the announcement. No one seemed to notice that Vor-On was

gone. With all of Kandor lost, who could keep track of every missing person?

Zod felt a chill as he confessed quietly to Aethyr, "I am about to make history. I can feel it."

She gave him a sidelong glance. "You've already made history. What you're about to do now is create a *legend*. I will help you make yourself into a veritable demigod."

Standing on a pile of boulders at the crater lip, Zod lifted his hands and shouted, "This is not a time for indecisiveness. This is not a time for debates and factions. This is a time for us to be strong under a single leader with a single vision." He shouted at the top of his lungs. "This is a time for Zod—the new ruler of Krypton!"

CHAPTER 42

∞☐◇‼◇⊸T̶♀◊ 42

When the distant early-warning outpost was completed on the empty plains, all twenty-three receiving dishes turned their detector arrays toward the open sky. They listened for the faintest whispers from the empty heavens. Optical telescopes studied the stars at night, while longer-wavelength sensors combed the neighborhood of space during the day.

In the design of the facility, Jor-El had provided for the streams of data to be shunted directly to his expanded research building back at the estate. Shortly after the Kandor disaster, his servants and groundskeepers had all departed for the refugee camp to pitch in. Now, except for himself and Lara, the estate was empty, deserted. He didn't mind at all. The two of them enjoyed their solitude, a time to recover from so many tragedies.

Very soon now, he was sure he would receive the compelling seismic data his brother had promised. In the meantime, Jor-El devoted a few hours each night to studying the breathtaking new images of space: pools of ionized gas coalescing into fresh stars, false-color plumes of cosmic jets squirting into the vacuum, globular clusters, the whirlpools of distant galaxies.

The most sensitive radio dish in the array picked up a constant stream of static punctuated by pops, brief whistles, and indecipherable clicks. Jor-El left the speakers on at all times in his laboratory, white noise in the background. Though Donodon had told him that space was

peppered with inhabited star systems and unusual civilizations, Krypton's neighborhood seemed empty and quiet.

Wanting to stay close, Lara joined him in the research building, and he was glad to have her here. At times he could see she still ached from the loss of her parents and young brother. Jor-El had felt a similar heaviness in his heart since the death of his father. Though the old man's lingering degeneration had been a long time coming, the sadness at losing him was no less.

Lara commandeered one of the broad lab tables for herself. After tying back her hair to keep it out of her way, she spread out sketchplates, notes, and piles of documents, working on her own historical documentation. "I like being out here with you."

"It's mutually beneficial," he said. "You can be very inspirational."

She continued diligently writing down lines of text, etching a rough draft before permanently inscribing the words in memory crystals. She mused aloud, "I've always kept a journal, but this feels more important now. Somebody has to chronicle these events for posterity. Can you think of a better historian than me?" Her mouth quirked in a teasing smile, warning him that he'd better not contradict her.

"I can't think of a better *anything* than you." Jor-El leaned over, curious to peek at how she might be portraying him in her journal.

She self-consciously covered the text, then gave him a mysterious look as if she'd been waiting for exactly the right moment. "I have other news for you, Jor-El. Special news—"

The background listening-post speakers crackled with a burst of static, a whisper that seemed unnatural. Jor-El discerned sounds that were indisputably words. Startled, he strained his ears. "What's that?"

The static roared again, faded, then cleared to be replaced by a deep, somber-sounding voice. "— anyone can hear me. I send this message because I have no other hope. Someone out there must listen." Another crackle and squeak of static drowned out the next words. "— repeat for as long as I can."

Jor-El raced to the control deck and sent a command to pull together other signals from the observation array. By combining the outputs of the twenty-three dishes, he hoped to strengthen this faint transmission, perhaps even find an optical counterpart. He and Lara both stared as a

blurred image formed on one of the holographic condensers, then sharpened to show a hairless emerald-skinned man with a heavy brow ridge.

"My name is J'onn J'onzz from the planet Mars. My race is dying.
My civilization is falling to dust. Please save us."

Having glimpsed a tantalizing fragment of the message, Jor-El spent
hours recording the repeated signal, barely blinking, never turning his
attention away. He used every known technique to filter out distortions
and anomalous spikes caused by cosmic background interference. The
transmission must have been traveling across space for years, if not centuries, and a few hours would certainly make no difference to the fate
of the forlorn Martian. But Jor-El was a man of action, and Lara loved
him for it.

She assisted him in hooking up equipment, recording data, adjusting connections. Finally, after the signal had been processed and ampli-
fied, the two of them stood together, listening.

On the crackling screen, the heavy-browed Martian said, "By the
time you receive this, my civilization will be dead. History has swept
across us like an unquenchable fire. We thought our race would last
forever. We thought nothing could harm Mars, because we had a perfect
society, an advanced people with highly developed technology. We were
wrong."

The green-skinned man bowed his head. "I am the only one left
alive, and how long can I survive? My wife, my family, all lost." The
skin on the alien's face rippled and sagged. His form shifted as if he
himself were composed of wavering flame; then he seemed to restore
himself. Lara didn't think it was a signal distortion; the Martian had
actually altered his own shape.

His message was old, from a far-off star system, yet his grief seemed
fresh. The Martian man overlaid old images of his beloved world as he
spoke, showing red cliffs and rock pinnacles, domed cities and dusty
arches now in ruins, green-skinned people like ghosts walking through
now-empty complexes, then fading into blurred smoke. Lara saw idealistic
images of another green Martian, a female with supple skin and a pointed

head crest, standing beside two children. They looked happy. She was sure these must be the alien man's family.

Then came monstrous white-skinned counterparts to the peaceful green people. The pale ones had severe features, angular heads, deep-set dark eyes, and sharp teeth.

The grieving survivor said, "All died . . . white Martians, green Martians. Except for me. I survived. I am alone. I beg you to help me—or if that is impossible, then please at least *remember*."

Remember. Just as Jor-El's father had said with his last breath.

The heart-wrenching message replayed, and Lara also felt the longing, the loss. She was reminded of Kandor and her own parents. "That magnificent civilization. Did you see their cities, Jor-El? Those people, how intelligent they were! And yet it's gone. How could that happen?"

Jor-El shook his head, unable to comprehend how the Mars in the transmission could have been swept into the dusts of time. "There's nothing I can do to help them, is there? It's too far away and too long ago."

Lara saw what he needed, and she knew she could give it to him. She had learned the news only that morning, and she'd been waiting for the right moment to deliver her announcement. There could be no better time than now.

"I know things seem bleak, but there is always hope." She smiled and hugged him. "I'm pregnant, Jor-El. I'm going to have our child."

CHAPTER 43

≈☐◇‼◇⊷T☐◊ 43

The next day, Jor-El went to his father's enigmatic translucent tower
and cracked open the temporary resin barrier he had used to seal the broken
doorway and lock the components of Donodon's dismantled ship inside.
In recent months he had been tugged in many different directions—by
the threat of the inquisition, the loss of Kandor, the death of his father,
the giant telescope array . . . and Lara's pregnancy! He was going to be a
father. Even now, Jor-El still hadn't had time to fully absorb the wonderful
news Lara had given him. They were going to bring new life to Krypton
in the wake of so much recent tragedy and suffering. One baby could do
little to counteract all that grief, yet Jor-El felt a new hope.

Now, after hearing the message from Mars, he was eager to begin
his long-delayed work of studying Donodon's vessel. The blue-skinned
alien had been a curious investigator; he would have wanted Jor-El to
learn as much as possible from him. Each one of the components the
Commissioner had delivered was like a piece of a much larger puzzle.

And maybe in his explorations Donodon had learned something
about the lost civilization on the dusty red planet. . . .

The thought of the curious, insightful alien explorer brought back
memories of his own father as a vibrant and incisive man. Both of his
sons had looked up to Yar-El, awed by all the things he had accomplished. For years, Jor-El had left the odd corkscrewing tower intact,
preferring to savor the mystery rather than digest the answers.

When Commissioner Zod had urged him to hide the alien's spacecraft from the Council, Jor-El had not taken the time to fully investigate the interior of the tower. Now he stepped inside and looked around, drinking in the details, smelling the cool and faintly metallic air.

Why had his father built this odd structure? The laboratory was a perfectly serviceable space, well stocked with analytical tools and references. Yar-El had designed and constructed this remarkable place, and then just sealed it off. Had the older man been waiting for something? His cryptic comment from years ago, that Jor-El would know when to enter the tower—what had he meant by that?

At the time he'd designed the structure, the older genius had already been caught in the claws of the Forgetting Disease. His behavior had gradually grown more irrational as his thoughts, memories, and grasp on reality slipped away. Jor-El had loved his father, but he had not understood what was happening to the man. The best doctors on Krypton had said there was nothing they could do. And that helplessness and confusion—that problem he could never solve—terrified Jor-El.

His father was far too intelligent not to grasp how the terrible illness would progress, how he would slowly degenerate until he lost his mind entirely. Jor-El couldn't imagine how the man had endured such knowledge.

On the far milky wall of the tower he saw the bold, even defiant serpentine family symbol inside its diamond-shaped outline. Yar-El had placed this mark prominently here. Even as the disease worsened, the older man had not forgotten who he was or what his family meant to him.

Fascinated, even compelled, Jor-El stepped close to the smooth interior wall, face-to-face with the large symbol. "What is it you want from me, Father? If only you had spoken to me back when it was possible." With a finger he traced the S-shaped curve.

And at his touch, the lines began to glow. A circular section of the tower wall surrounding the mark shimmered with a lambent light.

Yar-El appeared. His image stood tall and majestic in his scientist's robes. His silver hair had been brushed back, and he had placed a fine chain on his forehead. His voice was stentorian, his words fraught with meaning. Jor-El couldn't remember the last time he had heard his father speak with such power and conviction.

"Jor-El, my son, I have left this message for you. I created this tower for a purpose I can no longer see. I trust you to understand what I do not, for too much is slipping away from me now. This may be the last time my mind can hold all of these thoughts. I feel so much draining out of me like water through a sieve. . . . "

Jor-El realized what his father had done. The family symbol had been set down as a pattern covered with a veneer of message crystal! His own warm touch had activated it.

Yar-El continued, "I once felt sorry for those who could not understand my calculations or my theories. Can you imagine how much more terrible it is to know that you once had that clarity and understanding, but that it is now gone? No matter how hard I clutch at them, the memories flit away.

"With my analytical mind I achieved many wondrous things, yet I paid for those triumphs. The fire that burns brightest also burns out most swiftly. Our race is changing. I am an anomaly—as are my sons. Both sons.

"Beware. It is not enough to flaunt your genius. A truly integrated Kryptonian uses both heart and mind. By joining the two, you will achieve your ultimate potential. You can be a true superman."

The image flickered, and Yar-El shuddered. His intangible gaze turned until he was looking directly at his son. "I am sorry I could not be there for you. I know you, Jor-El. I know your brother. Hold tight to yourselves. I wish we could walk together into the future. Instead, the future is up to you."

"Father!" He reached out to the image. Old Yar-El bowed his head, closed his eyes, and vanished as the recording ended, leaving Jor-El inside the tower, feeling more alone than ever.

He worked for days, tinkering with the separate pieces of Donodon's ship, trying to understand how they fit together. The Commission for Technology Acceptance had not been terribly meticulous in keeping detailed records as they dismantled the vessel, and now Jor-El had to use his best efforts to put them back in the right place.

Despite numerous attempts, no matter how much care he used in taking apart component after component, the riddle of the alien's stardrive was beyond him. Even though Zod was waiting for him to make some great breakthrough, Jor-El could barely grasp the basics, and he was a long way from designing a copy so that Kryptonian industry could build a powerful space navy. That was Zod's ultimate goal.

Setting aside his work on the starship engines, he found a separate enclosed system, the amazing library database of the planets his alien friend had visited. Here, inside the navigation system, Jor-El could find the log entries of all the fascinating journeys Donodon had made.

The ancient message from dying Mars played over and over in his mind. Jor-El had hoped he would become inured to it, but he kept being reminded of how far that strange civilization had fallen. If the Council hadn't shunned such explorations, might someone from Krypton have been able to visit the red planet in time, so long ago? Had Donodon's people been able to do something?

Using the distant early-warning array, Jor-El had already pinpointed the origin of the Martian signal: a solar system with an average yellow sun so small and far away that it was barely visible in Krypton's night sky. With that information in hand, he plunged into Donodon's navigation logs, combing through the records of the alien's travels, star system after star system. . . . Yes!

In his explorations, Donodon had visited that yellow sun around which Mars orbited. According to his log, the alien explorer had also picked up the desperate message and gone to investigate, but even he had been too late. Donodon had stood alone in the thin, cold air of Mars, recording what he saw in the spaceship's database.

Staring at the display screen from the separate navigation system, propping the bulky component on the least-cluttered laboratory table, Jor-El played images of weathered rust-colored terrain and fallen cities that emphasized what the forlorn last Martian had already said. Though the continent-wide canals were dry and parched, they showed the mammoth scope of the lost race's achievements. Now iron-oxide dust coated everything, slowly erasing the marks of an advanced civilization.

He thought about showing this remarkable discovery to Commissioner Zod, but felt a strange hesitation. To what purpose? Zod would not care, and the Martian race had already been extinct for countless years. The Commissioner would no doubt dismiss the heartbreaking message by saying that the dead race was no threat to Krypton and was therefore irrelevant. Jor-El decided to keep this to himself.

When he advanced Donodon's log to the next entry, however, Jor-El was so impressed, so inexplicably happy, that he ran back to the manor house and woke Lara from a deep sleep. He excitedly brought her out to the tower chamber so that she could see for herself. She rubbed her eyes and followed him across the dewy purple lawn, then leaned against him as the two of them watched the screen that had been taken from the dismantled ship.

Jor-El played the record of the next place the wizened, intrepid alien had visited. "Watch this, Lara. It's a beautiful planet, sparkling and blue, so peaceful and full of life."

Though Mars was dead, the next planet closer to the yellow sun was covered with oceans and swathed in gauzy clouds. The continents showed a variety of terrain ranging from frozen ice caps to mountains, forests, grasslands—and cities . . . wonderful, vibrant cities. Donodon had not contacted these people directly, but preferred to view them from a discreet distance. Their civilization was young and thriving, on the verge of technological expansion.

The people had only recently discovered radio communications and happily broadcast their existence out into the universe without a care as to who might hear them. They played exotic-sounding music. They built tall buildings that scraped the sky. These people were full of energy, unhampered by stifling restrictions such as those that had been imposed by the Kryptonian Council.

When Donodon's surreptitious surveillance zoomed in close enough to show the inhabitants themselves, Lara drew a surprised breath. "They look just like Kryptonians!"

"Yes, the racial similarity is eerie." Jor-El leaned closer. He felt an unusual kinship with the people on the third planet from the yellow sun. They seemed imaginative, ambitious, innovative, not afraid to risk failure. Jor-El longed to contact these people, share information and solutions with them—much as Donodon had intended to do when he'd come to Krypton.

Jor-El and Lara found the place beautiful and compelling, reminiscent of Krypton, yet very different. These people called their planet *Earth.*

CHAPTER 44

The next day Nam-Ek arrived at the estate, brusquely handing a message crystal to a curious Jor-El inside the tower laboratory. The shimmering image of Commissioner Zod rose like smoke from Jor-El's palm. "I need your help now more than ever, Jor-El." His thin voice was insistent. "I envision a project so grand that it will take our best work to accomplish it. Come and help us create the future—the next capital of Krypton. Nam-Ek will bring you and your wife to me, to the ancient ruins of Xan City."

The bearded mute gestured insistently toward the special flying raft he had brought. The vehicle had fast engines and soft seats, open to the warm air, but with an enclosed canopy to protect them from hot sun or bad weather.

Jor-El and Lara looked at each other. She crossed her arms over her chest. "I don't like this. It didn't sound like a request."

Nam-Ek was stony-faced. He shook his head vigorously.

Jor-El stepped up to the mute. "I have important work here, and so does Lara. We can't just leave."

In response, the other man replayed Zod's message, then made an imperious gesture to the vehicle. Jor-El felt angry, but also uneasy about the lengths to which the Commissioner's bodyguard would go.

"You're not going to take no for an answer, are you?" Lara demanded of Nam-Ek.

The mute shook his head. His expression was implacable.

Though not pleased, Jor-El did not argue as they both climbed aboard the vehicle. Zod would have his way, and Jor-El was beginning to resent it more and more.

The flying raft hummed as it shot across the distance, heading toward unpopulated and sparsely explored regions of the continent. Nam-Ek stood by himself at the controls, only occasionally turning around to look at his passengers.

In spite of her surprise, Lara was grudgingly fascinated by the prospect of visiting such a famed historical site. "Xan City . . . why would the Commissioner go to an abandoned ruin like that in the first place? He never seemed much interested in history." Then she nodded. "I'll bet Aethyr had something to do with it."

When they finally reached their destination by late afternoon, Jor-El saw a small cluster of temporary shelters that had been erected in the crumbling old city. Aethyr directed them to the Commissioner's makeshift office. Inside, Zod stood surrounded by numerous wafer-thin windows that projected images of the city ruins, overlaid with drawings of a fantastic new city to rise from the ashes of the old. "Thank you both for coming so promptly."

Jor-El glanced at Nam-Ek, who stood with muscular arms crossed over his chest. "Your man seemed to think it was an order."

"Yes, he can be quite implacable. Nevertheless, I assure you this is crucial." Zod raised a hand, leading them out of his temporary office structure. "Come with me and see how I intend to keep Krypton safe."

Even Aethyr looked as if she would burst with anticipation. "Xan City is full of treasures left by Jax-Ur." She hung close beside Lara. "This will solve a mystery that's centuries old!"

Zod escorted them down a steep set of metal stairs to a labyrinth of underground chambers and then to a bustling central room. The chamber's walls were lined with copper-alloy sheets. Antique but sophisticated-looking control decks glowed with diagnostic crystals. High-resolution plates displayed detailed maps of the entire surface of Krypton.

Seven newly recruited technicians from the Kandor camp now sat at the panels, touching crystals, studying readings, and conferring among themselves. By the hunch of their shoulders and the set of their necks and arms, Jor-El could tell the technicians were tense in the Commissioner's presence. They had placed their faith in Zod, sworn their loyalty, and followed his orders.

"What is all this, Commissioner?" Lara asked, still gazing around.

"Weapons of such magnitude that they will keep us safe from all enemies."

Jor-El felt a lump in his throat. "What sort of weapons? Where did you get them?"

As if sharing a secret, Aethyr looked directly at Lara, who suddenly went pale with realization. "You found them? After all these centuries?"

Jor-El glanced quickly at his wife, and then he *knew*. "You found some of Jax-Ur's nova javelins?"

Zod met his eyes, calm and confident with just a flash of defiance. "All of them. All fifteen."

Jor-El remembered how naïve he had been during his first dinner conversation with Lara, when they'd talked about the terrible mark the warlord had left on Krypton. "Why would you need such power, Commissioner?"

"To repel an outside invasion, of course." Taking Jor-El by the arm, he marched to the other side of the control room, where he activated a palm crystal. An opaque shield in the copper walls slid aside to reveal one of the sleek nova javelins, so close that Jor-El felt he could reach out and touch it. "Intriguing, is it not?" Zod said near to Jor-El's ear. "You know you've always had questions about them."

Despite his uncertainty and Lara's obvious unease, Jor-El was captivated by the weapon's smooth lines, the tall golden stalk that still gleamed bright even after being buried for centuries. The fins at its base were like bent legs, sharpened to points; balanced atop a slender shaft was an elongated gold ellipsoid filled with destruction.

Jor-El was greatly uneasy to be involved with such destructive power. "And you need me to see if these ancient weapons can be repaired?"

"No, no—I believe they will function perfectly well. No-Ton and our technicians have been cleaning, tuning, and performing basic tests. Jax-Ur created weapons of enduring destructive power. You have to admire him."

Jor-El stared through the observation plate at the doomsday weapon. "Then what do you need from me, Commissioner? Why bring us all the way here to these ruins?"

"These ruins are our new home." Zod smiled. "I just wanted you to know that Krypton no longer needs to rely solely upon you. I hope this eases your burden. Aren't you relieved? Here Krypton's true government can have access to all the power we may require under any circumstance."

CHAPTER 45

Commissioner Zod's announcement that he would reestablish his capital at the site of Xan City was greeted with general favor. Groups of volunteers and refugees packed up and joined crowded convoys heading south, abandoning the temporary camp at the crater. Despite a few stubborn holdouts, most people were convinced they needed a fresh start, far from the scar of Kandor.

Before any major work crews arrived, though, Zod had Nam-Ek remove the monolithic old statue of the fallen warlord. He refused to rule in the shadow of a failed tyrant. He also ordered the statues of Jax-Ur's kneeling rivals to be taken away, though he whimsically decided to keep one of them in his new office.

Once all the heavy equipment arrived at Xan City, the cleanup and construction crews began their massive new project. With appropriate encouragement, they applauded the triumphant, breathtaking vision of a soaring metropolis, a replacement for Kandor. The sixteen members of Zod's Ring of Strength issued a great deal of propaganda and promises. The Commissioner displayed fantastic blueprints for his grand new city rising from the ashes of the old.

After clearing away the fallen columns and walls in damaged sections of the city, the new workers would rebuild what could be salvaged and create everything else from scratch. The Commissioner gave Jor-El and Lara their own quarters in one of the first reconstructed dwellings so that they could remain here to help; the scientist and his wife had no choice but to leave their distant estate behind and live here, at least temporarily, until the work of the new capital city was done. For his main administrative building, Zod ordered the reconstruction of a government palace in what had been Jax-Ur's central citadel.

Meanwhile, from far away in his fine house in Borga City, Shor-Em issued a shrill condemnation of Zod's seizure of power, outraged that one man—a "mere Commissioner"—should think that he alone could rule the people. Once again, he proposed Borga City as a much better alternative for the "interim" capital. Other prominent outspoken citizens joining his protest included Tyr-Us, son of old Jul-Us, from the metal city of Corril in the ore-rich mountains, and Gil-Ex from Orvai in the lake district. But they were far too late.

By now, it had been nearly two months since the Kandor disaster. Tyr-Us, Gil-Ex, and Shor-Em had taken *two months* to raise their objections to what he had been doing (and they offered no concrete alternative). Zod simply couldn't abide that.

No one could have imagined, much less implemented, a faster return to normalcy. Instead of the endless talk and governmental lethargy to which most Kryptonians were accustomed, *his* people saw tangible progress every day. *His* people had a new capital and an obviously visionary leader.

Meanwhile, pontificating from Corril, Tyr-Us (whose name must have been inspired by his constant tirades, Zod thought) called again and again for the Commissioner's immediate resignation, demanding that he return power to the "rightful heirs of Krypton." By that, presumably, Tyr-Us meant himself and other old-guard nobles, none of whom had done a thing to help.

The construction at Xan City continued unabated.

One day when a team of three young volunteers broke open a new set of deep and unexplored catacombs, they blundered into a huge nest of the topaz-shelled beetles. Within moments the three had been eaten alive, their screams broadcast by their short-range communications devices. By the time a rescue crew arrived, nothing remained but gnawed bones. The beetles attacked the rescuers as well, but the crew beat them back.

Afterward, Zod assigned a handpicked team led by Nam-Ek (who

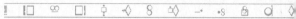

delighted in the task) to comb through the ruins and eradicate the infestation. Hundreds of thousands of the scuttling insects were wiped out, and the rebuilding began again. Zod announced his sorrow over the three volunteers who had been killed in the "regrettable construction accident."

But the task was large, even overwhelming, and Zod knew that some of his less-dedicated followers might want to slink back to their comfortable cities. Before the people could even consider giving up in the face of the daunting task ahead, he realized he had to give them a compelling reason to stay here.

Zod summoned all of his workers to the old Execution Square. The bright red sun presaged a sweltering day, but in the coolness of a fresh dawn the possibilities seemed boundless. Zod touched a voice-amplifier patch at his throat. "When faced with the greatest crisis in our planet's history, you came to me because you know that I am the future. I promised to protect Krypton against all enemies. I will show you why we need Xan City and why you can depend on me and no other to defend us."

He stepped onto the weathered block that had been the base of the ancient Jax-Ur statue. His words resounded like the booming pronouncement of a god, and he tried to make eye contact with as many people as possible. "*I* have the power to keep Krypton safe."

At his command, Sapphire Guards pushed the crowds back from the circular designs barely visible on the flagstones. With a hum and a shudder, the paved surface cracked along precise lines, and the people stepped away in trepidation. With ominous slowness, the half-circle silo covers scraped aside to reveal the ancient weapon pits.

Zod drew in a rich, deep breath, as if inhaling the awe of the spectators. Lights glowed from within the pits, illuminating the polished metal skins of the tapered missiles. Like the golden arrows of an angry deity, the fifteen nova javelins slowly climbed to the surface, simultaneously threatening and awe-inspiring. Three of the eighteen platforms were empty; these had held the weapons that had destroyed Koron.

Zod did not say anything for a long moment. He didn't have to. Everyone here knew that no other leader could promise as much. He would dispatch more fanatical supporters to all cities with the proof.

"Let Shor-Em and his cronies complain. I am a man of action. And I vow to use these nova javelins in order to defend my vision—*our* vision," he quickly corrected, "of Krypton."

The fifteen weapons gleamed in the ruddy sunshine, their narrow ellipsoidal warheads pointing toward the sky, waiting for a target.

CHAPTER 46

The city grew with remarkable speed. With so many political bridges to be built, the ambitious younger nobles of the Ring of Strength had gone to speak forcefully to other citizens across the continent, touting Zod's cause, emphasizing his mighty stockpile of nova javelins that could protect Krypton.

Inside the half-completed government palace, amid the clamor of carpenters and stonemasons, Zod summoned Jor-El and Lara. Some of the carved pillars along the interior walls were ancient and weathered; the new ones, careful imitations of the same design, looked out of place. Patches of stone resin sealed parts of the wall that had fallen down, covering up the long-faded frescoes that depicted Jax-Ur's triumphs.

The main roof had partially collapsed, and colorful fabric awnings covered the roof opening, peaked like a nomad's tent so the infrequent rains would run off. Gazing upward, Jor-El wondered if this was a conscious symbolism to remind visitors of how far they had already come from the temporary camp at the Kandor crater.

In the middle of the office, Zod had installed what looked like a weathered, lumpy boulder. Upon closer inspection, Jor-El could barely make out that it was the figure of a bowing man . . . bending his knee to someone? He wondered why the Commissioner had brought it here.

The Commissioner began by offering Jor-El provocative words. "I've decided that it is time your father received the gratitude and respect he always deserved. Do something for him, for me, and for all of Krypton. Show everyone what a true genius Yar-El was."

Jor-El had not expected this. "My father was a great man, but when he succumbed to the Forgetting Disease, many people called him mad. They turned their backs on him."

"And what I am offering will change all that," Zod said.

Lara was more cautious about the seemingly innocent offer. "My husband and I can't agree without knowing what you're asking."

Zod continued in a magnanimous voice. "Yar-El changed Kryptonian architecture forever. With his fantastic crystal-growth process, he created hexagonal columns of utmost purity and material strength. He built some of the most beloved landmarks of old Kandor. Now I want you to use your father's techniques to grow our new city's skyline as rapidly as possible." He looked wistfully down at his blueprints. "Once this city is finished and rivals even lost Kandor, Shor-Em and those other annoying voices will be silenced. We need to show them. Show them all."

Jor-El went to the broad window in the Commissioner's office and looked out at the well-preserved ruins, the partially rebuilt towers all around the square. He tried to envision how his father's architecture would fit in, immense spikes of transparent crystal, green and white and amber. "It would have to be done properly and with great care."

Zod clasped his hands together. "I knew you would share my vision. It will be good for the heart and soul of Krypton. This city can never be the same as Kandor, but it can serve as a new Kandor."

Jor-El began to run the specifics through his mind, performing calculations and estimates. "It is a long, slow process to grow crystals with proper stability, to anchor their structures and guide each facet along perfect intersection points. In the near term, it may be faster for you to erect traditional buildings using standard methods, while I continue this project in parallel. Eventually, this city will be as awe-inspiring as you intend."

"No, no! It must be swift and impressive. During my days at the Commission, I read your father's original archived records. He set forth an alternative technique, an accelerated growth process that uses several potent catalysts. Drawing upon the power of Rao, gigantic towers and immense spires can be grown within days. Is that not true?"

Jor-El shook his head. "That was a much inferior process, Commissioner, and my father discarded it. What it gained in speed, it lost in stability. Don't you want your capital to stand for centuries, even millennia? Longer even than the original Xan City? Such things can't be rushed. If we use the flawed catalyst technique, the buildings may last for no more than a generation or two."

Zod's brow furrowed. "Jor-El, if *Krypton* survives the next generation or two, then we will have all the time in the world. Once we get past this crisis, I promise to give you the full freedom to make any improvements you wish." He joined Jor-El and Lara at the window, gazing out at the bustle of construction. "Appearances are just as important as reality. No Kryptonian can doubt what Zod has done for them. I need to present my city as a new capital, a fait accompli—and soon."

Jor-El quickly looked at him. "Your city?"

"Krypton's city. Sometimes I grow a bit too passionate." He offered them an intense, unsettling smile. "Grow me these crystal buildings to quiet any naysayers, and in return I will name the tallest, most ornate spire after Yar-El."

"My father would not have wanted any accolades," Jor-El said. "Nor did he need them, especially not with buildings that are sure to be flawed."

Zod's expression darkened. "I insist."

Jor-El looked at Lara, who understood his need, and she nodded reluctantly. He said, "I will do this task in memory of my father, so long as we have time to make it right once we pass this current crisis." He narrowed his eyes, waiting for the perfect moment to raise the much more substantial issue of the data Zor-El had just sent him. "And there are other matters we need to discuss. When this is finished, I have certain priorities you must address."

The Commissioner sounded dismissive, as if a tit-for-tat arrangement was to be expected. "Perfect, my friend. I am forever in your debt."

CHAPTER 47

∞ ⟟⟠‼◇⟐T̰⟐ 47

Lara loved watching the wheels turn in Jor-El's mind as he pondered a new problem to solve. He had decided that he would harvest select seed crystals from the smaller structures on his estate and also from the magnificent palace in the arctic. Zod gave him the loan of a flying craft and sent him away to gather what he needed, telling him to hurry.

While Lara remained behind, she finally took the time to talk more with Aethyr. Inside one of Xan City's restored ancient buildings, the other woman's private quarters were far more spacious than Lara had expected. "I never imagined anything so ostentatious for you, Aethyr. Remember when you killed and roasted a snake once just because you didn't think we had enough camp rations to last us?"

"I called it the serpent of truth," she said with a smile.

"It certainly tasted foul." Lara screwed up her face at the remembered bad experience.

"You were the only other one who tried it. I've always respected you for that. It shows strength of character."

With a giggle that made her feel ten years younger, Lara said, "Do you remember Lyla Lerrol? She was so horrified that we had tasted the meat of a serpent that she wouldn't sleep anywhere close to us. Afraid we'd grow scales in the middle of the night!" Both of them laughed at the memory.

Aethyr suddenly became serious. "Commissioner Zod knows how

brilliant your husband is, but you can help us here, too. I've personally told him about you, Lara. You trained to be an artist—didn't you work with your parents?"

"I met Jor-El during a large-scale project at his estate." Lara's expression fell. So many things reminded her at unexpected times. "My parents were lost with Kandor."

Aethyr didn't look at all troubled. "My parents were lost, too, but they were the worst of the old Krypton. We have to forget all that now and move on." She poured them each a glass of ruby-red wine from Zod's personal stockpile, though Lara declined. She had not yet told anyone about her pregnancy. "You were never meant to be a mere assistant to a scientist. You have intelligence and skills all your own. In these times, Commissioner Zod asks all of us to give more than we've ever given before—to work harder, to contribute our best."

Lara was skeptical. "But what is it you need from me? Specifically? I am a historian as well as an artist. But everything I previously did seems very small now, in relation to Krypton's state of emergency." She considered revealing the personal journal she had kept, offering it as an official history of these troubled times, but an inner sense kept her from saying anything.

Aethyr casually took a gulp of her wine. "The loss of Kandor is the most devastating thing to happen to our planet since the destruction of the third moon. It has global repercussions for our economy, our government, trade, transportation, the whole balance of power. As the cornerstone of his rule, Zod has shown that he's the only man who can defend us against another such attack, but that is not enough for him. He sees this tragedy as a second chance for us. We Kryptonians can rise from the ashes and put ourselves on a new path."

Lara saw the other woman's fervor and recognized that she was sincere. "I still don't understand what you think I can do—"

Aethyr indicated the plain white walls of her chambers. It was obvious where patches of stone resin had been applied. She had hung dyed fabrics and mist-scarves from hooks pounded into the wall, but all the new buildings looked unfinished, unadorned—much too plain to rival the grandeur of Kandor.

"As Zod's personal artist, your work for us will be more vital than anything your parents ever completed. Even though Ora and Lor-Van are gone, let us show everyone that the glory of Krypton remains undiminished. Lara, we want you to take charge of the *design* of our new capital. Make it beautiful. No—*more* than that—make it awe-inspiring."

CHAPTER 48

On the night before Jor-El was to return, Commissioner Zod summoned his people to the former Execution Square, which he had renamed the Square of Hope. It was time to give his faithful followers another cause for celebration.

"Today we christen Krypton's new capital. Xan City is a mark of the past, a reminder of lost glory. Our new city, though built on the rubble of a once-powerful empire, must stand for our whole planet, our entire people." He looked around, scanning the faces. "Therefore, I name it . . . *Kryptonopolis.*"

With encouragement from the Ring members, as well as the diligent Sapphire Guards, the audience started to cheer. The Commissioner smiled at them all, reveling in their acceptance.

A voice shouted out from the crowd. "Why not name it Zod City, while you're at it? You've usurped everything else."

The crowd drew a quick gasp, turning to see who had spoken. An obviously agitated man stepped forward, long yellow hair streaming from both sides of his bald pink scalp. A long walrus mustache dangled down on either side of his mouth, giving him an absurd appearance. His robes bore a bold X-shaped crest denoting his proud noble family. Zod recognized him.

With a quiet hand signal, the Commissioner held back an angry Nam-Ek; the Sapphire Guards remained alert, ready to act. Zod spoke brightly, feigning welcome. "Gil-Ex, you have finally decided to leave your soft cushions and delicate banquet barges in Orvai! We can always use more help, even from one of the pampered older nobles. Join us at our real work. We can train you to do something practical for a change." Some members of the audience chuckled. "I only wish Shor-Em and Tyr-Us would also come to help, rather than complaining from their distant manor houses."

The mustached man scowled, and his pink scalp turned red. "I didn't come to join your efforts, Zod. I came to talk sense into the rest of these people." He looked around. "I want them to see what you're doing to our proud heritage. They don't want to live under a dictatorship!"

Listening to the undertone of murmurs from the crowd, Zod knew the people were on his side. He had trained them well, demonstrated his capabilities. And more and more joined him every day, though he knew that an annoying resistance kept growing like noxious weeds in towns and settlements where he didn't have sufficient control. Yet.

"Gil-Ex, these people can see quite well what I've been doing. That's why they are helping me. Open your eyes and look at what we've accomplished already! We work together as a team to make Krypton strong instead of frightened and weak. The old Council kept us defenseless. None of these good people wants that again, no matter what ineffective form of government you hope they will accept."

Gil-Ex sniffed. "True Kryptonians can see through your lies, Zod. They remember what is right and true about our civilization, and they won't let it be lost." He turned to the rest of the crowd, raising one knobby fist. "All of you, join me! You must reject the tyranny of Zod and his unjust seizure of power."

Koll-Em called out with withering scorn, "We're quite familiar with what the likes of you considered 'right and true about our civilization.' No thank you!"

From his assigned position in the crowd, Da-Es shouted out. "We know what dreams Commissioner Zod has for us. We prefer to follow dreams rather than delusions."

"Have you actually *been* to the crater of Kandor, Gil-Ex?" bellowed muscular Mon-Ra from another part of the crowd. "Have you witnessed firsthand how much destruction our outside enemies can bring against us? Have you bothered?"

Gil-Ex sidestepped the question. "We all know what happened there. I have no need to see for myself. I doubt my heart could bear it—"

"What's the matter? Afraid to get your hands dirty?" jeered Koll-Em.

"You complain about Zod, but what have *you* done to protect us?" called Ran-Ar, another Ring member.

The Ring of Strength continued to rile up the audience, and the crowd's mood turned ugly. It took Gil-Ex several moments to realize that he had chosen the wrong venue for his speech. Zod allowed the anger to simmer until it reached the point where he thought he might lose control. He didn't want them to turn into a mob against this one man, because such extreme reactions might provide the other dissidents with ammunition against him. Worst of all, it could make Gil-Ex into a martyr.

"Please, calm yourselves! This place is the Square of Hope. Here we cherish all that was best about Krypton—including the right to free speech, even when a person states something so patently absurd. Gil-Ex, these people do not support your opinion. I am disheartened by your stubborn refusal to recognize my good intentions. I cannot understand what I've done that causes you to object so vehemently, but I will hear you out. Maybe we can come to a meeting of minds." He extended his hand, sounding so cordial. "Come, we will talk in my tent."

Gil-Ex saw that he had no choice but to agree.

The next day, after Gil-Ex was gone—though no one had seen him leave—Zod issued a happy pronouncement. "The two of us spoke far into the night, and Gil-Ex finally realized his misunderstanding. Since he had isolated himself from the true effects of our tragedy, he was sadly ignorant of our planet's need. He had listened to lies and distortions from power-hungry men trying to cast doubt on our great work." Zod feigned a smile. Passion and sincerity oozed from him with every word. "When he realized that his own well-intentioned comments may have hindered the recovery of Krypton, Gil-Ex was in tears."

Zod's listeners absorbed this dramatic and unsettling turnabout.

They had followed the Commissioner to an empty, ruined city and had sworn their allegiance to him and his grand plans for Krypton. Because they themselves were wholeheartedly convinced, it wasn't unreasonable to believe that Gil-Ex had changed his mind, too. Some workers accepted the explanation with more caution than others did, but all of them gave Zod the benefit of the doubt.

The Commissioner put on his most sincere expression. "I had hoped Gil-Ex would become my ally, but I accept his decision to withdraw from public life. He wants the rest of us to continue without the shadow of his previous accusations." He bowed his head, barely able to hide his satisfied smile.

Over the next few days, other outspoken dissidents disappeared from isolated towns and villages, each leaving behind a heartfelt note of explanation. Some admitted shame, and many urged the people of Krypton to follow Zod.

He knew that even among his own followers a few might not believe the convenient stories. Outside, some people were bound to express their suspicions, claim evidence of conspiracies . . . and his own people would make such comments sound ridiculous. There would always be complaints, but complaints could be dealt with.

And so the Commissioner moved forward with fewer roadblocks. The construction of Kryptonopolis continued.

CHAPTER 49

∞⌕◇‼◇⌐⊤♀◊ 49

After a rushed two days, Jor-El returned from the arctic carrying seed crystal chips he had cut from the key spires of Yar-El's wondrous palace of solitude. From his laboratory at the lonely estate he took the catalysts he needed, metallic powders and liquid impurities that would be drawn into the lattice as the great towers grew.

The manor house, the research building, the mysterious tower that still held Donodon's spaceship—all were quiet and empty. As he surveyed the grounds, an eerie sense of déjà vu reminded him of the abandoned ruins of Xan City. Jor-El felt very alone without Lara. . . .

While he was there, he received a message from Argo City. Zor-El appeared flushed, both exuberant and angry. "I have the data, Jor-El. The accumulated readings are exactly what I expected, *exactly* what I saw before. The core buildup is progressing with astonishing speed, and a planetary explosion is imminent, possibly in less than a year!"

"Unless we do something," Jor-El said. He remembered how easily the Commissioner had approved his plans for the listening outpost. *I trust you to do what is best for Krypton, Jor-El.* "I will make Zod listen. Don't worry, Zor-El. We will take the necessary action."

Back in Kryptonopolis, he found Lara happily working with a crew of artisans to install the panels of an intricate frieze along the lintel of a government building. He watched her unobtrusively for a moment, his heart full of love for her. When she noticed him, Lara ran forward, wiping a smear of paint from her cheek. She excitedly told him how Aethyr and Zod had asked her to participate in the resurrection of the capital city. She felt it was a job to which she was immensely well suited.

Lara had expressed her doubts about the Commissioner's intentions, but Zod seemed to have won her over by giving her this grand project. Much the same way, he realized, as Zod had ingratiated himself to Jor-El by allowing him free rein to conduct the research he had always wanted to do. Tempting Jor-El with unfettered science and Lara with a history-making art project. He could see that the Commissioner was a very effective manipulator, but the man was also sincere in his passion. He and Lara had not seen any more altruism from any of the outspoken city leaders.

Taking the dark bag that contained the seed crystal chips he had harvested, he met with Commissioner Zod and three members of the Ring of Strength inside the government palace. On blueprint films, Jor-El described the structures he could create with the materials he'd found, and how much of the landscape they would dominate. "Once I trigger the accelerated process, the chain reaction of crystal growth will occur without any further guidance from me. I need to get it right the first time."

The Commissioner's eyes had a bright gleam. "I am anxious to get started."

Jor-El shook his head. "We've got to wait until nightfall to do our preparations. The seed crystals must remain covered until everything is ready. Once they're exposed to light, the chain reaction begins."

Zod glanced up at the deepening sky color through the tentlike fabric that covered the damaged ceiling. "Rao will set soon. Tomorrow, Kryptonopolis will no longer be my dream, but a shining reality."

In the dark of the night Jor-El set out his seed crystals at the four corners of the Square of Hope and atop Lookout Hill at the outskirts of the ancient city. He positioned each brittle seed carefully, measured, checked, and double-checked. Zod, Aethyr, and Nam-Ek accompanied him, watching every step of the process, their excitement tangible in the cooling night air.

An hour before midnight, Jor-El added the catalysts and liquid impurities, checked the angles and positioning yet again, and stepped back, satisfied. "Tomorrow," he told them, "be here exactly at sunrise."

The next day, when he and Lara arrived in the Square of Hope in the predawn darkness, Zod was already there, pacing impatiently. Nam-Ek stood motionless, as big as a statue; aloof, Aethyr lounged on a new stone bench. No-Ton and Koll-Em also joined them, rubbing their sleepy eyes.

The colors presaging sunrise flooded across the eastern sky. "Any minute now," Jor-El said. The air was thick with anticipation.

The roiling red fringe of Rao rose above the horizon, spilling crimson light across the landscape. When the first rays struck the seed crystals, the reaction was instantaneous. At the four corners of the Square of Hope the first crystals began to sparkle. Energized by the sunlight, they drank in the catalyst powders like dry sponges absorbing a flood.

A hexagonal spire shot upward, four times the size of the original crystal, and it kept growing, thickening. It spread out subsidiary crystal branches that followed the design Jor-El had programmed into the base lattice. The extraordinary rush of growth made a thunderous cracking and popping sound. Perfectly symmetrical with the upreaching spire, the crystal's anchor root plunged downward, drawing more material from the rocks and soil. Stone paving tiles at the square's perimeter buckled and broke.

At all four corners of the square, shining spires seemed to be competing with one another as they raced toward the sky, rapidly dwarfing the other structures in Kryptonopolis. On Lookout Hill outside the city, a fifth gleaming tower rose higher and higher.

Commissioner Zod's face showed deep satisfaction. Nam-Ek reacted with childish glee as the components continued to erupt and unfold like a puzzle made of diamonds and emeralds. By the time Rao had risen fully, the red giant shone down upon an entirely new city.

"This does indeed rival Kandor!" Zod clasped the scientist's shoulders. "You have done everything I expected—and more. I knew you would not let me down. Krypton owes you a debt greater than I can ever repay."

Jor-El seized the moment. He had been considering how to bring up the matter. "Then it's now my turn to ask you a favor, Commissioner. It is vitally important to our planet's survival."

Zod's eyes took on a calculating look; then his expression shifted again. "You have never asked for any kind of boon before. If it is within my power to grant . . . "

"As you know, my brother discovered dangerous instabilities in the core of our planet. The Council refused to take any action until Zor-El provided them with extensive data."

Zod nodded slowly, cautiously. "Yes, I was present when you and your brother made those claims. And the Council, as usual, chose to ignore problems rather than address them." His voice held a heavy undertone of caution.

"We've all experienced the increasingly severe quakes. More than one tidal wave has struck the coast, and massive volcanic eruptions continue in the southern continent. The core pressure is still growing—and now I do have a full set of data. The situation is precisely as bad as I feared. Trust me, Commissioner. The evidence is indisputable."

He could see Zod trying to decide how to respond. "Even if I accept your warning, what can we do about it?"

Jor-El's words came in a breathless rush. "I've been thinking about the old prototypes I submitted to your Commission. Do you remember an intense cutting laser I called a Rao beam? At the time I felt it would be useful for boring tunnels through mountains, for mining, and for construction. Your Commission decided it was too risky." He lowered his voice to a grumble. "As usual."

Zod tapped his fingers together, fully focused on Jor-El rather than on the still-growing crystal spires behind them. "I seem to recall it. But if the plans were confiscated, what will you do now? Start again from scratch?"

Jor-El gave him a wry smile. "Commissioner, just because you took my drawings and destroyed my prototypes doesn't mean that the *idea* is destroyed." He tapped his temple. "Every invention I ever created, every design and every process is right here, in my head. I remember them all perfectly."

Zod took a moment to process the startling revelation. "Intriguing."

He nodded slowly to himself, then responded with a thin smile, as if he had suddenly decided on a different strategy for playing this game. "And could your Rao beam also be configured as a weapon? Something we could fire at attacking alien ships if they should come against us? It would help the defense of Krypton."

Jor-El considered. "I suppose. Once the Rao-beam generator is erected, installed, and calibrated, I see no reason why its target point couldn't be shifted."

"And if I allow you to build this Rao beam, I presume you intend to drill some sort of shaft through the crust? Like a pressure-release valve?"

"That is the theory. The best drilling site may be the crater of Kandor, though the project will cause substantial damage to the area. There's no way around it—"

"That doesn't concern me. Kandor is already a no-man's-land. Best to put it to some use," Zod said. "But I am more troubled by the fact that your own brother has been less than accepting of me. Perhaps if Zor-El issued a statement of wholehearted support for me from Argo City?"

Jor-El wanted to snap at the Commissioner for worrying more about personal politics than the fate of the whole world. "Then show him that you're completely different from the weak Council. With your leadership, Commissioner, we can prevent a worldwide disaster. Aren't you the man who swore to take any action necessary to protect us?"

Aethyr leaned close to the Commissioner with a strangely hungry look in her eyes. She said in a quiet, breathy voice, "Zod . . . the savior of Krypton."

He seemed to like the sound of that very much.

CHAPTER 50

The visitor came to Argo City in secret. After crossing one of the bridges, he arrived in the middle of the night and made his way toward Zor-El's villa. Under his dark hood, he refused to reveal his identity, but insisted to the household sentry that the city leader would see him.

Zor-El dismissed the volunteer guards who had dutifully blocked the stranger's entry. He frowned at the mysterious guest. "You can't expect my guards to blithely let you enter as if you were an old friend."

The man came into the light and pulled back the hood. "But I am an old friend."

Zor-El was shocked to see the man's haggard appearance, the haunted look in his reddened eyes, his sunken cheeks, as if he hadn't slept or eaten well in days. "Tyr-Us! Why didn't you inform me you were coming? What's happened to you?"

"The same thing that will happen to all of us if we're not careful." He looked over his shoulder toward the sentries as if they couldn't be trusted, toward the night as if something dangerous were after him. "Please let me inside. I need shelter, just for a little while."

Zor-El hurried the man through the door as he snapped to his guards, "Make sure no one else enters my home. See that we're not disturbed." Their master's abrupt reaction seemed to frighten them more than anything else.

Alura saw the troubled expression on her husband's face, and quickly led him and Tyr-Us into a withdrawing room filled with exotic plants. She lit several solar crystals.

Tyr-Us stood weak and shaking in the middle of the room. He touched the enormous flowers with fingers that trembled with wonder. "It rejuvenates me to know that something is flourishing on Krypton while our government festers and rots." He drew a deep breath and squeezed his eyes shut.

"Tell me everything, Tyr-Us. When did you leave Corril? So many other noble sons have abruptly stepped out of public view. When I'd heard nothing from you in weeks, I thought maybe you had joined them."

Tyr-Us's eyes were wild. "I could have vanished, too! The Commissioner's thugs have been following me. I saw dark figures in Corril walking down the metal streets, pretending to be visitors, but they all had those armbands Zod's followers wear."

"I've seen them in Argo City as well. I don't like them."

"Watch yourself, Zor-El—for they are certainly watching you. You should cast them out of your city before they cause further damage."

Zor-El was disturbed by the suggestion. "I can't just arrest them and say that their views are forbidden, no matter how fanatical they may seem. That would turn me into a dictator as bad as you claim Zod is."

Alura picked a flower and pushed it into Tyr-Us's face. "Smell this." Involuntarily, the shaken man drew a quick breath, and the stimulant perfume made him stand straighter. "Eat these." She held out two berries, one blue and one red.

"What do they do? Will they drug me?"

"No, they will strengthen you."

Eyes narrowed, Tyr-Us looked at the berries. "How do I know I can trust you? How do I know I can trust anyone today, even the two of you?"

Zor-El grabbed the man's arm. "You know you can trust me because you *know* me. What has changed you so much? You're frightening us."

"You should be frightened! Do you know how many others have disappeared? Shor-Em has been attacked twice, but managed to drive off the assault. His guards were unable to capture or interrogate the ones who struck out at him. Fully fourteen of us who spoke out against Zod have 'retired,' and no one has heard from them again. Think of it, Zor-El. You know it makes no sense."

"Yes, I was surprised to hear that Gil-Ex had decided to support Zod. It made no sense after everything he'd been saying."

"You know he was a vain and self-righteous man. Do you think Gil-Ex would just quietly hide himself? Never. I am the son of Council Head Jul-Us, and I should have had a seat on the Council someday. So should you, Zor-El."

"I have Argo City."

"You won't if Zod takes it away from you." Tyr-Us finally ate the two berries and sighed. He looked at Alura. "I'm sorry to have distrusted you."

Two staff members brought in a hurriedly prepared meal and a large pitcher of herbal tea that Alura brewed for its strengthening properties. Tyr-Us was startled by the unexpected servants and looked as if he might bolt, but Zor-El took the tray of food and quickly dismissed the helpers.

The haggard man sat down on a bench surrounded by lush herbs, shaking his head miserably. "The risk increases with every person who sees me. Just by being here, I increase the danger to you both."

"Tell me more after you've eaten." Zor-El nudged the plates closer.

Tyr-Us seemed queasy and apparently uninterested, but once he tasted the food, he ate so ravenously that Zor-El feared he might become sick.

"You haven't supported Zod and his overthrow of the true Krypton government," Tyr-Us said between bites. "But you've been careful not to openly oppose him, either."

"Shor-Em thinks I should have done so long ago, but I had my own disaster here, remember. Argo City still has much rebuilding to do."

"If you had resoundingly supported our claims, you'd quite possibly be dead like all the others—like I am soon to be."

"Nonsense!" Alura said. "You can stay here. We will protect you."

"You can't protect me, and I'll only endanger you if I stay here. I won't do that." He looked up at Zor-El. "You are my friend, an ally. If we don't organize all of our supporters, soon Zod will have the whole planet in his grip. He'll do whatever he wants, and I believe he wants a war. If we ever receive another alien visitor like Donodon, Zod is likely to open fire just to test all the new destructive toys he's creating."

"You must be exaggerating. What proof do you have?"

"His agents continue to destroy all proof and silence any criticism. Can you afford to take the risk that I might be wrong? I need to hide, but I have to go somewhere they won't think to find me."

As Tyr-Us looked down at his empty plate, Zor-El had an idea. "There's an isolated dacha in the hills near my old family estate. My father lived the last years of his life there, but he died recently. My mother abandoned the house and came to live here in Argo City. No one goes there. No one would find you. You'd be safe, and you would put no one else at risk."

Tyr-Us's face lit up. "Are you certain?"

"We insist," Alura said.

Their guest suddenly became anxious again. "But you must not tell your brother. Jor-El is conspiring with Zod. He's helping him to conquer the world."

Zor-El scowled. "My brother is working for the good of Krypton. He always does."

"But he cooperates with the Commissioner. Many have seen it."

"Jor-El is a good man who has no interest in politics whatsoever."

"Zod may well be fooling him!"

Zor-El held up his hands. "My brother is not easily fooled, and Commissioner Zod *did* step up to lead the people during the crisis . . . which is more than Gil-Ex or anyone else did." He sighed. "Nevertheless, I will keep your secret. You have my promise."

The gaunt man nodded, relieved.

"We will find a place for you to sleep," Alura said. "We'll pack up some clean clothes and any supplies you need."

"It would be good to wash . . . and rest."

Zor-El led him to a room reserved for guests, and Tyr-Us was so exhausted that he fell asleep as soon as he collapsed onto the blankets. Without disturbing him, Zor-El and Alura set out clean garments and towels. Cleansing crystals in the adjacent bathing room would be ready for him whenever he chose. . . .

But the next morning when Zor-El went to check on his guest, Tyr-Us was gone. The desperate man must have taken the clothes, washed quickly, and slipped away without anyone seeing him. He left no note, no indication that he had ever been there—presumably to protect them.

Alura stared at the empty bed, the dirty clothes in a pile on the floor, which they would have to destroy. "Do you think he was abducted? Those people following him, did they get to him in our house? Past our guards?"

"Now you sound as paranoid as he did." Zor-El shook his head, ashamed at his sharp tone. "I'm sorry. I don't mean to belittle his concerns. Those other disappearances, especially Gil-Ex, are very suspicious. We'll keep watch on our own streets, step up the civilian guard to make sure you and I stay safe. I really don't know what to think about Commissioner Zod."

Later that morning, he received a surprise message from his brother. Jor-El wore a glad expression, and his blue eyes glittered. "Zor-El, I have good news! Just as I promised, I convinced Commissioner Zod to let us take action about the core buildup. Thanks to your data, he's agreed to allow the two of us to begin work on a massive project." From the communication plate, Jor-El grinned. "He will supply materials, manpower—anything we need."

Zor-El was taken aback, especially in light of Tyr-Us's dire warnings about the Commissioner. Though he had suspicions, he could not turn down a chance like this. He knew the danger in the planet's core, and saving the planet was more important than politics. "And what does he propose we do?"

"That's up to us. I have an approach we might take. Come and work with me. We can get started right away."

Zor-El remained silent after his brother had terminated the transmission, filled with conflicting thoughts.

Alura stood behind him, having listened to the entire message. "What are you going to do? Can you trust Zod, considering what Tyr-Us said?"

"I'll reserve judgment and see for myself if there are any strings attached to this offer. But I have to put the fate of Krypton above everything else. If the Commissioner means to prove that he's different from the old Council, and he's willing to let me do what I *know* has to be done, how can I let politics get in the way? We're talking about the end of the world."

CHAPTER 51

From memory, Jor-El redrew his plans for the Rao beam, which he had surrendered to the Commission long ago. Each subsystem, the gem-like concentrator, the beam focuser, the tall open-framed support der-rick—everything came back to him. Now that he applied himself, he even made improvements to the original design, and this time the Commission for Technology Acceptance would not censor his idea.

Before even discussing the overall plan with his brother, Jor-El dispatched construction teams up into the mountains overlooking the Kandor valley. Excavators plowed a road up to the highest summit of the range, the perfect spot from which to perform the high-energy drilling project. From the peak, the vantage offered an unobstructed view of the deep, ugly scar where the capital city had been gouged out, leaving an incredibly deep hole.

When Zor-El finally arrived from Argo City, the dark-haired man was taken aback to see how much Jor-El had already completed. "I thought we would be working on this together—sharing theories, calculations, designs."

Jor-El couldn't believe his brother's attitude. "When did this become a competition?"

"It's not supposed to be."

"Good. I don't care about glory or awards. I simply want to stop the core buildup, and I didn't think you would want me to waste any time.

Haven't we waited long enough already, or did you want to do things like the old Council?"

Zor-El was thrown off guard. Though he had a difficult time seeing past Tyr-Us's frightened accusations, this was his brother. Jor-El was a powerful scientist with many brilliant ideas, and his one and only priority was science. He was not a conspirator. "Sorry I jumped to conclusions. Yes, let's get this done before Zod changes his mind. What is your plan?"

Jor-El pointed down to the near-bottomless pit, explaining that the Rao beam was the only viable way to drill so deeply into the crust. "The thickness of the crust varies around the world, and here it's relatively thin. By my measurements, the crater is already almost a kilometer deep. We can use that as a starting point."

Zor-El studied the beam design and admitted that he could not have done better.

Jor-El continued, "The building quakes we keep feeling are the planet's attempts to relieve pressure where the stresses are greatest and the crust is weakest, as are the volcanoes in the southern continent. But if we create a second release point here, we may—and I emphasize *may*—dampen the instabilities in the core."

Zor-El scratched his dark hair, still thinking. "Have you given any thought to what happens once we start burning down into the mantle? How were you planning to hold the integrity of the shaft when the walls are melting in every direction?"

"That does pose a problem."

Zor-El gave him a steely look. "You aren't the only one who can invent things! Remember the powerful field I developed to protect my diamondfish probes? I expanded the concept to reinforce Argo City's seawall after the recent tidal wave. We can use the same field to maintain the integrity of our drilling core."

Jor-El's eyebrows went up. "Like a protective liner?"

Zor-El's hard expression broke into a smile. "You always understood me better than anyone else, Jor-El."

"Great minds think alike," he joked. "And Krypton certainly needs 'great minds' right now."

"To act decisively—something the old Council could never do."

Jor-El clapped his brother on the shoulder. "Then we should get drilling."

The tent encampment and outlying settlements were now entirely abandoned, the last stragglers sent down to Kryptonopolis. Fortunate timing, because once the Rao beam drilled through the crust, the lush Kandor valley would become a disaster zone. The scientist No-Ton was on-site as Zod's representative to observe the preparations, but the Ring member clearly felt out of his league, and left the decisions to Jor-El and his brother.

"We should calculate the projected magma outflow," Jor-El said. "How much will we need to release in order to bring the unstable core back to safe levels?"

"According to the data I collected, the eruptions in the southern continent were too widespread, and the depth was incorrect." In the days since gathering his data, Zor-El had completed extensive follow-up calculations. "By unleashing the magma here, though, we'll do more good than a dozen eruptions down in the southern hemisphere."

With the cooperation of numerous technicians and engineers and full access to any resources Jor-El requested, the Rao beam facility was completed with astonishing speed. On a high derrick atop the windy mountain peak, the intensifier crystals and lenses were ready to be aligned; once they were shifted into place, the crystals would focus the blinding, penetrating beam. Additional technical stations now occupied several nearby subpeaks, where huge collecting arrays of prisms and mirrors gathered the power of the great red sun each day.

White hair blowing in the stiff, cold breeze, Jor-El sat on a rocky outcropping near the control shack beside the high derrick, waiting for Rao to reach its zenith. "It's time, Zor-El. Are you ready?"

"I've been advocating this for months. Let's not stand on ceremony when Krypton could explode at any moment."

Calling for help from No-Ton and the technicians, the two men shifted the lenses into alignment. Drawing from the sun and from the solar generators, the huge central crystal dangled like a pendant within the framework, glowing, charging, until it spat out a razor-sharp beam. Faster than an eyeblink, it struck the crater with pinpoint accuracy, hit the deep bottom, and began drilling into the crust.

A chimney plume of vaporized rock, steam, and smoke boiled upward. Debris flew in all directions; hot rocks showered down, and hellish smoke rose from the drilling site. Although Krypton's straining core pressure demanded to be released, even the intense Rao beams would take days to penetrate the kilometers of crust to reach the molten mantle.

Hour after hour, the derrick shuddered with strain from the power output. The shaft burrowed deeper, and the two brothers waited side by side, watching from atop the summit.

CHAPTER 52

While Jor-El was gone for weeks setting up the huge Rao-beam project, Lara remained in Kryptonopolis to paint breathtaking new frescoes and assemble mosaics. Commissioner Zod expressed great support for her work. He said the glorious art helped to anchor his capital city's place in cultural history.

Aethyr's enthusiasm for Zod's "new Krypton" seemed boundless, though Lara wasn't sure exactly what role her friend played in the government. The other woman often slipped away unexpectedly; taking one or two Ring members and some Sapphire Guards, she would disappear for days and come back at odd hours. Whenever Lara asked about it, Aethyr remained evasive. "Sometimes a new government doesn't run as smoothly as it should."

Meanwhile, Lara intently studied the numerous buildings being erected or repaired, then sketched out her artistic plans for them. She transformed the blocky walls from plain, serviceable structures into truly majestic monuments that would surpass anything Jax-Ur had created long ago.

The five immense new crystalline towers had already altered Kryptonopolis, transforming the construction site into a dramatic work of architectural art. On Lookout Hill the tallest monolith gleamed in the red sunlight. Despite Jor-El's insistence that the gesture was not necessary, Zod had proudly named that structure the Tower of Yar-El.

Lara's main project was to embellish a structure designated as the new treasury building. She sent detailed plans to armies of her help-ful apprentices, then went to inspect the numerous decoration proj-ects under way across the city. In Kryptonopolis, Lara supervised five times as many workers as her parents had ever overseen. All this was entirely new to her, but she was sure Ora and Lor-Van would have been pleased.

She stopped to admire an intricate and colorful mosaic her crew was installing on the new Academy headquarters, to be named after Cor-Zod. The mosaic's pattern of carefully arranged pieces was still not obvious at a glance, although she had a clear picture of it in her mind.

"Magnificent." Zod had come up behind her, accompanied by Aethyr. "But Krypton has a new request to make of you, an even more difficult task." The Commissioner's resonant voice sounded personable.

Not sure what to say, Lara ran her gaze over all the workers engaged in assembling the mosaic. "I don't have time for anything else, Com-missioner. With Jor-El gone, I am already devoting every waking hour to this work."

"I would expect nothing less from the wife of Jor-El." Zod stepped close, and his presence fell over Lara like the shadow from a thun-dercloud. "You've already drawn your designs, and we have plenty of competent supervisors to ensure that the work continues without pause. However, Aethyr suggested you as the perfect person for an extremely important project, one with even more enduring relevance than any of these works of art."

"A different sort of art," Aethyr added.

Before Zod could explain further, one of the mosaic workers stum-bled and knocked over his basket full of cut tiles from the high scaffold-ing. He yelled a warning to the people below as hundreds of colorful chips tumbled through the air. Sparkling like a shattered rainbow, they pattered on the flagstones. The other workers groaned, not because any-one had been hurt, but because gathering up all the pieces would be so tedious.

The Commissioner turned away, clearly not wanting his devoted followers to see his stormy expression of contempt and disappointment, but Lara noticed. It took him only a fraction of a second to compose a fresh smile for her. "Aethyr tells me you have a background in history, and that your instructors at the Academy commended your writing talent. Most important, you grasp the context of the great events around us."

The compliment made Lara oddly uncomfortable. She did not tell him of the detailed personal journal she had already been surreptitiously keeping. "Yes, history and writing are among my interests."

Aethyr ignored the chaos behind them. "Lara, it is important to make sure that history remembers Zod properly. These are turbulent times, and when emotions run high, memory isn't always accurate."

The Commissioner nodded. "You are the perfect person to be my official biographer and the chronicler of my new reign, to set down the official version of events and determine how history remembers me— remembers all of us."

Lara was not so easily recruited. "You want me to write propaganda for you?"

"Not propaganda—the truth."

Aethyr interjected, "There is no such thing as completely objective truth, Lara. Everything the Commissioner does can be seen from varying perspectives. Though many of the complainers have now withdrawn their objections, some people like Shor-Em still argue with his decisions out of petty jealousy and a petulant resistance to change. You remember how much Jor-El has fought against that kind of backward thinking. We are in this together."

Lara crossed her arms over her chest, still not convinced. "I also remember, Commissioner, that *you* were the one who censored most of my husband's inventions. If not for you, Jor-El's discoveries could have benefited Krypton for many years. But your Commission held him back."

"That was not my choice, Lara. I followed the Council's guidance, and for that I admit my error. Have I not proved myself since then? Look at what I am allowing Jor-El and his brother to do right now. Drilling to Krypton's core! A project the old Council would never have approved, no matter how much data they reviewed." He looked at her intently. "Won't you give me the benefit of the doubt?"

Skilled artisans scurried around the base of the scaffolding like hive insects, busily picking up the mosaic pieces; within minutes, they had cleaned up the mess. "See how efficient Kryptonians can be if they work together and follow a single leader?" Aethyr said. "That's why we have to help everyone see what Zod can do for them. If you write our history properly, you'll be helping to save Krypton as surely as your husband's drilling project will."

Before she could reply, Lara fought against a sudden twisting in her stomach; she took long, deep breaths through her nostrils. At first she thought it was some instinctive revulsion to what they were asking her to do, but it was merely her pregnancy. Even though she loved to feel the baby growing inside her, she had recently begun suffering bouts of morning sickness.

Neither Aethyr nor Zod seemed to notice her discomfiture. Trying to calm her nausea, Lara spoke to them through clenched teeth. "We are still in the midst of such chaotic events. There's not enough perspective for a true history."

"One must start somewhere, and events are fresh in your mind." Zod brushed a speck from his chest. "I will grant you full access, so you can get the truth directly from me, instead of listening to any rumors you might hear."

Aethyr added with a snort, "Borga City continues to mount a smear campaign against the Commissioner, disregarding all we've accomplished. They completely ignore the fact that we have the nova javelins to protect Krypton. Zod has asked to meet with Shor-Em to discuss matters, but the man refuses."

Zod nodded gravely. "Fortunately, many of those who spoke out against me have been convinced otherwise. Gil-Ex was the first, as you know, and many others have respectfully retired into seclusion. Tyr-Us recently joined them, too."

Lara hadn't heard this. "*Tyr-Us* now supports you? That's an amazing turnabout."

"He saw that his outspoken criticism was harming Krypton's chances for recovery. We won't be hearing any more complaints from him."

Lara bit her lower lip, trying to hide her skepticism. "In order to make your chronicle accurate, I should speak to those men, include their points of view. Let them state in their own words what they originally thought and why they changed their minds. That will be a good way to provide a balanced perspective."

Zod was instantly troubled. "No, the focus should be on me and my goals. Wasting time on them is merely a distraction. For now, you have enough material to begin writing." He gestured toward the scaffolding. "I will assign other people to oversee these art projects."

"Wait! I—I haven't agreed yet."

"Of course you have, Lara." Aethyr patted her on the shoulder in a patronizing gesture. "Of course you have."

CHAPTER 53

∞ ⌂◇‖◇⌐Т̈◊ 53

The intense red beams continued to pound into the crater of Kandor, melting through the crust. Enclosed by the distant walls of the broad valley, trapped dust and smoke made the sky thick and hazy. Even up in the mountains, every breath tasted of ozone, burnt metal, and ash.

Though Jor-El covered his face with a snug breathing mask, his eyes still burned and watered. Zor-El stared into the ripples of thermal disturbance that radiated from the pulsing Rao beam. No-Ton and his technicians bustled about, amazed and intimidated by what they were doing.

All day, every day, as soon as the red sun rose high enough to charge the collectors, energy was funneled to the focusing point to generate the Rao beam. The drilling continued unabated until sunset, at which point the beam weakened and finally faded. After dark, the brothers ate premade meals in their temporary hut and reviewed the current day's progress and the next day's plans with No-Ton and his team. The two pored over cartography sheets and depth-analysis simulators to get a better picture of the inexplicable shifts in Krypton's core.

Each evening, Jor-El spoke with Lara in Kryptonopolis. Just seeing her image on the communication plate lifted his spirits. When she mentioned that Zod had asked her to be his official biographer, he had mixed feelings and sensed that she did, too. His brother expressed doubts about the Commissioner's motives and tactics, especially after Tyr-Us's warnings.

Jor-El told him not to worry. "Lara isn't easily swayed. She'll tell the truth, whether Zod likes it or not."

"He may well censor her."

Jor-El frowned, recalling many former encounters with the man. "Yes, he's done that plenty of times before."

The Commissioner sent brusque official messages encouraging Jor-El to complete his task as quickly as possible and return to his weapons development work. He even suggested that Zor-El come to Kryptonopolis and offer his help and insights, now that his concerns about the core pressure were being addressed. Zor-El gave a noncommittal answer, hesitant to reconsider his opinion of the man.

Several hours after sunset, the zone around the crater had cooled enough that the brothers could venture down to the drilling site and take additional readings. None of the other technicians wanted to accompany them into the hellish place. The smoky air was nearly unbreathable, forcing the two to wear protective goggles and filter masks.

In the charred darkness, Jor-El and his brother walked through the remnants of the empty refugee camp, feeling the eerie mood, the strange sense of loss. So much had been abandoned in place: support frameworks, sanitation pits, garbage dumps. Toxic soot covered the landscape for kilometers around. Rocks cracked, rumbled, and popped as they cooled. Waves of heat shimmered up from the impossibly deep hole. Jor-El hoped that later generations wouldn't curse them for causing so much destruction. Then again, if later generations survived at all, it would be due to their efforts here.

Zor-El walked ahead, intent on reaching the lip of the crater. From his pack, he removed a glistening scaled device, another of his diamondfish detectors. Once activated, it squirmed and twitched in his hands, its impenetrable armor flashing reflections from their handlights.

Zor-El touched a particular scale to activate a fuzzy, glowing envelope around the diamondfish. Leaning forward, he whispered, "Drop down to the warm depths, my friend, and tell us how far we have drilled." He tossed the diamondfish over the edge, and it tumbled, flashing, into the shadows. He tuned the handheld receiver and watched the trace as the diamondfish fell for more than four minutes down the shaft. When the mechanical creature finally struck the bottom, it took a moment to recover and get its bearings before it began sending back images of the melted rock.

Jor-El looked at the readings. "Yes, we should break through by midmorning tomorrow."

Zor-El remained silent for a moment and then said, as if the thought had just occurred to him, "I've revisited my calculations using a slightly different set of assumptions and initial conditions. There may be a . . . problem."

"You revised your calculations? Shouldn't I proof them? What did you find?"

"There's a chance—an extremely slight one—that instead of relieving the pressure in the core, this breach just might . . . crack open the planet. All of Krypton could explode like a punctured pressure vessel."

Jor-El stared at him in disbelief. "We're going to break through tomorrow, and *now* you raise this possibility?"

"As I said, it's a very remote chance, hardly worth mentioning," Zor-El replied, sounding defensive. "You know what's happening down there. We have a choice that's not really a choice at all. Even raising the question would have invited months or years of tedious discussions—discussions among people who haven't got the slightest understanding of the science. You and I are the only ones qualified to make the decision."

"For the whole planet?"

"Yes, for the whole planet! We either accept the risk that our actions *might* cause a disaster, or we do nothing and *ensure* a disaster. I'll take the chance."

Jor-El let out a long sigh. "Let me look over your calculations. If I don't find the risk acceptable, I'm calling a halt to our operations here."

Zor-El was not happy, but he conceded. Later, back in their habitation hut, they hunched over the light of a glowcrystal as Jor-El pored over line after line of his brother's mathematics. He did find one error, but it was in Krypton's favor, reducing the chances of disaster even further. Zor-El flushed with embarrassment, even though the results made the risk of planetary destruction orders of magnitude less likely.

Jor-El was still uneasy, but could see no better choice. "All right, I'm satisfied. We drill tomorrow, and we finish this."

CHAPTER 54

∞⛫◇‼◇⊸T̈◌ 54

The next day, the scarlet beams shot downward again, and after four hours, the valley floor began to rumble. The detectors in the substations went wild. Jor-El ran to his brother. "We're there!"

Zor-El went with him to the overlook and raised his viewing lenses to stare down into the Kandor valley. The Rao beams burned and burned. "Get ready. This is going to be spectacular."

He was right.

The deep crater suddenly became the mouth of a cannon, firing a fusillade of blazing yellow-white lava into the sky. Propelled by all the power bottled up within the planet, the stream of magma squirted straight up, higher than the mountains, higher than the clouds—and it kept rising. Curiously, some of the lava had exotic emerald streaks, like green ribbons wound through the plume of liquid fire.

"Shut down the Rao beam!" Jor-El shouted to the awed technicians. When they didn't move, he raced to the controls himself and swung aside the concentrating lens. The red energy bolt faded into the air, leaving only ripples of disturbance in its path.

The lava fountain continued to spew upward.

"If that column of lava reaches escape velocity, it will shoot all the way out of our atmosphere," Jor-El said. "Depending on how long this stream lasts, we might soon have a ring of cooled rubble drifting around our planet."

"Prepare for more meteor showers in the coming months," Zor-El said.

Jor-El grinned as he mused, "If the debris field spreads out all through Krypton's orbit, Zod will probably consider it another defense against invading alien ships."

"Then make sure you explain that to him."

Lightweight pebbles—more like foam than rock because of their many gas inclusions—began to patter all around them. As larger chunks started to crash to the ground, the technicians scrambled for shelter in the control huts. Zor-El dragged his brother into the nearest metal building, and from inside they listened to the staccato rattling on the roof, like a heavy hailstorm.

The lava continued to gush unabated for four days, and finally Zor-El's seismic instruments indicated that Krypton's core had begun to shift and relax, reaching a new and more stable equilibrium now that some of the pressure was released. Soon, when the fiery jet started to lose power, they would place a force-field cap on the core shaft to seal the lava geyser entirely.

Venturing down from the mountains to the perimeter of the debris field, Zor-El had taken samples of the unexpected green mineral to study, but its structure and the reason for its exotic transformation remained a mystery to him. "Our world is changing in ways that I cannot begin to explain."

Jor-El looked out across the valley, where brushfires had burned away vegetation and rendered the once-verdant area as stark as the surface of a moon. "We've caused some of those changes ourselves, Zor-El. What are the global consequences of what we've done? With all the ash in the atmosphere, the climate will change, the weather patterns . . . "

His brother's dark brows drew together. "Damage or destruction, those were our two choices. Now our planet will survive, thanks to what we've done. It may take centuries, but Krypton will recover." He raised his eyebrows. "In fact, if your Commissioner is so intent on being our savior, he can demonstrate his goodwill by sending teams to reclaim the landscape."

When Zod sent his congratulations and announced a procession from Kryptonopolis, Zor-El abruptly decided it was time for him to leave. His excuses were very transparent. "I've been away from Argo City and Alura for too long. Now that I know the planet won't fall apart, I've got a city to run."

"The Commissioner wants to issue a commendation to *both* of us. Neither of us cares about it—but if I have to endure it, then you have to be here, too. This is as much your triumph as mine."

Zor-El seemed very anxious. "No, you can take full credit. Zod's applause means nothing to me."

"And when have I ever asked for accolades?"

"Jor-El, listen to me. I *don't* want to stay, but you can use this to build your political capital. Someday you may need to make a request of Zod. Make sure he understands the debt he owes you."

On the high mountain peaks, the winds were always cold, despite the gushing lava geyser that continued to blast into the sky. Zod's celebratory procession arrived, accompanied by Aethyr, Nam-Ek, and a military escort. Jor-El watched the convoy of levitating vehicles wind their way up the crushed-rock roadway to reach the compound. He hoped to catch sight of Lara among them, but apparently she had remained behind in Kryptonopolis. He couldn't guess whether or not that had been her own choice.

By the time the group gathered near the tall derrick, Zod had had plenty of time to view the spectacular magma plume. He nodded solemnly. "This is most impressive, Jor-El."

Ferret-faced Koll-Em, the only member of the Ring of Strength who had come along, bustled to the cliff edge to survey the devastated valley. "It's spectacular! No other city leader would have dared to launch such a demonstration of power." He spun around to grin at Zod.

"It was a scientific imperative," Jor-El said. "*Not* a demonstration of power."

Koll-Em didn't seem to understand the distinction. "My brother could never have conceived a project of this scope or this urgency! You have saved the world, Commissioner."

Zod stroked his neat beard. "Is that what I've done, Jor-El? Saved the world?"

"Well, you . . . " For a moment the scientist didn't know how to answer. "By granting us your permission and backing for this work, you did something the former Council never could have managed. Our preliminary seismic readings suggest that the critical pressure is rapidly decreasing. So, yes, it would seem the world is saved."

"Good. You've already instructed No-Ton on how to seal the geyser when the time comes, haven't you?" When Jor-El nodded, Zod ordered the rest of the technical team to remain behind and monitor the lava geyser for the time being. He beamed at Jor-El. "Now that you're satisfied Krypton is safe, you can devote yourself to matters of more immediate importance. I believe there is a great deal of work—not to mention your lovely new wife—waiting for you in Kryptonopolis."

CHAPTER 55
㏄⚬◇‼◇⚬T̈◇ 55

As he left the mountain installation long before the Commissioner's entourage arrived, Zor-El had more than one reason to be uneasy. On the last day of drilling, No-Ton had made an offhand comment that Tyr-Us had also withdrawn his objections to Zod's rule, and then—like so many others—had "retired from public view."

Zor-El could not forget the genuine terror on the distraught man's face when he'd come to Argo City late at night. Tyr-Us would never have changed his mind. Never. Something was very wrong.

Anxious to be away, and oddly reluctant to express his true fears to his brother, Zor-El had departed from the mountains on his personal transport platform, but he did not return immediately to Argo City. Instead, he made a long detour westward to his parents' empty dacha in the foothills. He clung to the hope that Tyr-Us had simply dropped out of sight and that opportunistic Zod had fabricated a story to suit his own plans. If he could bring Tyr-Us out of hiding, Zor-El could prove that the Commissioner was lying.

He traveled the cleared paths in the blackwood forest and followed a creek into the heavily wooded dell where the familiar dacha stood. When he stepped off the flying platform and approached, he found the rustic house dark, the garden overgrown, the windows shuttered, much as his mother had left it when she'd gone with him and Alura back to Argo City. Although she had never complained about the years spent tending her catatonic husband, Zor-El knew his mother was relieved to be part of a community again.

He moved cautiously closer, in case a paranoid Tyr-Us had installed traps or warning devices. "Hello!" he called, going up to the door. "It's Zor-El. I'm alone." He waited, heard nothing. "Tyr-Us, are you there?"

The dacha remained silent. He tried the door and was surprised to find it unlocked. The latch was broken. Someone had forcibly entered, smashing part of the door, even though Zor-El had told Tyr-Us how to access the key. On the porch he found a gouge in the wood and a stain that might have been blood.

Alert for danger, Zor-El stepped inside. The house was dim, dusty, and utterly silent.

"Tyr-Us?" he called again, but it was a pointless exercise. One of the chairs was overturned. A cabinet door hung halfway open. The air itself seemed to shout of a violent struggle. In the slanted light he spotted an indentation in the wall, a splintered patch on the floor his mother had always kept so immaculate. A tiny scrap of torn fabric lay in a corner.

This dacha should have been a safe haven for Tyr-Us. Zor-El had promised the man a sanctuary.

But someone had found him anyway.

Someone had made him disappear.

Zod.

Zor-El clenched his fists. For his brother's sake, he had tried to give the Commissioner the benefit of the doubt, but now there could be no question of the man's guilt. All of the outrageous and ridiculous-sounding claims Tyr-Us had made must be true.

In a cold voice, Zor-El muttered, "Today you have made a very serious enemy, Commissioner Zod."

CHAPTER 56

⧜⌂◇‼◇⊶T♀◊ 56

Since being asked to write the official history according to Zod, Lara had spent days collecting her notes and her thoughts. She vowed to record her chronicle accurately and faithfully, regardless of what the Commissioner wanted.

In her student days, she had read and analyzed enough ancient epics and archaeological texts to know that would-be historians often colored their accounts, and later generations found it difficult to separate reality from wishful thinking. She wasn't going to do that. Hers would be a balanced perspective.

It was true that the old Council had caused the long stagnation of Krypton, and Lara did not intend to show them in a favorable light. It was true that after the disastrous loss of Kandor, Zod had been the only one to act swiftly and decisively. He had set up the refugee camp and within months had begun to construct a new capital. In that respect, Lara could not argue with his results.

It was also true, though, that the Commissioner had simply declared himself the absolute ruler of Krypton. Despite protestations from other nobles and city leaders, he refused to form a legitimate new Council, declined to listen to any advisers but his handpicked Ring of Strength. That wasn't right, either, and she would not excuse it in her account.

She had reviewed the angry charges issued by Shor-Em, Gil-Ex, Tyr-Us, and other outspoken dissidents. The disappearance of so many critics seemed too convenient, too coincidental. Zod's refusal to let Lara speak with them only strengthened her suspicions. . . .

She didn't know how to proceed.

Five days ago, Jor-El had returned from the drilling site, pleased and relieved that he and his brother had resolved the most serious threat to Krypton. Most of the population still did not know the scope of the ecological devastation caused by the lava geyser, and sooner or later there was bound to be a tremendous outcry. Zod didn't seem to think it would be a problem.

Back in the capital, he kept Jor-El busy with numerous projects, though sometimes her husband disagreed with the priorities and insisted on doing other work that he considered more important. So far the Commissioner hadn't pressed the issue, but Lara could tell the man was displeased.

Early one morning, before Jor-El set out to measure the intrinsic flaws in his newly grown crystal towers, Aethyr sent a priority message instructing them to come to the Square of Hope. "Zod is making a historic announcement. You'll want to record it in your chronicle, Lara." On the communication plate Aethyr's smile revealed brilliantly white teeth. "I'm so glad you're with us, on our side." Lara found it very difficult to take the compliment at face value.

Curious, she and Jor-El made their way across the bright new city. Hundreds had already gathered for Zod's grand announcement, whatever it was. Nam-Ek intercepted the two of them and cleared a path through the crowd to where Aethyr waited. "Come! Lara and Jor-El, you have a place of honor."

All sixteen members of the Ring of Strength had taken prominent positions near the speaking stage. Behind Zod, a tall, monolithic object stood in the middle of the square shrouded in opaque fabric. Lara stared, wondering when that thing had been moved into place.

After an excited hush fell over the crowd, Zod stepped to a podium in front of the shrouded object. He spoke in a booming voice. "Kryptonians, we must build landmarks rather than leave scars like the crater of Kandor." He turned meaningfully to the tall draped object, and the crowd's anticipation was palpable. "We must show any ill-informed enemy the face of our greatness."

Zod raised a hand sharply, and burly Sapphire Guards pulled the cables attached to the tarpaulin. The fabric fell away to reveal a massive statue, a towering noble figure with the defiant yet paternal face of the Commissioner himself. "Behold Zod!"

Jor-El stared at Lara in complete surprise. "Is this one of your art projects? Did you create this?"

"I didn't even know about it." Lara felt a chill that the man's ego would allow him to commission such a work. Zod must have kept this from her, and it could only have been intentional.

But the rest of the crowd had no misgivings. Prompted by the Ring of Strength, the audience began chanting, "Zod! Zod! Zod!"

He smiled confidently, letting the shouts and cheers wash over him. Finally he raised both hands for silence. He had an even bigger announcement to make. Taking Aethyr by the hand, he drew her up to stand with him. "This woman has been my partner, my adviser, and my confidante during our greatest tribulations. There can be no more perfect companion for me, nor for Krypton. And so today I accept Aethyr as my formal consort."

"Now that's another surprise," Jor-El said quietly against the background of cheering. "Do you think they love each other?"

"They are definitely cast from the same mold." Lara wanted to be happy for her friend, but her heart felt torn. Everything about Zod and Aethyr's relationship was different from what she and Jor-El shared. And yet those two also seemed inseparable. . . .

Zod had to shout to make his words heard over the din. "Not long ago, I was privileged to perform the marriage ceremony of two of Krypton's greatest citizens, Jor-El and Lara." He gestured toward the two of them, and the crowd dutifully applauded. "But who could possibly perform such a ceremony for me, for the leader of Krypton?" He spread his hands as if genuinely asking the audience for an answer. But he responded to his own question. "Aethyr and I have spoken our own vows to each other. I, Zod, hereby declare that we are legally and officially wed." He and Aethyr raised their hands in the air, then looked directly at Lara. "Let history record our union for all future generations to know."

Jor-El was startled by the presumptuous act, and a few members of the audience muttered, more in confusion at the unorthodox wedding than in outrage. Before the puzzled uneasiness could turn to expressions of disquiet at the implied arrogance of the announcement, Zod whistled.

A loud and brassy fanfare sounded from high windows in the rebuilt government structures. Doorways burst open and a parade of brightly clothed servants marched out carrying platters of fine foods: steaming meats, rich pastries, fruits and soft candies on skewers. Four graceful fountains recently placed at cardinal points around the square gurgled, then gushed a sparkling ruby liquid—wine from the storehouses.

The crowd laughed in disbelief at this unexpected largesse. Zod continued, "It has been far too long since Krypton had reason to celebrate, far too long since we cheered and feasted. Let our wedding day become a magnificent memory for everyone."

The people crowded forward to partake of the treats.

Stunned, Lara held on to Jor-El's arm.

Now formally married, Zod and Aethyr spent the long hours of darkness together in their shared palatial quarters. It was an unusual wedding night, as filled with schemes as it was with passion. They were kindred spirits, and sharing the future held far more than mere romance.

Their government palace was cluttered with hangings, paintings, and ornate furniture. This was not because Zod had any personal need for opulence (especially since Aethyr herself cared little about baubles and luxurious possessions), but because the ruler of Krypton was expected to live in ostentatious surroundings.

As they lay together on rumpled sheets of glistening websilk, Zod was both exhausted and energized by their passion and their shared dreams. He did indeed consider himself the savior of Krypton, despite the constant troubling complaints from the remaining gadflies.

Aethyr rolled over and studied his expression for a long moment. "You are bothered by something. I can tell."

"I pay little attention to the other would-be leaders. We've removed most of the loudest ones, and look how much stronger Krypton has become. What troubles me more, though, is that I've been sensing a certain hesitation in Lara. I watched her expression when we unveiled my statue. She did not seem altogether impressed."

Aethyr propped herself up on one elbow. "That's not surprising. Your statue is central to the Square of Hope, just as Jax-Ur's statue once was. We placed Lara in charge of the city's greatest artwork, and you left her out of the project. I would certainly be miffed if you ever did something like that to me."

"She has her history to write, and that is her priority." Zod let out a troubled sigh. "And sometimes Jor-El makes me uneasy, too. He does not follow my cause with his heart. He did not join us out of loyalty as you did, my dear, or the way Nam-Ek does."

She chuckled. "Nam-Ek would follow you off a precipice. He has no opinion about the politics involved."

"I once thought the same of Jor-El. Oh, he rationalizes his coopera-tion, but that can change. He thinks for himself—too much, I fear."

Aethyr snuggled closer, put her arms around Zod's neck, and stroked his face. "Jor-El is an extremely intelligent man with a strong moral code. He's probably guessed that you're hiding things from him."

"You're right. I will have to watch him closely."

CHAPTER 57

After discovering that Tyr-Us was truly gone, Zor-El did not dare
tell anyone where he was going. For too long he had given his brother's
benefactor the benefit of the doubt, but now he felt duty bound to formalize the resistance against the self-proclaimed ruler. And he had to
find a way to get Jor-El away from Zod before it was too late.

He arrived at Borga City and demanded to speak to Shor-Em. Zor-El
hid his personal floater vehicle on dry land, then sought out one of the
gondoliers who plied the canals through the marshes. After securing a
ride, he sat in the narrow boat, mulling over what he knew and what he
suspected about Zod. Fortunately, the gondolier asked no questions.

The boatman pulled up to a cluster of moss-draped pilings and
secured his craft to a silver ring. Zor-El looked up at the main scarlet
balloon at the center of Borga City, from which the satellite platforms
extended. Small inflatable elevators tethered to the piling were available to anyone who wished to use them. After thanking the gondolier,
Zor-El stepped onto the nearest platform and opened the valve so that
marsh gases filled the anchored balloon. When the elevator began to rise
quickly toward the main floating city, he adjusted the flow of gas until
the balloon reached the proper height. Zor-El stepped off.

On the interlocked platforms, the citizens of Borga City lived in
open-framework homes, little more than awnings stretched across poles.
Subsidiary bridges and platforms were held up by their own flotation

sacks, the separate districts named according to the colors of their centerpiece balloons.

Shor-Em and his city council met in the emerald district, a high-floating dock next to the scarlet central balloon. The dissident city leader and his noble advisers sat on an open deck, sipping from steaming cups of tea.

Seeing Zor-El, Shor-Em stood up from his cushions and exclaimed, "I hoped you would come! We need each other's support against this menace." He had curly blond ringlets that fell in a soft mane around his head. As was traditional in Borga City, the leader wore a thin gold circlet around his brow. His robes were sky blue, his skin pale. The seven other nobles with him wore similar clothing and identical worried expressions. "Have you heard about Zod and his *statue?*" The others tittered, openly showing their scorn.

Zor-El immediately got down to business. "Tyr-Us is gone. He came to my city, claiming that Zod's men were hunting him. I sent him to what I believed was a safe place to hide, but he has vanished."

The news caused great consternation among the gathered men, but Shor-Em was not entirely shocked. He called for more refreshments. "The Commissioner is already touting Tyr-Us as a miraculous convert, like all the others. None of us is fooled." Several of the blue-robed councilmen shook their heads in disbelief. "Do you think he murdered them all, just to silence them?"

"He might have, but I believe Zod is smarter than that."

"Ahem, he's not smarter than we are." Shor-Em proudly looked at his nobles. "Sit with us. We have important decisions to make."

After the loss of Kandor, many older noble sons had congregated here in Borga City, lamenting the lost glory days of Krypton. Instead of quietly disappearing as Zod had hoped, the blueblood nobles had become a persistent thorn in his side, though they had not yet managed to take any significant action.

Zor-El found it unsettling to sit on soft cushions while discussing matters of such gravity. It reminded him too much of how the old eleven-member Council would have dealt with the problems. Restless, he walked to the edge of the high platform and stared down at the marsh. Like a cloud of flying jewels, amethyst-winged butterflies flitted about in a huge group, their movements perfectly coordinated, as if they were a single organism. Not a single one missed its move. "If only Kryptonians could cooperate like that," he muttered.

"We will have to." Shor-Em nodded defiantly. "The Commissioner is already ahead of us. He has brainwashed his followers, but we cannot let him fool any more people. I have already expelled all of his fanatics from Borga City. I will not allow them to praise that terrible man. You should do the same."

"We all should!" cried another nobleman.

Zor-El was troubled. "Zod's supporters have also spoken in Argo City, but I do not have the right to silence them because I disagree. That's not what we stand for."

Shor-Em gave him a sour frown and slurped his tea. "You have the right to stop a merchant from selling poison, if he claims it is food. That's how I see it. All followers of the traitor Zod can go live out in the swamps, for all I care." He straightened the circlet on his brow. "But we need to do more, create a full-fledged uprising to strip Zod's power from him."

Zor-El smelled the mulchy aroma of swamp gases boiling up from far below. "If that is what you believe, then the leaders of other cities should be here. A rebellion must represent all of Krypton, not just Borga City."

"Ahem, if we were to announce such a conference, Zod's spies would hear of it, and he could strike us all in one place. No, I have decided that we will make up our minds here and discreetly pass the word. We must proceed with great caution."

Zor-El wasn't sure which course of action would prove wiser. "Many Kryptonians have had enough of great caution."

For hours he, Shor-Em, and the nobles talked. Passions rose, but they all had a similar goal. Finally Shor-Em made his firm summary announcement. "We will form our own government, a Council with eleven members of our own choosing. That will give the people a preferable alternative. We will return Krypton to what it should be, ruled in the time-honored tradition." He sounded brave, but somewhat pompous. "Commissioner Zod can rot in Kryptonopolis. The rest of the world will live under another banner—our banner."

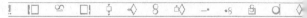

His fellow nobles applauded, reinforcing their own bravery, drawing strength from one another. Zor-El did not disagree, though he still had reservations. He seemed to be the only man here who understood how dangerous their course of action was going to be. "Zod won't like this one bit."

CHAPTER 58

No matter how carefully she applied her brushstrokes to the painting, Lara could not get the details right. She wasn't sure she wanted to. Every day, she grew more uneasy about the Commissioner's activities, especially since the unveiling of his statue. And now he had commanded her to paint this self-aggrandizing portrait.

From the moment the project began, Commissioner Zod had adopted a carefully chosen pose at his desk surrounded by important documents. Wearing a dark uniform of a more militaristic design than his usual clothes, he raised his chin and froze in position for Lara to paint his likeness.

"Aethyr was right to recommend you to me," Zod said, barely moving his lips. "You have remarkable talent in so many areas."

"I do my best, Commissioner." Lara couldn't think of anything else to say.

"If only everyone did. I was very pleased with your portrait of Jor-El out at his estate. You truly captured his heart, his nature, his soul." Zod's eyes flashed as he half rose from his chair. "It's imperative that you do the same for me."

"Please don't move, Commissioner." She swallowed hard and tried to focus on her work. "I'd like to capture that expression." Lara could never portray the same depth of nobility in a portrait of Zod because she simply didn't see it in him. He wanted a flattering likeness, yet Lara saw too much in him that was *un*flattering.

She wiped her brow, set down the pigments, and pressed a hand against the small of her back. Because of her growing pregnancy, she frequently had to shift position. Her stomach was now obviously rounded. At least the bouts of morning sickness had mostly passed. She poured herself a glass of cool water from a pitcher and quickly poured a second glass, which she offered to Zod first.

He accepted the water without thanks and frowned impatiently. "You took a break not long ago. My portrait must be on display for the public unveiling of the completed government palace in two days."

"It will be finished, Commissioner." Lara took a long drink, gathered her resolve, and returned to painting.

As if locked into place, Zod immediately assumed the same pose as before. "Since I have you here, I will tell you more of my personal background for your historical chronicle." Lara continued to work studiously on her painting. She had written some pages in the official document Zod had requested, but she spent more time jotting down unfiltered—and much more critical—impressions in her private journal. He continued, "Understanding my personality is the key to properly describing my actions and motivations. Generations from now, people will read your account of me, so it is imperative that you grasp how my mind works."

"I'm writing a history, Commissioner, not a biography."

"If it is a representative account of the most pivotal events, then my story must be your main focus. I suggest you start with a brief description of the life of my father. Cor-Zod was the greatest man ever to serve on the Kryptonian Council, and certainly the last effective one. I am following in his footsteps."

"Should I include some background on your mother as well? For balance?"

"Not necessary. Your chronicle will be long and detailed as it is, so let us concentrate on the important influences in my life."

Holding back a retort, Lara made a long, thick brushstroke in the background of the portrait. She felt a twinge in her abdomen, as if her unborn baby were also reacting to the chauvinistic comment.

Zod talked at great length about his father, crediting Cor-Zod with virtually every important decision the Council had made in the last fifty years. "I should have been the heir to my father's legacy, but I was cheated out of my rightful position on the Council. The other members accepted bribes or promoted cronies rather than valuing a truly competent man."

Unconsciously, he ran a finger along the line of his cheek. "Many people say I look just like my father. When we unveiled my statue, I felt as if I were looking at him again." He flashed a glance at Lara, who had frozen in her painting. "I get the impression you don't entirely approve of that statue. Why?"

Lara quickly searched for an acceptable answer. "The statue is a fine work. Yet by its very nature it seems . . . presumptuous. History has not yet issued its verdict on what you are doing."

Zod's face was as stony as that of his statue. "That is why I instructed you to write the history—to ensure that the verdict is favorable."

"You seem quite certain of me, Commissioner."

"How can I not be certain? I stood by your husband in his time of greatest need. I performed your marriage ceremony. Our bond is very close." He didn't speak the words, but she could hear it in his voice: *You owe it to me.*

"I see your point." Lately, she and Jor-El had been uncomfortably aware of additional Sapphire Guards, even members of the Ring of Strength, watching them, taking a close interest in their movements and activities. It made Lara very uneasy.

"And you see how unfairly I am treated by those who oppose me. So many ignorant dissidents!" His voice grew strident as he stood from his desk; Lara didn't chide him to resume his pose. "Did you know that Shor-Em has expelled all of my supporters from Borga City? He chased them into the swamps, just as he did to his own brother!" He sniffed in indignation. "So speaking one's opinion is now punishable by exile! Is that the sort of Krypton they wish to have, a fascist state?" He shook his head. "If we could take care of only a few main ringleaders, I am confident this ill-advised resistance would crumble."

"Take care of them? What—what do you mean?"

He caught himself, then belatedly chuckled. "I simply wish I could talk directly with my critics. I *know* I am doing the right thing for Krypton. And thanks to your chronicle, others will see it as well."

Lara concluded that she could do no more work on the portrait.

Though she had not intended it, her painting had captured a darkness about Zod—an expression of implacable calculation and hauteur. Nervous about what his reaction might be, she turned the work toward him. "It's finished, Commissioner."

He pondered the painting for a long moment. "Quite adequate. You have captured my true essence. It will go on display immediately in the government palace." He folded his hands at his desk. "Now that this project is complete, I am anxious to read a draft of your history."

"The events themselves haven't finished unfolding yet, Commissioner."

"I am merely referring to volume one. We must establish the facts and begin disseminating them."

CHAPTER 59

Though he had grave concerns about the Commissioner, Zor-El wasn't convinced that Shor-Em and his councilmen could solve the world's problems, either. The self-absorbed nobles didn't seem to be much of an improvement over the oblivious old Council. Despite this, he agreed to sign their defiant declaration against Zod. Given the situation, it seemed imperative.

Then he returned to Argo City to explain to all his people what he had done. And why.

Even before resting or changing his travel clothes, he called a meeting of the citizenry in the central fountain square. For those who could not attend in person, his image and words were projected on the faceted crystal walls of strategically located public buildings.

"When I look around me today, I no longer see my Krypton," Zor-El said to the attentive audience. "No one can deny that the Council in Kandor made serious mistakes in their naïveté and lethargy, but I won't correct old mistakes by making new ones. No tyrant can ever restore our civilization. The people who are hypnotized by Zod's charisma and fearmongering must be shown the truth. He has removed many of his critics, but I will not be silenced!"

Around him, the air was heady with the scent of blooming flowers. Alura stood by his side, as always, and now his mother had also come to live with them. Over the past two months, Charys had settled comfortably in Argo City.

He continued his speech. "I have clear evidence that Commissioner Zod's overzealous followers have committed grave crimes, perhaps even murder. Other leaders who spoke out against him have been kidnapped or killed. One of my close friends has vanished—it was the only way Zod could ensure his silence."

Worried muttering rippled through the crowd. "The evidence is simply too alarming to ignore, and so I have come to a difficult decision: Those who disseminate Zod's propaganda are no longer welcome in Argo City. They must leave, voluntarily or by force. I have to draw the line, take a stand." He nodded sternly. No one in the audience argued with him.

"Since our normal city guard is not equipped to meet this challenge, I call upon the rest of my citizens to form a Society of Vigilance. All of us must watch for threats from Commissioner Zod. He wants no organized resistance to his rule."

"So how do we stand up against him?" called an older leathery-skinned man from the audience. Zor-El recognized him as a wealthy fisherman who owned five ships, two of which had been destroyed by the tsunami.

"But we have no army!" said someone else. "And you can bet Zod is gathering one. While we're trying to rebuild Argo City, he's preparing for war."

"War on Krypton?" a young man said in a high voice filled with disbelief. "A civil war?"

Zor-El said, "Shor-Em is about to issue a declaration challenging the Commissioner for leadership. Many other cities, towns, and villages are also rejecting the authority of Kryptonopolis. Here in Argo City, I declare that we are an independent city-state. We do not accept the rule of Zod."

As soon as he spoke the words, Zor-El knew he had stepped across a line and dragged all his people along with him. He had thrown down a gauntlet that Commissioner Zod could not ignore.

Argo City had to be ready.

CHAPTER 60

∞ ⛢ ◊ ‼ ◇ ⊤♀ ◊ 60

As night fell after a long day, Jor-El and Lara ate a quiet dinner on the small, flat rooftop of their designated quarters in Kryptonopolis. Even here in the city, Jor-El loved to sit under the stars and stare up into space, letting his imagination roam free. For a while he could forget the close scrutiny he and Lara had been receiving from Zod's security. Out in the shadowy streets, he suspected someone was surreptitiously keeping track of him.

Now, near the horizon after sunset, they watched a silvery arc of cosmic mist, the periodic comet called Loth-Ur's Hammer, which returned to Krypton only once every three centuries. The event was marked on public calendars, and at any other time, the arrival of Loth-Ur's Hammer would have drawn far more attention, inspiring artists and astronomers, providing an excuse for celebrations and cultural events. The Priests of Rao might even have called it an omen. With the continuing political turmoil, though, the comet sparked very little popular interest.

In ancient times, Jax-Ur had named the comet after his cruel father. According to legend, the gauzy apparition had crossed the sky during the warlord's seizure of power; now the comet had returned, just as Commissioner Zod seemed to be following in the footsteps of Jax-Ur. The obvious parallels troubled Jor-El.

"I think Zod actually reveres the old warlord, though he tries not to let it show," Lara said. "Look at this." On her sketchpad she called up archived engravings from the ancient records of Jax-Ur's court histori-

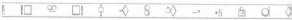

ans. In the middle of a great plaza called Execution Square stood a statue of the stern warlord looming over his subjects. "See any similarities?"

Jor-El stared at it. Even the position of the figure's arms, the expression on the face, and some trappings of the carved uniform were identical to Zod's newly erected statue. "It can't be a coincidence. And he has Jax-Ur's nova javelins, too." He shook his head and tried to enjoy the clear night, but his eyes strayed from the misty comet to the spangled remnants of the shattered moon. Nova javelins had done that. . . . But Zod insisted the weapons were to be used only for the defense of Krypton.

"The Commissioner is a brilliant man, but one moment he impresses me with his willingness to support new science or the way he handles a situation, and the next moment he bewilders me with one of his unconventional announcements. Zod wants to think he's the best thing to happen to Krypton, but he may be the worst."

"We'd better decide soon." Lara put a hand on her rounded belly. "Not only do we have the future of Krypton to worry about, but we're about to have a baby."

Jor-El stroked her stomach, and she placed her hand over his. He felt something move beneath his fingers. Lara pressed his hand down. "Did you feel that? It was the baby. It kicked." She winced. "Another one!"

"Our child is a strong one already." Jor-El felt such a sense of wonder that he promptly set aside all his other concerns, his political worries, and his suspicions. For the moment, that love was stronger than his doubts about Zod. He and Lara were going to be parents!

Keeping the baby's health paramount, Lara had been eating well and taking care of herself. Not content just to accept the advice of doctors, she kept herself well informed about the progression of her pregnancy. She wanted nothing to go wrong.

Jor-El had doted on her and pampered her. Every day he did his best to prepare the foods she craved, though he couldn't remember the last time he had done any cooking before her pregnancy. He allowed himself to enjoy these times with her and realized that he was happier now than he could ever remember being before.

In his younger years, Jor-El had thought that only scientific pursuits could give his life true satisfaction—the thrill of discovering new things, developing new ideas. But his feelings toward Lara, and his paternal instinct to love, protect, and teach this baby surprised him with their intensity. He promised himself that he would create the brightest possible future for his child. On Lara's beautiful face he saw an expression of complete fulfillment. Her smile seemed almost too big for her face, and he realized that his own smile was just as broad.

As Lara relaxed in her chair next to him, humming an old folk song, his attention wandered back to the pale smear of the comet's tail. Jor-El had never been able to switch off his analytical mind, his ever-curious observations. He had been so preoccupied with emergencies that he had never gotten around to studying this astronomical marvel in detail. Even so, evening after evening in Kryptonopolis he had taken a few moments to look at the majestic comet on its ancient path.

Tonight, though, he realized that what had been the smooth and graceful arc of a wispy tail now had strange knots and kinks. Even with his naked eyes, he could see that some areas in the head of the comet appeared brighter, as if jets had exploded from its frozen surface.

"Jor-El, I know that look on your face, so don't even try to keep secrets from me."

"I need to contact the telescope listening post before Loth-Ur's Hammer drops below the horizon. There's something I'd like to check." He and Lara left the open rooftop, climbed down the stairs, and went out into the brightly lit streets. She matched his brisk pace, wanting to find out what had piqued his interest so.

Though he would rather have been at the telescope array himself, or at least at the observatory monitoring center on his estate, he could get the information he needed from a substation building here. Using his codes to control the receivers remotely, he could realign the twenty-three receiver dishes in Zod's distant early-warning system in order to get the best images possible.

With Lara looking over his shoulder, Jor-El worked swiftly, entirely focused on the combined images from the telescopes. "I'm not an expert on cometary behavior, but this seems most unusual." He back-calculated the comet's path from the archive of images over the past several weeks, and then he plotted variances in its expected orbit.

From the largest optical magnifiers, he found a high-resolution image of Loth-Ur's Hammer. The silently tumbling comet was made of black ice laced with rocky inclusions and pockets of gas. White plumes volatilized out, erupting in unexpected jets of fine dust and frozen gases.

"Those are impressive explosions," Lara said.

"Yes . . . yes, they are." Jor-El summoned up the data recorded by the rest of the telescope cluster. The distant early-warning system had not been designed to look for anything like this, but Jor-El could sift through the recordings to find what he needed to know.

Because Krypton's swollen red sun was larger and more furious than at any other point in its history, the turbulent solar radiation had had a dramatic effect on the comet as it swung around Rao. The resulting explosions in the thawing iceball had shifted its rotation and changed its orbit.

Jor-El felt his heart sink as he went over his calculations again and again. "Just when I thought we were safe . . . "

"Jor-El, you're scaring me."

"You should be scared." He stared back at the now-ominous image of the immense comet. "Loth-Ur's Hammer has changed course. The comet is hurtling directly toward us, and if my estimates are correct, in four months it's going to smash into Krypton."

CHAPTER 61

Under a clear, star-filled night sky, Alura and Charys went out to install new light crystals on the Eloquin Bridge, the southernmost of the five graceful spans connecting Argo City to the mainland. The two women worked their way along the bridge, embedding clear white gems that glowed with inner fires. They had volunteered for the task because it was a way they could aid the new Society of Vigilance. The improved lighting would make it easier for volunteers to keep watch after dark.

Overhead, the intact moons had risen, and the remnants of Koron sparkled like frozen fireworks. The long arc of Loth-Ur's Hammer had already dipped below the western horizon. Alura and Charys were alone on the bridge, since few travelers passed back and forth this late at night. The Society of Vigilance patrolled the city now at all hours to make certain Zod's fanatics caused no trouble.

Over the past several days, anyone wearing a sapphire-blue arm-band emblazoned with Zod's family crest had been evicted from the city. Protesting as they left, groups of the Commissioner's adherents marched defiantly over the bridges out of Argo City, vowing that they would return once Zod had "consolidated" all of Krypton. Alura was certain that by now the Commissioner had received word of what Zor-El had done, and she was just as certain that many of his followers remained in the city, posing as normal citizens until they could find a way to wreak havoc.

The two women worked their way along the Eloquin Bridge in

silence, weighed down by heavy thoughts as they checked and installed illumination crystals. Finally Charys said with forced cheer, "So I am finally going to be a grandmother. Jor-El and Lara didn't waste any time. I can't wait to spoil that little baby."

Alura felt her mother-in-law's implied question hanging in the air. The darkness covered her blush. "Zor-El and I have talked about having children, and we will someday. I've always wanted a little girl. We keep waiting for a better time."

"There'll never be a perfect time if you always look for excuses."

Awkwardly Alura tried to change the subject. "Now that you're settled here, have you considered continuing your psychological studies? Weren't you writing a treatise on the anomalies in Krypton's population?"

Charys seated a palm-sized crystal in a connecting socket, and it glowed around her hand. "I still make observations. Our entire society is a laboratory. My own Yar-El deviated from the norm, and both of my sons qualify as geniuses. I only hope you and Lara can anchor the two of them, because Krypton needs their brilliance. Especially now." The older woman continued to muse. "Even Commissioner Zod is an example of political genius. He has both the foresight and the fortitude to be a great leader, but alas, like Yar-El, he has gone too far beyond the pale. A man like Zod is effective primarily in crisis situations. And so in order to hold on to his power, he has to create or maintain the state of emergency."

"And that's what he's been doing," Alura said.

The conversation stopped as a pair of shadowy men walked toward them across the bridge from the mainland. They carried no personal lights, which in itself seemed odd. Though crime was almost unknown in Argo City, Alura felt a shiver of fear. She had been edgy ever since her husband had cast out Zod's fanatics. Fortunately, the Society of Vigilance patrolled the bridge ramps to be sure no unwanted visitors crossed over during the night. Even so, Alura hesitated before installing another crystal, holding it in her hand.

Out of long habit, Charys nodded politely as the two men came closer. "Good evening."

One of the men said to Alura, without any pleasantries, "I know you. You are the wife of Zor-El."

"The other one is his mother," said the second man. "We'd better take them both."

Before either woman could answer, the first man lunged for Alura, arms extended, as if he thought he could just grab her and carry her off. She swung the fist that held the illumination crystal and opened her fingers at the last moment. The sharp-edged jewel smashed his left cheek just under his eye, and the man reeled backward, cursing. Something dropped from his hand and clattered on the span of the bridge. A stunner!

Charys lashed out with surprising violence at the other man, thrashing and flailing her hands as she yelled at the top of her lungs, "We're being attacked! Guards! Help!" The old woman startled her attacker by striking him hard in the nose with an openhanded blow, sending a gush of blood down his face. He roared and tried to throw himself on her.

Alura snatched up the fallen stunner and pointed it at the man fighting Charys. She shot quickly, without aiming, and the sizzling beam caught his legs below the knees, making him crumple.

She could already hear people running to offer their assistance. Lights began to glow in the sleepy buildings of Argo City as volunteers were alerted.

The man facing Alura got to his feet and wiped blood from his cheek where the crystal had cut him. He glared at the two women, spun, and bolted as fast as he could back across the bridge toward the mainland.

As Vigilance guards arrived, Alura pointed into the darkness. "One ran that way. See if you can capture him!"

Charys shook herself off, more indignant than injured. Alura turned to look at the man whose legs she had paralyzed. She was shocked to see that through sheer force of will, the fanatic had dragged himself to the edge of the bridge and used his arms to pull himself up onto the crossbars. "Stop him!"

Blood still streamed from his broken nose. With a defiant leer, he flung himself through the gap. He didn't scream, didn't shout any

last words, but simply plummeted into the darkness. After a very long moment, Alura heard the hard slap of a body striking the still water.

"Now we'll never know who they were," Charys said.

Alura looked toward the mainland in dismay. The other attacker had already gotten away. "We know exactly who they were."

CHAPTER 62

∞⌂◊‼◊⟵T̤Ϙ⟩ 62

With a tremendous sense of urgency, Jor-El went to see Zod early the next morning. The impending celestial impact was imminent and definite. Four months! Unless something deflected the hurtling ball of ice, it would smash into Krypton only days after the birth of his baby. It was straightforward celestial mechanics, and the numbers did not lie.

However, if Commissioner Zod pulled together all of his resources and diverted manpower from his other projects, Krypton just might be able to do what was necessary. After the obvious success of the Rao-beam project in mitigating the instabilities in the planet's core, Jor-El hoped the Commissioner would listen to his warning now. After all, the man prided himself on *getting things done.*

Jor-El strode purposefully toward the government palace, taking no time to notice the glory of the towering crystalline spires; he walked right past the intricate mosaics and murals that Lara had designed; he cut across the center of the Square of Hope, passing Zod's ominous new statue. Behind him, he saw a Sapphire Guard noting his movement.

With every minute, he could feel the comet coming closer.

Nam-Ek stood before the entrance to the Commissioner's offices, a barricade more impenetrable than any door. The mute's shoulders were squared, his heavily muscled arms crossed over his chest. Carrying copies of his records and projection crystals, Jor-El approached him. "I have important information for Commissioner Zod. He'll want to see me."

Nam-Ek shook his bearded head, clearly following orders to keep

visitors out, but Jor-El stepped closer until they were almost touching, chest to chest. "Has the Commissioner ever instructed you to keep *me* out? And have I ever demanded to see him without good cause?"

Nam-Ek shook his head to both questions, and Jor-El pounced on the brief hesitation. Slipping around the large man, he entered the cool, stone-walled office. Startled, the Commissioner looked up from a map on which he had marked the locations of Krypton's cities. He drew lines connecting them, adding up numbers—troop strengths?—beside each line, as if he were making some sort of military plan. With a grimace of annoyance, he pushed the papers aside. "I told Nam-Ek that I was not to be disturbed."

"Disturbed? What I'm about to say is very disturbing indeed." Taking charge of the moment, he found a clear spot on Zod's desk and set down his crystals, inserting them into the open slots in a projection device. "You asked me to monitor space so we could be forewarned about threats from outside. That is exactly what I've done."

Now the Commissioner gave him his full attention. "Are we about to be invaded?" Judging by his startled expression, Jor-El suddenly realized that even Zod had never truly believed there would be an attack; he had simply used the threat to unify a frightened people under his banner.

Jor-El displayed the high-resolution image of the steaming, tumbling comet. He spoke firmly, with no doubt in his voice. "This is Loth-Ur's Hammer. Outgassing from the main body has knocked it into a different orbit." Next he projected ellipses that showed the orbit of Krypton, the comet's previous orbit, and then he displayed a new red arc that exactly intersected Krypton.

Zod frowned. "What does this mean? What are you showing me?"

"Isn't it obvious?" He pointed to the intersecting lines. "Loth-Ur's Hammer will hit us—in four months' time."

The Commissioner sighed. "Another disaster? Did you not also insist that great Rao itself was going to go supernova?"

"It will." Jor-El did not back down. "But this is even more imminent—"

"And did I not fund a hugely expensive drilling project to release the pressure in our core with a tremendous lava geyser—a geyser that, incidentally, devastated the entire valley of Kandor?"

"Yes, and we averted a catastrophe. But what does that—"

"One catastrophe after another, Jor-El. What will it be next week?" He sounded both paternal and patronizing.

Jor-El couldn't believe what he was hearing. "Look at the data, Commissioner. Have No-Ton double-check everything, if you like. The conclusion is inescapable."

Unbelievably, Zod responded with sarcasm. "My conclusion is this: Any reasonable calculation will show that being threatened by a comet *now,* of all times, would be an inconceivable coincidence. Solar disturbances, tectonic upheaval, massive waves, *and* a threatening comet?"

"But that's just it, Commissioner—it's not a coincidence. These things are all related to each other by—"

But the Commissioner folded his hands and met the scientist's gaze. "This comes at a very bad time, Jor-El. All the sporadic and ineffectual resistance to my leadership is now becoming organized, and several major cities are forming an alliance against me. Your own brother has followed Borga City's lead in evicting all of my supporters, and after I humored him with his warnings of a core pressure buildup! Does he feel he owes me nothing?" His voice rose as his rant gathered momentum. "There has even been some talk among town leaders of talking military action to overthrow me. Me! After all I've accomplished for Krypton. This is a crisis."

Jor-El dug in his heels and stiffened with anger. "Not compared to the comet. You are faced with an impending disaster *far worse* than the loss of Kandor." He flicked his fingers dismissively at the nearest stack of papers on Zod's desk. "*This* nonsense won't matter unless all Krypton pulls together to find a way to prevent this disaster. But we must act soon. Maybe we can reconfigure the Rao beam to—"

Suddenly Aethyr, looking flushed and haughty, rushed into the office. "Zod, it has happened just as you feared. Another emergency."

The Commissioner came to his feet and stepped around his desk, taking Aethyr's warning more seriously than Jor-El's entire presentation. "Which one now?"

"Shor-Em." She pushed aside Jor-El's still-projecting device, cutting off the orbital traces and the comet images without bothering to look at them. She slapped a single amethyst message crystal into the center of the cleared surface and activated it. First blurry, then sharp, the projection showed Shor-Em looking effeminate yet noble with his curly golden hair and the circlet on his *fore*head.

The Borga City leader spoke in a pompous voice. "Zod's grandiose ambitions can no longer be tolerated. I, Shor-Em, am the true heir to the Kryptonian Council and announce the formation of a new government. Eleven members have already been chosen and will serve the needs of the people. I therefore declare Borga City the new capital of Krypton."

The Commissioner's face grew red with outrage as the message continued.

"Zod is only a pretender who seized power in our most vulnerable moment, while we reeled in shock. He took advantage of the situation. Is that the sort of leader Krypton needs? I think not. Zod sees no reason but his own. He does not abide by the rule of law.

"Follow me, and we will return Krypton to its former glory!" In the image, Shor-Em held up an ornate document, from which he read: "'We, the undersigned leaders, agree to abide by the laws of the New Council and hereby pledge to support the New Council with our loyalty and our resources.'"

The names of other population centers and their leaders began scrolling beside the man's image. Jor-El felt a cold lump in his stomach when he saw Argo City also listed there, and Zor-El's name. Zod seemed to have forgotten he was standing there.

Shor-Em continued with finality, "We will leave Zod to his old, dead city. His brief reign is ended." The city leader's image shimmered and vanished.

Aethyr stared at the ruddy fury boiling up in Zod's face. Jor-El tried to gain the commissioner's attention again, insistently holding up his crystals. He tried one last time, knowing it was futile. "Loth-Ur's Hammer is far more—"

Zod looked at him with both anger and anguish. He clearly wasn't sure of his decision, but forcibly convinced himself. "Jor-El, I will lose this war unless I act *now*." Leaving Jor-El behind, he followed Aethyr toward the door, already shouting for his Ring of Strength. "I don't have time for comets."

CHAPTER 63

∞⌐◊!◊⊶T♀◊ 63

Seeing Zod's reactionary response to the growing defiance of other cities, Jor-El worried that the Commissioner might cut off public access to the communication plates. He had hoped the man would put aside his own grandiose concerns when faced with an emergency that went beyond politics and personal feuds. But though he expected a rational reaction from Zod, he was not entirely surprised. Zod made decisions based on how they affected *him,* not how they affected Krypton. Jor-El could no longer rely on the Commissioner. He had to take his own action, find other help.

While Zod met in secret councils with his Ring of Strength, engrossed in planning a response to Shor-Em, Jor-El seized the opportunity to contact his brother. Zor-El would understand the threat of the comet, and he would see the games and stupidity as the insignificant distraction that they were.

Unfortunately, when his brother's face sharpened into clarity on the flat plate, he was formal, even stiff. "Give me good news, Jor-El. Tell me you've finally realized what Commissioner Zod is doing. Tell me that you'll come join me and Shor-Em and the legitimate New Council."

Jor-El was surprised by the vehemence in his brother's voice. "There's a new threat to Krypton, and Commissioner Zod won't do anything about it. Put aside these foolish rivalries and listen to me."

"Foolish rivalries? The future of our civilization is at stake. Can't you see what Zod is doing?" He raised a finger. "Where is Tyr-Us? Gil-Ex?

All those who have spoken out against him? Zod made them disappear, probably killed them. And don't quote that ridiculous explanation that they've 'retired from public view.'"

He had never seen his brother so angry. "Zor-El, what's the matter with you? Listen to me—"

"What's the *matter*? When Tyr-Us warned me about Zod, I thought he was paranoid. I told him to hide in our parents' dacha. But he vanished. The house was empty, ransacked. I saw blood. He's gone."

Jor-El struggled to absorb what his brother was saying. He had known nothing of this.

"Then last night our mother and Alura were attacked by Zod's fanatics in a failed abduction attempt."

Jor-El reeled. "Attacked? Are they all right? Tell me what happened. Are you sure the Commissioner's people were responsible?"

"They are both unharmed. My Society of Vigilance got there in time, chased away one of the abductors while the other one jumped off a bridge. Thankfully, we were prepared."

The white-haired scientist could not fit the pieces together in his mind. "Then how do you know they were Zod's men? Why would the Commissioner target our mother or your wife?" This made no sense to him.

"Because I evicted his followers from Argo City. I'm convinced Zod wanted hostages he could threaten to kill if I didn't capitulate."

"But if you have no proof, you can't make these wild accusations."

"You know it's true. You can't be so blind."

Jor-El drew a deep breath, gathering his thoughts. "In truth, I would not be surprised." Then he pushed stubbornly ahead, refusing to be sidetracked the way Zod himself had been. "Listen to me. This is science you can't ignore. Please!"

The other man remained steely and trembling with anger. "What could possibly be more important than a threat to my wife and our mother—"

"*This.* The end of all life on Krypton!" Jor-El inserted one of the projection crystals into the side of the communication plate and displayed the image of the comet, its jets of outpouring gas, and the deadly intersection of orbital paths. "Look at the orbits."

On the screen, Zor-El frowned as he immediately grasped the implications. "What does your precious Commissioner have to say about this?"

"He's more concerned about Shor-Em and Borga City. We can't rely on him." Jor-El couldn't keep the bitterness out of his voice. "While the comet hurtles toward us, Zod rallies his armies. I saw him studying tactical maps. He won't tolerate the way Shor-Em has challenged him."

"Are you talking about a military assault on Borga City? Is he mad? My first duty is to warn Shor-Em to prepare his defenses."

Jor-El was dismayed by his brother's reaction. "You, too? We'll all be killed if we don't stop the comet. That must be our only priority."

"If Zod attacks now, we will be embroiled in a civil war that's bound to last much longer than four months. No one will even look into the sky as Loth-Ur's Hammer comes right toward us. This is happening now, Jor-El, right now. We have to prevent it." His mood changed, and he sounded more urgent. "Come to Argo City and work with me. I couldn't save Tyr-Us from Zod, but I will not let him corrupt my own brother any further."

"Zod won't just let us leave Kryptonopolis. His Ring of Strength has been watching us carefully." Jor-El shook his head. "And he may be the only person on Krypton with the resources to save us. If there is even the slightest possiblility I can force him to see reason, or somehow use the tools in Kryptonopolis, then I have to take that chance. *We* have to take that chance. Everything else is just politics." He searched his brother's hardened face. "We used to laugh at people with misplaced priorities like that, Zor-El. Look at my data, I beg you. And then tell me where you want to focus your efforts. Give me your ideas. Otherwise, I'm on my own." He ended the transmission.

That night, sailing off the coast, Zor-El sat brooding with Alura on the benches of their gently rocking boat. He had told no one but his wife about Jor-El's disturbing news.

Their boat, a cat's cradle of silver struts and cables, glided across the calm sea. Ninety small sails of different geometric shapes were loosely connected to one another like a vast fabric puzzle, catching errant breezes from any direction. Glowing crystals lined the masts, turning the craft into a spiderweb of colors.

Zor-El stared at his beloved metropolis on the peninsula. Lit up at night, the spires and hemispherical buildings shone like a mirage. A faintly visible shimmer from the extended force-field barrier above the seawall distorted the stars at the horizon.

"It seems so peaceful out here, Alura." It was the first he had spoken in many minutes. "Quite a paradox."

The night breeze stirred her dark hair. "How did Shor-Em respond when you warned him about Zod's attack plans?"

"Borga City was already on high alert. Shor-Em will remain vigilant, but I have no idea how Zod intends to strike. My brother didn't offer any details. He was much more concerned about the comet."

Alura, as usual, was frank. "Shouldn't we be concerned about the comet? Jor-El is rarely wrong." The boat rocked as rippling waves passed them by. Deep beneath the water, a yellowish glow flowed and stirred, like a pool of sentient phosphorescent liquid, then dove deep.

Zor-El let out a long, sad sigh. "Yes, he's right. I looked at his data. There's no question about it." The black vault of night overhead was peppered with frequent meteors, many from the debris ejected by the spewing lava jet. What drew his attention, though, was the pearlescent cometary arc, as if some ghostly painter had used a wide brush to spread a trail across the night.

"So beautiful," Alura said. "And deadly."

"Jor-El saw something that none of us noticed while we were preoccupied with ourselves. He said I was falling prey to false priorities, just like I accused Zod of doing. And I can't dispute that."

"So what will you do?" Alura asked.

"How can I stop a comet? We don't have the technology. Anything powerful enough to do that would have been squashed by the Commission for Technology Acceptance long ago." He gritted his teeth as the thoughts grew more definite in his mind. "I can expand my protective barrier. Maybe it can save our city from a cometary impact."

He nodded, already planning how to install simple generators. He could raise a whole hemisphere to cover Argo City. "I could offer the barrier to other cities as well. If Jor-El's worst-case scenario happens, at least some of us might be saved." Their boat continued to drift on the gentle currents, but Zor-El knew it was just the calm before the storm. "Unless the whole planet is smashed to bits."

CHAPTER 64

Inside Zod's newly designated war room, Aethyr and Koll-Em studied terrain simulations modeled out of transparent gel. Beside them, Nam-Ek looked on with silent interest. The dark blue fabric of the big mute's uniform was stretched tight across his muscles; a crimson sash draped from his left shoulder to a gold belt at his waist.

"The marshes around Borga City are going to pose extreme difficulties for frontal assault," Aethyr pointed out. "The ground is uncertain, the canals are a maze, and the mud will prevent us from using heavy siege machinery."

"Then we'll bring in wave after wave of large floater platforms filled with soldiers." Koll-Em sounded eager. "My weakling brother won't put up much of a fight. He talks a lot, but I doubt his meek followers would find the courage even to throw pebbles down at us from their balloons!"

Zod said with finality, "There will be no direct military assault."

"Then how are we going to defeat them?" whined Koll-Em. "My brother has defied you. You can't simply ignore that."

"I will not ignore it. But I plan to use a much more efficient method to eradicate them and, at the same time, demonstrate my power to the rest of Krypton."

"What do you intend, my love?" Aethyr's eyes flashed.

Zod ran his fingers over the gel-formed topographical sculpture, caressing them from the mountaintops down to the marshy drainage in the east. "Jor-El has given me the very weapon I need to cauterize this wound. Come, we will take a small party and head north to the mountains. The people of Borga City will never see it coming."

Only a small force went to the nearly deserted Rao-beam facility. The group consisted of no more than a dozen men, mostly chosen from the ranks of the former Sapphire Guards.

After crossing a wasteland of soot, chunks of lava rock, and burned vegetation at the edge of the Kandor valley, Zod's troops pushed up the steep and narrow mountain roads to the installation. No longer in operation, the tall metal-framed derrick creaked and hummed as breezes whined through it. The focusing lenses, prisms, and powerful Rao batteries had been taken off-line, but still sat ready.

Several weeks ago, the lava geyser had died away to a burble, which No-Ton had covered with a small force-field cap, precisely following the instructions Zor-El had left behind. A small scientific team had remained to monitor the now-sealed hole. Hearing the troops arrive, the technicians emerged from their battered and dented prefab shacks that huddled among the cold cliffs. No-Ton stared at the Commissioner's group in surprise.

Zod announced boldly, "We require this installation for the defense of Krypton, to strike a blow against an enemy even worse than Brainiac— an internal enemy." When the others didn't seem to know how to respond, he continued. "I have tried unsuccessfully to be reasonable. Now there can be no other solution than to eliminate the festering sore of Borga City."

Standing atop the ridge, Zod turned from the blasted valley of Kandor and looked down the other side of the divide, to the east. Beyond the foothills, numerous stream-carved drainages created swampy lowlands. The target was nestled close to the horizon, nearly at the limit of the Rao beam's range.

Zod turned to size up the derrick framework. When Jor-El had built the Rao beam, he had designed it to aim the beam down into the crater of Kandor, nothing more; he had not installed automated systems for altering the direction of the carefully aligned beam. Now the whole structure would have to be swiveled around using brute force. "Nam-Ek, turn that heavy projector mechanism. Remember what I showed you on the map?"

The big man's muscles bulged as he strained against the cross-hatched structure, swiveling the thick bars that held the focusing lenses. Zod shook his head at the clumsy and imprecise method. "A disappointing oversight," he said aloud. "We neglected to plan for the possibility of other targets."

No-Ton bustled about in distress. Though he was part of the Ring of Strength, the noble-born scientist paid more attention to engineering matters than strategy meetings. "Commissioner, could I please have more technical details? This is very delicate equipment." He glanced sidelong at Nam-Ek, who continued to wrestle with the machinery. "It could take a day or more for proper realignment and recalibration, depending on the target."

Zod drew a deep breath of the razor-edged cold air. "Can't you do it faster?"

The scientist stiffened. "Do you want it fast, Commissioner, or accurate? I can do either one, but not both. Which would you prefer?"

Aethyr came up beside Zod and spoke in a hushed voice. "Another day won't make any significant difference, my love, but a mistake would be quite embarrassing. Let No-Ton do what he says he needs to do."

"Very well." Zod unfurled his filmpaper map and held it against the gusting breezes. "These are the coordinates. This is your target."

CHAPTER 65

After warning his brother about Loth-Ur's Hammer, Jor-El ignored all other tasks Commissioner Zod had set for him. In fact, he ignored the Commissioner entirely, instead spending the rest of the day engrossed in his calculations, estimating the mass of the approaching comet, analyzing spectra from its wispy tail to determine its chemical composition . . . trying to determine how much damage the impact would cause. He plunged into the problem wholeheartedly.

At first Jor-El considered modifying his small solar-probe rockets to carry powerful explosives (as Zod had originally ordered him to do), but he swiftly realized that the comet was too massive to be deflected or destroyed by even a thousand such missiles. In fact, the explosions would likely fragment the icy mass into several equally deadly chunks that would also bombard Krypton.

He needed to have an army of engineers and technicians to work on the problem—and he knew he could succeed, if only Zod would give him the manpower and equipment. It would be a project like erecting the giant telescope array on the plains or the Rao-beam installation in the mountains. He *could* do it.

But he had to make Zod see the magnitude of the disaster. Jor-El simply couldn't do this work alone. Though he doubted he could penetrate the man's stubborn fixation, he needed to try. His face set with determination, he marched back to the government palace, prepared once again to debate with the Commissioner. He would demand to know why Zod—or at least his misguided fanatics—had attempted to abduct Alura and Charys, as Zor-El had claimed.

The government palace seemed empty, though. A Sapphire Guard stood outside the door, rather than burly Nam-Ek. "I am here to see Commissioner Zod. He'll want to meet with me right away," Jor-El said, hoping it was true.

The guard, whose face was mostly hidden beneath his round, polished helmet, obviously recognized the white-haired scientist. "The Commissioner is not here. He is dealing with the dissidents."

Jor-El suddenly recalled all the military plans Zod had apparently been making. Zor-El was right to be concerned. "He went to Borga City?"

"No. He headed north to the crater of Kandor."

Jor-El left, disturbed. What would the Commissioner want there? Something from the old refugee encampment, perhaps?

When he arrived back at their designated living quarters, he found Lara deeply alarmed. She had pushed aside her work on the writing table to expose the inset communication plate. She met him at the door and pulled him over to hear the message. "Listen to this! It just came from No-Ton."

The private-channel image sharpened into the distraught face of the other scientist, who spoke under his breath. "The Commissioner has seized the Rao beam. Tomorrow he plans to blast Borga City! He means to make an example of Shor-Em."

A rush of cold anger and fear coursed through Jor-El. "Isn't the comet going to destroy us fast enough? I can't believe Zod would do something so insane."

Lara looked intently at him. "I can. He sees only his own priorities. We have to warn Borga City, evacuate the people."

Jor-El tried to envision all the inhabitants of the giant floating city fleeing into the marshes. It would take days to get them out of there, days to convince them to move in the first place. But he did not allow doubts to paralyze him. He was *Jor-El,* and they would listen to him. He'd have to make them listen. He would save them . . . for another day.

He contacted the city leader directly, demanding to speak to Shor-Em even though he was in the middle of a banquet. When the blond-haired leader frowned at him on the communication plate, Jor-El delivered his warning in a rush. Shor-Em blinked, then chuckled nervously. "Surely you are overreacting. That is not how we respond to political disagreements on Krypton."

"I am deadly serious. And you have very little time to get all your people to safety, as far away from the city as possible."

"That can't be necessary. Allow me to—"

"Do something *now*, Shor-Em. The survival of your populace requires that you act immediately!" Jor-El was shouting at the screen, and the other man flinched. "Laugh at me in the morning if I am wrong."

Even when the city leader muttered something that sounded like agreement, Jor-El was not convinced. And so he contacted other people in Borga City, any links he could find on the communication system. He repeatedly sounded the alarm, convincing as many men and women to listen as he could.

Next, he contacted Zor-El and enlisted his aid as well. "Even with the comet coming toward us, this is happening *now.*" His brother knew more officials and administrators in Borga City, and soon the alarm spread from person to person. Lara hunkered over the communication plate, promising Jor-El that she would continue to access any person she could find in the distant metropolis.

He kissed her quickly. "I have to go up there myself—face Zod and demand that he not do this. Only I can stop him."

But he feared that the Commissioner had stopped listening to him.

He departed immediately on the fastest floater raft he could find and flew through the night. He wrestled with his own arguments, seething at what Zod was trying to do. By the time his vehicle arrived at the mountain outpost, dawn's first light had begun to creep into the eastern sky. Very little time remained.

Nam-Ek had swiveled the derrick into its new position, and following orders, the technicians had shifted the focal point, reinstalled the solar batteries, and aligned the prisms and lenses. Flushed and anxious, No-Ton was giving the equipment its final test while waiting for sunlight to brighten.

Jor-El's abrupt arrival startled Zod. The Commissioner's smile looked like a curved blade. "I did not call for you."

"The *situation* called for me."

No-Ton stepped hesitantly closer to the other scientist. "I contacted him, Commissioner. I felt it might be necessary for you to . . . discuss your plans with him."

Zod scowled. "My plans are my own, and my mind is made up."

Jor-El trudged across the compound and stopped under the tall derrick structure. Cold wind blew his pale hair back from his face. Above him, the massive central crystal hung suspended at the nexus of where the solar beams would reflect and converge. "What are you doing with the Rao beam, Commissioner?"

"Only what is necessary. The fabric of our society is unraveling because of a few ragged ends. Those traitors in Borga City want to throw our world into anarchy. They established their own sham Council strictly to set Kryptonians against each other. How can we afford that?" He sounded so reasonable. "You saw Shor-Em's defiant message. Your own brother was duped by that inflammatory declaration and signed it." Zod struggled to regain his composure, fighting back a murderous fury, and took a deep breath. "Because we owe Zor-El much, and because you love him, I am willing to withhold judgment on Argo City. For now. I will give you one chance to talk sense into your brother. But for the people of Borga City, I hold out no hope. No hope at all."

The mountain winds made the Rao-beam derrick creak, as if it were shuddering. Zod raised his head, as if inspired to continue his speech. "Our old, weak society produced far too much deadwood—people who exist but do not *live,* whose hearts beat but do not pound! They are not like you and me, Jor-El. They must be swept away before a new Krypton can be born from the ashes." Staring into the blaze of the rising red sun, he spoke to Aethyr. "Power up the beam! We have waited long enough."

With icy confidence, she issued the necessary commands. The prisms in the beam apparatus began to hum with a harmonic tone, and the batteries hungrily gulped the raw energy.

Growing desperate, Jor-El grabbed Zod by the arm. "Stop this, Commissioner! You can't mean to destroy a whole city."

With an expression of distaste, Zod plucked the scientist's fingers away from his sleeve. Deaf to further protestations, he gave Jor-El a withering frown. "Do not act innocent. You created the Rao beam and presented the plans to me. You knew full well that the technology could be used in this way."

"The Rao beam is a tool, not a weapon!"

"Any tool can become a weapon."

"But—against our own people?"

"Against our *enemies,* whoever and wherever they might be. And when this is over, maybe we can look at the approaching comet that has you so upset." He seemed to be offering a small consolation prize.

"This is not why I helped you. It goes against all that I believe—"

Aethyr interrupted them smoothly. "The beam is ready, Zod. You may give the order."

"It is given."

"Stop!" Jor-El tried to push his way to the control shack, but two Sapphire Guards grabbed his arms. He thrashed against them. Even though he had sent out his most urgent warnings, even though he had begged Shor-Em to evacuate his people and Lara had continued to make calls, he knew for certain that there hadn't been enough time. Many would have gotten away, believing the call of Krypton's greatest scientist, but others would have tarried. He doubted Shor-Em had taken him seriously at all. "Commissioner, if you do this you are not the savior of Krypton, but its *destroyer*!"

Zod gestured across the mountains and into the eastern marshes. "Fire!"

Appalled, Jor-El yanked one arm free from the guards, struggled to drag himself toward the control shack, but the familiar whining hum sang up through the energy conduits of the derrick. At the last instant, he averted his eyes from the dazzling heat and from the horror.

The Rao-beam projectors spewed forth a gout of pure red light. Zod watched with clear contentment on his face as the scarlet lance shot toward the lowlands on the horizon. The beam, powerful enough to cut through a planet's crust, slammed into Borga City.

From their vantage point in the distant mountains, Jor-El saw only a flash, but he knew exactly what was happening. The incinerating beam engulfed the huge balloons that supported the city's interlocked platforms. The explosion would be instantaneous and terrific, igniting the giant cavities of volatile marsh gas that bubbled up from below. He hoped, prayed, that most of the people had already fled, racing to safety across the marshes.

But he knew they weren't all safe. He couldn't bear to think of the burning bodies falling from balloon platforms, the fiery eruptions raging across the swamp. He knew it signified thousands of deaths at the very least, people whose only crime was to disagree with Zod's leadership.

Though the devastation was complete in moments, Zod let the beam continue to pound its target, minute after endless minute. Any evacuees who had remained in the area would be watching in horror at the horrific pummeling, the destruction of everything they had known.

When he was finally satisfied, Zod told No-Ton to shut down the apparatus.

Moving ponderously, as if weary beyond description, the other scientist shifted the prisms away from the focal point. The air still thrummed with vibrant energy. Leftover ripples of heat dissipated from the column of ionized air along the beam path.

"We have annihilated one nest of traitors," Zod said. "Let us hope this ends the nonsense, once and for all."

CHAPTER 66

∞⚷◊‼◊⚬T̈Q̈◊ 66

While the foolish dissidents in other population centers were shocked and sickened by the obliteration of Borga City, Zod used the opportunity to strengthen his position. Even before his small victorious group paraded back into Kryptonopolis, he had made his preparations.

Aethyr raced ahead to distribute glorious propaganda so that his followers would learn of the event in exactly the way he wished. Towering information screens portrayed the retaliatory strike as reasonable and necessary. Most of the citizens of Kryptonopolis would already accept whatever Zod told them; anyone who expressed concern or seemed overly distressed—particularly if the person had connections to Borga City—was efficiently removed from the crowds and quietly reassigned far from the others.

Zod returned to his capital, bearded chin held high, eyes bright with victory. Nam-Ek strode boldly beside his master, his muscles bunched, his hands clenched into fists the size of large rocks.

No-Ton and the other technicians had also been recalled from the isolated mountain outpost; Zod didn't want any of them near the Rao-beam generator, at least until the uproar had died down.

Riding among them all, watched carefully by the guards, Jor-El looked broken and deflated, as if deeply ashamed that his invention had been used in such a manner. The pale-haired scientist kept his gaze turned away, but the Commissioner noticed an occasional flash of anger in his eye. Maybe Jor-El wasn't as much under control as Zod had hoped. He wondered if the defeated mood might only be an act. What if Jor-El decided to turn his considerable talents against Zod?

On the journey back, Jor-El had defiantly revealed that he'd sent a warning to Borga City, that he'd informed Shor-Em of the impending destruction. At first Zod had been outraged by the defiance, but then he grudgingly realized that survivors—witnesses—would only tell the tale and emphasize the lengths to which the Commissioner would go. No one could doubt his seriousness now. The many refugees would spread out, seeking food and shelter, and Zod was not inclined to help them. They still had to prove they had learned their lesson.

Fortunately, according to initial reports, Shor-Em and his haughty sham Council had insisted on staying inside the city. They had been annihilated along with everyone else who believed in them. A perfect solution. This had indeed been a successful undertaking, and he would make certain everyone knew it.

As the small band of troops passed between the crystal towers and into the Square of Hope, Zod raised his hands and his voice. "Borga City and its corrupt and dangerous leaders brought this fate upon themselves. It was a painful decision for me, but now we must put an end to this debilitating struggle, this civil disagreement. There are some survivors, innocents who evacuated in time, and they are dispersed to other cities. Let us hope they have accepted the truth now. Krypton is at last safe from traitors to our way of life."

The members of the Ring of Strength and their deputies lined the streets of the capital. They automatically responded with shouts and cheers. Koll-Em was the loudest of them all, barely able to contain his vindictive joy that his older brother had just been vaporized.

Zod gave a preoccupied nod, as if he were talking only to himself. "In seven days I will hold a vital summit in Kryptonopolis. I command that all city leaders present themselves to me. Anyone who does not attend will be seen as an enemy of Krypton." He marched forward with his loyal followers, sweeping into the government palace with Aethyr and Nam-Ek beside him.

Jor-El pointedly remained outside.

Lara was physically sick after hearing of the destruction of Borga City. She clutched her rounded stomach. "All those people! Even if two-thirds of them escaped in time . . . "

Jor-El rocked her in his arms. "I don't know what to believe anymore, but I certainly don't believe *him*. He will not focus on any problem other than how to achieve his own ambitions." He felt the crushing weight on his conscience of having created a tool that killed an entire city. "Zor-El was right. For too long, I tried to convince myself that the Commissioner was the lesser of two evils, that his actions would ultimately benefit Krypton. But after this . . . after his minions attacked our mother and Alura . . . " He raised his head. "Now I've got to do something about it. I can't hesitate. The responsibility is mine."

Lara reacted with alarm. "Zod will be watching you more closely than ever."

He shook his head. "Speed is my best ally. If I slip away tonight while the Commissioner is still reveling in his victory, I can blindside him. He withdrew everyone from the Rao-beam installation. Now is my chance." Jor-El held her by the shoulders, feeling steel inside. "What kind of world will our baby be born into if I let Zod wipe out entire cities on a whim? Whatever happens to me, at least my child can be proud."

"Then I'm going with you, whatever it is you intend to do."

"You can't, Lara."

Her eyes narrowed indignantly. "Just because I'm pregnant doesn't mean I'm incapable. I won't let you leave me out in the cold."

He smiled with great love for her. "That's not why I want you to stay. I need you here to cover for me. Give me an alibi if Zod suspects anything."

"Oh, he will suspect—but I'll find ways to deflect him."

"Lock down our quarters. If anyone asks, tell them I cannot be disturbed, that I'm focused on my cometary calculations. Zod should believe that." He kissed her. "I'll be back as soon as I can. Hold off any questions until then."

In the darkest, quietest hour of the night, Jor-El crept through a window in their bedroom and furtively made his way out of Kryptonopolis. He dodged the overconfident Sapphire Guards patrolling the streets. After Zod's recent show of strength, most of the people were cowed and cooperative. But not him.

When he reached the Rao-beam facility high in the mountains, the ever-present smoke and soot in the air made him think of the funeral pyres of burned innocents. He shuddered. This Rao beam had been constructed to save Krypton from the pressure buildup in the core, not to annihilate entire civilian populations. Zod had smeared Jor-El with their blood, and he felt violated.

Though the rig's solar-generating crystals were dim and the focusing mirrors had been removed, enough charge remained in the central battery for Jor-El to do his work. In his hubris, Commissioner Zod had left the facility empty during his "celebration" in Kryptonopolis, but soon he would surely send a contingent of soldiers to guard the equipment. Jor-El had to act swiftly.

Working alone in the dimness, he knelt to remove the access panel from the central generator. He shifted internal crystals, rewired control circuits, and built a feedback loop. Sparks began to swirl inside the main dangling crystal. Then he climbed up the high derrick, hand over hand on the cold metal bars, to the heart of the Rao-beam projector. After using a prybar to twist the focusing rods into near-impossible angles, Jor-El scrambled back down. The metal handholds were already growing hot as the beam projector built up to an overload.

Zod would never again use this device as a weapon. Jor-El would make certain of that.

He sprinted back toward the empty monitoring shacks as the crystal throbbed. Internal lightning bolts ricocheted in its facets as the giant gem swayed in its cradle. Shards of the scarlet beam flashed off the prisms, then turned in upon themselves. When the buildup reached its critical point, Jor-El expected the mechanism to burn out.

But it was more spectacular than that. Wild and chaotic red beams splashed onto the crystal heart, striking the focusing rods and reflecting at the wrong angles. Spearpoints of light sprayed in all directions.

Jor-El ducked into the shelter behind the dented shack moments before a swerving beam melted the roof clean away. The tall derrick began to shudder and thrum wildly. The vibrations increased.

Strafing crimson bolts struck the support girders, cutting off the derrick's legs, and the whole structure began to topple toward the steep cliffs. With a groan that sounded like a dying scream, the structure tilted farther over. Only one support leg remained fastened to the boulders now. The central crystal dangled, spun, and finally broke free of its support cable. It shattered on a cliff ledge far below in a hail of blazing light and broken glass.

The flurry of beams died away, but gravity and leftover thermal energy continued to take their toll. With a wrenching noise, the last of the support legs tore free. Steel bolts sheared off, and the entire construction scraped down the cliffside like sharp fingernails on a polished slate board. The twisted derrick finally came to rest, while boulders pummeled the wreckage.

Unnerved yet exhilarated, Jor-El went to the edge of the precipice. He could barely make out the tangled ruin wedged into the boulder field far below. At last he felt satisfied. He had disarmed Zod, at least temporarily.

Now he had to race back to Kryptonopolis before anyone noticed his absence. His alibi needed to be perfect.

CHAPTER 67

∞ ⟡ ‼ ◇ T̤ ⟨ 67

After the annihilation of Borga City, all those who had signed
Shor-Em's inflammatory declaration knew they could not stand against
Zod. They had already seen the towering nova javelins, and now the boiling scar in the middle of the marshes was a stark reminder of what any
continued defiance would earn them. The many survivors of the city lived
in squalid temporary encampments out in the marshes, while others made
their way to Corril, to Orvai, to the villages in the mountains or river valleys or the coasts. After the disasters of Kandor and Argo City, this was
one more wave of people who saw their very planet falling apart.

Now Zod had to convince them that he was the only person who
could hold their civilization together.

Bowed and beaten, the sullen city leaders traveled to Kryptonopolis
for the summit meeting, as commanded. Though not entirely contrite,
they were clearly afraid to cause any trouble. The refugees and witnesses
of the blasted city had already spread the word, told of the horrors they
had seen. They feared Zod now—feared him completely.

He observed the supposedly meek representatives from his government palace. He wanted to kill them one at a time until someone
revealed who had committed the sabotage at the Rao-beam installation
on the very night of his triumph. His inner fury had not abated since
he'd learned that some terrorist had wrecked the facility. The gall! He'd
had no immediate plans to use the beam weapon again—mainly because

no other major city lay in the correct path—but Zod was outraged that someone had defied him. He could not tolerate that.

Loyal Sapphire Guards brought the individual rebel leaders into his office as they arrived, nineteen of them so far. The intimidating guards had clubs and hand weapons, but Zod's control was firm enough that the mere threat of violence made actual violence unnecessary. Each city leader stood before him; some looked broken, while others retained a foolish but impotent anger.

"Who sabotaged my Rao-beam installation?" Zod demanded of them one at a time. "Who committed this traitorous act against all of Krypton?"

No one gave a satisfactory answer. No one knew anything.

Since these men had capitulated so swiftly and willingly, Zod was certain they did not have the strength of character to do anything so bold and defiant. They paid lip service to their resistance but didn't have the spine to stand up to him. They were, however, pleased that some mysterious stranger had dared to do something they had not. Three of the men who showed a last spark of defiance warranted additional questioning, and Koll-Em took great glee in inflicting pain. Again, none of them knew anything.

For good measure, at Aethyr's suggestion, Zod also called in No-Ton for questioning, as well as all the technicians who had originally worked at the installation. When destroying the Rao beam, the saboteur had known exactly what he was doing. Since he was a member of the Ring of Strength, No-Ton was indignant at the very idea of the Commissioner's suspicions, and Zod was quickly convinced that none of those workers had been involved, either.

When he summoned Jor-El, however, Zod was surprised to sense a change in the scientist's mood. Before he could even ask, Jor-El said, "Is it a crime for me to be thankful that you have lost a deadly weapon? You have ignored the real threat of the comet. Loth-Ur's Hammer is coming in less than four months. You have just wasted another week. I beg you to turn your attention to that far more critical situation."

The Commissioner sighed. "As you requested, I passed the data on to a team of scientific advisers. They have assured me your projected orbits are inconclusive. There is nothing to worry about." In fact, he'd been hard pressed to find any scientist besides Jor-El with a working knowledge of celestial mechanics.

Hearing this, Jor-El's disbelief was quickly replaced by a wash of anger. "Commissioner, when have you ever questioned me before? Can you afford to take the chance now?" Zod was troubled. Indeed, he had accepted Jor-El's science and theories in every previous instance, but now he obviously didn't want to believe. Jor-El pressed the issue. "Are you sure the others aren't just telling you what you want to hear?"

"Does that make the conclusion wrong?" Zod rose to his feet. "I admire your science, Jor-El—I always have. But you do not see the larger picture. If I pull back all of my manpower right now to work on this theory of yours, then the other city leaders will pounce like carrion dogs! I don't dare show weakness or hesitation. My glorious plans for our future will go up in smoke if I lose Krypton!"

"If we don't do something about the comet, we will all lose Krypton."

"If you're right."

"I'm right."

"You sound rather arrogant and self-assured."

"I'm right."

"In that case, do everything in your power to help me achieve a swift and decisive resolution to this civil war. Then I would have no other distractions." Zod lowered his voice, abruptly changing the subject. "You know something about what happened at the Rao-beam facility. I can see it in your eyes." He realized he would have to play this carefully. Too much was at stake, and he had too many unfinished projects for which he needed Jor-El's expertise. While the Commissioner had a host of other scientists and engineers in his employ, none of them could hold a candle to Jor-El.

The ivory-haired scientist didn't answer, and Zod suddenly drew the obvious conclusion. Jor-El was protecting his brother! Yes, of all the city leaders he had summoned, Zor-El remained among those conspicuously absent. Zor-El knew the installation's vulnerabilities as well as his brother did. Yes, Zor-El the firebrand . . . intelligent like his brother, but also a loose cannon, prone to precipitous actions without thinking through the consequences. Destroying the Rao beam was exactly the sort of thing such a man would do.

But Zod had learned not to ask questions when he did not want to know the answers. He couldn't afford to lose Jor-El. Not yet. "I will be watching you carefully." He called the Sapphire Guards waiting outside his office door. "Take him back to his quarters. Make sure he and his wife are prepared and cooperative for our presentation later today."

Aethyr came to wait with Zod in his office as the fateful hour approached. He stared out the window into the plaza where crowds had already gathered. "This is the dawn of a bright new day," he said to her, as if starting his long-anticipated speech.

Aethyr's red lips pressed together in a frown. "It would be brighter if Zor-El had come."

Zod's expression darkened. "I have already decided that we must deal with Argo City. I am convinced Zor-El is the one who destroyed the Rao beam."

She was startled but not surprised. Zod straightened his dark uniform. "Come, it is time." He took her by the arm. Surrounded by guards, he and his consort walked together out to see the noisy crowds in the Square of Hope.

Zod took his place at the foot of the towering statue, with Aethyr and Nam-Ek nearby. The Sapphire Guards had cleared a wide area around the beaten city leaders. Zod wondered how many of those defeated men knew the story of what Jax-Ur had done to those he had vanquished. A smile crept onto his lips.

On cue, Aethyr turned to face him and shouted, "We all bow to Zod." She bent her knee before him and lowered her head. Nam-Ek followed suit, the massive silent man submitting to his leader.

"We all bow to Zod," said Koll-Em as all sixteen members of the Ring of Strength did the same.

The Commissioner raised both hands as if dispensing a benediction. "And now, my city leaders, all those who join us in a united Krypton— kneel before Zod."

Hesitantly at first, ashamed and obviously feeling coerced, the gathered leaders got down on their knees. Like ripples spreading out from a stone dropped into a still pond, all the people in Kryptonopolis submitted, dropping to their knees around the colossus statue.

Zod found it all quite satisfactory. "Shor-Em once sneered that my title of Commissioner was insufficient for a man who would rule Krypton. In this one thing, he was correct. So I no longer call myself a Commissioner, for my Commission is gone. Nor will I take the title of Council Head, for that would serve only to remind us of our weakness.

"Defending Krypton requires an entirely different sort of thinking—military thinking." He drew a deep breath. Some of the people turned their faces to gaze adoringly at him, while others averted troubled eyes. "From this day forward, I shall be General Zod."

General Zod. The title felt so appropriate, so perfect. That announcement should have been the climax of his day.

But then, stealing his glorious moment, the newly grown crystal spires around the square began to shimmer. Flares of light skirled along the facets like electrical bursts, tracing lines of inclusions and flaws.

"What is this?" Zod demanded, forgetting that the voice amplifier patch remained at his throat. His alarmed voice rolled like thunder across the square.

People milled about in confusion; the defeated city leaders cringed, as if this were some sort of punishment from Zod. The crystal spires shone brighter, and the smooth facets began to display an image, a dark-haired man with a steely expression. Cold claws raked down Zod's spine as he recognized the man.

Zor-El's voice boomed out. "You do not speak for Krypton, Zod! Argo City defies you. I defy you. And in their hearts, I know that all those here defy you." His image shouted at the uneasy crowd. "Zod is a criminal against our race. May his reign be as short as it is unwelcome. He tried to abduct or kill my wife and my mother—my wife and mother!" He made a sound of disgust.

Zod shouted, "Stop that signal! How is Zor-El doing this?"

Out in the audience, Jor-El turned quickly away. Lara whispered something in his ear. Then Zod knew that the pale-haired scientist must have modified the tall crystal structures to function as gigantic communication plates.

Before Zod could call the Sapphire Guards to seize Jor-El for interrogation, the Argo City leader called out through his many identical images projected through the facets, "I call on all Kryptonians, all true Kryptonians, to stand against this man who claims to 'protect' us by destroying our cities, who resorts to murder to prevent anyone from criticizing him. Zod has shown his true colors."

The face of Jor-El's brother flickered and vanished. The crystal spires stopped glowing. And the uproar began.

CHAPTER 68

After humiliating General Zod in such a spectacular and public forum, Zor-El knew that his days were numbered. He had to build up Argo City's defenses and bring together any others who would fight the tyrant.

While the destruction of Borga City had driven many people into frightened submission, it had also galvanized an uneasy ragtag rebellion into a genuine force. Shor-Em had not gone far enough, and he had never dreamed how Zod would be willing to respond.

The Borga refugees had lost everything, and now they joined any resistance they could find, offering to stand and fight against the tyrant. As they drifted to temporary new homes, they began to build an army that was much more widespread than anything the General had imagined.

In his private villa Zor-El met with powerful merchants, industrialists, deputy leaders, and other volunteers who wanted to join the new resistance. A handful of people had come directly to him after he'd warned them to evacuate from Borga City, making no secret of the fact that they owed him their lives. More and more volunteers came from all across Krypton, and determined members from the Society of Vigilance vigorously sought to weed out any spies sent by Zod.

"General Zod already has an army, powerful weapons, and most of Krypton under his thumb," said Gal-Eth, the vice mayor of Orvai. He had bristly blond hair and a ruddy face. He had fled his beautiful city in the lake district after the reluctant replacement for the lost Gil-Ex had trudged off to bend his knee in submission to Zod. "How can we protect ourselves against that?"

"We're the people of Krypton," Zor-El said. "We can do the impossible."

"It's been a long time since we did the impossible," grumbled shaggy-haired Or-Om, a prominent industrialist from a small mining town in the mountains north of Corril. "The old Council beat that out of us for so long that we forgot how to be innovative."

"Then we'll find a way to remember," Korth-Or insisted. His sandy-brown hair was streaked with gray, as if he had rubbed ashes it in; his face was narrow, his lips generous, and he spoke with a faint lisp. He had escaped with his family on the night before Zod destroyed Borga City. Korth-Or had temporary quarters in Argo City, but he made no secret that he would have been much happier on the march against General Zod.

In the bright morning, Zor-El faced the sunlit room full of anxious but determined men and women. Alura had placed verdant potted plants along all the walls. "Those of you who can, go back to your own cities," he advised the secret group. Korth-Or sat fuming with indignation, reminded that he had no home. "Speak to your populations, find volunteers. We have to gather an army strong enough to stand against Zod—and soon—or we are lost."

"Are you sure we aren't lost already?" Or-Om had been imagining disasters since long before Krypton had actually faced one, and it had taken much convincing for him to join this gathering, leaving his industries behind. "Our resistance to Zod was based in Borga City, and now that's gone."

Such talk angered Zor-El. "The resistance is here now. But if that's how you truly feel, then go to Kryptonopolis, and bend your knee to Zod. Be my guest."

No one took him up on the offer.

As soon as she found the mysterious message crystal left just inside the villa's portico, Charys carried it to Zor-El in his high tower laboratory.

He had been struggling day and night to increase the scope of the force field. When it was no more than a small bubble around the diamondfish, the design had been simple. But to form a whole hemispherical dome over Argo City was a nearly insoluble problem. Red-eyed, he continued to test his shield, raising the shimmering barricade higher and higher above the seawall. There must be no weak point against an attack from Zod's minions.

His mother held out the crystal, and he realized exactly who had sent the message. "It's from Jor-El." He had been angry after their recent argument about Zod, but his brother had also made possible the defiant transmission through the facets of the towering crystals, and—much to Zor-El's astonishment—he had also revealed that he'd sabotaged the Rao-beam generator. And Jor-El was absolutely right about the threat of the comet, and he had sent urgent warnings to Borga City, which allowed many of the people to escape.

Charys thrust the crystal at him. "You can't change the message by avoiding it."

As soon as Zor-El cupped the message crystal in his warm hand, the image began to form. The ivory-haired scientist spoke to him insistently, "We need to help each other. No matter how terrible Zod's actions, we both know that our most pressing problem is Loth-Ur's Hammer. Our time grows shorter day by day, and we've already lost a month during which we should have pooled all our resources and brainpower to divert the comet. Zor-El, you and I might be Krypton's only hope, the only ones who can see."

Charys did not take long to speak her mind after the message faded. "He's right—and you know it. You've got to help him."

He shook his head slowly. "You're my conscience and my sounding board, Mother, but what if Zod forced him to send that message? Jor-El has a wife, and they're about to have a baby. General Zod has ways to coerce him."

She stared intently at him. "And do you believe that?"

He looked at her for a long moment before he finally shook his head. "No."

"The two sons of Yar-El can find a way. Share your defensive shield with him." Charys gestured to the calculations strewn on his table. "Maybe he'll show you how to expand it to help other cities."

"I can't do that! Do I dare risk letting the shield fall into Zod's hands? He would use it to make his defenses impregnable. How can we ever defeat him if he hides behind an impervious barrier?"

He stepped out onto the open balcony where he breathed in the cool evening air. "Even if I accept what Jor-El says, it's best to let Zod believe that the two of us remain at odds. What if he tries to use my brother as a bargaining chip? What if he threatens to kill his wife and unborn child unless I capitulate?" He looked into his mother's deep-brown eyes. He knew in his heart that Zod would not hesitate to do exactly that.

"Then we just can't let that happen," she said.

Filled with a mixture of inspiration and dread, Zor-El went back to his work. He refused to give up, refused to sleep until he had solved at least one critical problem.

CHAPTER 69

The time for subtlety had passed. Now that he had named himself General, rallied his followers, and coerced his critics, Zod pulled together his weapons and manpower. A sullen Jor-El worked his daily assignment in the underground control rooms, where General Zod had instructed him to ensure that the nova javelins would function properly.

And Aethyr remained vigilant for any weak points in their government. She watched Lara closely, and waited, and finally made her move.

Lara was her friend—former friend—yet now Aethyr feared the other woman was becoming a liability. And if that were the case, she intended to find out for herself and expose Lara. It would be so much worse if Zod should discover it first.

Aethyr chose her time well. Because of her pregnancy, Lara had regular appointments with her doctor, a dry and humorless woman named Kirana-Tu. Aethyr waited until Lara went to the new Kryptonopolis medical center before she and Nam-Ek approached the private dwelling. In Kryptonopolis, no door was blocked to the consort of General Zod; they easily bypassed the locks.

With Nam-Ek watching at the door, Aethyr moved through the main chamber, poking around until she found the long table where Lara had set up her writing pads, stylus, and recording sheets. Her eyes lit up with curiosity. Here was the great chronicle that Zod had commissioned, the firsthand historical record of events.

Aethyr swiftly scanned the lines of text. Lara had concise, clear handwriting, not overly flowery or effeminate. Later editions of this work would no doubt include calligraphy and holographic enhancements. Someday every student on Krypton would be required to memorize the life of Zod. However, as she skimmed page after page, Aethyr found the summaries of events to be lackluster, forced. She was quite disappointed.

And suspicious. She knew her friend better than that, knew that Lara did not hold back her opinions. The very absence of any sort of commentary or the slightest of veiled criticisms made Aethyr wonder what the other woman could be hiding.

Hiding . . .

"Nam-Ek, we must search this place. Find out what they are trying to keep secret from us." The authority of General Zod gave her all the confidence and justification she needed. With an eager grin, the big mute nodded and began to tear the dwelling apart.

In a hidden and sealed drawer in a private bureau inside the bedchamber, beneath the writing surface, she found a journal. Lara's real record.

Now, as she read from line to line, Aethyr's heart fell and her anger rose. What should have been a glorious biography lionizing a great leader was full of harsh criticisms and insults. Lara blatantly accused Zod of foolish mistakes, character flaws, and grave hubris! She portrayed him as a bloodthirsty tyrant.

Aethyr stood cold for a long moment, debating what to do. Finally she gathered up the pages. She would make absolutely certain that the public could never read these lies.

"Come, Nam-Ek. We must see the General immediately."

Aethyr dropped the papers on Zod's desk. She made no apology for interrupting his strategy session for a retaliatory strike on Argo City. "Read this. Lara wrote it."

He picked up the sheets. "What am I looking for?"

"Choose a page at random. It should be quite apparent."

She watched the General as he read first one page, then another, then a third. He didn't say a word, but he grew coldly, murderously furious.

CHAPTER 70

The female doctor pronounced Lara's baby healthy and strong in its third trimester. "You should have no complications."

Lara let out a wry laugh, though the sheer tension in her mind made any sort of laughter difficult. "No complications? That'll be quite a change, considering how our lives have been going."

"What do you mean?" Kirana-Tu asked, not understanding the joke. She was supposedly one of the best obstetricians on Krypton, but she had little awareness of outside events. Lara smiled to herself, reminded of Jor-El's single-mindedness when he focused on a complex technical problem.

"By the way," the doctor added, as if it were an irrelevant detail, "the baby will be a boy. I thought you'd like to know."

"A son!" Lara couldn't wait to tell Jor-El.

Again, the doctor missed the reason for her patient's excitement. "Well, it had to be one or the other. Would you have been just as excited if I told you it was a daughter?"

"Of course." Lara was now even more convinced that the two of them would have to slip away from Kryptonopolis and escape from Zod's oppression. But she also knew they were being watched carefully.

Pleased to have such a clean bill of health, and her news, Lara left the medical center only to find Aethyr and Nam-Ek waiting for her. Both wore implacable expressions. Nam-Ek took one large step forward and grasped Lara's arm with a broad hand. His grip was like a shackle.

Her heart skipped a beat. "Should I ask what this is about?"

Aethyr stepped forward, looking as if Lara had entirely betrayed her. "If you need to ask, then you are more foolish than even I guessed. Be sure to include that in your seditious historical chronicle."

"So, you read my journal?" Lara quipped, knowing she could not deny what she had written. Suddenly she could no longer hold in her pent-up dissatisfactions and her rage at what Zod had done. "Was my grammar incorrect? The spelling? Maybe you didn't like my descriptions. Too many adverbs? Or perhaps I should have taken more creative license in describing Zod. But you did want this to be a *history* instead of a fantasy, right? Or did I misunderstand you?"

Aethyr didn't answer. Nam-Ek hustled Lara toward the Square of Hope.

Lara went on, though she knew it would do her no good. "I particularly liked my account of the annihilation of Borga City. Quite vivid prose." The big mute pulled her arm so hard she nearly stumbled.

"I wanted to add interviews with all those dissidents who so cheerfully changed their minds and conveniently retired, but I couldn't find any of them. Not a one! Do you suppose something terrible happened to them? Maybe we should tell the General. He'll get to the bottom of it."

Aethyr said, "Silence! I won't hear you speak of him that way."

"Oh, his actions speak well enough for themselves."

Nam-Ek was so angry he issued a grunt.

They reached one of the towering emerald crystal spires at the corner of the square. Not long ago, Zor-El's defiant face had been transmitted from these facets, linking into electronic resonance and communications circuits that Jor-El had added to his father's original blueprint. Now the gleaming towers had been stripped of all outside connections, power sources, and amenities.

The lattice design had created intentional voids, cavities, and chambers to be modified into rooms. Eventually, these towers were earmarked to become crowded administrative buildings, but at the moment the spiky turrets acted only as showpieces to demonstrate the grandeur of Kryptonopolis.

Nam-Ek shoved Lara into one of the openings. She stumbled into a transparent-walled office . . . no, a cell. She whirled, still shouting bit-

terly to Aethyr. She couldn't stop the words pouring out of her. "If you bring me filmpaper, I can keep writing. The General asked me to finish the chronicle right away. I wouldn't want to disappoint him!"

"Sarcasm will not help your case, Lara."

She tossed her amber hair. "Did I have a case? Does that mean there will be a fair trial? An objective court? I look forward to speaking in my own defense."

Aethyr added a growth crystal to the wall and applied a small power source. "Zod isn't going to make a spectacle of you. You aren't important enough to warrant that sort of treatment." Crystals began to grow, and angular spears closed off the room. As the last of the gap sealed shut, Aethyr added, "The General doesn't want you. He wants Jor-El. And with you locked away in here, your husband will have no choice but to cooperate."

Jor-El had a sickening feeling about why he had been summoned before Zod. He could think of several reasons why he might be in trouble. He stood straight-backed and unyielding, saying nothing. He had been planning to flee with Lara, to escape so that he could work with his brother in Argo City, but now he feared it was too late.

An angry General Zod sat in his heavy office chair with his consort at his shoulder, as silent and intimidating as Nam-Ek. Glaring at Jor-El, Aethyr lovingly stroked her husband's uniform. High above, the fabric pavilion coverings of the roof flapped and fluttered as a dry wind picked up.

Zod tapped his fingers together pretending to search for words, but Jor-El could tell that he had practiced his little soliloquy. "I need you, Jor-El. I have always needed you. But more than anything else, I need you to support me. I need you to be my staunchest ally, rather than someone who participates only halfheartedly."

Jor-El remained silent and rigid. He had too many secrets, too many plans in the works. Even now, sensing his personal peril, he could not forget about the giant comet coming . . . but Zod seemed intent on destroying Krypton first.

The General got up from his desk and paced around him. "Until now, I have acted as an indulgent parent with an exceptional child. I have allowed you to play with whatever interested you."

"What interests me is what's most important to Krypton. Right now, our greatest threat is Loth-Ur's Hammer, not your critics! If that mountain of ice and rock smashes into our planet, *everyone* will die—yet you ignore it."

Aethyr moved like a viper about to strike. "Be quiet when the General speaks to you."

Zod waved her back. "Remember that I have followed your career for a long time, Jor-El. First you warned that our sun could go supernova at any time. Next, you and your brother claimed our planet would explode. Now it's a comet. This threat is a hobgoblin of your imagination—or worse, a plan to divert my attention so your brother's rebellion can gain strength." He narrowed his eyes. "I know you secretly sympathize with the dissidents, and I will not be deceived by your comet."

Jor-El squared his shoulders. "You are wrong, General. Dead wrong. If there's any deception here, it's you who have deceived yourself."

Zod sounded weary. "From this day forward, I expect you to work with unwavering dedication on the nova javelins. You will inspect all fifteen, repair any defects, and ensure that the missiles are ready for launch at a moment's notice. The charts and coordinates from Jax-Ur are out of date and inaccurate. I charge you with the responsibility of updating all their navigation systems." He ran a finger along his lower lip. "I may need the weapons sooner than I expected."

"I refuse."

The General cut him off. "To ensure your dedication to the greater good, I have taken your wife into protective custody. She is being kept safe inside one of the crystal towers where, also for the greater good, she can write no more of her malicious distortions of epic historic events. There is no need for her or your unborn baby to be harmed—so long as you remain cooperative."

His heart pounding, Jor-El stared at the General, who stared back. Using Lara as a fulcrum, Zod could move him however he wished—and the General knew it. In a voice as cold as an ice crystal, Jor-El said, "Before I do anything, take me to Lara. I must see for myself that she's unharmed."

Aethyr's tone was dangerous. "You do not give orders to Zod."

The General did not break eye contact with Jor-El. "I give you my word she is quite unharmed."

Jor-El shook his head. "You have given me no reason to trust you."

Zod sighed, making it seem as if he was doing the scientist a great favor. "Very well. Seeing her will convince you faster than arguing would."

Jor-El maintained his stiff demeanor as he marched alongside the General, matching his brisk, military pace.

The towering shard of green crystal loomed over the edge of the Square of Hope, riddled with small cavities and inclusions. Zod led him through the main entrance and along curving, faceted tunnels to where Lara was sequestered. Angled crystal spikes had been grown across the doorway like overlapping prison bars. Jor-El could see his wife's form through the translucent walls. He ran toward her, to Zod's apparent amusement.

Lara heard him coming. She pushed her hand between the crossed crystal bars, and Jor-El clasped her cold fingers. "Lara, are you safe? Has he hurt you?"

"Other than sealing me in this cell? No—I don't think he will."

"Make no mistake, I *will* hurt you," Zod said from several paces away, "but only if it is the only means to achieve my goals."

Jor-El ignored him. "I'll find a way to get you out of here."

She squeezed his hand. "Don't let him manipulate you. You know what he's capable of. He'll use me as a hostage—"

The General came forward and added another growth crystal to the wall. With a series of snaps and cracks, the intersecting spears thickened and began to fill in the gaps in the lattice. Lara snatched her hand back before the bars closed around it.

"There." Zod assumed a cordial manner. "Now we can get on with our real work."

CHAPTER 71

Looking down at the contoured gel model of Argo City in his war room, Zod couldn't hide his pleasure. "Intriguing. This presents a strategic nightmare for them. We can easily cut off the whole peninsula, and Zor-El will have to capitulate."

Aethyr shrugged. "Then our victory is a foregone conclusion. The only question is how long the siege will last."

Nam-Ek looked down at the three-dimensional model, as if memorizing the miniaturized terrain. Zod had also studied reports from informants, including many of his original supporters who had been ousted from the city.

"Argo City is basically an island, connected to the mainland only by this thin strip of land, a bottleneck. We can blockade the city with a relatively small number of troops and equipment. These five bridges"—Zod traced the gentle arcs that led across the narrow bay from Argo City to the mainland—"are strategic weak points. Our soldiers can capture and hold them, effectively amputating the rebels from the rest of the world."

"There's the ocean on the other side," Aethyr pointed out. "They have docks and boats."

"But where can they go—fishing? They have no navy, no warships." He pursed his lips. "But you make a valid point, and I prefer to be thorough. Maybe I should deploy aquatic craft so we cut them off from the ocean as well." Nam-Ek grinned; Zod could tell he was eager to see the

boats. "None of the new structures they've built since the tsunami are proof against attack. We can bottle them up just like Kandor and then begin our bombardment. Once the way is clear, our army will invade the city."

"Why don't you just build a new Rao beam?" Koll-Em looked hungry to see another swift cleansing blast.

"Destruction is easy but there is little satisfaction in it. What kind of conquest leaves nothing but rubble? I am the savior of Krypton, not its destroyer." He smiled wryly at his twisting of the words Jor-El had spoken. "The victory is much greater if I bring Argo City under my rule. That city is like a jewel in a crown."

All the construction crews in Kryptonopolis had been reassigned to the task of strengthening General Zod's impressive army. Technicians assembled large numbers of conventional weapons. His own scientists and engineers were swiftly redesigning and refitting normal vehicles. Teams worked round the clock to convert large construction crawlers into armored artillery launchers and siege vehicles; floating passenger platforms were transformed into troop transports.

The Sapphire Guards and the Ring of Strength recruited, even coerced, every one of Zod's able-bodied followers to undergo weapons training, don uniforms, and join the great campaign. The army could cross the continent and be at Zor-El's doorstep within a week after they mobilized.

Three days later Zod's assembled armies gathered outside of Kryptonopolis, ready to march. Jor-El observed the fanfare with skepticism. Were these people truly so excited to go attack another sovereign city? Had they been so duped by Zod's delusions? Yes, he realized; they probably had. By now, anyone who had openly expressed disapproval had been quietly reassigned elsewhere . . . or had vanished entirely. The rest demonstrated their enthusiasm, or at least made a good show of it.

Jor-El stood alone, his emotions balanced between anger and helplessness. He ached for Lara, knowing she was a hostage to ensure his cooperation, and he could do nothing about it. His love for her had made him vulnerable. Fortunately, it also made him strong. If she'd had longer to talk with him, Lara would no doubt have insisted that Jor-El forget about her, and do what was right and necessary.

He vowed to save her. He would also save Krypton. There was no other option.

Wearing his crisp new uniform with the hauteur of a man in complete control, Zod marched up to Jor-El. His voice was low and taunting. "No matter what gadgets or defenses your brother might have concocted, Argo City cannot stand against me."

"My brother is an intelligent man. He may surprise you."

"Ah, but my armies were equipped by an even more intelligent man." Zod smiled. "I was able to use the designs of the great Jor-El himself." He made a gesture.

At the edge of the city, large warehouse buildings opened up, their heavy doors sliding into recessed ceilings to expose hangars filled with military equipment. Armored machines emerged, some crawling on heavy treads or thick wheels, others hovering above the ground with levitation pads. Jor-El struggled to grasp what he was seeing. The vehicles were loaded with missile launchers, ray projectors, thermal cannons, digging devices, and canisters that could only be powerful explosives.

"You see, Jor-El, you aren't the only one who remembers the innovative concepts you delivered to my Commission. So many dangerous inventions . . . so much potential for destruction. Don't you agree?" Just as Zod had kept the creation of his ostentatious statue a secret from Lara, he must have had separate teams working to produce these weapons without Jor-El's knowledge.

"I recognize some of those designs, but—how? The Commission confiscated my plans! You destroyed them."

"I lied—for the good of Krypton."

More and more exotic weaponry rolled out, making the General's already overwhelming army seem ten times more threatening. "You will remain here in Kryptonopolis under close watch, but rest assured that when Argo City falls to me, you will have had a clear hand in its defeat."

CHAPTER 72

∞⌐◊‼◊⊷T̈◊ 72

Zor-El knew that General Zod's army would be coming with all the
force it could muster. At Borga City, the General had already shown how
far he was willing to go. Now Argo City would surely face annihilation
as well.

Though he had already anticipated Zod's response, Zor-El received
confirmation of his worst fears when Jor-El sent him a desperate message burst. Jor-El was being held under guard, and Lara was a prisoner—exactly as Zor-El dreaded—but even so, his brother found a way
to communicate . . . as he always did.

To control information and to prevent word from leaking out, General
Zod had shut down all outgoing communications from Kryptonopolis.
The message grid had been cut off . . . and yet Jor-El tapped into it, sending a pulsed burst into the continent-wide power network. The message
only worked once, melting down several nodes, but the ominous text had
played out on the screens of Zor-El's seismic monitors.

"Zod's armies are coming."

So they prepared for the onslaught. Zor-El's people responded with
heartwarming dedication and sacrifice. The Society of Vigilance had
swelled in recent days, recruiting many members from the angry Borga
City refugees, and everyone in the city was on alert. Scouts patrolled the
mainland up and down the coast and many kilometers into the interior,
watching for the oncoming army from Kryptonopolis. It was only a matter of time.

Ironically, Zod had succeeded in unifying Krypton against a common enemy—*him*. Never before had so many people, so many cities, cooperated so fully toward a single goal. The widespread, and hollow-eyed, survivors from the annihilation of Borga City were only one more reminder of the crimes. Other than his lockstep followers in the new capital, everyone else had turned against the General. Zor-El watched with grim satisfaction as his people pushed themselves beyond their limits; they used their imagination, shook themselves out of their long-standing malaise, and retreated from the quagmire of stagnation. The spirit of Krypton had been reawakened.

In his observation tower, Zor-El had finished his intensive calculations, but he felt little joy in his solution. During a time like this, he and his brother should have been laboring side by side with the assistance of No-Ton and every other scientist on Krypton. Instead of deploying his shield to protect against the oncoming comet, he would now have to use it to defend against an invading army.

Utterly exhausted despite the satisfaction of success, he turned to his wife. "Sometimes I wonder what the point is. Even if we save our city from Zod, Loth-Ur's Hammer is still going to smash the whole planet in a month."

Alura stroked his cheek with a sky-blue blossom, then gently trailed it across his face, down his nose. He felt a rush of rejuvenation from the tailored pollens and perfumes. "You do it because you never give up hope. You may indeed find a way to save Krypton, or save one city, or even save a single person. That is the point."

A young auburn-haired woman rushed into the tower chamber; sweat-damp garments clung to her arms and body. "I just came across the Alkar Bridge from the mainland. Our scouts spotted an incredible force of troops and gigantic vehicles coming toward the coast at great speed."

Before he or Alura could ask questions, the young woman spread a thin, flexible sheet of filmcrystal on the tower wall, where it adhered to the smooth stones like a newly installed window. She smoothed a wrinkle and touched a corner so that surveillance images began to play. With the General standing proud and invincible in the lead craft, the vanguard of Zod's troops advanced on floater platforms followed by large rolling vehicles, like dragons covered with thick armor. Next came wide-barreled artillery launchers, attack vehicles studded with spikes and unidentified weapons. Behind them came rank after rank of uniformed soldiers.

Never before had Krypton seen such an army.

"General Zod must have rallied everything against us." Alura's voice cracked.

Zor-El shook his head, his face grave. "I doubt we're seeing everything. Count on the General to hold a few thoroughly unpleasant surprises in reserve."

Though the young scout was still panting from rushing to him with her report, Zor-El gave her no time to rest. "Sound the alarms through the streets! Get everyone in Argo City ready. We have drilled for this, and now it's time. I want Or-Om, Gal-Eth, and Korth-Or with me to help me guide our defense. If the General defeats us here, their cities will be next."

Wiping sweat-streaked auburn hair out of her eyes, the young woman ran from the tower room.

Next he turned to Alura. "Can you see that my mother is safe?"

"And where, exactly, is safe?"

"I wish I knew." Zor-El put his arms around her. "At least the waiting is over, and we can plan accordingly. I'll transmit immediate messages to our supporters in other towns. I don't like to use Argo City as bait, but while Zod is attacking us, the rebellion has to begin everywhere else across the continent. Zod can't fight us all at once."

"He'll try." Alura looked back at the filmcrystal window that displayed the massive armed forces from Kryptonopolis. Zod's military outnumbered them at least ten to one. She lowered her voice. "You're going to have to take drastic action."

"I didn't want to, but now there's no choice. It'll be a difficult siege."

"We can endure, no matter how long it lasts. With my efficient greenhouses, our waterways, and our local energy sources, Argo City could be perfectly self-sufficient for years."

He felt a lump in his throat, thinking through the cascade of consequences. "There can be no turning back. My beautiful city will never be the same afterward—even if we do somehow survive the comet."

"Zod has already forced us into permanent change. It's not your fault."

The red sun shone like a great burning eye on the events about to unfold. To the east, the sea was strangely calm, and Zor-El tried to draw peace from it, but his stomach was knotted.

So far, he had heard nothing more from his brother besides the terse warning message. Kryptonopolis had been locked down tight even with Zod's army gone. Posing as loyal followers of Zod and wearing sapphire armbands seized by the Society of Vigilance, volunteer couriers had slipped into the new city. Each one carried a small message crystal that, to most observers, projected innocent images of family members who had vanished with Kandor. Zor-El, however, had hidden secondary messages in the crystals, schematics and detailed explanations of his work with the protective shield. Now it was his turn to help Jor-El. That secret message was tailored to activate only upon contact with his brother's DNA markers, which were the same as his own. None of the couriers had returned.

Zor-El took Alura's hand, and they walked out of the tower. It was time to be with the people. "We've done all that we can. For the rest, we have to rely on hope and luck."

"That's not a very scientific-sounding statement."

"Even in science there's a certain element of chance."

Nervous, yet resigned, crowds had gathered in Argo City's streets and squares. Many stood on balconies overlooking the five graceful bridges, watching the dust cloud and shadows that marked the forward progress of Zod's army. It wouldn't be long now.

"Clear the bridges," Zor-El ordered. "Bring everyone inside the city. Those who want to take their chances on the mainland should evacuate now." Staying in Argo City under siege might not be any safer, but this was where he had cast his lot. Zor-El would rely on his technology, his own abilities.

And he had a surprise for the General.

Massive floating platforms loaded with armed troops drew up to each of the five emblematic bridges, and Zod's warriors disembarked, each contingent led by one puffed-up member of the Ring of Strength. Rumbling siege equipment, heavily armored vehicles, and mobile weapons took up positions along the thin spit of land that formed the narrowest part of the peninsula. Very quickly, all of Argo City was blocked off. But the General held his army back, as if hesitant to fire.

Zor-El smiled at Alura. "He must be worried about what I have up my sleeve."

"Why are you waiting? You know what you have to do." Her dark eyes were full of worry. He thought she looked achingly beautiful. "Are you having second thoughts? We may have only a few moments before the attack begins."

He laughed. "Zod won't attack—yet. I know his type. He'll make a grandiose speech, threaten us, and try to make us quake in our shoes. He's convinced that we have no chance."

At the forefront of his army, General Zod rode on a command platform surrounded by impenetrable transparent panes that would protect him from any stray weapons fire or overt assassination attempts, even from his own people. Aethyr and Nam-Ek flanked him as the floater pulled up to the central bridge. He looked ready to cross and lead a full-scale invasion. Zor-El, who had moved to a tall building on the bayside edge of the city, crossed his arms and looked down from a balcony at the tiny figure of the General.

Zod spoke into a high-powered amplifier that made his voice so loud that the words clapped against the clouds overhead. "I do not wish to damage this glorious city, but your defiance harms all of Krypton. If I do not receive your surrender within one hour, we begin our bombardment. Your people shall suffer terribly. Think of them."

Zor-El had installed voice amplifiers of his own on the observation balcony. His defiant response, picked up by repeaters and speakers everywhere, thundered through the city, across the bridges, and along the peninsula, so that every member of the invading army could hear.

"I don't need an hour, Zod. My people and I made up our minds long before you arrived. You cannot have this city, and I will not let you harm my people." Raising his hand, he gave orders to his waiting technicians. *The irrevocable act.* "Activate the shield."

Suddenly a shimmering golden dome extended from the seawall. Made out of crackling static and solidified light, it rose in a huge arching vault, reached its apex high above the tallest towers, and slammed down, severing the five bridges like an executioner's axe.

The southern edge of the force-field dome sealed itself on the bottleneck of the narrow peninsula, throwing up curtains of dust as it did so. In shock and disarray, Zod's army scrambled back from the crackling wall.

Cut in half, the five bridges, precious landmarks of Argo City, slowly groaned and twisted as the severed spans slumped downward. With the tension released, their cables whipped about, and the majestic bridges plunged into the water of the narrow bay.

Protected inside their shimmering dome, the people of Argo City let out a collective sigh of awe and dismay. Zor-El stared with sickened satisfaction, but no triumph, as tears streamed down his face.

CHAPTER 73

∞⚐⬦‼◇⊶⊤♈♌ 73

After Zod took his army on the march, the only ones left in Krypto-nopolis were too young, too old, or too infirm to fight. Even these people were allowed no rest, but forced to continue work on Zod's projects. Koll-Em had been placed in provisional control, bitter at being left behind but pleased with the taste of power and responsibility. Token squads of Sapphire Guards patrolled the streets, merely as a matter of form. They expected no trouble.

Jor-El was their only worry.

The knowledge of Lara's incarceration wounded him like a cold knife in his side. Even with Zod gone, he knew that Koll-Em and a few of the more brutal Sapphire Guards would not hesitate to harm his wife in order to coerce him.

Still appalled that Zod had copied inventions from plans the old Commission had supposedly destroyed, Jor-El decided to inspect the weapons shops under the pretext of finding parts for the nova javelins. The buildings and hangars were now relatively empty since the army had taken everything along. He examined the construction bays, the fabrication machinery, the chemical synthesizers. The place stank of fuel exhaust, harsh solvents, a variety of volatile compounds, and machined metals.

He was disgusted, yet not entirely surprised, to recognize the unique chemical composition of the main explosives Zod employed in his new artillery. They were based directly on the high-energy propellent he himself had developed for his solar-probe rockets. Jor-El had puzzled over that same distinctive molecular signature when trying to prove his innocence in the matter of Donodon's death. He had found traces of this very explosive in the wreckage of the seismic scanner. Now he knew where it had come from. Zod, or more likely his henchman, Nam-Ek, had used his own rocket propellent to blow up the device.

Jor-El already had plenty of reasons to turn entirely against the General, and this merely gave him one more.

As he searched for some way to disrupt Zod's plans, he felt very alone. He had sent his desperate warning transmission to his brother, and he hoped it had served its purpose. Kryptonopolis had received no news from the General's army since it departed, but even if Zod hadn't shut down the communications grid, all transmissions had been disrupted. Rao had undergone a suddenly violent phase, spewing unstable flares that interfered with standard communications. The vehement solar storm made Jor-El wonder if the red giant might be about to go supernova. He had not been able to send up a probe rocket for many months. Of course, no one else on Krypton could be torn away from their more parochial concerns. As usual.

Under careful supervision, Jor-El spent his days grudgingly working on the nova javelins, as Zod had commanded. The ancient warlord's maps and charts were indeed out of date, and—under better circumstances—Jor-El could have compared the old measurements with his new modern ones to develop fascinating tectonic theories. Now, though, he had explicit other orders for the missiles.

He deciphered complex systems that even No-Ton did not understand. The two men analyzed and reconfigured the guidance systems, then ran repeated tests to reset the navigation and targeting controls. Mechanically, the systems were functional again, but spatial and ground-based coordinates had altered in the thousand years since Jax-Ur's reign.

Though No-Ton was also a member of the Ring of Strength and should therefore have been considered trustworthy, Koll-Em insisted on monitoring every test for himself, much to Jor-El's annoyance. The edgy young noble didn't understand any of the operations, but kept an eye out for anxiety on Jor-El's face as an indicator of deceit. Even when No-Ton assured his fellow Ring member that Jor-El was doing as he'd been instructed, Koll-Em lurked about and watched.

Jor-El didn't consider the reluctant No-Ton to be an ally, but he knew that the other scientist also had reservations about what General Zod was doing. Fortunately, No-Ton was in such awe of Jor-El's technical expertise that he did not question misleading statements that the white-haired genius confidently put forward as "facts."

When Jor-El finished his activities in the nova javelin bunkers, he shoved sheets of incomprehensible numbers and projected trajectories into Koll-Em's hands. "As you can see, everything is in order." The angry young man would never be able to interpret them.

Leaving the underground chamber, he ascended to the surface, emerged at the edge of the Square of Hope, and boldly walked to the complex glassy spire where Lara was being held. An uncertain-looking Sapphire Guard blocked the way. "I am here to see Lara," he said.

"No one is allowed to enter."

"I am allowed to enter. I am Jor-El."

Koll-Em hurried up, flustered and trying to show that he was in control of the situation. "Oh, let him inside. Seeing his hostage wife will remind Jor-El why he has no choice but to assist us." His thin-lipped grin was little more than a slash across his face.

Jor-El gave him a scornful look. "There are *always* choices. But sometimes every choice is flawed."

Close on his heels, Koll-Em followed him down the colored glassy corridors. "It's not too late for you, Jor-El. If you help us achieve a smooth victory and thwart Argo City's resistance, General Zod may yet forgive you. You could still have an important place in our new order."

"Before or after the comet destroys Krypton?"

Koll-Em was clearly uneasy. He respected and feared Jor-El's scientific talent. "Zod will protect us. He can do anything."

Jor-El rounded on him. He did not comprehend the young man's attitude, his enthusiastic assumption of his position of power. "General Zod killed your brother. He annihilated Borga City, yet you still support him. Aren't you angry?"

"My brother only got what he deserved," Koll-Em sneered. "Time and again over the course of our lives, he belittled me, held me back, ignored me." The nervous veneer of his bravado could not entirely conceal his real feelings. "Borga City is gone now, just like Kandor. What happened has happened. We can't wallow in the past. We must look to the future."

Disgusted with the pointless parroting of Zod's propaganda, Jor-El kept walking until he reached the barricaded door to Lara's cell. A lattice of thick crystal entirely blocked the opening. The translucent walls blurred the details of his wife's lovely face. Nevertheless, when she spotted him she moved quickly to the faceted wall. "Jor-El! I knew you'd come." Her voice carried through the clear crystal.

He pressed as close as he could. "I came to make sure you were still safe."

"She's safe *for now*," Koll-Em taunted from behind him.

"May I have a moment of privacy with my wife?"

"No, you may not. Who knows what secret information you two might exchange?"

Jor-El placed his palm flat against the wall of interlocked crystal; behind the blurry barrier, Lara did the same. "Be strong, Lara. We'll get through this."

"Tell me what's happening out there. Is Argo City safe?"

Koll-Em grabbed his shoulder and pulled him away. "She doesn't need to know all that." The Sapphire Guard began to manhandle Jor-El back out.

"I love you!" he called to her.

Lara's voice vibrated through the facets. "Do what you have to, Jor-El!" She pressed herself against the crystal barrier, but he couldn't see her clearly.

He longed to look at her face, to touch her. "I don't intend for my child to be born inside a cell."

"Then you'd better help this war end very soon," Koll-Em said.

The fear and suspicion that permeated Kryptonopolis now worked in Jor-El's favor. He went about his plans, feigning bold confidence; any furtiveness would only invite suspicion, and he had no intention of explaining himself.

The new devices he had secretly assembled were simple enough, remarkably brilliant in fact. He intended to pass along his appreciation to Zor-El—if they both survived the next few days.

In a small pocket, he still held the fragment of a message crystal he'd received from a haggard-looking secret courier shortly before the army marched for Argo City. The hidden recording it held from Zor-El offered vital information: "Others might be uncertain of your loyalties, Jor-El, but you are my brother. I believe you'll do the right thing with these designs."

He'd been saddened to learn that this was the third covert message Zor-El had tried to send him. None of the other volunteers had found him, and Jor-El never saw the haggard messenger again. Had he slipped away, been forcibly recruited into the army, or been killed? Every day, Jor-El expected to be thrown into a crystalline cell himself; he prayed at least it would be next to Lara's.

Moving as if he were walking on fragile glass, he determined an appropriate installation point on the perimeter of the city, another one in the Square of Hope, another outside the main offices. After slipping into the government palace, he measured carefully and found a hiding place to install the last small object in the large main chamber that Zod had been using as a kind of throne room.

Just as he finished, Koll-Em stormed into the room. The man's pointed face flushed upon seeing Jor-El there. His loose brown hair had a wild look. "What do you think you're doing? This is a restricted area."

Jor-El stood up to him. "General Zod asked me to run a special scan. I am confirming that no assassination devices have been planted in his absence."

"The General told me nothing of this!"

Jor-El let a mysterious smile creep across his face. "Precisely who do you think he's worried about? You've made your ambitions clear, not even showing mercy to your own brother. The General has every right to be suspicious of you." He pressed his point. "Shall we contact him now? We might be able to break through the interference caused by the solar storm. General Zod won't be pleased by the interruption, of course, but he will confirm what I'm saying. The call will also give me a chance to inform him of certain suspicious items I found in your own quarters."

Koll-Em paled. "What items? You were in my quarters?"

"I was doing my job."

The young man seethed for a long moment. "I don't trust you, Jor-El."

"The feeling is very mutual. And Zod trusts neither of us." Then he added with an ironic smile, "All hail, the new Krypton."

He walked out of the government palace, leaving Koll-Em fuming with helpless anger.

CHAPTER 74

∞⚏◊‼◊⟵Ṭ♀◊ 74

Like a slap in the face, the force-field dome over Argo City made General Zod's cheeks burn. He knew that Zor-El and his people must be laughing at him from inside the city. He did not find it intriguing at all. "Bring forth our weapons and blast through that barrier. Show these deluded fools that they cannot resist Zod."

Aethyr chose her words carefully. "Are you willing to destroy Argo City after all? How much do you think that force field can withstand?"

"We shall see."

Unable to control the anger he felt on behalf of his master, Nam-Ek marched forward, fists balled, and pounded against the crackling barrier. His strongest blows barely elicited a humming sound. Frustrated, the mute stepped back, scowling at his knuckles and flexing his tingling hands.

"Pull back! Prepare for our first bombardment."

When the initial rounds exploded against the golden dome, the shock waves blew backward with such force that the sound nearly deafened the soldiers who stood too close to watch; holding their ringing ears, the men staggered away. The most powerful detonations produced little more than ripples of color across the force field.

Zod's army cheered hopefully as the next group of demolitions experts planted even more powerful bombs. They unleashed a truly apocalyptic chain of explosions, also to no effect.

"Try the bridges. Maybe those are weak points." He still couldn't

344

believe Zor-El had actually cut off the magnificent spans that had been the pride of the city for many centuries. The remaining superstructure, half out of the water outside the protective dome, resembled the skeleton of a beached sea beast. Zod fumed, incensed that he'd underestimated the sheer irrationality of Jor-El's brother.

Taking a different approach, he ordered his construction engineers to dig tunnels under the narrow neck of the peninsula. If they could get under the protective dome, they would come up from beneath. But no matter how deep they dug with their best tunneling apparatus, they still encountered the shimmering barrier many meters underground; the force field had sliced easily through dirt and stone. His diggers emerged from their tunnels, dirty and discouraged.

The General now began to grow impatient. Sensing his mood, Aethyr pushed him. "You are the savior of Krypton, my love. You don't take half measures, and no one thwarts your will with impunity."

"Correct on all counts." The two of them stepped back onto the command platform, cruised back over the troops, and turned to survey Argo City. Under the seething red sun, the very *intact*ness of the defiant city mocked him. "Bring forth our heaviest weapons. The city is forfeit. Let loose a bombardment that will make even the ghost of Jax-Ur shudder! I want a complete and utter holocaust here."

Argo City remained silent behind the faint hum of the force field.

His army lined up seventeen wide-bore thermal cannons, pointing the flame launchers' muzzles toward one section of the barrier. Conventional crystal-tipped penetrators were loaded into field guns on the bottleneck of land. Catapults, vibrational thundershocks, flash-enhanced mortars—everything was aimed toward the thrumming dome.

When General Zod gave the command, every weapon fired at once. The sound and the fury roared through the skies. Flames and flashes billowed upward in blinding intensity. Aethyr watched the furious explosions; their colors and heat reflected off her skin, as if suffusing her with energy. Nam-Ek wore an expression of boyish delight. Zod didn't blink, refusing to miss a moment of the spectacle.

Raging flames and caustic smoke surrounded the golden dome. The General tried to *will* the force field to collapse. His armies kept launching their weapons, exhausting half of his arsenal.

But when the smoke cleared, the dome remained intact.

A sickening sense of failure assailed Zod, threatening to overwhelm him. Finally, he barked orders for the attack to cease. Continuing the pointless waste of firepower would simply make him look like more of a fool. He could lay siege to Argo City and starve them out, though that might well take months or years, depending on their stockpiles. And all the while, his military would be embroiled here, squandering valuable time, as other towns took advantage of the situation for their own petty rebellions. By remaining entrenched, waiting for the shield to flicker and come down, Zod himself—the great ruler of Krypton—would appear weak, ineffectual. He would be a laughingstock.

Though the words burned like bile in his throat, he said, "We return to Kryptonopolis. Immediately."

Aethyr was shocked. "No! We cannot retreat. Think of how history—"

"We are *not* retreating. We are modifying our tactics. If these weapons are ineffective, we must resort to something more powerful."

Zod's great military force loaded up the troop-transport platforms and turned around the heavy weapons and field artillery. He was sure the people of Argo City understood that he meant to come at them again with a vengeance. They could stew over that while he made his final preparations.

CHAPTER 75

General Zod's army swept back into Kryptonopolis like a swarm of hungry chewerbugs from the Neejon plains. Some of the soldiers were outraged, some ashamed. All had been thrown off balance. Even the most devoted followers could not believe Zod had been so easily defeated.

As soon as Jor-El saw their expressions, he knew that the tyrant had failed to conquer Argo City, that his warning had arrived in time, and that Zor-El's shield dome must have held. His relief was tempered, however, by the certainty that the General would try something even worse.

Immediately upon his return, Zod shut himself inside his government palace. During the days it had taken him to move his troops back across the continent, the General's anger had not cooled. In the meantime, fully seventeen other cities and towns had declared their independence and arrested Zod's supporters. Dealing with them all would force Zod to stretch his armies much too thin.

The flustered soldiers flooded through the streets and hurried to their communal habitation structures. Exhausted and uncomfortable, many of them stripped off their uniforms. Jor-El could tell that most of the civilian population was unnerved by what they had seen during the brief siege. And they all knew that the conflict wasn't over.

In the meantime, feeling lost without any concrete, objective information about what had happened at Argo City—and completely cut off from his brother—Jor-El checked an anomalous reading from his distant early-warning array, only to discover that his brother *had* sent him a coded message, disguised as an astronomical signal. Chuckling at the unorthodox method, Jor-El learned that Argo City had deactivated the shield as soon as the invading army retreated. While the dissidents were preparing their response, Jor-El saw how he could help, and he secretly transmitted his idea to Zor-El. Now, if the separate pieces could fit together . . .

Finally, after leaving Kryptonopolis in tense uncertainty for half a day, Zod emerged from his headquarters looking taller, harder, a whirlwind contained within a crisp new uniform. He seemed more indomitable than ever.

Jor-El noticed that the most dedicated groups of soldiers and Sapphire Guards were strategically stationed throughout the streets in a determined show of strength. Zod's planned announcement must be so calamitous that the General himself feared his own people might rise up against him. Tensions were at a breaking point. By now public opinion in Kryptonopolis was turning against him, though the Ring of Strength held any criticism in check with intimidation. For now, at least, their tactics were sufficient, but Jor-El could see that Zod's hold on the people was starting to crumble.

Anger made the General's razor-edged voice loud enough that he no longer needed special amplifiers. "We must show those backward thinkers of Argo City that General Zod will not be trifled with. Clear the Square of Hope!"

Jor-El felt utterly alone in the huge crowd. How he longed for Lara to be there beside him. Watching the General's expression, he knew that his worst fears were about to be realized. Zod was about to step off a cliff into damnation.

"The people of Argo City have made their choice. I will launch one of the nova javelins against them," he announced with finality. "May Zor-El and his people find mercy under the red light of Rao, for they will find none from me."

As he issued his fateful order, General Zod experienced neither guilt nor glee. Only satisfaction and liberation.

Based on what had happened to the moon of Koron long ago, Zod had a healthy respect for Jax-Ur's warheads. By his best guess, even one of the javelins would disintegrate the whole peninsula and vaporize part of the continent around Argo City, shield or no shield. It would leave a scar a hundred times more vast than the crater of Kandor.

Zor-El would get what he deserved.

The General envisioned what might happen as the nova javelin struck. The force-field dome would collapse, and waves of incinerating heat would reduce the population of Argo City to ash. Even if the dome somehow held, the ground all around would be flash-melted. Quakes would rip apart the surface, flatten the buildings into piles of rubble. The sea would boil, and molten lava would roar up from beneath Argo City. Zod could imagine the cacophony of terrified screams in the brief instant before they were cut off. Those deeply satisfying thoughts had finally convinced him to take this terrible action.

And so he gave the order.

In the Square of Hope, one of the circular coverplates hummed, vibrated, and split apart to reveal the weapon underground. Slowly, one of the golden warheads rose out of the pit like a rapidly growing spike-weed. Coolant steam curled around the golden shaft; the fuel tanks had been fully charged.

Zod could not tear his eyes from the beautiful weapon. "Set the coordinates for Argo City."

"Set coordinates for Argo City!" Koll-Em snapped.

No-Ton, still down in the control room, responded that the weapon was ready. His voice held a faint quaver.

Zod spotted a shaken-looking Jor-El standing alone in the crowd, his pale hair in disarray. *Good.* "Prepare to launch." His heart pounded with anticipation, and he watched with fire in his eyes and in his mind. He felt very alive.

But before the javelin could launch in a plume of exhaust and flames, the circular door of a second weapons pit split open. Another nova javelin rose slowly into the open air.

The already nervous crowd began to mutter. Aethyr looked at Zod in alarm. "You can't launch two of them. You could crack open the whole planet."

"I did not order this," Zod shouted. "Abort the second launch!"

Instead of retracting, though, the second nova javelin continued to rise until the lift platform also locked into place. Then, unexpectedly, a third pit opened.

And a fourth.

Zod's soldiers shouted in dismay. Even they could grasp the terrifying consequences of launching so many doomsday weapons. Every person on Krypton had seen the smashed moon in the night sky.

"Stop this! Abort the launch!"

Another coverplate opened, and another, until finally all fifteen nova javelins stood starkly in the open air like a hideous forest of death. The golden rockets pivoted slightly on their launch rods, acquiring their target.

This could not be happening. Zod knew only one person who could help. He bellowed into the crowd. "Jor-El, I command you to stop this!"

But the scientist simply spread his hands. "The controls were old and unreliable, the systems deteriorated. You've brought about your own downfall, General Zod. And now you've doomed the rest of us with you."

"No!" With an ineffectual shout, Zod ran toward the access doorway that led down into the control tunnels, knocking aside the terrified people who stood in his way.

Before he could get inside, all fifteen nova javelins launched.

CHAPTER 76

Blinding shafts of yellow light and fire spat from exhaust cones. With an earsplitting rumble and a high-pitched whine, the doomsday weapons hurtled into Krypton's sky.

"Stop!" Zod yelled at the air, as if the ancient devices might obey his order.

The trails of fire and smoke climbed upward, scribing Krypton's epitaph upon the heavens. The General paused and stood white-faced, unable to tear his eyes away. Nam-Ek stared in fascination at the exhaust plumes and vapor trails, apparently thinking they were beautiful. Aethyr fell to her knees. The streaking missiles raced high across the sky. The end was surely coming.

Zod pushed his way down the stairs and raced along the sterile, white-walled halls to the control chamber. There, No-Ton and four technicians stood in pasty-faced helplessness before the banks of guidance systems. Zod stormed in and hammered at the controls, trying to realign the target vectors. The systems did not respond.

He grabbed No-Ton by the front of his laboratory tunic. "We've got to stop this! Destroy the weapons. They must have a self-destruct mechanism."

No-Ton lashed out at Zod, no longer intimidated by the man. "After the incident at the Rao-beam installation, you specifically ordered us to deactivate any systems that could be used to sabotage the nova javelins. You *instructed* us to disconnect the self-destruct capability because you were afraid someone might stop you from launching them."

Zod cursed. "Then change their course! Get rid of them somehow. They will blow up all of Krypton."

"General, there is *nothing* we can do!" Frantic technicians yanked out crystal after crystal from control decks, but it did no good.

Filmscreens transmitted high-resolution images from the telescopes and monitoring dishes in Jor-El's distant early-warning array. The nova javelins continued to burn, thrusting higher.

"They should reach the zenith soon and begin their plunge to Argo City," the scientist said, his voice oddly brittle. "After that, the whole planet will break apart. The chain reaction could take minutes, it could take a month. This is uncharted scientific territory for me." Zod didn't like the flare of defiance in No-Ton's eyes. The scientist sniffed. "If there's anything you wish to say to your followers, now may be your last chance to do it."

Zod desperately needed to find someone else to punish for this debacle. "Why did this fault occur? I ordered only one weapon to be launched. What caused them all to take off? Who is responsible?"

"What does it matter? Maybe the weapons were all linked somehow. Maybe this is a final trick that Jax-Ur played upon later generations, his revenge against anyone who uncovered his stockpile. There's no stopping it now."

"Get Jor-El in here!" Zod shouted.

One of the female technicians gasped. She bent over the display screen. "General! Look at this." The telescope array tracked the progress of the nova javelins, and on the image, the sky had turned darker, more purple, full of stars. "The parabolic trajectory is wrong. The javelins have changed course!"

Zod shoved his way closer. "How so? Where are they headed now? What part of Krypton will they strike?"

"It doesn't matter," No-Ton insisted. "With that much firepower, any impact will blow the whole planet apart."

The technician shook her head vigorously. "No, they've achieved escape velocity. They're . . . they're heading out into space."

Zod couldn't believe what he had heard. "To space? Are we safe, then?" He spun toward No-Ton. "Is it an accident, or was it planned?"

"I set the coordinates for Argo City myself, General. As you ordered. The missiles have completely deviated from their program."

Clustered like a flock of migratory birds, all fifteen nova javelins soared out of the last wisps of Krypton's atmosphere and clawed their way free of the planet's gravity well.

"Are they just going to disperse?" He felt a sudden, giddy hope. "Will they detonate where they can cause no harm?"

No-Ton sat back, pale with disbelief. "Who can know, General? This is beyond me. When the rockets run out of fuel, they might eventually circle around and fall into Rao. We could have a reprieve after all."

The words reminded Zod of the instabilities Jor-El had long predicted in the sun. If fifteen nova javelins plunged into the red giant, might such incredible explosions finally trigger the sun to go supernova? He wanted to scream in frustration.

The observing telescopes increased their magnification, and the view shifted. Now Zod finally saw the intended target of the doomsday weapons. No-Ton and the other technicians gasped. Zod clenched his fist. "Damn him!"

Aethyr stumbled into the control room, looking drained and terrified. "I wanted to be with you at the end."

Zod showed his teeth in a bitter smile. "There will be no end. Not today."

A haloed ball of ice and rock filled the screen, surrounded by a vaporous coma and a long feathery tail. Loth-Ur's Hammer.

Like precisely targeted arrows, the nova javelins streaked toward the heart of the comet. All fifteen struck within seconds of each other. The combined explosion released five times as much force as the blast that had obliterated Koron. Filters automatically drowned out a percentage of the glare before the screens themselves overloaded. Outside, the distant detonation created a brief new sun in Krypton's sky.

All that remained of Loth-Ur's Hammer was an expanding cloud of energized gas and the sparkling residue of the greatest weapons display Krypton had ever seen.

The comet was vaporized, no longer a threat. The world had been saved.

The weapons had been sabotaged.

And Zod knew that Jor-El was the man responsible.

CHAPTER 77

꧌⛆◊‼◊⵪T̥◊ *77*

In the confusion and chaos after the missile launches, Jor-El could have escaped from Kryptonopolis. He could have raced back to his estate or fled to Argo City. But he would never leave Lara behind.

Like the ancient philosopher Kal-Ik, who had spoken the truth even though he knew that Chieftain Nok would execute him for it, Jor-El had done what was necessary. Even though he had saved the planet, General Zod would quite likely kill him. This was a betrayal of unprecedented magnitude.

Nam-Ek came for him, his face a thunderstorm of rage. Jor-El had expected a full squad of Zod's Sapphire Guards and several members of the Ring of Strength, but the burly mute alone was more than capable of hauling him off to the government palace. Unafraid, and proud of what he had achieved, Jor-El prepared to face his nemesis. He would not back down.

Ever since Zod had erected his pretentious statue, the government chambers had begun to take on the appearance of a throne room. Now, that was where the General waited for Jor-El. Zod sat in a squarish, bulky chair on a raised platform with Aethyr at his right hand, icy and beautiful.

Nam-Ek released the scientist with a forward shove, making him stumble. Jor-El caught himself and tried to regain his dignity by straightening his white robes. He touched the curved S family symbol on his breast, drawing strength from a lineage that dated back to Sor-El and the time of the Seven Army Conference. Without a word, he met Zod's gaze.

Sour-faced Koll-Em entered the throne chamber pulling Lara roughly along, despite her advanced pregnancy. When she saw Jor-El, Lara broke free of the man's sweaty grip and ran to her husband. He held her, kissed her lips, and buried his face in her amber hair, certain that Zod meant to execute them both.

With a glower, the General curtly dismissed Koll-Em. When the young noble pouted at being left out of this confrontation, Zod responded with a look that made him scuttle away in silence. Finally the General said, his voice a low burn, "I would ask you to explain yourself, but I am not interested in your answer."

Jor-El was not intimidated. "You're alive now because of what I have done. Shouldn't you be grateful?"

"You defied me!" Zod launched himself to his feet as if he himself had become a dangerous projectile.

"I protected all Kryptonians from your criminally stupid decisions." Jor-El took a step closer to the blocky chair. "And now it's time for you to be removed from power. I should have done this long ago."

Zod froze at the audacity of his statement; then he began to chuckle. Beside him, Aethyr laughed aloud, and even Nam-Ek guffawed wordlessly. Jor-El ignored them. "General Zod, your rule is at an end."

Zod exchanged glances with his two companions, as if one of them could explain the joke. "And how will you accomplish that? I am intrigued. You have always been a thinker, a man of ideas rather than actions."

Jor-El raised his eyebrows. "Actions? I am the one who destroyed the Rao-beam generator so you couldn't use it again as a weapon." Aethyr and Zod looked even angrier than they had been before, but he continued. "My brother and I coordinated our plans for stopping you. In the days since your armies withdrew from Argo City, Zor-El has pulled together an extensive resistance from all across Krypton. Your senseless attack was enough to goad many other city leaders into action. Even now they are marching on Kryptonopolis."

Zod laughed with scorn now. "A ragtag handful of poorly armed rebels? They can't possibly stand against me. I have been building my

military defenses for months, and my whole army is here. We have weapons based on your own designs and wave after wave of expendable foot soldiers."

Jor-El smiled. "Perhaps. But I have better technology and greater imagination."

Zod looked at Aethyr and Nam-Ek, suddenly uncertain. Jor-El touched the controls hidden inside his loose robe.

The force-field generator he had placed near Zod's throne activated. A small dome immediately appeared, trapping Zod, Nam-Ek, and Aethyr inside a hemispherical prison three meters in diameter. Nam-Ek roared and threw himself at the curved wall, but his blows bounced off ineffectually. Zod also hammered and shouted, but it did him no good.

"Zor-El smuggled me the plans," he explained to Lara. "The field will contain the General until my brother and his army arrive."

Her beautiful eyes were still troubled. "But the rest of Zod's forces are out there. Even if a rebel military is coming, they can't defeat all of Kryptonopolis."

"They can if we divide the General's followers into much smaller groups." He pressed another button, and a second force-field dome appeared, greater in circumference. This one slammed down over the whole government palace.

Then he activated the third dome, larger still, stretching halfway across the Square of Hope and capping the others like a set of nested eggs. There, it cut off the hundreds who had gathered out in the streets, separating them from their weapons and military equipment. By design, the force-field barrier crashed into the tall statue of Zod, severing it in two, and the pieces toppled to the flat tiles.

Two more domes extended in stages out to the perimeter of Kryptonopolis, again dividing the remaining soldiers.

Watching the furiously cursing Zod in his shimmering prison, Jor-El felt tremendous satisfaction. He held Lara, pressed her rounded belly against him, and knew that his son would be born on a free Krypton after all, a world that no longer faced the threat of imminent annihilation.

"Now we wait, Lara. You and I, here together."

CHAPTER 78

∞ ⌐◊‼◇⊶T̈◊ 78

Zor-El's allied rebels were converging on Kryptonopolis when they saw the nova javelins streak into the sky. He paused to stare up at the curving vapor trails while his companions gasped in dismay and awe. He swallowed in a dry throat. Within moments, if the missiles found their target, all of Argo City might be vaporized. When Zod's armies had departed, unsuccessful, Zor-El had deactivated the force-field dome. Seeing the missiles approach, they could always switch it back on again, but would it withstand *nova javelins*? Alura could be dead, and his mother, all his friends and acquaintances, all of Argo City's great works—gone in a few moments.

But he trusted Jor-El would do as he had promised.

Now, as the golden missiles vanished into the distant sky, Korth-Or spoke, his lisp growing more pronounced with his agitation. He had already lost his own city. "So Zod really did it! The bastard."

"Should we wait? If the world is going to end today, what good does it do for us to attack Kryptonopolis?" Or-Om shook his shaggy head in disbelief.

Zor-El drew his dark eyebrows together. "Because if the world doesn't end, then every moment will count." They had gambled everything on this surprise turnabout, and he would hold on to hope.

His multipronged army continued toward the capital city with its hodgepodge assembly of vehicles and equipment—tools that had been hastily converted into weapons, passenger craft refitted to become military vehicles and soldier transports. The fighters came from the refugees of Borga City, as well as dozens of other cities and towns; Zor-El had drawn the bulk of them from his own citizenry. Now the armed group moved inexorably toward the former Xan City, knowing they would be outnumbered. But Zor-El told them to have faith.

And they did.

Then the army saw the huge flare high in the sky. Even in broad daylight, the searing blue-white detonation cast second shadows, overwhelming the red sunlight. Blinking and rubbing their eyes, the anxious rebels stared in awe at the spreading glow that marked the destroyed comet in space. They cheered and whooped, but Zor-El allowed them no time to celebrate. "Onward! We can't slow down now."

When at last they reached the city, Zor-El took in the breathtaking view of the rebuilt capital now encased under a nested set of shimmering domes—exactly as he had hoped to find it. General Zod's supporters were all bottled up inside the force fields. "Now it's time to do some mopping up."

The rebel army encountered several hundred stragglers around the perimeter of the outermost dome. They were trying to batter their way in, assuming that Zod had shut them *out*. Zor-El smiled at the irony as his troops quickly rounded up the confused men and women. Most surrendered without a fight; some struggled, but they were easily disarmed and taken prisoner.

Zor-El had brought several dozen smaller force-field generators, which his army used as holding domes to keep the groups separated. Afterward, it would be an arduous task to sort out which of these people belonged fanatically to Zod's cause and which had been only reluctant fighters.

By the time the rebels overwhelmed the stragglers and encircled the outermost dome over the city, Zor-El's rebel army had acquired twice as many weapons as they had arrived with. Then, fully armed, they prepared for the next phase, spreading out around the force field's perimeter. When Or-Om, Korth-Or, and Gal-Eth announced that their separate groups of soldiers were ready, Zor-El found the hidden shield generator exactly where his brother had told him he intended to install it.

With a last glance around to be sure his fighters were prepared to face Zod's men trapped between the next two domes, he deactivated the outermost shield. Because of the large area between the two shells, Zor-El knew that this would be the largest single crowd of enemy soldiers; each successively smaller dome would contain fewer and fewer fighters. Divide and conquer.

Several frantic members of the Ring of Strength were inside, cut off and struggling to understand what had happened. As the force field vanished, Zor-El's troops pushed forward, but Zod's Ring members rallied their followers to attack. Some fired their weapons indiscriminately, but many of the reluctant soldiers simply surrendered.

Zor-El's rebels isolated the hot spots and disarmed the numerous men and women who obviously had never wanted to join Zod's army. Working inward, he deactivated another force-field dome and advanced to the Square of Hope, where the bisected Zod statue lay like a fallen idol on the ground, and within an hour, the newcomers had subjugated all the people inside that shell. By now they had disarmed the majority of the opposing army, and their own casualties were minimal.

However, when he shut down the subsequent dome that encompassed the government palace, a sudden fury of armored Sapphire Guards led by a screaming Koll-Em nearly overwhelmed them. Some of Zod's loyalists used beam lances, new weapons corrupted from Jor-El's original designs, to incinerate the first line of rebel soldiers. The sheer violence drove back Zor-El's fighters, and they were forced to leave their dead on the ground.

He cried out, "Pull together! Take them out before they kill any more of us." Ten of his fighters had already been cut down.

"For Borga City!" Korth-Or shouted, still pushing forward.

"For *Krypton*!" Gal-Eth added.

Ferret-faced Koll-Em had no interest in surrendering or even surviving. The Sapphire Guards continued to fire their deadly beam lances. Taking careful aim, Zor-El shot his own weapon, sending a burst of thin crystal darts into Koll-Em's chest. With a scream that faded to silence like the air leaking out of a balloon, the head of the Ring of Strength collapsed to the stone steps outside the government palace.

Weapons fire pummeled the last Sapphire Guards, powerful enough to breach their armor. After a flurry of noise, silence descended again.

Zor-El bowed his head. "How many did we lose?" He listened as names were called out, soldiers checking bodies and counting smears of smoke and burned flesh on the ground.

"Fifteen," said Gal-Eth.

"That's fifteen too many." Zor-El looked ahead of him at the government palace. General Zod would be inside. All of them had their weapons drawn as they pushed into the imposing building.

But as the victorious rebels marched into Zod's throne room, Zor-El saw his brother holding Lara, paying no attention to the faint shouts of the three prisoners trapped inside their small dome.

CHAPTER 79

∞ ⊡◇‼◇⊶⊤♀◊ 79

Despite their exhaustion, Zor-El and his rebels spent many hours interviewing the prisoners who had been herded into separate containment domes. They winnowed out the armored Sapphire Guards and the remaining Ring of Strength members, keeping them under a separate prison dome as the most dangerous captives.

Other hapless citizens insisted they had meant only to help in the wake of the Kandor disaster. They had come under Zod's spell, plunging one step after another down a slippery slope. Artisans, builders, civil engineers, people of all classes had just wanted to do the right thing.

In the aftermath, the people of Kryptonopolis reviled General Zod's actions. Torn blue armbands littered the ground, still showing Zod's family crest. Soldiers discarded the military uniforms the General had forced them to wear; they piled the garments in great mounds in the Square of Hope and set them alight in large bonfires. All of the former city leaders who had bent their knees and submitted to Zod abdicated in shame.

Inside the throne room Zod, Aethyr, and Nam-Ek remained trapped in their hemispherical bubble, irate and totally helpless. In addition to Koll-Em, two Ring members had been killed during the fighting. Jor-El spoke on No-Ton's behalf, explaining how the man had alerted him to the Rao-beam attack on Borga City and how he had subtly resisted the General in numerous ways. The remaining twelve were placed in restraints and brought forward, heads bowed, so they could observe their General in his total defeat.

Before any sort of trial could begin, however, before the Ring members could plead their cases, beg for mercy, or snarl justifications, Jor-El and Lara made a chilling discovery.

Inside the government palace, Lara turned in slow circles, studying the architecture of Zod's primary office. Looking at the intersection of walls and using her artist's spatial perception, she realized that something was wrong. "This wall isn't where it's supposed to be, Jor-El. See this load-bearing column here?" She stepped around the weathered statue of Jax-Ur's kneeling victim and studied the perfectly interlocking wall blocks. "He's hidden something behind here. There must be a latch or a lock."

Already dreading what they might find, Jor-El tested the panel, listened for sounds of resonance, then returned to Zod's desk. With his arrogant confidence, the General would not have worried about being discovered in his own office. He would have made the controls easily accessible.

Inside one of the drawer panels, Jor-El located a small set of crystals, one of which caused the stone-block wall to slide aside to reveal a staircase that led down to a deep vault. He and Lara looked at each other, neither convinced that they wanted to see what Zod had hidden, but both knowing they had to go down there.

Though she was in the last few weeks of her pregnancy, Lara still moved with an agility that allowed her to keep up with him. At the bottom, they found a dimly lit set of chambers with thick walls and numerous alcoves, stands, cases, and sealed chests. The objects were arrayed like exhibits in a museum.

Jor-El recognized a handheld device—a reflective scrambler that could block incoming communications, effectively preventing anyone from sending a message. He himself had invented the device years ago, but the Commission for Technology Acceptance had banned it. Just another one of the inventions that Zod had kept for himself.

With widening eyes, Jor-El went to the next display deck and found the original plans for the Rao-beam generator, then rocket engine designs, satellite launchers, thrust enhancers, heat concentrators. Jor-El wondered how often Zod had censored scientific work for the express purpose of keeping it for his own private arsenal.

"I should have ignored the Commission, never brought any of my inventions to Zod." His throat was dry, and his eyes burned. "Damn the old Council and its foolish rules!"

Lara had moved out of view into a small side chamber. Her voice shook when she called out. "Jor-El, you'd better come in here. You need to see this."

In a small room of its own, Jor-El saw the greatest secret that General Zod had been hiding. Along with a complete control console studded with crystalline rods, a silver-ringed frame hovered in the center of the room, holding open the singularity Jor-El had created.

The Phantom Zone.

And in the flat opening between dimensions, he saw hundreds of despairing faces crowded against one another, flattened and overlapping. Their open mouths shouted. Their eyes pleaded.

He didn't need to recognize any of the faces to know who they were. "So this is what happened to anyone who spoke out against Zod."

Some of the more vehement dissidents had probably been killed outright—he guessed the brutal work of Nam-Ek there—but the Commissioner would have considered the Phantom Zone to be a much neater, more satisfying way to dispose of his enemies.

Jor-El froze, feeling his anger increase even further. "We have to get them all out of there."

When the imprisoned faces spotted the two of them, their expressions changed as they begged, but the dimensional barrier muted all sound. Jor-El went to the control console and raised his hand, trying to reassure the trapped ones.

"I'll help you release them." Lara's lips quirked in a smile. "I've done this before, remember?"

On the control panel, he changed the polarity of the crystals so that the glowing red shards became green. Amber shifted to white, reversing the flow into the Phantom Zone and releasing the first prisoner. As if he'd been ejected from the other universe, a man spilled out of the vertical, flat circle, so weak he collapsed to his knees. Trembling and unable to speak, he looked at Lara and Jor-El with haunted eyes. Lara helped him up.

Jor-El recognized the man as Tyr-Us, son of the old Council Head

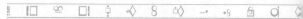

Jul-Us, and a friend of Zor-El's. He had vanished under mysterious circumstances.

The remaining faces continued to clamor in total silence while Jor-El worked the control crystals. A second man, balding with a long walrus mustache, collapsed onto the stone floor. His eyes looked sunken and hollow. Gil-Ex. "We've spent . . . an eternity in there. It's Zod. Do not trust Zod!"

"No one needs to worry about Zod anymore."

Jor-El continued to release prisoners from the Phantom Zone. One after another, they emerged, terrified, breathless, and glad to be freed from the maddening dimension. Dozens of those who had tried to issue warnings against Zod, those who had complained about his policies . . . those who had supposedly "retired from public view."

The last to emerge was a servant named Hopk-Ins who had worked in the halls of the Commission building in Kandor—the first person Zod had exiled to the Phantom Zone, just on a whim.

One by one, the rescued people staggered up the stone steps, out of the dim museum chamber, and into the fresh air and warm red sunshine, emerging to a whole new Krypton.

CHAPTER 80

∞⸆◇!!◇⊷T̈☌〈 80

General Zod seethed inside the transparent prison. Together, defeated, he and his companions stared through the impenetrable dome at the accusers who paraded through the government palace—*his* government palace. They had tricked him, brought him down, and Jor-El had betrayed him most of all.

The people eyed him with expressions of lingering fear, disgust, even hatred. The hatred puzzled him most. He was, after all, the savior of Krypton.

"I feel like an animal in a zoo, on display for foolish visitors to gawk at," he said to Aethyr. "Maybe it was merciful for the Butcher of Kandor to slaughter all those animals." Nam-Ek flashed him a startled glance.

"Unlike the Butcher of Kandor, these people will never have the nerve to take any definite action," Aethyr said. "They'll debate us and study us for years."

"And all the while, we will be trapped here." Zod's whole body trembled with the effort of containing his emotions. He wanted to shout at them, but that would only entertain the watchers and make him appear weak. He did not intend to appear weak.

Nam-Ek, though, had no such self-control. Every hour or so he let out a wordless roar and pummeled his fists uselessly against the dome shield. A few in the audience chamber glanced up at the disturbance. Several were embarrassed; others simply ignored him. Two officials smiled confidently at the force field, then went about their business.

Zod wanted to kill them all.

One by one, as if wrestling with their fears, the dissenters who had been imprisoned within the Phantom Zone came to glare at the General. Puffed with bravado (since he was caged), they railed at him, cursed him. At first he laughed at their ridiculous posturing. Eventually he ignored them.

Zod paced the cell like a prowling predator. Aethyr watched him, her lips curled. Now that they had been arrested and he could offer her nothing, Zod wondered if she would still love him. What if this woman had simply agreed to be his consort because of the mantle of power he wore?

But Aethyr did not denounce him.

Several times, their captors had expanded the dome to encompass a few small amenities. They had food, water, a bucket, and little else. There were no tools Zod could use to plan an escape. He had only his own voice and powerful personality to influence his captors. At one time, that might have been sufficient, but not anymore.

He deserved reverence, not humiliation, after what he had accomplished for Krypton. No one else would have taken the necessary actions after the loss of Kandor. History would prove that he had saved his race from their own indecisive helplessness. He had done what was right, had nearly reached the pinnacle of achievement—when it all came crashing down. If he had made any bad decisions, he would not admit to them.

Keeping Kryptonopolis as a provisional capital, the people scrambled to form a new government . . . or, more likely, rehash the old one. The bumbling leaders were looking to precedents that had already proved weak and useless. Gil-Ex and Tyr-Us talked openly about forming a new Council, just like the old one in Kandor. Apparently, during their time inside the Phantom Zone, their delusions had grown. They remembered nothing. Idiots!

Zod vindictively hoped that some outside invader would attack Krypton right now, just to prove him right. After all, *he* was perfectly safe under this protective dome. . . .

After two days of turmoil, the provisional government announced the beginning of Zod's trial. The General stood straight, clasped his hands behind his back, and raised his voice to be heard through the humming shield. "You have given me no time to prepare. I must have counsel. I must have access to my accusers. This goes against the laws of Krypton."

"We *are* the new Kryptonian law," said Gil-Ex, still looking ridiculous with his long mustache and his glistening pate. "You've had enough time to contemplate your crimes. Plead your case, beg forgiveness if you wish. No one doubts your ability to speak articulately."

Aethyr gave a bitter laugh. "Oh? And what about Nam-Ek? He hasn't spoken a word since he was a child."

The members of the provisional government looked flustered at that. Zod knew these men would do whatever they wished to do. He didn't press the matter.

Large filmplates were set up around the force-field enclosure, and Zod knew that this spectacle would be transmitted to viewers across all of Krypton. How the weak masses relished seeing a mighty man fall.

His accusers came forward one at a time. First Gil-Ex described how, after he had spoken out at the construction camp of old Xan City, Zod had asked for a private discussion. But Nam-Ek had seized him in the tent, and the two had thrown Gil-Ex into the Phantom Zone. "An awful place! No light, no movement, no heat or cold. I didn't even have an existence." His face flushed red. "It was just empty silence except for the other prisoners trapped there, all of us disembodied."

Tyr-Us spoke next, trembling as he explained how Zod's secret minions had hunted him for weeks. Having sought help from Zor-El and other like-minded critics, he tried to find safety, but had finally been captured in Yar-El's empty dacha. He, too, had been thrown into the Phantom Zone.

No-Ton discussed in a stuttering voice how he'd been forced to help blast Borga City with the Rao beam and then modify the nova javelins, which had almost destroyed the planet. Next came the bent-backed and scrawny servant Hopk-Ins, who sobbed as he told the story of Zod using him to test the Phantom Zone.

General Zod quickly became deaf to their string of complaints, the whining, the pathetic calls for sympathy. He closed his eyes to their pitiful expressions as they recounted their ordeals. The accusations droned on in an endless litany.

Zor-El showed images of the abortive attack on Argo City. Lara described how she had been imprisoned, both to coerce her husband's help and because she'd written the truth in her journal.

Finally, Jor-El stepped forward and fixed his eyes on Zod's. Before the scientist could speak, Zod shouted at him, "Are you their puppet now, Jor-El? Have they offered you a position on the new Council? Was that what you wanted all along? Political power?"

Jor-El seemed surprised. "Political power? Hardly. I merely wanted to save Krypton, even as you did your best to destroy it." With a proud and wise demeanor, he turned to face the men who acted as judges. "Yes, Zod did all the terrible things you've heard in other testimony. He seized power in our time of greatest need, and he maintained the state of emergency to keep his followers close. He should have let Krypton settle back into a normal rule of law and government."

"You are just as much to blame, Jor-El." Zod could not keep the smugness from his voice. "*You* built the Rao beam that destroyed Borga City. *Your* weapon designs armed my entire military. *You* repaired the nova javelins so they could be launched. *You* created the Phantom Zone, where so many political prisoners were held. Without you, I could never have wielded such power."

From behind the force-field barrier, he watched the scientist's flustered expression, but Jor-El did not back down. "Your Commission warned that even simple inventions could be corrupted and misused by an evil man. That evil man was *you, Zod.*" He turned back to the group of glaring judges, many of whom now seemed to regard him with uneasy suspicion. "Under the auspices of his Commission, Zod banned technologies that would have helped Krypton, while hoarding the designs for himself. He stole my inventions, corrupted advances that should have benefited everyone, and developed weapons that he turned against his own people."

From inside the dome, Zod shook his head. How he despised the man and his revisionist view of events. Instead of shouting further, General Zod clamped his lips together and waited. He was painfully reminded that Jax-Ur, too, had been defeated by the disloyalty of a trusted companion. He took no satisfaction from the historical parallel. *Damn Jor-El!*

Not surprisingly, the ruling of the provisional Council was unanimous. When his sentence was read, Zod didn't even need to hear it. He spoke through the shimmering barrier. "These other men are fools, Jor-El, and I expected nothing else from them. But *you*—you have truly betrayed me."

Jor-El didn't even look at him. He spoke to the judges. "I, too, cast my vote against Zod. He will always be a threat to Krypton."

"You could have saved yourself considerable time," Aethyr snapped at the gathered judges. "You knew what you would conclude before the proceedings began. You didn't even allow us to speak in our own defense."

Tyr-Us looked brave now that Zod was safely bottled up. He raised his chin. "And what do you wish to say? How can you defend your heinous actions?"

Zod silenced Aethyr with an abrupt wave. "Give them no further sport."

Korth-Or took one step closer to the dome. He was still simmering with accusations, still seeing the holocaust of when his Borga City had been destroyed. "Aethyr-Ka, do you still wish to stand with General Zod?"

"Do not use my family name! They were dead to me long before they vanished with Kandor." She stepped to the edge of the shimmering field. "Yes, I stand with General Zod."

"And you, Nam-Ek." Or-Om sounded compassionate. "You were a mere pawn in these actions. We believe you are mentally flawed. We can perhaps find some leniency if you will renounce Zod. Signify by nodding or shaking your head."

Nam-Ek was incensed by the very suggestion. He balled his fists and shook his head vigorously.

The leaders of the new government stood together as Gil-Ex announced in a booming voice, "General Zod, there is no more fitting punishment than for you to be confined permanently within the Phantom Zone. There, you will forever endure the torment that you forced upon us."

Zod did not give them the satisfaction of a defiant retort. Armored soldiers came forward, muscular men who had replaced the Sapphire Guards.

They surrounded the small imprisoning dome. A crew of anxious-looking workers brought the silver ring out of the museum chamber.

Despite his proud demeanor and unshakable strength, Zod felt a chill. He wished Aethyr and Nam-Ek had indeed renounced him, so they wouldn't have to suffer the same fate.

From where he stood Zor-El activated the force-field controls, and the small dome disappeared. Briefly freed, Nam-Ek was ready to hurl himself upon the guards and perhaps die in a hopeless attempt at escape. But General Zod touched the big man's arm and shook his head. The mute relaxed, complying with his master's wishes, as always.

Gal-Eth said, "Take one last breath of Kryptonian air. Smell the sweetness of freedom that you are leaving behind."

Zod spat at them.

He glared out at the crowd, focusing his anger on the one person he hated the most. "Jor-El, we could have saved Krypton. We could have led these people out of their own stupidity, but you betrayed me. You betrayed *them*! You doomed them all! I could have made this into a world that my father would have admired, but you and all future generations will pay for your shortsightedness. This is on your head, Jor-El—your conscience! I curse you for that. I curse you and all your descendants!"

Jor-El stood coolly, as if he were actually *proud* of what he had done, and he made no reply.

Ignoring his rant, the guards took Aethyr by the arms. When she struggled, they seized her legs as well and carried her bodily toward the silver frame that enclosed absolute emptiness. Zod grew wild, feeling the last shreds of his long-cultivated control slough away. "No!"

They threw Aethyr into the blank plane, and she vanished instantly, to become only a flat disembodied face filling the Zone.

Next, it took five men to push Nam-Ek into the singularity.

Finally, the guards came for Zod. With every fiber of his being he wanted to fight, to scream and shout and not allow these hated people a moment of victory. However, he knew he could not escape the guards, the howling mob. Even if he broke away, they would hunt him and kill him like an animal. And if he kicked and thrashed, forcing them to pick him up bodily and throw him into the Phantom Zone, he would only appear childish. Humiliated and worse—*impotent*. He was Zod, *General*

Zod, and he could never allow himself to look powerless, especially in front of these people whom he despised.

By taking control of the situation, he placed himself in charge for one last time. Better yet, he snatched the power and authority from these weaklings who had betrayed and defeated him. He had only one possible option, and Zod vowed to do this on his own terms. His own terms! Let historians record this ending with awe!

Unexpectedly, he spun and broke away. Rather than allow his enemies to touch him, not accepting *their* punishment, he had only one place to go. With a last glare of hatred directed toward Jor-El, General Zod dove headfirst through the silver rings.

He heard surprised and outraged shouts from the throne room . . . until absolute, infinite nothingness swallowed him up.

CHAPTER 81

∞⌒◇‼◇⊶T♀◇ 81

In the middle of the Square of Hope the broken statue of Zod lay like a stone corpse covered with dark fabrics. The provisional Council would soon find some way to dispose of it permanently. The public would not feel satisfied until the offensive relic was destroyed.

In their wild and relieved celebrations, the people also turned their anger against any reminders of the old dictatorship. Individual vandals, as well as larger mobs, targeted other examples of civic artwork Zod had commissioned. Lara was helpless to prevent them from defacing the intricate mosaics, sculpture walls, and elaborate murals she had so meticulously designed.

"Stop this desecration!" She tried to push her way to the largest mural wall, moving awkwardly because of her pregnancy. "It's *art*!"

"It's propaganda for Zod—and we have had enough of that," someone snarled at her.

"Propaganda? Just *look* at it—what's left of it!" But they refused to accept that even the most straightforward images did not contain subliminal ideas in support of the overthrown government. Her words went unheeded, and the rampant destruction continued.

Offended on her behalf, Jor-El demanded to speak with Tyr-Us, who seemed to be in charge of the provisional government, but the man made obvious excuses not to see him. The scientist finally barged in, appointment or no appointment. "Why would you let vandals destroy my wife's artwork? They're scenes from *history*. Lara designed them herself—"

"But Zod commissioned them," Tyr-Us answered impatiently. "We want no leftover reminders of that regime. Can you blame the people? It's better to simply start fresh. If your wife would like to submit alternative designs to our cultural committee, she is welcome to do so." He seemed to think he was doing her a favor. "However, we have many eager craftsmen who wish to contribute. Your wife may have been General Zod's pet artist, but she will be on equal footing with the rest of our people from now on."

Jor-El stiffened. "Why would you punish Lara? I don't understand your attitude at all. We are only trying to help—"

"Really?" The man seemed on the verge of saying much more, but then insisted that Jor-El leave. "I have more important things to do than listen to your complaints."

Striding through the streets, Jor-El next encountered Gil-Ex surrounded by a group of advisers. The advisers looked up, startled, when the white-haired scientist stepped forward. "Gil-Ex, who should I speak to about all the technologies Zod hid in his secret chamber? Krypton might still benefit, but only if someone with the proper vision applies those theories in a constructive way. I could be of service on such a committee."

Gil-Ex was surprisingly cool. His bald pate flushed pink, and the tips of his long mustache quivered. "That won't be necessary. We have others to perform that task."

"But who would be better suited?"

"Someone who wasn't the righthand man of General Zod."

For a moment, Jor-El was speechless. "I helped overthrow Zod. Without me, you would still be inside the Phantom Zone."

Gil-Ex cut him off. "Without *you,* the Phantom Zone would never have been created in the first place."

The remaining pieces fell together for Jor-El, and now he saw why members of the provisional government were rebuffing him. "Thank you for your time," he said in a clipped voice and stalked away. Though he didn't turn around, he could sense Gil-Ex and his advisers watching him.

Lara was infuriated when he told her what had happened. "They're distorting history! That's exactly the sort of thing Zod wanted me to do—and I refused! How can the new Council *want* to make the same errors? They're as bad as the General himself."

Jor-El shook his head. "They will never see it, and you gain nothing by making such claims." As he sensed the direction the political winds were blowing, he realized that he himself might end up being a scapegoat. "They want our world to be exactly as it was before the loss of Kandor, but they've forgotten that the old Krypton wasn't perfect by any means. I thought we would have learned something from all that has happened."

CHAPTER 82

After so many nightmarish months, Jor-El wished he could just go home to his peaceful estate, pursue his own interests, and wait for the birth of his son. It wouldn't be long now.

Lara couldn't agree with him more. "I want our baby to be born in the manor house."

But with the new government being formed, Jor-El could not simply abandon the people and leave the course of Krypton's future to chance. He wanted to make certain the new leaders learned from their mistakes and did not fall into the backward thinking of the old Council. He suspected that the provisional government was already stumbling down the wrong path.

He'd had no interest in politics before, but now he had a chance to change the direction of society. Despite his reservations, he was willing to become a guiding force so that Krypton would look ahead, explore the universe, and become part of galactic society, just as Donodon had invited them to do.

In the sky overhead, Rao continued to swell and churn, erupting with more spectacular flares than had been recorded in centuries. The turbulent red sun concerned him, and it had been far too long since he'd sent up a solar-probe rocket. Perhaps he could convince the new leaders to take long-term action and prepare for Rao's eventual demise. He had already shown his proposed arkship plans to No-Ton, and the other scientist had gone wide-eyed at the very prospect of evacuating an entire planet.

Two days later, inside the refurbished government palace, Lara sat with him in the front row as the provisional government met to formally establish a new Council, choosing representatives from cities across the continent. Tyr-Us sat at the head of a long table with ten empty chairs. He acted as the de facto head of the proceedings and seemed to accept his role as a matter of course. He was the son of old Jul-Us, and he had suffered greatly for standing up to Zod. Jor-El knew the others would find the man comforting.

Because of his ordeal in the Phantom Zone and his track record of being one of Zod's first and most outspoken detractors, Gil-Ex also accepted a seat. In what was almost certainly a measure of sympathy for their similar suffering, four more of the prominent dissidents recently released from the Phantom Zone were also elected. As their names were called, the four came forward to take empty chairs at the Council table.

For their parts in the great battle that had overthrown Zod, Or-Om, Korth-Or, and Gal-Eth also accepted seats on the new Council. Jor-El was surprised when they offered the next seat to No-Ton. Though he was a former member of Zod's Ring of Strength, they found the other scientist acceptable because of his "notable resistance to the General's dangerous orders." No-Ton didn't seem to have expected the appointment, either.

"And for our last seat on the new Council, we are proud to nominate Zor-El from Argo City," Tyr-Us said. Although he was glad for his brother, Jor-El was perplexed and concerned that they had brushed him aside.

Zor-El stood from his bench in the speaking hall, his face etched in deep thought. He held his left arm out in front of him, contemplating the burn scars there. "I have had experience with the cumbersome nature of the old Council. By requiring that even the simplest votes be decided by consensus rather than a simple majority, many important—if controversial—matters died without resolution. We can no longer run Krypton this way. You all know it." He looked around the gathered representatives and nominees.

Gal-Eth grumbled, then nodded his head. "Dramatic change has been forced upon us. We may as well make the best of it."

Or-Om, the mining industrialist, gave a brief and loud burst of applause. "I agree. If I ran my companies the way the old Council ran Kandor, I'd never get anything done. Let's make a change for the better."

"I propose that decisions be made by a simple majority on the new Council," said Korth-Or. "It's the only way we can move forward."

Tyr-Us frowned as if the very idea of such a major shift pained him, but he saw the mood in the room and grudgingly nodded. "Are there objections?" No one raised any issues. "So that decision, at least, is unanimous. A simple majority, six votes out of eleven, will decide matters under debate. Now, Zor-El, please join us at the Council table so that we can begin our first session."

The dark-haired man flashed his brother a mischievous smile. "But I did not accept the position you offered, Tyr-Us. Argo City is more than one man could wish to rule—at least this man. Now that the protective dome has been deactivated, I have five bridges to rebuild, along with agricultural fields that were trampled by Zod's army, and a whole sea-harvesting industry to restore. Thus, I regretfully decline."

The new Council members could not have been more surprised. After a moment of uproar from the table and the audience, Zor-El shouted until they listened to him. "But I nominate my brother, Jor-El, to take my place. No one has done more for Krypton in the past tumultuous year than he has. You should have granted him the very first seat on the new Council."

Jor-El felt a wash of gratitude. Everyone in the audience was looking at him.

Then he was completely taken aback by Tyr-Us's venomous reaction. "Impossible! Jor-El collaborated with our greatest enemy. He provided General Zod with terrible weapons. You all heard Zod during his trial—without Jor-El, that evil dictator would never have come to power."

Gil-Ex interrupted the tirade with one of his own. "Jor-El created the Phantom Zone, where so many of us were trapped. None of us can forget that! For that one act alone, he should never be forgiven."

"And he built the Rao beam that destroyed Borga City, slaughtering hundreds of thousands of innocents!" said another one of the former Phantom Zone prisoners on the Council. "You assisted him, Zor-El, but that vile invention was his own creation, was it not?"

Or-Om added in a low voice, "As I recall, wasn't he also responsible for the death of the alien visitor in the first place? That's what set in motion this whole chain of events."

"Brainiac stealing the city of Kandor—" Tyr-Us began, his face red.

No-Ton interrupted, his voice sounding nervous. "Excuse me, but you can't blame Jor-El for that. Donodon's race had nothing to do with the arrival of Brainiac."

"Can we be sure of that? Zod is the only one who told the story. Who can believe anything he said?"

Zor-El shook his head. "Already you prove my case. If I had any doubts about declining your invitation to join this Council, you have just dispelled them all. Are you delusional? Have you forgotten—"

But Jor-El rose slowly to his feet, gesturing his brother to silence. "I can speak for myself, Zor-El." He turned to face the Council table, with its prominently empty chair. He took a step closer. "Yes, I was there at the beginning, and I cooperated with Commissioner Zod to save the people at Kandor." Feeling heat flood his face, he stared at the ten seated members one at a time. "Where were the rest of you? Any of you? Kandor was *gone,* our planet was under threat of another alien attack, and Zod was trying to save people and defend Krypton. Of course I helped him! Many good citizens came to offer aid in whatever ways they could.

"Donodon was my friend, and his death was an accident. Or maybe not entirely an accident—I found evidence that Zod himself may have been responsible for the explosion."

"For what possible reason would he do that?" said Gil-Ex in a scornful voice.

"To throw the old Council into a panic so that he could more easily seize power." Jor-El began to address their other accusations, one by one. "Yes, the Rao beam was my own invention. My brother and I used it to relieve the pressure in our planet's core. I could not prevent Zod from seizing it as a terrible weapon, but I did sabotage the Rao-beam generator and stop him from ever doing it again. Where were the rest of you?

"Because I could not make Zod see the threat of the oncoming comet, I reprogrammed the nova javelins to destroy Loth-Ur's Hammer, rather than Argo City or any other city on Krypton. Thus, I saved our planet yet again." He found he was shaking with anger. "And still you doubt my motives? *I* am the one who brought about General Zod's downfall. I set the trap to imprison him in a force field, allowing the rest of you to take Kryptonopolis." He let the moment of silence hang and then said, "Therefore, I accept the nomination to become a member of the new Council. I will continue to devote myself to the betterment of Krypton. As I have always done."

Zor-El applauded as his brother walked defiantly toward the last empty seat at the Council table. No-Ton also clapped, and a smattering of applause rippled through the audience. Or-Om, Gal-Eth, and Korth-Or, who had accompanied Zor-El on his march against Kryptonopolis, shrugged and also agreed.

Tyr-Us and Gil-Ex looked decidedly uncomfortable as the ivory-haired scientist sat at the long table. Finally the new head announced, "Very well, this Council is in session."

The day after the new government was formed, Zor-El bid farewell to his brother and Lara. Jor-El said, "Are you sure you won't stay with us until the baby is born? You'd be perfectly welcome back at the estate, far from all this turmoil."

"That's more tempting than an offer to sit on the new Council, but I must decline." He let out a good-natured sigh. "Our father asked us to have children, remember? How am I ever going to have a son or a daughter if I never spend time with my wife?"

Jor-El laughed. "I trust that's a scientific problem you can solve for yourself."

When the Council called its first official meeting, all the people of Kryptonopolis were encouraged to attend in person, or to watch the proceedings projected on the facets of the giant crystal towers, to which Jor-El and No-Ton had restored power.

Determined, Jor-El took his seat at the end of the long table, though he still felt awkward and unwelcome there. At least half of the Council members looked askance at him, especially those who had been imprisoned in the Phantom Zone. He could understand their resentment: His own ordeal in that empty dimension had been extremely disorienting and unpleasant, and he had been trapped there only a few hours. These others had been lost in the void for months.

And General Zod would spend the rest of eternity on the other side of the singularity. Zod was the one to blame, not Jor-El.

Lara arrived early enough to get one of the front seats so that she could see her husband. Even with her extremely rounded abdomen, she remained graceful and beautiful, though the hard bench seemed uncomfortable for her. Giving him an encouraging smile, she squirmed to find a better position.

Jor-El had already requested a leave of absence from official business so that he could take Lara away to the estate. She was due very soon, and the doctor, Kirana-Tu, had offered to be available for the delivery.

Jor-El realized he hadn't even been given an agenda for this session, but Tyr-Us began the meeting, sounding ponderous. "To take the first step forward for a new Krypton, we must sweep away the ashes of the past." He looked around him. "Five members and I propose a symbolic gesture, but symbols are important. The Phantom Zone is a dangerous object, and it must be destroyed so that it is never misused again." He seemed very pleased. "Six of us have already held a vote, and so we carry a majority." He looked over at No-Ton, Or-Om, Korth-Or, Gal-Eth, and Jor-El. "We would, however, be pleased if the decision were unanimous."

The others were taken aback, even affronted at the sudden blatant partisanship. "How can we vote?" cried Korth-Or. "We haven't even heard your proposal yet!"

"This is not the way our business should be conducted," Gal-Eth said in a more cautious voice. Even in the audience, muttering could be heard.

Gil-Ex looked very satisfied with himself. "Previously, Council business required all eleven votes to be carried. Now, because of the motion introduced by Zor-El and approved unanimously, we need only six votes."

Tyr-Us said, "We have much business to complete, and we felt this was a swift and efficient way to proceed rather than waste time in debate when we already had the votes necessary."

Jor-El was greatly disturbed, not just because of the obvious political machinations but because of their misconceptions about the underlying science. The Council members didn't understand what they were suggesting or how to implement it. He looked down the table to face the others. "Excuse me, but no matter how many votes you manage to find, the Phantom Zone *can't* be destroyed."

Gil-Ex shouted him down with surprising vitriol. "We've had enough of your corrupted technologies, Jor-El. You can't change our minds."

"Wiping out the Phantom Zone—*your* Phantom Zone—is the only way we can restore hope," Tyr-Us added, only slightly calmer. "This act will also guarantee that Zod and his cronies never escape."

Jor-El shook his head, not rising to the level of insults. "I didn't advise against it. I'm simply stating a fact: The Phantom Zone is a stable singularity, a hole into another universe. It cannot be destroyed, no matter how much you may want to do so."

The audience members began to grumble. "Thank you for your insight, Jor-El," Gil-Ex said, his voice like ice. "But I'm certain we can find a way. We don't need your help."

"The vote has already been carried," added one of the former Phantom Zone prisoners. "Time for the next item of discussion."

Sighing, Jor-El saw that he would not win the argument. Sadly, he realized that this would likely be how the new Council often conducted business. He turned toward Lara, searching for a friendly face—and was astonished to see her hunched over, her face clenched in pain. Both of her arms were wrapped around her stomach.

He jumped to his feet from behind the table. "Lara, what is it?"

She tried to reassure him with a smile, which didn't convince him at all. "The baby. Labor contractions."

He hurried around the table to the first row of seats, not caring that he caused a disturbance. Tyr-Us called for order in a scolding voice. Jor-El grabbed his wife's arm. "We've got to get you out of here. I'll find the doctor."

"Don't . . . overreact." She clamped her teeth together and sucked in a quick, hissing breath. "I'm sure we have time. But you'd better get me to the estate soon."

Forgetting about the stubborn Council, ignoring the looks and the whispered comments from others in the benches, Jor-El ushered his wife out of the chamber. The meeting would have to continue without him. At the moment, he had far more important concerns.

It was the happiest moment in her life and the perfect ending to a long dark string of events. The birth of a baby son, healthy and strong.

Once back inside the manor house, Lara retired to their bedchamber as her labor progressed. The female doctor hovered inside the room during Lara's hours of contractions. Jor-El held his wife's hand the whole time.

Afterward, though Lara was exhausted and drained, her amber hair streaked against her face with perspiration, Kirana-Tu insisted it was a relatively easy delivery. "So typical, you barely needed me here." Lara lay back in the bed and held her baby in the crook of her arm, biting back several choice comments for the humorless doctor.

Jor-El's chef had returned from serving the masses in Kryptonopolis, clearly disgusted with how his master had been treated by the Council. Fro-Da wanted to settle down at the estate again, where he could worry about nothing of greater consequence than his sauces, braised meats, roasted vegetables, and spiced fruits. To do his part for Lara, he had studied traditional records and developed a special fortified soup that would help the new mother regain her strength.

The next morning, Lara insisted she needed fresh air. Holding the baby, Jor-El walked slowly with her out to the open porch where she could smell the fragrant breezes and look out over the flowers, the fresh-cut purple lawn, and the splashing fountains. Resting in a comfortable chair, she cradled the infant in her arms. He was wrapped in a red and blue blanket sent to them by Charys from Yar-El's old possessions.

Jor-El stared in wonder at the little boy's face. "After so many astonishing events, I never imagined that the high point of my life would come so unexpectedly."

"Unexpected? You've known for almost nine months you were going to be a father."

"But I didn't know it would feel like this. Before, it was always a theoretical proposition."

"You and your theories, Jor-El," she teased.

"But this one has struck me here." He put a hand to the center of his chest. "I can't explain it."

"You don't need to explain it. Just *feel* it. That's what I've been trying to show you all along."

He gave her a bittersweet but satisfied smile. "I vowed that our son would be raised in a better world, and I intend to keep that promise. I'll see that our boy reveres truth and justice."

The infant's blue eyes were open and clear, and Lara was sure he was studying his parents. She wondered if he would remember this moment.

"Truth and justice," Lara mused. "Remember the obelisks, the paintings I made to symbolize the most important facets of our race?"

"Yes, you used Kal-Ik to symbolize truth and justice. I felt a lot like him when I stood up to Zod." Jor-El looked at her, and they were both considering the same thing. "So you think Kal is a good name?"

"I think it's a perfect name for our son. *Kal-El.*"

"Who am I to disagree?" He bent down and kissed the baby. He had dark hair, with a small but persistent curl at his forehead. "Welcome to the world, Kal-El."

Giving his wife a tender kiss, he took little Kal in his arms and held him.

CHAPTER 84

Jor-El retreated from public view for a few days after the birth of
his son. At home, he doted on baby Kal-El, savoring the delights of
watching him discover small marvels, like holding his parents' fingers,
splashing in warm bathwater, and making experimental sounds. Jor-El
wondered if Yar-El had experienced the same simple pleasures after his
two sons were born.

Jor-El returned to his laboratory and revisited the many half-finished
projects he had abandoned over the years. As a scientist, he couldn't
simply stop the ideas from coming into his head. Zod's Commission for
Technology Acceptance was forever gone, but Jor-El expected no more
openness from the new leadership, even though he was ostensibly part
of the Council. The six old-guard members could always vote down his
suggestions.

Though some of his fellow Council members blamed Jor-El for their
troubles, others respected him just as much for what he had done in the
past. He was *Jor-El*, and he did not care about glory, wealth, or fame.

Since Lara was recovering well and the baby was healthy, he knew
he had to return to Kryptonopolis and get back to work on the Council.
Many of the members were the older sons of entrenched noble families
that had been disenfranchised by Zod's iron regime, and they were likely
to idealize the old, stagnant ways. Without his guidance, he dreaded
some of the decisions they might make.

Before he could leave home, an urgent message from No-Ton and

Or-Om shattered the calm. In Jor-El's absence, many scientific responsibilities had been shifted to the other scientist's shoulders, and No-Ton was the first to admit he felt inadequate to bear them.

On the communication plate, the two men stood close to each other, their images clear. "This isn't a social call," Or-Om said gruffly, scratching at his newly cut hair.

No-Ton seemed almost frantic. "The Council just issued an edict banning *all* of your supposedly dangerous technology, Jor-El."

He felt a cold wave of disgust. He had already been afraid of dark and reactionary days ahead. "Just how do they define dangerous technology?"

"Anything invented by *you,* presumably." Or-Om shook his head. "Since they don't understand any of it, they don't want to take the risk."

"I wasn't there for the vote," Jor-El said. "I didn't hear any of the discussion. I wasn't given a chance to speak on my own behalf. I will demand a reopening of the debate."

"Your vote wouldn't have made a difference," No-Ton said. "Tyr-Us has his majority of cronies, and he means to demonstrate how 'different' he is."

Now Jor-El did not try to hide his anger. "They already destroyed my wife's art in Kryptonopolis without a valid reason. Now they mean to erase everything *I've* done? They can't just delete me from the historical record. Surely I have more supporters than that? How could they forget so quickly?"

"Right now, people are afraid to speak out," No-Ton said. "The Council is still vigorously rooting out any remaining supporters of Zod, and no one wants to fall under a veil of suspicion."

"We could bring Zor-El back to stand by you," Or-Om suggested. "He won't put up with this nonsense. He never should have gone back to Argo City."

"I'm coming to Kryptonopolis. Maybe I can sway them in the next official meeting. I can't ignore this."

"It's more urgent than that!" No-Ton interrupted. "You already know that the Council means to destroy your Phantom Zone. Tyr-Us and Gil-Ex are irrational about it. Korth-Or and Gal-Eth both debated with them, but the six won't change their votes."

Jor-El replied with a sigh, "But they can't destroy it. I've already explained that."

No-Ton was trembling as he spoke. "Tyr-Us has decided to throw the silver rings down the shaft in the crater of Kandor. He thinks the magma should get rid of the Phantom Zone well enough. I . . . I'm not certain about my physics, but I fear that—"

Jor-El reeled backward, feeling as if a tall dam had just shattered and a wall of foaming white water was rushing toward him. "But if they do that, it will sink to the very core! The Council members don't understand what they're doing. They never have. The consequences could be devastating."

"They have made up their minds, Jor-El," Or-Om said gruffly. "Tyr-Us has already taken the Phantom Zone up to the crater."

The valley around Kandor was black and devastated, the once-beautiful landscape now a vast, leprous scar. Lava boulders lay scattered everywhere, as if a giant had tossed a handful of black crumbs across the ground. A smoky haze hung in the sky, trapped by an atmospheric inversion.

At the edge of the crater, Jor-El disembarked and let the floating vessel drift. He began to scramble along the steep rock-strewn path; the group of determined Council members had already picked their way down. Tyr-Us, Gil-Ex, and the other four Council members who had been imprisoned in the Phantom Zone were clearly determined to undertake this ill-advised action.

Work crews had cleared away part of the hardened lava pillar left behind by the eruption, exposing the shaft sealed off by Zor-El's protective field. The containment barrier held the still-pressurized magma below the surface. The somber self-important men stood next to a large object covered with a draping fabric, the silver rings enclosing the Phantom Zone.

"Wait!" Jor-El sprinted across the hellish ruins of the crater floor, waving his arms. When he stumbled and cut his palm, he ignored the blood running down his hand. "Stop! You must not do this." Armored guards blocked his way. They seized Jor-El's arms, but he continued to throw himself forward. "Let me go. I am a member of the Council." He pulled free. "Do not put the Phantom Zone into the shaft! You'll never stop the aftereffects."

The six members of the new Council looked at him with exasperation and resentment. "Once again, Jor-El threatens us with his science," Gil-Ex sneered.

"This is the *truth*. You are about to cause an irrevocable disaster!"

Tyr-Us screwed up his face into an expression of extreme distaste. "Obviously, he doesn't want us to destroy the Phantom Zone. Either he has an overweening pride in his own work, or he has an insidious plan to use the rings."

One of the other four said, "Maybe he wants to release General Zod. We can't let him do that."

"Ask any of your own scientists if you don't believe me. Ask No-Ton or Zor-El! Tyr-Us, my brother is your friend. At least talk to *him* first—but listen to *somebody*." The guards stopped him again when he tried to push forward, so he kept shouting from where he was, desperate to get through to them. "The Phantom Zone is a singularity. It's an opening into another universe. I created it by using a great concentration of energy, and it feeds on energy. If you throw it into our planet's core, the singularity will have more than it can possibly consume. It will grow, and it will keep growing. You'll never be able to stop it."

Gil-Ex rolled his eyes. "Jor-El is predicting the end of the world—again!"

Jor-El's knees went weak. Even though time and again he had been proved right, no one believed him. "I'm begging you—at least consider what I have said. If you do this, there's no turning back."

Two of the men removed the fabric to expose the silver rings and the flattened furious faces of Zod, Nam-Ek, and Aethyr trapped in the empty dimension.

Tyr-Us smiled. "We have pushed the lava down into the shaft using Zor-El's barrier. We'll drop the Phantom Zone in, cover it with another energy field, and dump these rings into the depths, where no one can ever retrieve them." He let out a long, slow sigh. "Zod will be gone, the Phantom Zone will be gone, and we can all breathe easily again."

Jor-El thrashed and struggled, but he could not stop these foolish, naïve men from carrying the object toward the deep hole. He let out a last cry as they placed the silver rings into the protected shaft, and he caught a final glimpse of General Zod's vengeful expression, snarling at them.

Pleased with themselves, the Council members switched off the lower field, releasing the singularity into the fiery lava core. The Phantom Zone disappeared into the blazing pit.

When it was entirely too late, the armored guards released Jor-El, and he sank to his knees on the sharp black rocks. He began to calculate how much time remained before Krypton destroyed itself.

CHAPTER 85

In the few weeks since defeating General Zod, Argo City had made tremendous progress. One of the severed bridge spans was temporarily repaired so that mainland traffic could cross the bay to the peninsula. Zor-El began to feel that his city was thriving once more. He had real hope again.

Until Jor-El told him what Tyr-Us and the others had done.

Continuing solar flares caused bursts of static and signal breakup on the communication plate, but his brother's news was shockingly clear. "I couldn't stop them, Zor-El. Every day, every *hour* counts now." His brother's face was pale and distraught. "The Phantom Zone is going to kill us all."

Jor-El sent a series of images and calculations. "As it sinks to the core, the singularity will drain more and more energy from the mantle. When it reaches the critical point, the opening into the Phantom Zone will expand geometrically, like a huge hungry mouth. It will swallow the entire core of Krypton instantaneously, leaving a great void. The remaining matter will suddenly collapse inward, and the shock waves will rebound. The whole planet will be blown apart."

Zor-El brushed his dark hair out of his eyes, refusing to give up. "Then you and I will find some way to stop this disaster. We've got to."

"Take all my data. *Please* find something I've done wrong. Show me my error." Jor-El swallowed hard. "I calculate that we have three days left."

As solar static threatened to disrupt the transmission, Zor-El stored the information. If Jor-El was right, no one and nothing could retrieve the singularity now that the Council had dropped it down into the shaft.

And Jor-El was almost always right.

After the signal broke up, he sat with Alura in his tower room, tugging at his hair and reviewing his brother's calculations. He racked his brain to think of some factor Jor-El had forgotten to include, some flaw in the initial conditions. But each result was as disheartening as the last. He tried to force the equations to yield different results.

Every time he ran a simulation, he watched the singularity expand until it engulfed the core of Krypton. Then the whole planet collapsed and broke apart like an empty eggshell. "There's not even the slightest chance, Alura. Nothing. Jor-El rarely makes mistakes in his calculations, and he hasn't now."

No errors.

Less than three days.

He wrapped his arms around his wife and pulled her close. Looking out across the sea, they held each other as darkness gathered. "What can we possibly do in three days? Even if we had all the resources of Krypton and the full cooperation of everyone in the world?" He stroked her dark hair. "Do we even tell our people? My mother? Do we inform them all that they'll be dead soon? It could spark a worldwide panic. Maybe it would be better if we just allowed them a few more days of peace and happiness."

Alura pulled back. "You can't do that, Zor-El. You've always trusted your people before, and they've always believed in you. They put their lives on the line to support your decisions. You can't hide this from them. It's not right."

When they told Charys, she agreed wholeheartedly.

And so Zor-El issued his statement. Despite the late hour, gongs were rung, people came out to their balconies to listen. With his wife and mother beside him, Zor-El paraded solemnly down the long, flower-decked streets. Every time he took a step, he was acutely aware of the ground beneath his feet. Somewhere deep below, a hungry monster was devouring the heart of the planet.

He followed the whispering canals, breathed in the perfume of the beautiful plants, and announced with utmost sincerity that the end of their world was coming.

Zor-El did not sleep, still struggling to find a solution, even a hint of a possibility, but he found very little hope to cling to. "I have the shield that I used to protect us from Zod. I can cover Argo City with a protective dome. We can hide under it and hope that will make enough of a difference."

"My greenhouses could support our population for a long time—but what chance would we have? How can your golden dome, however powerful, save us when all of Krypton crumbles? What possibility is there that any of us will survive?"

He bowed his head. "Almost none." Then he clenched his fist, struck the table, and looked up again with fiery eyes. "But what other choice is there?"

She gave him a wan smile and repeated his words. "Almost none."

CHAPTER 86

The huge telescope dishes stood as silent sentinels, still watching for now-irrelevant threats from space. With Krypton's time slipping away minute by minute, Jor-El went to the distant early-warning outpost, hoping for inspiration. The twenty-three receivers looked like gigantic flowers, their petals spread wide to drink electromagnetic signals. Soon they would all be swept away.

Lara accompanied him out to the site, holding the baby as they walked toward the observation array. She refused to leave her husband's side, knowing they had so little time left together. Kal-El nestled in his mother's arms, looking at the sights around him as if trying to see every detail of Krypton before it was too late.

Jor-El whispered to his baby son, "Kal-El, I am so sorry that you'll never be able to grow up, never meet your potential. I wanted to give you everything, but I can't hold the world together for you."

Lara fought back tears. "It's not your fault, Jor-El. The other members of the Council closed their eyes to the truth. They didn't *want* to see it."

"They feared my knowledge rather than respecting it. Tyr-Us and the others were so tied up in politics and alliances and feuds that they couldn't imagine a man might speak the truth just because it's the right thing to do. And now their willful ignorance will kill them."

No-Ton, Or-Om, and Gal-Eth—the Council members who did believe Jor-El's dire prediction—begged him to suggest a project they could undertake—even something desperate and high risk, no matter how little likelihood it had of succeeding.

Although their chances were vanishingly small, Jor-El gave No-Ton and his companions his old plans for the arkships to be used if the red sun threatened to become an imminent supernova. Working with complete abandon, racing for their lives, a frantic army of engineers, builders, and other volunteers from all walks of life stripped down buildings and tore apart bridges, then used the structural girders, alloy plates, and curved crystal sheets as raw materials to build the vast vessels.

No-Ton tried to cajole Jor-El to join them, promising him passage for himself, Lara, and his son. But Jor-El had done the projections, and he knew that there simply wasn't enough time to build such ships. He had to find another way.

Standing at the base of the vigilant telescopes, Jor-El suddenly wondered if someone else might listen, even though the Council had not. He could alter the big dishes in the great array, convert them into powerful phased transmitters, and shout a signal into the interstellar gulf, begging for aid, for rescue.

But Krypton had only two days left. Even with a transmission spreading out at the speed of light, no rescuers could possibly hear him and respond soon enough. In the time remaining, Jor-El's call for help would barely reach the boundary of Rao's solar system.

Even so, when he explained his idea, Lara suggested that he try. "At least someday others would know what happened to us. Maybe our tale will save some other race from their own closed minds."

"Like the last message from Mars," he said.

"J'onn J'onzz may have been very much like you, Jor-El."

The plight of the lone Martian survivor had certainly wrenched his heart. He had never imagined Krypton's fate would be so similar—and so imminent. When Donodon had visited Mars, the blue-skinned alien had found only dust and the echoes of a lost civilization. If only he had Donodon's help now.

At that moment, Jor-El would have welcomed a fleet of ships from the kindly alien's race. With those ships, they might have—

Suddenly his eyes flew open wide and his heart began to pound. "Lara, we have to get back to the estate! There's a chance—a small chance, but only if I can do it in time." He could barely catch his breath as the ideas thundered forward. With a shaky hand, he touched their baby's face. "Maybe I can save us after all."

The estate was quiet and empty. Jor-El had excused his few remaining servants so they could be with their families during the end. Only his chef stayed behind, claiming he had nowhere else to go. "This is my home. I'll stay here, if it's all the same to you." Neither he nor Lara could complain.

Jor-El hurried to the exotic translucent tower his father had built. Inside, with an intensity brought on by desperation and hope, he plunged into work he had left unattended for far too long.

All the components of Donodon's small spaceship sat in the middle of the tower room where Nam-Ek had brought them. Over the months he had made halfhearted attempts to reassemble the vessel, but the Commission had not given him much of the ship's framework or the "nonessential" pieces. Now, he carefully catalogued and organized the components, separated according to mechanisms that Jor-El understood and those that remained unexplained. Alas, the "unidentified" pile was much larger than the other. When he'd worked side by side with Donodon, Jor-El had learned much about the alien vessel, but the two had been intent on the needs of the new seismic scanner, not on understanding the details of the exotic starship. Now he had to do it himself.

Kal-El rested comfortably in a crib Lara brought into the tower. Their time was now measured in hours, and Jor-El felt the oppressive loss of each second that slipped away. Every breath he took brought him one breath closer to his last.

Red-eyed with weariness, Jor-El tried to decipher the alien engines and systems, relying on logical guesses. It would be impossible to manufacture other vessels like Donodon's to begin a mass exodus from Krypton—but if he was lucky and worked hard enough, perhaps he could reassemble and expand this one, placing the still-functional components in a single ship.

He remembered when Donodon had originally demonstrated the controls of the vessel, proudly telling him that the spacecraft was so sophisticated it could fly itself, explaining that its life support could

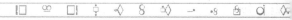

adapt to other races. But Jor-El didn't know *how* anything worked. He couldn't unravel it in time.

"I could install the heart of Donodon's small ship in the framework of a larger vessel. Large enough for the three of us." He looked intently at Lara. "Just the three of us. It might work."

"What about the rest of the people on Krypton?"

Jor-El hung his head. "It's not possible, Lara. In my entire life I've rarely admitted that, but this is one of those times. Do I save my family . . . or do I save no one? Those are the only two choices now."

"Tell me how I can help." Lara assisted him, working herself to exhaustion helping him and taking care of their baby. There was no time for sleep. Fro-Da kept them fed, but didn't ask what they were doing. Believing his master's conviction that the end was near, the chef found contentment in his daily routine.

Jor-El took components from several of his enclosed personal vehicles—a dome from a floater raft, seats and cabin from a groundcar, concentrated food supplies, medical kits. He needed to make a structure large enough for two adults and a baby, to last them for the unknown length of an interstellar voyage. Even the expanded ship would be cramped for an extended journey, and he had no idea how long their flight would be or even where they might go. But if Jor-El succeeded, then he, Lara, and the baby would be alive . . . at least for a little while longer. Alive. At the moment, that was the most Jor-El could strive for.

Taking precise notes, Lara captured images of his every step to make certain he could put the components back together. Jor-El finished reconnecting the engines, the power source, the navigation grid, and the planetary databases. Those were the most important parts.

Using a levitator crane, he installed the systems into the makeshift vessel he had constructed, a ship large enough to save the three of them. Though he tried not to, he continued to glance at the chronometer, feeling each moment drop away to vanish forever. He worked faster.

Meanwhile, Lara tackled another important task. From the library on the estate, she began to load as much of Krypton's knowledge as she could cram into memory crystals—history, culture, legends, geography, and science. She couldn't save the planet itself, but she could save its essence. She included the long and detailed journal recordings she had kept for so many years, the story of Kandor, her romance with Jor-El, the dark reign of Zod. The ship would take not only the three of them, but also all the information they might need.

With very little time remaining, Jor-El hooked up the engines and the power source to the large vessel. With Lara beside him, her expression hopeful and her faith in him complete, he tried to activate the systems.

When nothing happened, he tried again.

The power drain was too large. The sophisticated systems that had been precisely designed and calibrated for Donodon's small blue-and-silver spacecraft refused to recognize the much larger vessel built to accommodate Jor-El and his family.

The rapidly assembled ship would not function. The engine readings flickered, powered up, but failed to reach sufficient levels. The navigation computers refused to recognize the new framework he had built. Everything automatically shut down.

The ship would not function.

Sweating, fighting down panic, Jor-El double-checked all of the systems, reconnected each component. But still nothing. He had made no errors that he could find.

Donodon's ship was a marvel that even the alien explorer had not entirely understood. All of the components fit together in a pseudo-organic way, and Jor-El realized with a sinking heart that some part of the old vessel must have been a vital link in the chain. The exotic engines could not simply be pulled out and plugged into something larger.

It was a disaster. The expanded ship would never fly.

He slumped back, nearly knocking over one of his tables. Lara didn't have to ask him what had happened. She saw and understood. "You tried, Jor-El. We all tried."

"It isn't enough! There has to be some other way." He wrestled with dismay and hopelessness for the better part of an hour, when he did not have an hour to spare. Finally he came to a cold but necessary conclusion. He looked at his wife. "We'll take it apart—put the components back into a ship as close to the original size and shape that I can manage. They'll still function the way they were initially built. They have to."

"But the ship will be too small, Jor-El. It can't save all of us."

He drew a deep breath. "No. But at the very least it can save Kal-El."

The red sun of Rao dawned on the last day of Krypton.

The ground began to shake. All through the previous night, Jor-El hadn't been able to drive the vivid pictures from his mind, knowing what was happening at the core of the planet. For days, the Phantom Zone had swallowed more and more incandescent lava, and by now the singularity must be dangerously close to its critical point.

Jor-El did not give up. Even though he knew the energy drain on the cobbled-together components was too great to accommodate two adults and one child, he refused to accept that he couldn't make it function. He *needed* to save Lara and the baby; he simply couldn't imagine—or allow—any other outcome.

Working feverishly, he stripped out some of the systems, reduced the mass of the vessel's framework, and recalibrated the life-support controls to work with two passengers. He and Donodon had crowded together in the original tiny vessel . . . but that had been only for a short flight from Kandor to his estate.

He was willing to sacrifice himself in order to save his wife and child. But he *must* save them.

Again, though, he could not succeed. While Lara watched, her face pale and drawn, he made a second attempt to power up the internal systems of the modified ship. She bit her lip, rocking the baby in her arms, and she realized what he was doing. "You're going to stay behind, aren't you? But you want me to go with Kal-El."

"You have to." His tone had a ragged edge of raw desperation, and it allowed for no argument.

Even so, the built-in generator systems could not power up to the bare minimum requirements. A tear slid down his cheek from reddened eyes as he just stared at the vessel, feeling as if it had betrayed him.

"I can't do it. The only possible craft will be barely large enough to accommodate a baby. I can send Kal-El away from Krypton and pray the life support keeps him alive." The very idea sounded hopeless.

"But we can't send our baby out alone," Lara said. Her voice was almost a moan. "He'll be helpless and lost."

"That is why I so desperately needed you to go along. I failed." His whole body shuddered with the enormity of what he faced, what they *both* faced as parents. "But would you rather we didn't try? Would you rather we kept him with us so that we die together along with all of Krypton?"

She shook her head. Her eyes sparkled with tears, but both she and Jor-El knew the answer. "No, he is our son. If there is even one chance in a million that he can survive, then we have to take it."

"I was sure you would say that." He had faith in what Donodon's technology could do, and he clung to the slenderest hope that Kal-El would find a way to survive, a new place to call home, a people to accept him. "We will do what we have to."

Working swiftly together, he and Lara guided the new, much smaller starship out of the tower lab and onto the lush purple lawn. Constructed of a sturdy framework inlaid with the toughest Kryptonian structural crystals, many of which he grew using his father's best techniques, the ship looked quite different from Donodon's. During the urgent restructuring, Jor-El had made last-minute improvements to accommodate all of the memory crystals, all of the items Kal-El would need, wherever he went. The craft was as much Jor-El's design as the alien's, and the single life-form—the baby—finally did not cause the safety shutdowns to engage. To his great relief, he saw that at last the power levels were stable. The engines functioned.

There was a chance.

Jor-El and Lara had spent precious moments on an important task, each recording their heartfelt wishes and advice into a special crystal, dictating letters that their son would hear one day. As he grew older, Kal-El would have only these few hints of who his real parents had been. It had to be memorable.

With so much to say, Lara found herself at a loss for words when she recorded her message. Jor-El had struggled as well, reminded of how he had lost his own father to the Forgetting Disease and how Yar-El had found the strength and focus one last time to record a poignant message sealed into the wall of his mysterious tower. How could Jor-El do any less for his own baby?

Standing out in the open beside the small ship, Lara gazed around the beautiful estate, choked with emotion. "This is where we first met. This is where so much has happened."

"And now here is where everything is coming full circle," Jor-El said.

The ground shuddered beneath them, a wrenching, disorienting twist that made the couple stumble. He and Lara caught each other, kept each other from falling. Jor-El knew it would only get worse—and swiftly. Soon they would have no choice but to send the infant away forever.

After he had completed his frantic work on the new spacecraft, Jor-El then spent another hour poring over his calculations until his head pounded and his eyes ached. He had to be absolutely convinced he wasn't wrong, that there was no flaw in his reasoning. If he sent his innocent, helpless baby off into the unknown, and Krypton did *not* explode, then he would never forgive himself for what he had done. Kal-El would be lost to them forever.

Lara loaded the last few memory crystals into the strange hybrid ship, remaining brave. "Where will we send Kal-El?"

He gave her a rare smile. "I think I found the perfect place."

She suddenly remembered. "Earth? That beautiful world near Mars. In Donodon's recorded images, those people looked very much like Kryptonians."

"We can't tell exactly how different Kal-El will be from them. Simply growing up under a yellow sun may impose unpredictable physiological changes. Who can say? But on Earth, maybe our son won't be alone. Maybe those people will accept him."

She forced strength in her voice. "At least it's a chance."

When the crystal-inlaid ship was prepared, they had only to pack up the baby, say their farewells, and make sure that Kal-El got safely away before it was too late.

The ground shuddered more violently than before, and Lara fell to her knees on the grass. The surface heaved as if some monstrous subterranean thing were squirming, breaking free. The baby began to cry. These tremors were just the precursors. All of Krypton's continents were buckling, twisting as the world's interior spasmed.

Fro-Da came running out of the large manor house still wearing his apron; flour and cooking oil had spilled down his chest. The chef blinked as a jagged black crack snaked its way up one thick wall. Then, for reasons he must have considered urgent, he rushed back into the building. Jor-El shouted a warning, but his voice remained unheard as the load-bearing pillars buckled. The entire wing of the house fell in upon itself, burying Fro-Da with his kitchens.

In the Redcliff Mountains by the now-abandoned Rao-beam outpost, the cliffsides cracked, and avalanches slid down the slopes. House-sized blocks of stone broke free and tumbled into the valleys.

The sky overhead became a turmoil of spoiled-looking clouds, dust, and fire mixed with a fresh outpouring of gases from volcanic eruptions in the southern continent. Monster storms had begun to brew in the atmosphere, tumbling over one another as they raced across the landscape like unleashed hrakkas.

The whole engine of the planet's core shut down.

On the nearby plains, the telescopes and observation arrays shuddered and groaned. Girders and support stalks snapped, and the broad dishes slowly collapsed to the ground, breaking apart and crumbling under their own weight. In control rooms, all the images crackled into static and went off-line.

Fissures split the grasslands, spreading like fanged mouths. The floor of the crater of Kandor swelled into a huge dome much larger than Zor-El's force-field cap, and then split like a festering blister. The reawakened lava geyser shot a pillar of liquid orange fire to the sky.

A flat communication plate mounted on the curved wall inside Jor-El's tower laboratory crackled to life, sending an urgent transmission. Though he and Lara stood outside on the open lawn, Jor-El could hear the shouts and pleas of people begging him to help. But it was too late. As the ground heaved with another sharp shock, the tower twisted. A long, jagged crack shot up the side of the curved wall, and the communication plate tumbled over to shatter on the floor.

"It's time," he said to Lara, who clung protectively to their baby. "We can't wait any longer." Tears ran down her face, and Jor-El realized that he was weeping, too.

Lara wrapped their son tenderly in the blankets of their great house, the finest blue and red fabric emblazoned with the prominent symbol of Jor-El's family. "Kal-El, you have to go, or you'll die with us." She trembled, then straightened. This was their only hope.

Now that the baby was to be the only passenger, they had outfitted the interior of the ship like a cradle, a protective nest that would be monitored by the alien's life-support systems. Kryptonian crystals surrounded the cradle, memory crystals with the cultural and historical recordings Lara had copied, the seeds of Yar-El's architectural crystals, and the crystals that held Lara's journals. As the last item, she placed the special shard with the messages from both of them in with the baby. "This is so you'll know we loved you, Kal-El."

Lara gave her infant son a final kiss, brushing her lips against the delicate skin of his forehead. Her voice hitched as she said, "I wish you well on your new planet, Kal-El. I hope you find your way among the people of Earth. I hope you manage to be happy."

The planet continued to tear itself apart. "It has to be now," Jor-El said. Thunder in the sky competed with the cracking explosions and eruptions. The ground shook, and another split opened the wall of a nearby building, causing it to collapse. "We have to save him."

Lara desperately reached forward to touch the baby one final time. Suddenly thinking of his father's last utterance, Jor-El leaned in and whispered, "Remember." Then he took his wife's hand and drew her back from the ship so that he could close the hatch. Kal-El's blue eyes stared at his parents as the humming mechanism sealed the craft. The life-support systems switched on, ready to provide warmth, food, light, air.

With a whistling sound, four huge chunks of lava rock that had been ejected in a nearby volcanic blast slammed like bombs into the ground around them. One smashed entirely through the ceiling and skylights of the research building.

"He'll be safe, Lara." They stood bravely together watching the starship's automated systems lift the craft gently off the ground. "He will be the last son of Krypton."

The levitating ship turned on its central axis until it locked onto its optimal trajectory. The crystals on its hull shone in the red sunlight. The craft paused for just an instant, and then it rose up and away from the ugly-looking storms that approached from the east and north. Lara caught her breath and reached upward in a final gesture of farewell.

With a sudden flash of acceleration, the craft shot away, and Kal-El was gone.

CHAPTER 88

{Kryptonian symbols} 88

To Zor-El, the impending loss of Argo City, of Krypton, made everything seem more beautiful, all details crystalline sharp, each memory vivid with meaning.

His mother sat on a broad, flower-filled terrace and absorbed the world around her, all too aware of the approaching end. In a way, Charys seemed oddly contented. Zor-El said his goodbyes and left her alone.

He wanted to walk with Alura through her greenhouses, to hold her one last time and just wait together. Zor-El had always been an impatient man, insisting on action rather than complacency, but now there was nothing left to do. He understood vividly what was happening far beneath his feet. He stood on a ticking bomb and could not find a way to defuse it.

Another city might have reacted with wild riots, frantic last-moment hedonism, rampant vandalism, but Argo City was brave. The people had accepted the news with remarkable stoicism. He was proud of them.

Zor-El and Alura had walked along the streets, enjoying the gardens that hung like verdant curtains from the balconies and walls. Unaware of the catastrophe about to occur, the blossoms spread their petals wide to entice flying insects to pollinate them. Every breath tasted sweet. Even with the solar storms, the red sunlight felt warm and nourishing. Zor-El's dark eyes sparkled with tears.

Some stubborn fishermen had taken their boats out onto the water, as if this were any other day. Soon, Zor-El would have no choice but to activate the force-field dome, for whatever protection it might offer. It was likely to be a futile gesture, but it was all the protection he had to offer.

He returned to his tower and watched the readings come in from his distant seismic devices. Deep in the core, the singularity must be on the verge of its sudden, critical expansion. By the time the seismic signals reached his detectors, as soon as the acoustic waves could travel up through the mantle and resonate in the planet's crust, the fatal shock wave would already be on its way.

As he watched, the needles jumped, shuddered, and went off the scale. His heart leapt in tandem with the traces. "It's happened, Alura. Krypton's core just vanished into the Phantom Zone." He drew a deep breath. "Our world is about to implode."

Even now, huge portions of the interior were rushing to fill the void. The crust itself would crack and crumble, falling inward under its own immense gravity.

Loud sirens shrieked through the city. People rushed back inside the perimeter that the force-field dome would cover. Gondolas and powered sailing craft plunged through the city's canals to reach the protected area. Several large fishing boats, either unaware of the alarm or purposely ignoring it, remained where they were.

Zor-El remembered how peaceful it had been that night out on the water with his wife, spreading their gossamer sails and drifting under the starlight. If the world was going to end, he could understand why those fishermen were content to spend their last moments out on the ocean.

One final craft raced into the mouth of the largest canal; sailors jumped from their small vessel and ran along the docks and up the stairs on the seawall. Their abandoned craft floated away.

Zor-El was amazed at how swiftly the knotted black clouds converged overhead. The ground bucked and lurched, and the sea became suddenly stormy, stirred from deep below. Waves crashed into one another, building higher and stampeding toward the coastline. Already a series of enormous waves approached, much larger than the tsunami that had caused so much damage almost a year earlier. Waterspouts, giant pillars of silvery foam, whirled about, careening toward the coastline.

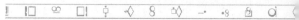

"I'm activating the dome."

From the control bank, he powered the generators, and the crackling shield appeared, sweeping over the boundaries of Argo City like a huge umbrella and slamming into the ground. Now they were completely isolated. This shield had held against General Zod's weapons, but Zor-El had no way of testing or calculating whether it would be sufficient to save them now. And even if this chunk of land somehow managed to remain intact, how could Argo City possibly survive if all the rest of Krypton were demolished?

The waterspouts circled like predators searching for anything to devour. An assault of waves obliterated the small gooseneck of land connecting the Argo City peninsula to the mainland, turning them into an island at last.

Tidal waves raced toward them, as if pursued by some terrible demon. A waterfall appeared in a line across the ocean as the deep crust broke open, leaving an enormous fissure, an empty hole that all the seas of Krypton could not fill. The first line of giant waves stumbled upon the fissure and poured down into the inconceivable depths. As the ocean struck the hot magma, an endless army of cannons seemed to fire shot after shot.

Another eruption vomited plumes of *emerald-green* lava, strangely altered minerals that proved to Zor-El that the transformation in Krypton's unstable core had continued even after he and his brother had released the pressure.

He already missed Jor-El, and he wished he'd had the chance to see their newborn baby. Shortly before all communication cut off, his brother had told him his desperate plan to send the baby off to an unknown planet. Sadly, Zor-El wished he and Alura had had a son or a daughter of their own, if only for a few years. . . .

He wished many things, and now it was too late.

A gargantuan wave crashed over the top of the protective dome, sending up spume and mist all around. Ironically, Zor-El saw a rainbow overhead cast by Rao's bright light. The chunk of land holding Argo City rose above sea level, broken free as some force from beneath pushed them away.

The catastrophe continued.

Kryptonopolis began to fall. The people in the glorious new capital had witnessed the loss of Kandor, then the rise and fall of the power-hungry Zod. But they could not grasp the magnitude of what was happening to them, to their world.

Tyr-Us called all members of the reconstituted Council for an emergency session, but the handful who showed up merely sat at the table, stuck with awe and disbelief. No-Ton, Or-Om, and Gal-Eth had gone to pursue their own last-minute plan for survival. Thunder rumbled both from the sky and from the ground beneath their feet.

As wide cracks opened in the newly paved streets, the remaining Council members began to blame one another for not listening to Jor-El, back when they could have prevented the disaster. The others had heard, and ignored, Jor-El's distraught pleas before throwing the Phantom Zone into the core shaft. Preoccupied with their own concerns, they had dismissed the warnings. They had not believed something so terrible could happen.

"Contact Jor-El again!" Gil-Ex wailed. "Give him anything he wants. The Council will support him now, so long as he tells us how to save ourselves."

"It is too late," Korth-Or said. "Can't you feel it?"

"It is never too late," cried Tyr-Us. "We are the people of *Krypton.*"

But if even Jor-El could save them, what chance did they have?

The five rapidly grown crystal spires of Kryptonopolis began to shake. Fissures shot like lightning bolts through the transparent facets. Due to their accelerated growth, which Zod had insisted on, the crystalline towers had been unstable from the outset, filled with impurities and structural weaknesses.

High turrets broke and fell under their own weight, sending a rain of razor-sharp fragments into the panicked crowds below. Those who could not flee swiftly enough stood transfixed as huge blocks of transparent stone fell down onto them and shattered on the ground with an explosive impact.

On Lookout Hill outside of Kryptonopolis, the tallest spire, which Zod had insisted on naming the Tower of Yar-El, withstood the wrenching shock waves for several minutes longer than the other structures, but it too broke in half and collapsed in a sparkling blast.

In the Square of Hope, the coverplates on the now-empty nova javelin pits crumbled and fell inward like trapdoors; panicked Kryptonians dropped screaming into the pits.

A zigzag split appeared across the center of the square, widening until it swallowed both halves of the fallen statue of General Zod. The dictator's carved stone face slid over the edge and vanished into the depths of the dying planet.

Inside the government palace, the remaining Council members wailed for help. Pillars buckled. Walls slid down into rubble. Tyr-Us finally shouted, though no one was listening, "We were wrong!"

Moments later, the whole imposing building collapsed, burying them in an avalanche.

Outside the city, the giant frameworks of half-completed arkships trembled and thrummed, amplifying the tremors in the ground. No-Ton shook his head in sad dismay. There was no way he could get the work done any faster.

The ships had been constructed with remarkable speed. His work crews had labored with a breathless anxiety, knowing their very lives were at stake. *They* had believed Jor-El's dire predictions. Using ready materials and structural components ripped whole from existing build-ings, they had raced to erect the frameworks.

Two of the arkships were mostly covered with metal plating, like the scales of a giant reptile, but their interiors were incomplete. The ships had no life-support systems and scant food supplies. The teams had worked independently, chaotically, without an overall plan.

No-Ton wept. Seven hours ago he had withdrawn all the construc-tion teams and ordered them to focus all efforts on completing a single arkship. Just one . . .

With a powerful seismic shift, one of the frameworks shuddered, look-ing like the metal skeleton of an enormous prehistoric beast. Letting out a chorus of groans, one of its sides buckled. A girder gave way, pulling in hundreds of huge rectangles of hull plating to collapse in a roar of metallic thunder. Thousands of workers were trapped inside. Teams abandoned their posts, rushing to the rescue, hoping to pull the injured from the wreckage.

A sharper quake knocked over a levitating crane. Another ship col-lapsed. Even the most secure armored compartments could offer no shelter from an imploding world.

A wide, dark fissure tore the surface of the planet and swallowed the well-meaning rescue crews; more and more dirt and rock collapsed into the depths. Red and yellow sulfurous steam blasted upward from the hot, exposed wound.

With a shrieking cry of distressed metal, the last of the huge arkships collapsed, slumping over next to No-Ton. The arks—the last chance for him and all these people—would never fly.

Jor-El and Lara watched the lone spacecraft dwindle to a speck in the sky until it finally vanished. "Kal-El is safe."

"At least one of us escaped." Lara took his hand. "And at least we're here together." Though Jor-El could conceptualize the scope of the disaster, the staggering number of deaths, right now his heart held only his wife and his son.

A line of emerald-tinged lava gushed from a newly opened crack in the estate grounds. The plains were on fire from the initial eruptions. Whole mountains were being swallowed up.

Holding each other, he and Lara watched the collapse of the structures around them.

The milky corkscrew tower trembled and swayed. Jor-El was astonished by how much material strain the structure endured before it finally crashed down. Its apex grazed the side of Jor-El's main laboratory, bringing down another section of the building.

The long walls shattered, ruining the ambitious murals that Lara's parents had painted. To Jor-El it symbolized how easily Krypton's history was erased. Would anyone remember them? Out in the entire galaxy, would Krypton simply be forgotten?

Eleven of the twelve obelisk stones collapsed, dropping facedown onto the purple lawn or the neatly manicured hedges. All of Lara's carefully thought-out artwork now fell into dust and shards. Feeling the ache in his heart, Jor-El realized just how much those works had meant to him.

The last flat stone, the one containing the perceptive portrait of Jor-El with his finely chiseled features, white hair, and far-seeing gaze, toppled over.

As the quakes increased in violence, giant sinkholes opened up. The manor house itself slid down into an ever-widening crater, and liquid fire sprayed higher and higher. Hot winds laden with ash and dust tore at them like a hurricane from hell.

Jor-El and Lara held each other tightly. He caressed her face, her amber hair so beautiful as it danced around her eyes, her cheeks. "How I wish I could have had more time with you."

Her tears were gone now as she faced him in their last moments. "The time we had was filled with as much joy as I could have asked for. I have no regrets. I love you."

His blue eyes were clear, and even with all of Krypton in uproar around them, he saw only Lara, only her face. "I love *you*." She seemed to glow in the red sunlight filtered through the sheen of his tears. He wanted this moment to last forever.

He leaned forward to kiss her, shutting out even the catastrophe with their love. They closed their eyes, and the world ended around them.

CHAPTER 90

The lone crystal-studded ship sailed off into space, escaping Krypton's atmosphere and leaving the dying planet behind. Inside the small vessel, a single baby, warm and protected in the blankets his parents had given him, blinked his innocent blue eyes.

The crystals around him contained all the memories and knowledge of Krypton, though Kal-El didn't know it yet. He had few experiences, but they were sharp and bright in his hungry mind. Through circular observation panels, the boy could watch. Though he did not understand what he saw, the spectacle would be forever burned into his memory.

With its core now gone, Krypton became a red and brown sphere laced with cracks of fire, like a partially extinguished ember. It began to collapse slowly, even gracefully, drawn together by the invisible hand of gravity, the empty rind of a fruit being crushed inward.

When all of the infalling mass slammed together at the center, the shock waves set up an equal but opposite reaction. The mortally wounded world began to rebound. Broken shards of continents and the flying remnants of oceans tore apart what remained of the gauzy atmosphere.

Krypton exploded with a flash of red and a flare of emerald green. Fragments hurtled outward in all directions.

Even as Kal-El's ship raced onward, the vessel's hull resounded with hundreds of impacts. The automated systems compensated, taking evasive action, increasing speed. The remnants of the baby's dead planet cooled into a handful of strewn glitter in the icy void of space.

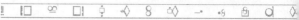

The alien stardrive activated, accelerating beyond lightspeed, rippling space and drawing much of the planet's debris into a vortex behind it.

The ship raced away until Rao was no more than a very bright star in the firmament. Safe and alone, the last son of Krypton sailed toward a blue planet orbiting an average yellow star.

Earth.

Kal-El's new home.